D0435177

FAIR IS
THE ROSE

FAIR IS THE ROSE

Meagan McKinney

Delacorte Press

Published by
Delacorte Press
Bantam Doubleday Dell Publishing Group, Inc.
1540 Broadway
New York, New York 10036

Library of Congress Cataloging in Publication Data

McKinney, Meagan.
Fair is the rose / by Meagan McKinney.
p.   cm.
ISBN 0-385-30915-5
I. Title.
PS3563.C38168F3   1993
813′.54—dc20   92-27232   CIP

Manufactured in the United States of America
Published simultaneously in Canada
May 1993
10 9 8 7 6 5 4 3 2 1
RRH

For Somebody's Darling

And for Tom and Tommy,
my two darlings.

ACKNOWLEDGMENTS

To Betsy McGovern and Tommy Makem for providing the beautiful songs, and for my dear friend Pat
Warner, member of the Mississippi 3rd, who likes me
even if I am a damned Yankee.

And lastly, for Damaris Rowland, Associate Publisher
of Dell Books, and for my agent, Pamela Gray
Ahearn, who, like millions of other women, see the
feminism, beauty, and strength in the romance novel
(and refuse to take no for an answer!). Thank God for
all of you.

WEARING OF THE GRAY

The fearful struggle's ended now,
And peace smiles on our land.
And though we've yielded,
We have proved ourselves a faithful band.
We fought them long, we fought them well
We fought them night and day.
And bravely struggled for our rights
While wearing of the Gray.

CONFEDERATE CAMP SONG

Chapter One

June 1875

It was a bad hanging.

And if there was one thing Doc Amoss hated, it was a bad hanging. He surveyed the seven white-draped bodies laid out in his small office. Even these men, the infamous Dover gang, had deserved the respect of a sharp snap to the neck and a swift journey to damnation. But this hanging hadn't been clean. At least, not at the end.

Doc shook his head, pushed up his spectacles, and went back to work. He'd spent all day with the Dover gang, first watching them be hanged, one by one, until their seven bodies dangled from their nooses, limp and solemn in the haze of dust kicked up by the horses. Afterward he'd helped cut them down and haul them to his office. The small town of Landen didn't have an undertaker, so it was Doc's job to ready them for burial. It'd taken all afternoon to wrap five of them. He was now on the sixth.

Doc leaned toward the spittoon, missed it, and left a pockmark in the dust on the naked floorboards. Outside, beneath the peeling sign *Haircut, bath, and shave, 10 cents—Surgery done Fast* he could see to the end of town where seven men dug seven graves in the anonymous brown sweep of eastern plain.

The shadows grew deep in his office. It was late. He pulled off the sixth man's boots and checked his mouth just in case the fellow had some ivory teeth the town could sell to pay for the hanging. Doc wrapped him, then crossed his name off the list.

Now there was no avoiding it. The last man had to be attended to. The seventh and worst.

Macaulay Cain. Just the mention of that name made a chill shiver down Doc's spine. He'd seen it on enough wanted posters to spell it backward and forward. He'd never wanted to mess with the likes of the notorious gunslinger. God and his sense of justice. Just when the hanging went bad, it went bad on Macaulay Cain.

Doc reluctantly looked over to the seventh white-draped figure. In all his days he'd never seen a man so difficult to put atop a horse and get a noose around his neck. Cain had required every one of the sheriff's deputies and even at the end, when his face was covered by the black bag and the men were ready to put the whip to his horse, Cain struggled and demanded that they wait for that telegram, the one he claimed was going to clear him.

The one that never came.

"Son of a bitch." Doc hated a bad hanging. It made a man feel right uncomfortable inside just thinking about the horse rearing and Macaulay Cain twisting in the wind, no broken neck to put him out of his misery.

When all was done, the deputies had brought Cain to the office. They cut the hands free and crossed them over his chest in a reverent manner. But Doc was the one to take the black bag off the head. No one else would do it. In a really bad hanging the tongue gaped out and the expression was frozen into a mask of terror as the poor bastard struggled to breathe while the noose tightened around his neck. The deputies visibly flinched when Doc removed the bag, unsure of what they might see. But before the sheet went over Cain's head, they all were relieved to see the expression loose and peaceful beneath the outlaw's scruffy growth of beard.

Resigned to his task, Doc walked over to the last body. The sheriff would be there soon to take the gang away for burial. He'd best be quick.

He bent to get a length of rope to tie the shroud. The room was quiet except for the buzz of green flies against the windowpanes and the sound of Doc's breathing. He leaned over the body, hand outstretched to grasp the sheet.

Then he felt it.

Another man might not have taken note of the small drop of blood that plopped onto Doc's black store-bought shoes. A man less trained in the medicinal arts might never have given it a thought, but John Edward Amoss had spent forty of his sixty-odd years learning one thing: Dead men don't bleed.

Sure, in a hanging there was always some oozing around the neck, but not enough to run off the table and plop right onto his toe.

The hairs on the back of Doc's neck rose. His hands itched to remove the sheet, but his feet were wiser. He stepped back.

Too late.

The hand shot out from beneath the sheet and clamped around his neck. Doc squeaked like a prairie dog caught by a coyote, but no one heard him. The townfolk had all gathered on the prairie waiting for the burial.

A long moment passed while neither man moved, Doc and the infamous gunslinger poised like statuary. In the silence Doc heard the man's labored scratchy breathing as Cain greedily filled his lungs.

Unable to help himself, Doc croaked, "You coming alive just now, son?"

The outlaw swept the sheet from his face. He looked bad. Too bad for a miracle. His voice was painfully hoarse. "Yeah. Sure. I'm the Second Coming."

Doc nodded, too scared to laugh.

"The telegram. Where's the goddamned telegram?" the renegade choked out, his words barely discernible.

"Nobody cleared you, son. No telegram came." All the while Doc said this he kept thinking about the twelve men the Dover gang had been convicted of shooting and wondered how many of those men were this one's doing. He wondered too if in the end the final toll wouldn't be thirteen.

Cain's hand tightened around his neck. Doc could hardly swallow.

"You lying to me?" The outlaw's features tightened, already pale with the trauma of the hanging.

"I wouldn't lie to you at a time like this, son."

Cain looked straight at Doc. Then he smiled, the smile never reaching his eyes. "I reckon I'll have to take you with me, Doc. I'm hell-bent to get outta this hanging town. One way or the other."

The man quit smiling. His wrists bled, his neck bled. And by God, thought Doc, he has cold eyes.

Doc swallowed. Not easily, with the man's steely grip on his throat. "They ain't going to hang you again. They owe you. We all agree. It was a bad hanging."

"Bad all around," the man spat.

Doc didn't answer, his eyes drawn to the man's neck. The rope had sure made a bloody mess.

"You got a horse?"

Doc drew his gaze away from the wound. "Yep. Out back. Good solid Indian pony. Take her."

"Gun?"

"Ain't got one. Don't rightly believe in them. Being a doctor and all."

"Then I'll take you with me. I gotta have some insurance." The man massaged his sore throat, then swung his legs over the side of the wake table. The fringe of his chaps was almost all sheared off, a sign of a renegade. Men running from the law sure as hell couldn't waltz into town to repair a harness. They used their fringe for everything from buckles to boot-laces.

Doc swallowed, conscious of the hand on his throat, the hand that at any minute could close and choke the life out of him. Fear made the blood drain from his face. "How far do you think you'll get with me dragging behind you?"

The outlaw stared. Those frigid gray eyes assessed Doc's paunch and balding head. "I need time" was all he offered.

Doc understood. "I won't tell. Not for a while anyways. That'll buy you some time. Get on out of here."

Those eyes narrowed, reminding Doc of a wolf's he'd once seen in the dead of winter. "Why would you do that for me?"

"I don't believe in hanging a man twice is all. You survived it. Must be for some reason. I ain't playing God."

The man pinned Doc with those eyes as his hand pinned him by the throat. "I need five minutes," he finally rasped. "If I don't get it, if you don't give it to me, I'll come back from the grave to get you."

"I swear you'll get your five minutes if I have to barricade the deputies from the door." Doc nodded as best he could.

Cautiously the man slid to the floor, his hand still clamped to Doc's throat. Together they walked over to the back door. For one brief second the two men looked at each other, a strange understanding passing between them. Just like that wolf, Doc thought, remembering how he'd lowered his rifle and the wolf ran off, leaving only the memory of those shattered-ice eyes.

The outlaw was at least a foot taller than the doctor, lean, hard, and capable from years in the saddle. There was no reason for Doc to say it, but he whispered it anyway, his throat still constricted from the power of the man's grip. "Good luck to you, Macaulay Cain."

The outlaw glanced at Doc, his expression startled. He looked as if he was about to say he didn't need any good luck from a man who had tried to hang him. But instead he took his moment, like the wolf, and he cleared the back door in a dead run. He leapt onto the startled Appaloosa in the corral and hightailed it west as if he were part Indian, with no need for a saddle or bridle to take him to the mountains that jagged up from the blue horizon.

And Doc watched him. Strangely anxious to see him free and gone, like that wolf in the snow.

Red is the rose
That in yonder garden grows
Fair is the lily of the valley
Clear is the water that flows from the Boyne
But my love is fairer than any. . . .

IRISH FOLKSONG
WRITTEN BY TOMMY MAKEM

August 1875

When traveling she always wore black. Widows were never questioned. They said all that needed to be said in the color of their weeds. Christal Van Alen had learned to wear black. She had learned the trick of wearing the black cotton gloves so no one would see she didn't have a wedding ring and therefore no late husband. And she had learned to wear the long black netting over her face, labeling her as a widow, veiling her features, obscuring her age. Dressed as she was, she rarely got inquiries, or conversation. It was safer that way. One would think that a woman traveling alone would want the friendly solicitations of her fellow passengers. But she'd learned, too, in her time out west that the only thing more dangerous than a renegade band of Pawnee was a stranger too inquisitive about her past.

The Overland Express coach hit a rut in the road, shoving her into the sharp corner of an object next to her on the seat. She eyed it, a small replica of a bureau that was the pride and joy of the hefty furniture salesman who held it.

She straightened, almost envying the salesman his wide girth. The stage accommodated six passengers, but the man next to her had been charged double fare because of the room needed for his samples and his large size. Squeezed between him and the side of the stagecoach, Christal could barely keep her skirts from being crushed. Her petite stature was no help. While the salesman was so heavy he hardly bounced around at all, she was thrust onto the corner of that tiny bureau at every jolt.

Clutching her grosgrain purse, she resumed her position, sitting primly, ankles crossed, hands placed one on top of the other in her lap. The ride grew smoother and she chanced a look at the other three passengers who had boarded the coach with them at Burnt Station.

One was an old man with a placid grandfatherly face. She thought he might have been a preacher when he reached inside his breast pocket and pulled out a book of Scripture. But then she noticed that the inside of the book was carved out to hold a small metal flask, which he eagerly swilled from, and she wasn't so sure anymore.

The young man next to him—a kid, really—looked anxiously out the window as if he was ashamed of riding in the coach instead of doing the manly thing by pulling his weight alongside on a cow pony. His traveling companion might have been his father, a grizzled character with a faded indigo vest and a large wiry gray beard that would have benefited from a pair of shears.

No one chatted. The "preacher" drank; the man in the blue vest dozed; the salesman stared at his little bureau as if thinking of his next account. Another jolt of the coach sent her once again into the vicious corner of the bureau. This time she sat back rubbing her ribs.

"Name's Mr. Henry Glassie, ma'am."

She looked up to find the salesman smiling at her again. He was a very pleasant-looking man, one whom she could believe provided good companionship on a long, dusty ride across a prairie such as this. But she didn't want companionship. She preferred silence. She could hide in silence. At least from everyone except herself.

She stared at the man through the anonymity of her veil. Bitterly she wondered if the kindness would flee from his eyes if she told him who she was. That her face was on wanted posters from Maine to Missouri. That the gloves she wore to hide her lack of a wedding ring also hid the scar on her palm that was sketched onto every one of those posters. She'd seen the last poster in Chicago. That had been three years back, and Wyoming Territory seemed far enough west to be safe, but every day she worried that it might not be. She'd been held captive in a nightmare in New York. Now she was running from that nightmare and from her own face. And from one violent man who would see her dead before she could utter the truth about a crime she didn't commit.

"Madam, if I may be so honored to address you as . . . ?" The man raised his eyebrows as if imploring her for her name. She could see he was determined to get conversation from her.

"I am Mrs. Smith," she answered in a low, polite voice.

His smile widened. "A lovely name, *Smith*. So proudly democratic. So easy to remember."

She almost smiled. He'd all but said her name was common —which it was. That was why she had chosen it. Yet Mr. Glassie made her feel complimented. He possessed the tools of a brilliant salesman: a silver tongue and a smooth presentation, and his comportment, his fashionable verdigris suit, and the large pearl stuck in his black four-in-hand tie, all proclaimed he was very successful at what he did.

But poor widows didn't buy much furniture, and conversation quickly trickled away, much to her relief. She was left once again to look out the window at the ironing board–flat prairie. Every now and again she removed her handkerchief, reached beneath her dark veil, and dabbed the perspiration that beaded along her brow. The sun burned overhead, and dust blew in the open windows, coating her gown with a gritty blond powder. They had just started out. Noble was a long day's ride. She was anxious to get there.

She'd heard a lot about the town of Noble the last three years. All her hopes now rested there. She was sick of running and she'd heard Noble was a good place to hide. A lot of gambling, a lot of women, and nobody asking questions. Not even a sheriff. They hadn't had one in years. People talked about Noble the way they talked about South Pass and Miners Delight; the town had sprung from nowhere with the rumor of gold and had faded just as quickly. But Noble's hedonistic ways lingered on and now it served cowhands and men heading north to Fort Washakie from the Union Pacific. She thought she'd be happy there for a while, working in a kitchen, dealing faro, even selling dances if she had to, in a small, nowhere town with no lawman to point fingers. It wasn't her first choice to sell dances for a living; the men were usually rough and sometimes they smelled. But she'd do it if there was no other work; her first thoughts were always on survival. And there were so many worse ways to make money. Especially for a woman.

Christal's eyes clouded as if she weren't seeing the scenery any longer. *Vice.* She hated thinking about the word, but it followed her like a shadow that persisted even when the sun had gone down. Way back in the olden days of a life she hardly remembered anymore, a word like *vice* never would have entered her vocabulary. Words like *vice* weren't in her family's dictionaries. In her world, vice was kept permanently untranslated and unexplained. For a young, well-bred Knickerbocker girl from Manhattan it was meant to be as meaningless a word as something written in shantytown Irish Gaelic—a language most definitely not taught at Miss Bailey's Conservatoire for Young Ladies, the exclusive girls' school on Fifth Avenue where once her destiny had led her.

But destiny had somehow come off its tracks, and now, instead, she was in Wyoming, living a life she never imagined, understanding vice all too well because she'd spent three painful years trying to avoid its clutches.

"Oughta be riding shotgun too, Pa. Them Sioux—never know when they gonna act up." The boy's voice brought her out of her dark thoughts. He looked at his pa, who was trying to sleep beneath his hat.

"You're a genelman now, Pete. We got money. We don't ride shotgun no more. Soon as we get to St. Louie, we gonna buy us some clothes and be genelmen once and fer all."

"We ain't got no escort, just the driver and the shotgun. What if we get stopped? This is Sioux territory. And them Cheyennes, everybody knows they're all riled up—"

"Noble's spittin' distance from here. They don't need you, Pete. That's what we paid 'em fer. And what you gonna do when we get on that there locomotive in St. Louie? Try and push it fer 'em?"

"Aw, Pa," Pete groaned. He gave an embarrassed glance in Christal's direction; then, as if he was glad for her veil, he turned to the window, appearing to scout for braves.

Indians. Her scalp tingled every time anyone even said the word. In the territory she'd crossed she'd heard blood-curdling stories about the Kootenai, Flathead, Shoshone, Blackfoot. They were horrible stories, stories that gave her nightmares. But nightmares weren't so bad when one was living a nightmare. She wasn't afraid of Indians.

Then the coach stopped.

At first no one knew what had happened. There was just a silence, a stagnant pause that held nothing but the flavor of anxiety. A pair of boots thudded against the top of the stage, but Christal realized that was only the man who rode shotgun shifting position.

"Why have we stopped?" Mr. Glassie asked, clutching his bureau and looking around as if someone inside the coach would know the answer.

"We ain't s'pose to stop at Dry Fork." The grizzled man in the blue vest frowned, then poked his head out the window. He opened his mouth to shout at the driver, but for some reason the words collapsed in his throat. When he drew back inside the coach, the muzzle of a rifle was pointed directly at his nose.

Christal gripped her purse until her knuckles were white. Suddenly all those stories of Indians and outlaws came back to her with an immediacy that left her stunned. Her mouth went dry. Through the mist of her veil she saw the preacher slam his Bible shut, shock, not inebriation, slackening his features. Pete looked as if he were foolishly about to take on whoever held his father at gunpoint. Outside, she heard the horses stamp, nervous with strangers in their midst. A second later the sound of a scuffle battered the top of the coach. There was a sudden silence; then a rifle thudded to the ground.

A hand, a very un-Indian grimy white hand, reached inside

the coach and unlatched the door. Christal drew back in fear. A scuffed boot came up to rest on the threshold, and its owner leaned on his knee. "Howdy, folks." The man smiled, showing a mouthful of bad teeth. He was unshaven and dirty, with mean dull eyes that quickly surveyed the passengers. When he saw his threat registered, he laughed.

"Is this a holdup?" Mr. Glassie gasped, holding his miniature bureau like a shield.

From behind the black veil Christal watched the outlaw, her heart hammering in her chest as if it would break free of her corset.

"Cain!" the outlaw shouted, lowering the rifle. "They want to know if'n this is a holdup!" He laughed again and pulled his bandanna over his face to mock them.

"See here," Mr. Glassie blustered, but before he could get out the words the outlaw was pulled aside and another took his place.

Christal had never seen such a man before. As an outlaw, he looked much like the other one, taller perhaps and more broadly built, but he was unshaven, with several days' growth of dark beard on his chin. His shirt was dusty and worn, a faded scarlet bandanna was tied around his neck, available to cover his face should the need arise. But he was different, memorable, more dangerous than the other man. His eyes made her heart stop. She had never seen such steely eyes, eyes that made it feel like January in July.

"Men outside," he grunted. Those eyes turned to Christal, pinning her to her seat. She knew he couldn't see her face beneath the veil, but that was small comfort as she squirmed beneath the chilling gaze.

To her relief he turned away to direct the male passengers. Her shoulders slumped after the assault of that stare, and she expelled the breath she hadn't even realized she'd been holding.

"Is this a holdup?" Mr. Glassie persisted, unwilling to remove himself from the coach until the situation was clearer. "As you men can see, we've a lady on board. We can't just trot off this coach and leave her behind without someone—"

"I said men outside." The outlaw with the cold gray eyes shot Mr. Glassie a glance of ice. The salesman didn't need more than that to convince him to relinquish his bureau and get out of the stage.

One by one, they filed out. Pete kept a defiant look on his face, as if to say "I ain't afraid of you." His father looked anxious, as if he'd come so far only to have all his dreams dashed in a robbery. From the window Christal looked at the preacher. His hands were shaking as he held them over his head. Her own hands were slick with cold sweat as she held on to the window.

She looked in the distance, hopelessly seeking help. The bridge at Dry Fork was obviously where these outlaws had been hiding as their target had rolled toward them. Christal spied their horses tied beneath the bridge. She counted five.

". . . am a representative of the Paterson Furniture Company of Paterson, New Jersey, and my company shall hear about this outrageous treatment, my good fellows!" Mr. Glassie announced as the first outlaw searched him for weapons. The second, the one with the steely eyes, patted down the old man's blue vest while Pete glared.

"I'm a poor man, a poor man, mister," Pete's father chanted while being searched. "Ain't no need in stealing from me 'cause I'm a poor man."

"No weapons, Cain," the first outlaw called out.

Cain, the man with the steely eyes, nodded. He lifted up Pete's coat. Finding a six-shooter stuck in the waistband of the boy's jeans, he took it and pushed the boy aside.

"Listen up." Cain shot a couple of times into the air. Everyone gave him full attention, including the driver and the man who rode shotgun, who were now on the ground. "You men'll be walking the rest of the way. Just follow behind the stage." Cain looked to the two riders who were bringing the horses up from the Dry Fork bridge. "The boys'll see you get there."

"Where?" Pete asked bravely.

Cain shot him a stare. "A town called Falling Water. You ever heard of it, kid?"

Pete hardened his chin. "Sure. It's a damn ghost town. Nobody been there for years."

"That's right. But you'll be there."

"You kidnapping us?"

"Yeah."

"Why?"

Christal clutched the door, waiting for the answer. She wondered whether this was merely a simple robbery, or something more complicated and sinister. Her mind played out one scenario after another. The worst was that somehow, some way, she'd been found by her uncle.

"The Overland Express has its payroll coming in Tuesday. We're holding you all for ransom." Cain stuck the kid's six-shooter into the waist of his own chaps. "You men walk behind the stage. If you get outta line, Zeke here's got permission to bullwhip you." The man named Zeke edged his sorrel toward the group. In his right hand was an enormous, wicked-looking whip, the kind that could easily flick the skin from a man's back.

Christal watched the numb horror seep into the other passengers' expressions. She was frightened, but she took consolation in knowing that her uncle wasn't behind any of this. If Baldwin Didier had found her, she wouldn't live to see tomorrow. With these outlaws, she had some chance.

"You can't hold us that long! Tuesday's four days away!" Mr. Glassie exclaimed, obviously thinking of his accounts.

Cain shrugged, obviously not caring.

"Who are you, my good man, that you think you can do this to us?"

"Macaulay Cain."

Pete gasped. "Macaulay Cain! Macaulay Cain was hanged in Landen over a month ago!"

"Some say that."

"And some say Macaulay Cain got out of the hangin' and met up with the Kineson gang. Is this here the Kineson gang?" the boy's father inquired, dread on his face.

"It could be, and if you're right, you'd best not be causing trouble." Cain's words were so low, Christal wouldn't have been able to hear them if he weren't standing right next to the stage. The menace that edged the man's raw voice sent a chill down her spine. She quickly saw she had been too confident. These men were outlaws. They'd done awful things, perhaps even killed men. They were wanted, desperate. And she was a woman alone.

Another man rode up from the bridge. Leading the last two horses by their reins, he hitched the two to the coach and fell in with Zeke. Christal was nearly hanging out the window when Zeke pushed the six men, including the driver and the shotgun, to the back of the coach where she could no longer see them.

Christal bit her lip and resumed her seat. If there were two horses hitched, one of them belonged to the outlaw who would be driving the carriage. That left one other gang member either to walk or . . . to ride in the carriage with her.

A sudden overwhelming panic seized her, and she wanted to run out of the coach and fall in with the other passengers. She didn't want to be alone in the stagecoach. More than that, she didn't want to ride with one of the outlaws, particularly the one with the cold gray eyes.

"You better treat that widow right. We ain't gonna stand for you mistreatin' her," she heard Pete demand from behind the carriage. His words tugged at her heart. He was brave to say such things. She couldn't remember the last time a man had cared about her welfare.

The sound of a high-pitched laugh crawled down her spine. "She'll be all right. She's going to ride with me."

"I'll be riding with her." A second voice brooked no debate.

There was a long, resentful pause before the other outlaw said, "Sure, Cain. You go ahead and get a peek at her. She's probably too old to fiddle with anyway."

The coach creaked as the iron-clad wheels waited to roll again. The number of horses had doubled, and there was that much more jangling of harnesses. Zeke cracked the bullwhip, but it must have been for intimidation because none of the passengers cried out. Still, the sound reverberated over the open prairie like a gunshot.

Christal's heart hammered with dread. She had a small muff pistol in her purse, so named because ladies in London carried such miniature guns hidden in their muffs when they were forced to walk through less than savory neighborhoods. But she had only been able to afford the pistol because it was more than fifty years old and carried only one shot, unlike the modern repeating gun. It would be foolish for her to reveal the gun now, in the coach surrounded by outlaws. Her only chance was to swallow her fear and wait. So she clutched her small grosgrain bag and watched the door open.

The outlaw named Cain jumped in, rifle and all. He slammed the door behind him and knocked twice on the roof with the butt of his rifle, and the stagecoach lurched to a start. Without acknowledging her, he slouched down on the dusty velvet seat opposite, kicking Mr. Glassie's prized bureau to the center of the coach so he could stretch his legs out on it.

She stared at him through the veil, her blood thrumming with fear. He rested his rifle across his knees, drawing her eyes to the length and power of his legs. He wore chaps, the leather rubbed smooth along the inside of the thighs from long hours in the saddle. The brass spurs lashed to his boots irreverently scarred the fine wood of the bureau. He was dirty, covered in dust and sweat. His presence filled the carriage with the scent of fired gunpowder, which stained his hands and shirt. She expected a bad animal-odor from him, as she would have from that first outlaw who had the rotten teeth. Instead there was a musky kind of man smell to him that repelled her and intrigued her at the same time.

It was hot in the carriage. The sun was now at high noon, and the dust kicked into the window with a new ferocity. Christal longed to pat away the perspiration on her face, but she didn't. She kept her hand on her purse, her palm curved against the pistol's curled handle, and watched him covertly from behind the veil. The sweat trickled down her temples and between her corseted breasts.

He stared out the window, rubbing the sweat from his eyes with his thumb and forefinger. Finally, he pulled at the faded scarlet bandanna, untying it so that he could wipe his face.

She gasped. The man's neck was circled with an angry ragged scar. She could think of only one thing that could give a man a scar like that.

That cold, steely gaze riveted on her. He touched his neck and flashed a cynical smile, revealing strong white teeth.

He leaned toward her. "You ever felt the noose around your neck, ma'am?" His laugh was rumbling and husky.

Unconsciously, her hand went to her neck. The other hand, the hand with the scar hidden by her black glove, curled as if to protect itself. She swallowed, not wanting to think of her past, of Baldwin Didier. Her uncle wanted to dance on her grave. He would have seen her hanged if he could have. Instead she'd been spared by her youth. She'd been in Park View Asylum until three years ago.

The outlaw sat back and perused her black-clad figure. Without warning, he raised his rifle and pointed it at her. Her heart stilled. She waited for him to pull the trigger, but he put the muzzle beneath her veil and began to lift it.

Her gloved hands gripped the barrel to stop him. She needed the protection of the veil. Just looking into those eyes told her so. She didn't want him to see her face. She didn't want to be that vulnerable.

She slapped at the gun, but he held it firm. Suddenly trapped by the terror of the looming muzzle, she stared at him, still hidden by the gauzy black material.

He tipped up the veil. In a flash, the netting was up and off her face.

Surprise and appreciation flared in his eyes. He clearly didn't expect what he saw, a blond nineteen-year-old girl whose eyes clashed defiantly with his.

He didn't say a word. They stared at each other for one long moment, each assessing the other. She was afraid, but experience had taught her never to show fear. She presented a face as haughty and cold as a marble statue, an easy task for a girl bred of the aristocracy of Knickerbocker New York. He stared right back, an enigmatic expression in his eyes.

She turned her face away and gazed out the window, dismissing him as she might a servant.

He placed the barrel against her cheek and forced her to turn her head back to him.

Her eyes glittered with anger and fear. She met his gaze once more. His eyes were as cold and steely as the smooth rifle barrel laid across her cheek. Then he did the strangest thing. Slowly he lowered his rifle. Her heart lurched when he reached over, but he did so only to cover her face once more with the veil. He sat back, gave her one inexplicable glance, and again looked out the window, absorbed in thought.

"Why did they hang you?" she gasped.

He turned back to her, his gaze slamming into hers as if the veil were no longer there. She believed his every word. " 'Cause maybe I needed hanging."

She drew back against the seat, her fear a small choking sound in her throat. His smile was both mirthless and satisfied. Then he resumed looking out at the wide stretch of prairie as if she were no longer there.

Chapter Two

The ride became hilly as they headed west and the flat prairie of sage and wheatgrass grew vertical into forests of lodgepole pine. Through the open window, Christal could hear the other passengers grunting and cursing to keep up with the stage, but as the terrain grew difficult, their voices became more and more faint. Until silence reigned.

The stage climbed into the threshold of the Rockies. Granite peaks iced with snow towered in the distance, and atop one particularly steep incline of the road where the backbone of mountains melted into sky, Christal swore she could see into heaven. But the going was difficult, and she had little time to be in awe of her surroundings. The coach lurched and lunged along an ill-used path, and she spent most of her attention clinging to her seat in fear she might land on the floor, or worse, in the outlaw's arms.

Finally, the stage lurched to a stop. She stole a glance out the window; all she could see were more pines, more boulders, and the rocky trail ahead, pitted and gorged by the weather. Frightened, she turned accusing eyes to the outlaw sitting in front of her.

Cain removed his booted feet from Mr. Glassie's prized bureau, hardly disturbed by the rough ride. He didn't look at her. Instead, he threw open the door and motioned for her to get out of the stage.

Half of her was desperate to scramble out to see if the other passengers had caught up, but the other half didn't want to move and risk releasing her grip on the handle of the pistol inside her purse.

"I don't see your feet moving, ma'am."

She stared at him. Even through her veil, she could see those amazingly cold eyes. Bravely, she stepped out of the stagecoach.

To her surprise they were in a town. There were three buildings ahead, two of them decrepit and skeletal, blue sky peeking through the walls like pieces of a puzzle. The third had once been a saloon, but the top of its false front had long ago tumbled to the ground and blocked the entrance. She raised her hand to shut out the sun's glare. A sign still hung over the saloon's swinging doors, so full of bullet holes it was illegible. The sound of rushing water from the gorge behind the saloon was the only clue to her whereabouts. They had said they were taking them to a ghost town named Falling Water. Clearly they had arrived.

She turned to look at her captor. None of the other passengers was visible down the dusty road, but three men with shotguns appeared from behind the saloon. Cain stared at them, his expression unreadable.

"Where are the rest?" one of the men asked, an outdated Sharps rifle crossed over his chest, ready.

Cain jerked his head in the direction of the road. "Coming."

The men let out a holler, then picked their way forward through the fallen planking, their uneasiness melting into jubilation.

"We got 'em, eh! We got 'em!" one man chanted. The other hooted, while the third rushed up to Cain.

"Found a room to lock 'em in, Cain, just like you asked." The man was thin and pimply. Even though she was hidden by her veil, he gave her a skeevy smile that made her draw back. "It's at the top of the saloon. Couldn't ask for better. No, you couldn't ask for better."

"Where's the key?" Cain demanded, not touched by the

men's excitement. He held out his hand. The man obediently handed it over.

"What we got here?" The second man came around, a big, ugly brute with greasy hair tied back with a strip of leather. He had more than curiosity on his face when he reached out to lift her veil. Christal skittered back only to land solidly against Cain's chest.

"Enough," Cain growled to the brute.

The man retreated.

Cain continued, putting an ironlike arm around her waist, either to keep her from fleeing or to keep them from attacking. "We got work to do before the others arrive. Boone," he said, motioning to the brute, "get the horses watered." He turned to the man with the smile and the third, an older man near sixty, who was just now stumbling over the last of the planks. "You two go get a stag. I'm going to get hungry and I get mean when I'm hungry."

The two nodded, swung their shotguns over their shoulders, and disappeared behind the saloon. Boone took another glance at Christal before he and the outlaw who had driven the stage walked the horses to the paddock south of the saloon.

She was again left alone with Cain. It was just him and her, empty buildings, blowing dust, and sky. She swallowed, her throat as dry as the road. She didn't want to be taken anywhere without the other passengers, and her mind whirled, desperately trying to think of some way to flee. Her hand tightened on her little grosgrain purse, her finger quietly searching for the trigger, but before she found it Cain's manacle grip took her arm. Her instinct was to run, and she stumbled back, trying to gather her skirts to do so, but he had her in both hands and began dragging her toward the saloon before she could gasp a protest.

"Where are we going?" she demanded, struggling to release his viselike hand on her arm, her heart beating a staccato rhythm in her chest.

He stopped. He ripped the veil from her face and threw it

in the road. A wind kicked up, and it rolled away like a tumbleweed.

"I needed that veil," she said, her defiant expression hiding the fear that pumped in her veins.

For the first time she saw a small glimmer of compassion in his eyes. Quietly he said, "Yeah, you ought to hide that face from these men. But in the end it isn't going to do you any good. And right now I want to see who I'm talking to." He squeezed her arm and shoved her in the direction of the saloon. Her purse—and her pistol—dangled just out of her reach from her only free hand.

A small path had been cleared in the fallen lumber. He forced her through the swinging doors and let her go. Christal walked a few steps, hardly believing her eyes. The saloon was no better than the road. Pale blond dust covered everything, the raw floorboards, the bar, the rickety chairs.

"Up the stairs."

Her breath caught in her throat. She whipped around to face him. She wasn't going to go up to the saloon's bedrooms with him. She would shoot him dead on the spot rather than let him rape her.

"Go on," he said.

She glanced around to see if there was a way to escape. The only door was blocked by him.

He stepped forward, the planes of his face hardened by the saloon's deep shadows. "What's your name?"

"Christal," she whispered, not looking at him.

"Christal what?"

"Christal Smith."

A shadow of a smile touched his lips. "Not *Mrs.*?"

"Yes. *Mrs.* Christal Smith," she spat.

"How long has he been dead?"

She almost asked "who" but quickly collected herself. "My husband's been dead six weeks."

"You couldn't have been married long."

She didn't answer.

He shrugged. In a low rumble he said, "We all gotta die."

She wondered if she heard compassion in his voice. If it was there, she prayed she could appeal to it. If it wasn't, with his cold eyes, God have mercy on her soul.

"Do you want to know who I am?" He crossed his arms over his broad chest. His shotgun had been left in the stage, but he didn't need it by the looks of the two six-shooters slung low on his hips.

He stepped toward her.

She tried to keep her voice cool and even. The closer he walked to her, the farther he was from the door, the better her chances of escape. Slowly she said, "I know who you are."

He smiled. "Who, then?"

She eyed the door one last time, her nerves on fire for her escape. "You're Macaulay Cain. The outlaw."

He took one more step; she bolted. She ran as if from wildfire, hope blooming when she cleared the swinging doors. But he easily tripped her in her cumbersome skirts. She tumbled to the dirt road and her purse and the pistol within it fell in the dust, maddeningly out of her reach.

He dropped to his knees, straddling her, and pinned her arms over her head. She struggled, his face dark and anonymous against the glare of the sun. Her knee jerked up to kick, she pushed against him like a filly trying to buck him off, but he only chuckled. She could have shot him just for laughing. Groping for her purse with what little leeway the grip on her wrists gave her, she could almost feel the silk cord of the handle. Her fingertips reached it, but with immaculate timing, he thrust her arms to her sides, far away from the vicinity of her purse. She was trapped.

Her breath coming in short, angry puffs, she stared up at him. He paused. Then he touched her hair.

She released a moan of fury. Captured as she was, she couldn't stop his hand from stroking the thick tangle that had fallen out of its pins. He picked up a curl and the pale color made a striking contrast to the dark hairs that sprinkled across the back of his hand. "Let me go," she spat.

"Your hair's like butter, did you know that?" His mouth pulled at the corner, as if he were biting back something he didn't want to feel.

"I said let me go."

He fingered her high collar that proved she was too impoverished even to sport a cheap cameo. Cupping her chin, he forced her gaze to his. "Now that I can see them, you got beautiful eyes too. The color of sky. Did your husband ever tell you that?"

"What business is that of yours?" she asked in a low, angry tone.

He ignored her retort. His hand fell to her waist. She squirmed; he didn't give an inch. He caressed the shoddy black crepe of her basque, then ran his knuckles across the swag of bombazine at her hips. His voice became husky. "And your waist is very small. Very small," he repeated, almost against his will.

Slowly his gaze rose to her breasts. She could see in his expression that he liked the way they rose and fell with anger and exertion. He liked it a lot.

She screwed up her lips to spit. No one was allowed to look at her that way. No one.

"You spit at me, ma'am, and I'll make that Yankee general Butler look like a goddamned knight."

Fury met ice. Her knowledge of the war was limited, but she knew who Butler was. He had the women of New Orleans locked up as prostitutes when they dared spit on one of his troops. Her lips parted in surrender.

She released an angry squeal of frustration, and he hoisted her onto her feet. She grappled to get her purse, but he scooped it from the dirt by the silken cord. He took hold of her waist, and she scratched and kicked and hit to keep from reentering the saloon without her weapon, but the man's enormous strength controlled her as if she were nothing but a doll. She lost the battle.

He dragged her through the swinging doors and stepped onto the stairs, shoving her in front of him. She fought like a cat to be freed, but he took one step, then another, and another, his boots hitting the boards like a drumbeat.

"No," she gasped, and pried at his hands on her arm and her waist, but he put down her rebellion once and for all by heaving her onto his shoulder. She kicked and wiggled until the froth of her petticoats was nearly to her thighs, but to no avail, she couldn't get free. At the top of the stairs, he entered a room, dumped her on a soiled feather mattress, and dropped her purse on a chair, out of her reach.

She stared at him in the dust that billowed from the mattress. He blocked the path to her purse, rendering her pistol useless. She had no way to win; he was going to rape her.

But he would have to kill her first. She wouldn't go without a fight.

He leaned over her, his tall form intimidating. She met his gaze; her eyes glittered with defiance. She'd spent three years protecting herself from men like him, three years of struggling and running. Women around her surrendered their honor in the name of hunger and need, but she hadn't, even though she'd gone hungry because she couldn't find enough decent work to still the gnawing in her belly. But she had never succumbed to whoring. And she never would. Her outside was hard and cool and aloof; she was the creature her life had forced her to be. But it was all to protect an inner core that was soft and fragile, gently reared and decent. Inside she was still the girl she'd been in New York before her uncle's crime had ruined her life, a girl who wanted to trust and give, to love and be loved in return. And this outlaw wasn't going to rape her and take that fragile inner girl away. Not while she still lived and breathed. She would preserve that girl at all costs. Because if he destroyed her, he'd shatter all reasons for fighting and surviving. If that girl was gone, Christal Van Alen could never go home. And she could never be that girl again.

He touched her jaw and looked as if he wanted to say something. But she refused to hear him out. Like a Roman candle, she lit into him, vowing to break an arm to keep him off. He grunted something and tried to stop her, but terror momentarily gave her a strength and speed she didn't normally possess. Her fists punched at his body, drumming wherever she thought it would hurt. She did her best to inflict damage, but it was disheartening to meet with so much rock-hard flesh.

And her heart sank when she saw nothing in his expression, no pain or anguish; nothing except surprise. But still he didn't have control over her. So she kept fighting, until he caught one flailing arm. Then, in a learned reflex, she took her free hand and slapped his face so hard it gave him a split-second pause.

"Hellcat," he rasped before easily capturing the offending hand.

"I won't let you do this, I won't!" She opened her mouth to bite him. He jerked back and nearly roared in anger.

Finally, their gazes locked in a standstill, they came to a pause. She looked up at him, noting his mouth was set in a grim line. He rubbed his jaw where she hit him and there was a patronizing anger in his eyes, as if she were a truant child.

"Let me give you some advice, Mrs. Smith," he whispered harshly, "you're a beautiful woman and you better know right now who to obey. We've got a lot of lonely men in this camp."

She bit her lower lip, refusing to allow him to see it quiver.

He leaned closer. She saw every silver fleck in those incredible eyes. "You think you're brave, but you're not. Without me you haven't got a chance. Out here, a man can smell a woman a mile away."

"Wh-what do you mean you can smell me?"

His hand touched her hair. His eyes never left her. "What I mean, lady, is that I can *smell* you. Everything about you. Your hair was rinsed in rosewater, probably this morning. I'd say you don't wear this gown often—you got it out today—because I can smell the lavender you packed it in to keep away the moths. You don't wear perfume and I suspect it's because you can't afford it. But you still smell better than anything because when I move close to you you have that woman smell and if I described it to you any more you'd slap me again." His voice grew ominous and low. "What I'm saying to you, lady, is this all makes a man think. And *want*."

"I'll fight you," she whispered.

He laughed mirthlessly. "You won't win." He turned grim. "But if you listen to me and *me alone*, you might get to Tuesday without having to be passed around like a used rag. Understand?"

Her face paled; her eyes kindled with fear. She nodded. She did understand. He wanted the sole right to rape and abuse her. But she would defy him all the way. To her last breath.

He stood. A swell of panic hit her as she waited for him to strip off his dusty shirt. She crawled to the back of the bed, ready to bolt the second she felt him come down on the mattress. She heard him say, "It's going to be a hard week, Mrs. Smith. Brace yourself."

Then he walked out, bolting the door behind him.

Stunned, she stared at the closed door for almost half a minute. By some miracle, she'd escaped being raped. And by a man whose eyes said he'd never felt pity or warmth in his entire life.

But it had only been postponed. He would return. When there were no more men to direct, or passengers to deal with.

Panicked, she ran to the chair that held her purse. Her fingers trembled so badly, she almost couldn't open it, but soon the pistol was in her possession. Then, dragging the rickety chair to the far corner, she sat, and with her black-gloved hands, she pointed the gun at the door.

Christal moved in the darkness of the bedroom like a shade, her black-swathed figure blending with every shadow. She'd been in the room for hours, until daylight melted away, along with her hopes of being rescued. She still wasn't sure why the outlaw had left her unscathed. Pete had mentioned the gang was named after a man called Kineson. Cain probably had to answer to him, so he'd been forced to miss his chance. But surely he'd try to make up for it. She pulled her arms across her chest and shivered.

A lamp shone beneath the locked door. She stepped to the other side of the bed, unsure whether she was terrified or relieved her fate was finally to be decided.

Cain entered the room, lantern in hand, the glow illuminating his lean features. His face was as barren of emotion as the room was of furniture, but she stared at him, thinking he was what the saloon girls of her acquaintance meant by a handsome devil. In his case the emphasis was on *devil*.

He held up the lantern to better see her. She was duly heartened to see the brief flare in his eyes when he saw what was in her hand.

He said quietly, "You're full of surprises, ma'am."

She stared at him from across the bed, her face pale and determined.

His eyes lowered to the pistol. "That's the smallest gun I've ever seen. It's old." His gaze met hers. "You've only got one shot."

"That's enough."

"Yeah, that's enough. If you don't miss and just wound me." He took a step toward her.

"Stay back." She shoved the gun out in front of her.

He paused.

"Give me the keys." She held out her hand.

He dangled them. "Where you gonna go, girl, way out here with nobody around?"

"I'm going to go very far away from you."

He chuckled. It wasn't a very jovial sound. "There's a lot worse out there than me."

"I'll worry about that when I come to it." She took a brave step forward. "Give me the keys."

He eyed her, the keys jangling as he swung them like a pendulum. She shivered, then realized she was standing near a broken pane in the window where cold mountain air rushed in. She sidled from the window, never taking her eyes from him.

"You want these?" He gripped the keys in his palm.

She nodded.

"They're all yours." He threw them at her, putting all his weight into the throw. The iron keys shot through the air like a bullet, too quick for her to catch, and smashed through one of the window panes, showering her in glass.

She gasped in dismay. But she didn't take her eyes from him. She'd expected to be tricked.

But if the diversion wasn't enough for him to take the gun, it was enough to gain ground. Instead of being across the bed, he was now not two yards from her.

"Go on. Leave, girl," he taunted. "Run on downstairs and get the keys where they lie in the dirt. I'll stay right here, and you can lock me up when you get back."

Her hand trembled as she raised the gun toward him. Their gazes clashed. Her eyes were somber and determined; his, mesmerizing, menacing. She couldn't tear her gaze away. "I'll shoot you if you come closer," she said.

"You can't control this situation all by yourself. There's too much you don't know. You'll get yourself killed. Give me the gun, girl." He inched forward.

She waved the pistol to warn him back.

He didn't surrender an inch.

"Do you want me to shoot you?" she asked, disbelief threading through her voice. He was a madman to test her the way he was.

He whispered, "But you're messin' up my plans, Mrs. Smith. I can't let you do this."

"You have no choice. Get back!" Her hands quaked. She wrapped both of them around the pistol to steady it.

He moved forward, like a wolf hunched down, eyeing its prey. She bit her lip, desperately wishing it hadn't come to this. She'd never killed a man. She didn't want to have to kill him.

Her back met the wall; she hadn't even realized she'd been backing away. He took another step, then another, all the time keeping her gaze captive to his.

She pulled down the hammer.

He stopped.

The seconds passed like years while they stared at each other, assessing. He behaved as if he didn't quite believe she was capable of pulling the trigger. But she knew she was, and she desperately wished he would retreat. To her unspeakable relief, he took one small step back.

Then he lunged for her. She screamed and pulled the trigger. But her hand was slammed against the wall. Just in time to save him. The bullet ricocheted only once before it burned into the ceiling.

"How—how did you know I was going to shoot?" she cried, frustration and anger tight in her throat.

"It's all in the eyes, Mrs. Smith." He drew his body closer to hers, as if to threaten her. "If a man's got a gun on you, you don't watch his hand. You watch his eyes." He released her with a violent shove. She scrambled out of his reach, still brandishing the now useless pistol.

He walked over to the bed where her black grosgrain purse lay. "No!" she gasped, but he paid her no mind. He opened the bag and dumped the contents out onto the mattress. Out fell a small ivory comb, two bits in change, and five paper-wrapped cartridges. As if all too familiar with the task of muzzle-loading a gun, he bit off the twisted tops of the cartridges, spit the paper on the ground, then poured the gunpowder and bullets out the window to the dirt below.

"You got any more of these?" he asked, turning to her.

"No," she whispered in despair.

"All right, then. C'mon." He took her arm and pushed her in the direction of the door.

"Where are we going?"

"Down to the camp," he answered gruffly. "The stove was taken from this place when it was abandoned. Seeing as how you're a woman, you'll be doing the cooking. Down there."

She wished she could have said she didn't know how to cook, and that he would have to find someone else to play servant. She hadn't been raised in the brownstone on Washington Square to be a scullery. Music and drawing had filled her days. Needlepoint occupied her evenings. Even now she could picture her mother in her chair by the parlor windows, looking so much like Alana, her sister, concentrating on her sewing. Though it had been six years, she could picture every detail: her mother's blond hair pinned neatly in a large bun at her nape, the indigo paisley shawl Father had bought for her in Paris draped over her shoulders, her brown silk gown rustling softly as she bent over her needlepoint frame, counting

stitches on her Berlin woolwork as she warmed herself by the
fire.

The fire.

Christal's eyes darkened. Her gaze met Cain's. She knew
how to cook, all right. Because the cozy picture in her mind
was just that, a vision, a memory, alive no more. And in the
past years, she'd done enough work in saloons to know what
to do with a hot stove and a bag of army beans.

They left the saloon, but not before Cain scooped up the
keys lying in the dirt, now dusted in black gunpowder. He
showed her a path that curved to the rear of the buildings
and dropped rapidly into a gorge. The sounds of gushing
water grew louder as they made the descent, but the going
was slow, the wan yellow light of the lantern barely illuminating the steep, rocky path.

Cain let her walk unfettered by his hands until a gleam in
her eye must have betrayed her desire to flee. Like a jailor, he
took hold of her arm and guided her down. She rebelled at
the iron grip, but her skirts tripped her more than once, and
her booted feet skidded on the bone-dry earth. Once, she
almost slid the entire fifty feet to the bottom of the gorge, but
he was there to steady her. And force her to continue.

Soon they were in the gorge, where a distant firelight flickered through the pines. They approached it and she could
see the light was from a freestanding stone chimney, the mining cabin long since burned down. Gunmen were everywhere, darting in and out of the half-moon of firelight as they
passed by the chimney. She counted nine of them including
Cain. There was only one she hadn't seen before, a barrel-
chested man with white hair to his shoulders and a large mustache. When he stood, he was almost as tall as Cain, and in his
fringed leather jacket he could have been the main attraction
in Buntline's production of *Buffalo Bill*. But he was no actor
playing a cowboy. The fringed leather jacket gleamed with
brass buttons cut from an old Georgia infantry coat. And the
man had eyes like a Doberman pinscher, a terrifying dog
she'd seen once in a New York exhibit.

She looked around anxiously for the other stage passengers. Behind her, Cain said, "All right, take 'em on up to the room and lock them in there. Boone, you can bring 'em grub when there is some." Then Mr. Glassie was shoved into the crescent of firelight, his beautiful verdigris suit pale green from the dust of the road. What horrified her was not his nervous expression, nor the way he stumbled from fatigue, it was the iron manacles that bound his hands and feet, in turn chained to Pete, then to his father, then the preacher, and lastly, the Overland stage driver. The outlaws had seen to everything. None of the passengers was going to escape and ruin the plan. She was the only one who had a breath of a chance.

The passengers filed past her like a chain gang. Helplessly, she watched Pete demand she go with them for her own protection, but the outlaw holding the bullwhip silenced him just by raising his hand. The chains scraped and rattled in a miserable melody as the men disappeared along the path that led up to town. Fear ripped through her heart.

"So this here's the woman."

Christal's blood ran cold. She turned and found the white-haired man staring at her. Then she realized all the men were staring at her, and the campfire talk had died.

One of them licked his lips. The hairs pricked at the back of her neck. Terrified, she stood like a statue, unable to move.

"She's gonna do the cooking, Kineson."

Cain's voice, deep and gravelly, broke her trance. Her presence of mind returned, and she realized he'd called the white-haired man Kineson. Kineson was the man the gang had been named after.

Fear ran up her spine as she met those predatory eyes. She took a step back, but Cain stopped her flight. With nowhere to run, she came face-to-face with the gang leader.

"Git to it, girlie," Kineson said, nodding to the fireplace. A malicious grin cracked his face. "I got a big appetite."

He laughed, and she wanted to spit in his face, but Cain pulled her to the fireplace. She twisted out of his hold and shot him a look that should have knocked him dead. Begrudgingly, she began her task, wishing that each and every one of the gang members were turning on the spit instead of the deer that roasted there now.

Her nerves stretched to the breaking point, she muddled through finding a pot and some canned beans in an old burlap bag. She dumped the beans in a pot and set it on the fire. Every man's gaze was glued to her, as if they were a pack of rabid curs.

She then felt a tug at her skirt. She spun around and saw that the men had sat in a circle around the fireplace, trapping her. Except Cain. He leaned on the fireplace, casually examining one of his revolvers. Again the hand grabbed her skirt. She stepped away from the outlaw, her eyes flashing with hatred, but, surrounded, she left one only to end up next to another gunman who in turn tried to look up her skirts. The men laughed and quickly made a game out of it. Panicked, she was near to crying, but her tears froze in her eyes. If she broke down, they'd have her.

So the game continued, the outlaws closing the circle around her, enjoying her desperation and fear. She ran from one part of the circle to another, and another, never finding escape. Then the game ended. Kineson's hand snaked beneath her petticoats and grabbed her ankle. She couldn't free it. He yanked and she landed in the dirt, the breath knocked clean out of her.

The men howled with laughter. Kineson reached for her, but before he could touch her, Cain jerked her off the ground. She fought him, scared out of her mind that he was going to attack her, but instead he said gruffly, "You got things to do. Do 'em."

She caught her breath, her gaze unable to leave him. If she didn't know better, she'd have thought he'd just saved her. He'd never been part of the game. He'd been off in the shadow of the chimney, watching. Until she fell.

She returned to the pot of beans, an insane gratitude sweeping over her. She was crazy to feel such a thing toward Macaulay Cain, her captor; for all she knew, he'd ended the torture for the sake of a timely dinner. She sneaked a glance at him. He had returned to the chimney and once more studied his revolver as if the incident had never occurred. She snatched up a wooden spoon and scraped the center of the pot where the beans had burned, chastising herself for even thinking the man had helped her.

"Cain . . . you know . . . sometimes I wonder who the leader of this here gang is . . . you or me." Kineson stood, his eyes full of threat.

The gang quieted in the speed it takes to snuff out a candle. All eyes turned to Kineson and Cain, who still stood nonchalantly at the fireplace polishing his revolver.

"You gonna answer me, boy?"

Cain slowly lowered the revolver and raised his eyes. Christal held her breath, the forgotten wooden spoon in her hand poised over the pot. Conflict was simmering faster than the beans.

"This is the Kineson gang. They haven't named the damned thing after me." Cain's every word was cool and concise.

Kineson eyed Christal in the manner of a victor. He smiled and sat down. "Just you remember that, boy."

Cain's quiet words were like thunder. "I'm no boy. Just *you* remember that or you'll be in your grave before you can."

Everyone froze. The next move was Kineson's. Christal slowly slid her gaze to the gang leader.

Kineson stared at Cain, unease in his eyes. There was a strange imbalance between the two men. Kineson was clearly the leader, but the man they all seemed to fear the most was Cain. Cain had the ability. In a gunfight even she would put her money on Cain. Kineson knew he'd win too. He didn't challenge Cain at all. He merely scratched his jaw and called for a drink, putting an end to the incident.

But Christal soon saw it was far from over. The gang returned to normal and she continued to cook the beans, and once, when no one else saw her looking, she found Kineson's gaze nailed on Cain, hatred burning in those terrible eyes.

Chapter Three

It took a century for the beans to cook. In that time the men spoke to one another in low tones, every now and again sliding a look to Cain, who cleaned his gun by the fire. Kineson ignored everyone but Christal. She couldn't make a move without feeling his gaze drive right through her.

A man picked up a banjo and began to strum. Eventually he began to sing. The words ran through Christal's blood like ice.

> *I'm a good ol' Rebel soldier, and that's just what I am;*
> *For this "fair land of freedom" I do not give a damn.*
> *I'm glad we fit against it, I only wished we'd won,*
> *And I don't want any pardon for anything I done.*

The war had been over for ten years. She could hardly remember it, it had touched her so slightly. Life had continued as usual in New York for the elite Knickerbocker class. Irishers were the ones sent to fight the South, and even when they abolished the draft, the Irishers were still the ones to go, for that was the only work they could get. Christal didn't know a single soul who'd been affected by the War Between the States. Until she listened to the outlaw sing his Rebel song.

I hates the Constitution, this great republic too.
I hate the Freedmen's Bureau, in uniforms of blue.
I hate the nasty eagle, with all his brag and fuss
And the lyin', thievin' Yankees, I hates 'em wuss and wuss.

Her only real memory of the war was holding on to her father's hand in the crowd while Lincoln's body rolled down Fifth Avenue. She'd been nine years old, and it had been very confusing to her why someone would shoot the president. But the West had taught her a lot about the war. Bitter Confederates were known to have banded together to raise the South once more. They started out robbing and thieving to fuel their politics, but quickly they degenerated merely to fueling their own greed. Their cause became skewed; still, like John Wilkes Booth, they held on to it to the bitter, dying end.

I followed Old Mas' Robert, for four years, near about,
Got wounded in three places, and starved at Pint Lookout.
I cotch the rheumatism a-campin' in the snow,
But I killed a chance o' Yankees—
And I'd like to kill some mo'.

The man's singing rang in her ears. The Kineson gang was nothing more than a bunch of outlaw southern sympathizers. Thinking back, she recalled that even Cain's words sometimes relaxed into a drawl. The ill-fated passengers of Overland Express had landed in the hands of a bunch of outlaw Confederates.

One by one, all the men started singing until Christal fought the urge to put her hands over her ears.

Three hundred thousand Yankees are stiff in Southern dust;
We got three hundred thousand befo' they conquered us;

> *They died of Southern fever, and Southern steel and shot,*
> *And I wish it was three million instead of what we got.*

She looked over at Cain. He'd stopped polishing his revolver. On the last verse, he sang the words with the rest of
the men, a faraway, melancholy look on his face.

> *I can't take up my musket and fight 'em anymore;*
> *But ain't a-goin' to love 'em, now that is sartin sho';*
> *And I don't want no pardon for what I was and am,*
> *And I won't be reconstructed, and I do not give a damn.*

Nervously she stirred the beans, all the while praying they
never found out she was from New York. She cringed when
she remembered Mr. Glassie telling them he was from Paterson, New Jersey. That didn't bode well for him.

The men called for their meal. Rebelliously she sloshed
beans onto plates, and they settled down to eat, like bears
stuffing their maws. Exhausted, she stood by the fire and
wondered if the time to escape wasn't at hand. The men were
preoccupied with filling their stomachs.

Where she would go, she didn't know. She secretively
glanced at a copse of aspen beyond the firelight. If she could
flee into the copse, she might be able to hide from them in the
darkness. If her luck held that far, perhaps tomorrow she
might stumble upon a miner's camp or a trapper who would
help her.

Slowly she counted the men to make sure their attention
was on their plates and not her. It was; even Kineson's lascivi-
ous looks had ebbed with the need to appease his hunger.
Her blood pounded with excitement. Again she looked into
the darkness to the copse of aspen. Then her gaze slammed
into Cain's.

Since they'd gotten to the campfire, he'd done his best to
ignore her. He was not ignoring her now. She could see in his

face that he knew she contemplated escape; she could also see the slight smirk on his lips, taunting her to try. He might have unintentionally stopped the men from harassing her, but she knew he was as serious about the kidnapping as any of them. And if she ran, he would catch her.

Her shoulders slumped. She was running out of ideas. Desperate to think of another avenue of escape, she became so absorbed in thought, she didn't see Kineson until he stood in front of her.

He smiled. Anxiety shot through her veins like liquid fire. She turned away, but the chimney blocked her path. Trapped, she tried to push him away, but he was too strong. He held her face with his hands and looked down at her pale, fear-ridden features. She pulled his hands off of her but it only further amused him. He smiled again, then reached for her, this time using a brutal grip around her waist while she struggled to keep him from kissing her.

"She's mine, Kineson."

Kineson looked behind him. Cain stood there, his right hand relaxed at his thigh, clearly ready to shoot the man's brains out.

"Get him off me," she gasped, her blue eyes frightened and angry. She looked to Cain, but his eyes turned ice cold. It was clear he didn't care to help her, only to retain what he considered his property.

Nonetheless, Kineson was furious. He spat, "What you mean by that, Cain? Why you helping this girlie? You making a claim on her?"

"Yeah." Cain crossed his arms lazily over his chest.

"You ain't gonna share?"

"No."

Kineson stared at him. Cain returned the stare, unflinching. Between them, they fought a silent battle. But it was a standoff. Neither man relented. Soon Kineson's hand seemed to itch for his revolver. He put his palm around the pearl handle, then looked at Cain's hand. A mistake. Cain's notoriety as a gunman came from speed, precision, and, as Christal now knew well, the fact that he could read a man's eyes and be the one to shoot first. Kineson caught Cain's stare again, and she could tell the gang leader himself knew he was disadvantaged. Kineson stepped aside.

Christal could hardly believe it. The gang had taken its name from Kineson; Cain was only one of his minions carrying out the kidnapping. But now she wasn't sure who the real leader was. Kineson could be intimidated by Cain, as the rest of the men could.

Kineson turned and abruptly pointed to her, his white hair and mustache a contrast to his angry red face. He blurted out to Cain, "She's yours for now, but I ain't gonna lay so low as to see you giving her charity. She's a prisoner and don't you forget it." With a furious nod he said, "Go on, then. Have a go at her. Make her your woman. But do it now or stand aside."

Cain's magnificent cold eyes turned to her. Kineson had offered a test of his loyalties. He would rape her and pass, or save her and fail. She felt a chill crawl down her spine. His expression was shuttered, unreadable. Her mind fooled her. For one brief second she thought he looked as if he regretted what must be done, but the emotion, if it existed at all, was gone before his hands reached for her.

She ran from him, shoving away his hold, a cry catching in her throat. Her fear gave her unexpected strength, and she pushed through the circle of men to the outer fringes of firelight. Cain had told her to obey him, and that he might prove willing to protect her from being raped by the men in the gang. But never had he said who would protect her from being raped by him.

She was almost into the safety and darkness of the woods before he caught her. In a rough, quick motion he swung her into his embrace, then crushed his mouth down on hers. The men hooted and hollered the more she tried to fight. Her fists pushed against his chest, but it was like trying to move granite. Her head jerked right and left as she tried to avoid the bruising kiss. But she was losing. His lips moved forcibly on hers, and his unshaven jaw scorched her soft skin wherever there was contact.

Then his tongue lunged into her mouth. She should have

bitten it, but the shock left her momentarily stunned. She broke his hold by twisting her head away. In the dim firelight, she stared up at him, terror surging within her.

His face was devoid of compassion. Nothing would stop him. He had a job to do, to rape and humiliate her and prove his loyalty to the gang, and he was determined to do it. He was going to rip away her pride and dignity and self-respect, but to him that would be a small price to pay for a few minutes of pleasure.

He kissed her, and this time she had the presence of mind to bite him. She sank her teeth into his probing tongue, he jerked his head back, and she could see blood on his lip. "Christ," he muttered, looking at the crimson smear on his hand where he'd run it across his mouth. That was all the pause she needed. She bolted. His hand snaked out to hold her and ripped the shoulder of her bodice. Tiny jet buttons sprayed over the grass, leaving him and the rest of the outlaws a good view of the full white flesh that peeked over the lace of her corset cover. By instinct, her hands covered her chest. A fatal error. He quickly had her in his embrace again, triumph in his eyes, but strangely, no satisfaction.

"God have mercy on your soul if you will have none on mine," she whispered, her words like acid before he silenced her with another kiss. Subduing her with superior strength, he forced her mouth open again, and she could taste the salty metallic essence of his blood, smell the animal scent of him, a rutting scent like that of territorial wolves. She released an inward sob.

She fought him with all her strength, but she was no match for him as he had proven in the saloon. Quickly her hands hurt from hitting him, her lips were sore from trying to break free. Little by little her strength waned, and she came under his control. Until she realized she was going to lose. He had her. All he would have to do would be to lay her on the ground, throw her skirts over her head, and rape her in front of everyone through the open seam in her pantalettes. The innocence she had protected and nurtured within her core would be destroyed, and after tonight the girl she used to be would be gone. And another girl, one damaged and diminished, would be there to take her place.

Her legs buckled beneath her; his hand wrapped over her derriere and held her up. Behind them the men continued to jeer and laugh and applaud Cain's dominance. Distantly, she wondered what kind of monster would do this to a woman. His thumb pressed against the bottom of her breast as he held her waist, but, growing numb, she hardly felt it. She was in a daze by the time he stopped kissing her and led her out of the perimeter of light. Just beyond the firelight, there was a ramshackle lean-to ready to fall to the ground. He pushed her behind it, as if somehow he had some shame and wanted his privacy.

Behind the lean-to, she heard catcalls, then the men began to fall silent. The show was over; they made do with listening. Cain pushed her to the ground. The pine needles, dry from the summer heat, crackled beneath her skirts, but the ground was cold and its chill gave her one last moment of strength. She struggled with him, ripping the underarm of her sleeve. The gang seemed to like the noise of tearing fabric, for they mumbled and one man let loose a laugh. Finally his hands caught hers and pinned them to the ground. He covered her.

He lay there, his tall, lean body heavy upon her own. Her breath came hard and fast as she waited for the onslaught. At any moment, he would start fumbling with the buttons on his jeans. Desperately she tried to separate herself from her body, so that the damage might only be physical.

"Cry out," he breathed into her ear, shifting his weight and grunting in the process.

She shut her eyes and refused his perverse request, glad she couldn't see him in the dark.

He groaned and shifted his weight again. "I said cry out, moan, whimper," he whispered. "Do it."

Her eyes flew open. She couldn't see his face, and now she cursed the dark. It seemed trickery, but she could have sworn there was something in his voice that seemed willing to help her.

He shifted again and his legs lay between her parted thighs.

She felt every inch of his hardened frame, but he had yet to unfasten his trousers or lift her skirts.

"I said whimper, God damn you," he grunted, and rustled the pine needles some more.

She whimpered.

It didn't take much for it to be convincing for she was shaken and confused. The sound came out as a wavering, feminine plea, and she could hear the men twitter beyond the lean-to, excited by her submission.

"Again," he groaned, now grunting in earnest.

She suddenly understood what he was doing. A sob caught in her throat. This outlaw played God with her life, her doom or salvation utterly under his control. And now he'd chosen to spare her. He was a criminal, sparing her from crimes he himself would commit, yet she was overwhelmed by a strong, insane gratitude that he chose to spare her at all.

He grew louder and more urgent. She began to weep, unable to deal with her conflicting emotions. Finally, he released a savage sound from deep in his chest, and lay over her, silent, waiting to see if they were believed.

The only sound was her soft crying. Beyond the lean-to the men were quiet. Then they began to talk as if they hadn't been listening at all.

Her senses came back to her. She could feel Cain's weight upon her. Her back felt like ice, but her chest where he covered her was warm. He breathed heavily. They were so close, she could feel his heart pounding.

"Why—?" she whispered, but he touched her lips, silencing her.

His words were low and harsh. "If you speak of this, you'll get me killed. Worse than that, you'll get yourself killed."

She nodded, but still she questioned why he'd helped her. He had every reason to carry out the rape, and he'd given an elaborate show to convince the other men. Yet he hadn't harmed her. Despite how she rebelled at the thought, she wondered if maybe he wasn't a bit like herself, that maybe his hard, cold renegade exterior hid another person, a person raised decent and kind, one who knew about compassion and mercy, yet who'd been forced by injustice to hide and seldom emerge.

Her emotions rent into tatters, she watched as he rolled off her. Tears still fell down her cheeks. Her nerves were over- wrought, her feelings utterly confused. Macaulay Cain was the devil incarnate. He'd kidnapped her and treated her little better than a slave. Yet when her fate had been in his hands, he'd saved her and now his charity appeared five times more than it actually was because it came from an outlaw, a man who was not expected to show charity at all.

He sat up and his fingers caught in the tear at her shoulder. Hesitantly, he caressed her there, just once, his callused fin- gers on tender skin. Then he heaved himself to his knees, pulled out his shirttail, and unbuttoned his trousers. She shiv- ered, the warmth of his body gone. He dragged her to her feet, and she wiped her tears, her emotions still in turmoil.

Grimly he pushed her in front of him as he had so many times that day. They walked back into the firelight, she look- ing stunned and ravaged, he, satisfied and dominant, slowly buttoning his pants and tucking in his shirttail. The outlaws were pleased. Kineson looked at her disheveled appearance and said snidely, "Here comes the merry widow now."

They all laughed. Except Cain. He gave her an undecipher- able look, then returned to polishing his gun.

She sat by the fire, unable to think of anything but what had just happened. The men began to retire to their bedrolls and an outlaw brought back the dishes the passengers had used up at the saloon. Grateful to have something to occupy her, she gathered all the tin plates scattered among the men, removed her black cotton gloves, careful to hide her scarred palm, and washed the dishes. When she was done, she put on her gloves, then sat by the fireplace, her head leaning wearily against the rock.

She hadn't eaten all day, and she was exhausted. But she had no need for food or sleep. Fear left her every sense at- tuned to only what was around her, not within her.

There were more and more snores as the outlaws drifted to sleep. From where she sat, she could feel Kineson's gaze on her as he lay in his bedroll. After a long time, she finally had the courage to look over at him. She was unspeakably relieved that he, too, had fallen asleep. Briefly she mulled over the possibility that all the men would fall asleep and she could sneak off into the woods. But she knew it wouldn't happen. Cain was not going to allow it.

She watched him place his bedroll alongside the back of the fireplace, the choicest spot in the entire camp. She wasn't surprised the gang allowed him such a spot, only that such a hardened outlaw would require the comfort of the fireplace. But then her heart skipped a beat when she realized he might want it if he were sleeping with a woman. Her gaze never left him as he bent and untied the thongs around his thighs that secured his holstered guns. Slowly he unbuckled the holster. He held it with one hand and reached for her with the other.

She should have expected he would make her sleep with him. The gang considered her his woman and it was necessary to keep her from escaping; still, she drew back, and he had to force her down onto his blanket. With unexpected chivalry, he put her next to the heat of the fireplace, his own back to the cold night air. The holster he stuffed between them, shoving it low where he could get to his revolver quickly. Then, without a word, he pulled the blanket across his shoulders and closed his eyes.

An hour passed as she stared at the back of the fireplace. She was warm, unbelievably warm, so warm that she actually had to fight off sleep. But what kept her awake was the thought of those six-shooters pressed into her buttocks. She couldn't get around the notion that if she could take Cain's gun, freedom would be hers.

Another hour passed. Slowly she turned on her side and faced him. His breathing was regular and deep. Inch by excruciating inch, her hand slid down the blanket until it reached the smooth handle of one revolver. The rapid fire of her heartbeat drowned out the distant lone howl of a wolf. Her finger wiggled through the trigger guard until it rested on the trigger. Her other hand reached down and took hold of the holster. She pulled on the gun. A hand clamped down on her wrist.

"You go reaching down there, Mrs. Smith, you just might find something."

It was too dark to see his face. She released a small moan as he squeezed her wrist. A pain shot through her arm. She surrendered her hold and tried to draw back her hand, but in punishment, he wouldn't let her. He held her hand down between them until she felt the hardness. It singed her hand.

Crying out, she struggled to pull away. This time he let her, shoving her away while he removed the holster from between them. She began to scramble out from beneath the blanket, but before she could, he thrust her back against his chest and threw his arm around her, its weight effectively rendering her own arms useless. The holster was in his hand, the guns right beneath her nose, so close, yet so far away.

She could tell by his breathing that it took him a long time to go to sleep. Unable and unwilling to move, she lay against him, his hardness burning through her skirts into her flesh. They lay there for a long time until, seemingly out of the blue, he asked in a low, surprisingly gentle voice, "You have any babies missing you right now?"

She could barely whisper, "No."

He released a long breath, almost as if in relief. Then, being an outlaw, he went to sleep just as he awoke. Quickly.

In the darkness, the memory of his near rape came back to her. Unbidden, she recalled his movements, his groans, and finally that deep animal sound that had seemed to emanate from his very soul. He made her feel things she wished she didn't. She cursed him, unable to move beneath the rocklike muscle of his arm. Sleep took a very long time to come.

Chapter Four

"Git along there, girlie, and fetch me another biscuit," Kineson said, looking as if he might kick her.

Christal wiped the sticky blond strands of hair from her eyes and shot him a killing stare. Having no choice, she slid another biscuit from the frypan, put it on a plate, and walked over to him.

The morning was cold but Christal barely noticed as she patted her face, flushed from the heat of the campfire. The sun was up late in the mountains, and it just now fired the tops of the aspens. To the west the sky was a clear azure, but the granite face of the gorge cast a long shadow over their camp. She cast her gaze up the rocky path that led to the town. She could just barely see the roof of the saloon at the top of the gorge. The other passengers might have an escape plan, but she would only be able to go along if she knew what it was, and she longed to speak with one of them. Her gaze slid to her captors. Boone lounged alongside the chimney, watching her with his brutish eyes. The oldest outlaw—she didn't know his name—flexed his knees while he walked around camp, as if he was prone to rheumatism. Three men sat around the fire eating biscuits, Kineson included. She didn't know where the others were.

"How come you never take those gloves off, girlie?"

She handed Kineson the biscuit plate and ignored his question. When she turned from him, though, she curled her palms, the black cotton gloves stiff from sweat and grease.

Cain walked in front of the chimney, suddenly appearing. His hair was slicked back as if he'd just bathed, and she noticed that, wet, his hair looked black. He hadn't shaved, but he must have performed some sort of morning ablution in the falls that thundered beyond the copse of aspen. Which was more than the rest of the gang did. Rags and fleas, the trademark of the Confederacy, was their trademark as well. Their stench repelled her.

"Get some of them biscuits. You can take them to the saloon." Cain hardly waited for her to pile them on a tin plate before he took her arm and led her up the path.

She tripped and stumbled, dreading the day ahead. Her attempts at escape had proved futile, now it seemed her only hope was waiting for Tuesday—if Tuesday ever came. Though there was a part of her, a very small part, that trusted Cain after what he had done last night, still he was the outlaw, and she his captive. She desperately needed the assurance that she would survive the kidnapping. If Overland Express came through with the ransom, she could wait it out until Tuesday —with his protection. If things were to go wrong, she needed to know how bad they might get.

It was difficult to balance the biscuit plate and climb. She stumbled on the rocky path, loosing several black, half-cooked biscuits before his hands reached out to steady her. But when she was righted, she shunned his hold as if he were a leper. She didn't like his hands on her. His touch was like a primeval memory and against her will, she began to remember the morning.

At dawn, she had awakened and felt icy air at her back. Shivering, she sat up and found Cain buckling on his holster, staring at her. His face became clearer in the whitening shadows. She noticed his eyes had lowered to her hair. Self-consciously she ran her fingers through the tangle. It was a mess; most of her pins were gone from her struggles. As if he could read her thoughts, he'd reached down and ripped another piece of fringe from his worn chaps. He handed it to her, a strangely considerate gesture, and she accepted it, hating the rush of gratitude that hit her.

And hating the way his stare quickened her pulse.

The remembrance of that stare even now distracted her. Her skirts tangled in her boots, and she tripped. The biscuit plate flew from her hand as she grabbed a branch to keep from sliding back down the trail. But the sharp, broken branch caught on her glove and scratched down her palm. She moaned in pain.

He caught her and extracted her hand where it was caught on the twig. Tersely he said, "Get rid of those damned gloves."

"The biscuits," she gasped, ignoring her bleeding hand. The idea of having to go back to the camp and make more sickened her.

He looked down at the burned, doughy biscuits strewn across the dusty path. As if recalling breakfast, he shook his head. "A little dirt can't ruin that cooking."

In any other situation she might have been insulted, but it was true, her cooking was deplorable and she was glad. The Kineson gang deserved to be poisoned.

She stooped to pick up the biscuits and brush the dirt from them, but he stopped her. "I said, get rid of those gloves."

"No—" She barely got the word out before he dragged her to her feet and pulled the glove off her left hand.

His gaze dropped to her hand, a hand suspiciously devoid of a wedding ring, and before she could stop herself, she stumbled to volunteer a reason. "I—I needed money after my husband died. I was forced to sell my ring."

He stared at her intently, as if homing in on her nervousness.

"How long you been married?"

"Two years." The lie came quickly.

"He's been dead six weeks?"

"Yes."

He looked down at her finger and rubbed where the ring should have been. His mouth twitched with a smile, as if he'd trapped her. "There's no white skin."

She didn't comment. To confess anything more would hang her.

He grabbed her right hand and pulled on the torn glove.

A shot of fear ran down her spine. She couldn't let him see the scar. The wanted posters might have somehow followed her west, and if he had ever chanced to see one, he'd know there was an enormous reward for her.

She snatched her hand away, more ready to fight than to reveal what was beneath her glove. Grappling with him, she smeared blood on his shirt, but he paid it no mind, as if he were used to it and used to fighting with her. He took her hand again and this time held tight. He pulled off the glove, his eyes glittering as he gazed down.

The scar took most of her palm. It was strangely beautiful; an exact shape of a rose, burned into her hand. She watched his reaction carefully, heartened that she only saw curiosity and, perhaps, a little shock in his eyes. But no recognition.

He released her hand. Slowly his eyes met hers. She could tell he wanted to ask her a lot of questions; also, that he knew she wouldn't answer. Without saying a word, she knelt and began to pick up the biscuits lying in the rocky path.

His eyes followed her every movement as if that would uncover her thoughts, her past. But she'd spent four years keeping secrets, and she kept them now. She picked up each blackened biscuit and blew off the dust, the memory of her tragedy kept painfully locked in her heart.

She'd been thirteen when the fire occurred. Her family, the Van Alens, was one of the exclusive and illustrious Knicker-bocker families of Manhattan, wealthy but restrained, living quietly in their old town house on Washington Square. Her life back then now seemed unreal, it seemed to spring from a storybook. Her parents had loved each other, and their daughters, Christal and Alana, had loved them. They were a close family who often welcomed their late aunt's husband, Baldwin Didier, into their home as if he were a blood relation. He was a frightening man in many ways to a young girl. With his gray Vandyke beard and his piercing blue eyes, Christal remembered not liking him. But he was also a man-about-town, and she remembered her parents laughing quite gaily over his dry comments, happy to have his company if only for the entertainment it offered.

But while Clarisse and John Van Alen laughed with their brother-in-law by the dying evening fire, Baldwin Didier was coveting. Rumor had it that the Van Alen legacy held immense wealth: enormous stock in the old Dutch West India Company, holdings in the Knickerbocker and New-York Bank, parcels of land that stretched from Wall Street to the Harlem River.

And very few relatives. Especially since Clarisse's sister, Didier's late wife, had died of stomach ailment.

One night when Christal had recently turned thirteen, she awoke to the acrid smell of smoke. She leapt from her bed and followed the smoke to her parents' suite. The rooms were in flames. And Baldwin Didier stood over the bed, a pensive cast to his face as he stared at her parents lying in state beneath the bed's flaming canopy.

She cried out. Didier fled. She prayed he was going for the fire wagon, but she knew it wasn't so when she stumbled to her parents in the smoke-darkened room and saw the blood, and the gold candlestick dented by the pressure of their skulls.

Christal now believed it was at that point her mind snapped, refusing to recall what she'd seen, an unfortunate occurrence because her lack of memory, a fine guardian from trauma, was also the ruthless traitor that put her in the asylum. With her memory gone, she could produce no evidence to absolve her of the killing of her parents. And that she was in the room when the fire occurred was certain. One had only to look at the palm of her hand.

The interior of her parents' suite was fitted with a set of Parisian silver repoussé doorknobs, each in the likeness of a rose. Her memory had returned before she ran away from the asylum, and now Christal could relive every terrifying minute in the suite. She'd known instinctively that her parents were beyond help, and with flames licking all around her, she'd run to the door to escape. But Didier had locked it.

Like a captured animal, she'd twisted the iron-hot doorknob until her strength was gone, and her hand indelibly branded. She recalled sliding to her knees in her white cotton nightgown gone gray with smoke. To this day, she didn't know if prayer had revived her, or something else, but somehow she crawled to the windows that fronted Washington Square and opened one. With smoke blinding and choking her, she felt her way onto the stone ledge outside. It was only a few feet to her bedroom window, and she crawled to it, unafraid of the twenty-foot drop to the street below, crying and gasping for breath in the clear night air, her entire body and soul in shock from what she had just witnessed. And strangely, she couldn't remember her hand hurting, yet it must have, terribly, for she'd worn bandages on it for almost six months. But even now she couldn't remember the pain.

The firemen found her huddled in her wardrobe, black from head to toe with soot, her right hand dangling uselessly at her side. Her mind rejected what she had just gone through, and she found she couldn't remember enough to answer the police's questions. The fire had raged so hot that her parents' bodies had been burned beyond recognition. There was no evidence left of their bludgeoning, nor of Didier's crime. There was just the doorknob burn on her hand, damning her by placing her in the bedroom when her parents died, and the amnesia, further damning her by proclaiming her insane.

A cloud of accusation hung over her until her uncle Baldwin mercifully bargained with the police to place her in the posh asylum out in Brooklyn. And no wonder he'd been merciful. With her sister Alana's fortune under his control, Christal's memory gone, and the rose indelibly burned into her hand, one of his own victims had given Baldwin Didier the alibi he'd needed to commit the perfect crime.

Christal shook with anger every time she thought about the fact that he had gotten away with such a heinous crime. Now her very reason for living was to see that he was found out, but it was up to her and her alone, and the going had been slow and difficult. She refused to seek Alana's help and perhaps endanger the only person in the world she loved. Christal could still picture her sister's expression as Alana visited her in the asylum, Alana's face, pale and beautiful like their mother's, but unlike their mother's, etched with concern, hardened with determination. Alana had never believed the terrible accusations surrounding her sister. She had fought tooth and nail for years to get Christal removed from the asylum. And though Alana had never been successful, her faith kept Christal going when she despaired. And because of this, her love for her sister went beyond even her love for herself.

Cain motioned for her to begin climbing again, interrupting her thoughts. She balanced the biscuits in one hand and held her skirts in the other. She climbed, assaulted once more by remembrance.

Her memory had returned when she was sixteen. The asylum had thought she'd truly gone mad when she began raving about her uncle's crime. They'd injected her with morphine until she almost believed they were right. But she'd convinced the night orderly to dispense with the shots, and in the wee hours of one morning three years ago, she'd dressed in a stolen nurse's uniform and departed the asylum for good. A fugitive.

She glanced back at Cain. Meeting his gaze, she still found no recognition of who she was, just the glint of curiosity. With no gloves to hide it any longer, she curled her palm over the scar. For years she'd wished she could be rid of it, but it was always there, like a shadow, ready to convict her of unspeakable crimes she had not committed. Once, she'd even thought of burning the rose scar off, but when she'd gotten the poker red-hot and held it up to her hand, she hadn't the courage to endure the pain. She'd tossed the poker into the fire and sentenced herself to a life on the run.

Her heart ceased its hammering in her chest. She wondered why she'd been so afraid. Out west, they were all fugitives. She glanced back at Cain. Of one kind or another.

In town, an outlaw paced the front of the saloon, on watch. Cain nodded to him, and they entered the swinging doors.

The saloon was hardly recognizable. The dust had been disturbed in so many places that for the first time she could see wood. The footsteps up the staircase looked as if an army had trod there.

She walked up the stair with Cain and knocked on the door. Zeke answered, his bullwhip replaced by a Winchester.

Christal handed him the biscuit plate. She peered over his shoulder and counted passengers. They all looked weary. Mr. Glassie was sweating though the morning was still cool. The preacher's hand shook when he reached for a biscuit, obviously wishing it were a glass of whiskey. The driver and Pete's father slept, their heads lolled against the peeling plaster wall, the rattle of their chains waking them every time they shifted position.

Her gaze met with Pete's. The boy was slouched in a corner, scared but defiant. Anger stained his cheeks when he gazed at her torn bodice. "Why ain't she here with us?" he demanded, refusing the biscuit plate. He tried to rise to his feet, but Boone, the other outlaw in the room, shoved him back to the floor.

"She's Cain's woman now, that's why," Boone said. By the look Boone tossed at her, Christal knew he'd been at the campfire last night.

"You ain't got no right—!" Pete cursed at Cain, but Boone kicked him in the stomach.

Christal started to go to him, but Cain grabbed her by the waist and held her back. "You can't help that boy," he said gruffly.

"Don't hurt him!" she cried out.

Boone looked to kick Pete again. Cain said, "Leave him," and Boone obeyed. It was clear he didn't like the fact that the order had come as a result of her plea, but even he knew Cain ruled with an iron hand.

"They had any water today?" Cain asked.

Boone shook his head.

"Then go fetch some."

Boone nodded.

Cain gazed at the passengers. Satisfied by their condition, he grabbed her hand and left, ignoring Pete's baleful stare.

They descended the staircase. Unable to stop herself, she said, "What's the chance we'll all see Tuesday?"

Cain glanced at her, his mouth a grim line. "Why don't you just worry about whether *you'll* see it or not?"

Her gaze locked with his. She thought about last night, how he'd saved her. "You won't let us die," she whispered with conviction.

He looked away. His eyes grew cold and restless. "I don't make any guarantees."

Cain paced his Appaloosa along the train tracks. They were down on the plains, beneath a rickety water tower, the sun shining hot on their backs. He studied the tracks, the ditches, the lay of the land. By instinct, Christal knew this was where Overland Express had been told to drop the payroll.

"Are you the one to meet the train?" she asked, riding bareback on the Ap with him, his arms encircling her. After they left the saloon, he'd hauled her on his horse, and they'd ridden down to the plains, not speaking.

"Kineson'll be there with me. The rest'll either be over there lying in the grass or back at the saloon."

He reined the Ap to the left, and they crossed the tracks. Christal white-knuckled the mane. Riding in Cain's arms made her nerves hum. She could feel every muscle in his chest, every sway of his hips against hers as the Ap jogged. There was strength in his body that far surpassed her own. The only way to escape him would be through her wits.

"What happens after you and Kineson have the money?" She dreaded the answer to that question, but the crime of kidnapping and robbery was so great, she couldn't rid herself of the terrible fear that Kineson wasn't going to allow any witnesses.

Cain paused. His face hardened.

In a quiet steady voice she asked, "Do they plan on killing us?" When he didn't answer, she continued with "I say *they* because—"

"I know why you said it."

"We were just passengers on that stagecoach. We don't have any involvement in any of this."

"You're the means to the end. Kineson and I were in the same Georgia regiment that got blown to hell at Sharpsburg. Terence Scott, the man who owns Overland, was the commander of the Union regiment that went against us."

Cain was from Georgia. She stored the little tidbit of information for future use. "So you're getting back at Mr. Scott this way? By stealing from him? You're cowards."

She readied herself for his anger, but Cain only said, "Terence Scott's a damned bluebelly and Kineson's a Secesh. There ain't nothing to be done about it." This time she noticed the slight drawl.

"You can do something," she insisted.

Finally the anger came. His voice was like acid. "I do what Kineson tells me to do. You remember that fact as if your life depends on it, because it does, Mrs. Smith, it does."

"You don't always do what he tells you." She remembered last night. He was just about to refute it, but she said, "We could escape, Cain. You and I, we could go back to Camp Brown and tell the authorities where the men are. I'll see that they exonerate you. Mr. Glassie, Pete, they'd be so grateful to be freed, I know they wouldn't press charges."

He looked her dead in the eyes.

She couldn't keep the desperation out of her voice. "You *can* do it. That man last night, he didn't want to hurt anyone. You're in with a bad lot. The war is over, Cain, and you and Kineson, you're never going to resurrect it."

"What do you know about the war? You're just a Yankee girl that was probably too young to even remember it."

She gasped. "How—how do you know I'm from the North?"

He smirked. "You got *Yankee* written all over you. You don't dress too proud, but you're used to money and nice things. I can see it in the way you carry yourself. You got your nose up in the air all the time. I don't know any Southern women who can afford that anymore."

She was shocked that he knew so much about her without her telling him. He knew she wasn't one of his own, and that would make her plea more difficult. But he had still helped her last night, even when he knew she was a Yankee. There was a good man inside him somewhere. If she could find that man, maybe she could save the lot of them. "If we run, Cain, if we escape, maybe we could help you. Mr. Glassie's company would be grateful, and"—she thought of Pete's father claiming he and Pete had struck it rich—"maybe we passengers could get some money together and give you a reward. You could go home to Georgia. Make a new life for yourself."

"I haven't got a home anymore. Sherman made sure of that when he went to take a piss in the Atlantic."

She paled. She was losing ground fast. This man had nothing to lose and nothing to gain. There was no reaching him. Finally she said, "You must have something you want that we could give you."

He looked at her, his gaze lowering to her torn and dirty bodice where it drew tight across her bosom. His glance nearly burned into her skin. He didn't speak at all. He didn't have to.

She grew quiet. She would never bargain with her body. The honor and pride inside her was something she would live with, or die with.

His eyes raised to see the defiance in her own. He quit his staring. "I'm not going to set you free no matter what you do, no matter what you give me." He stared out at the wide grassy prairie that surrounded them. "If I rode into town with you, they'd see me hanged for this one for sure." He pulled down the dingy scarlet bandanna tied around his neck. The raw scar still shocked her. "I'm not going to have another bout with the hangman and win."

She played her last desperate card. "If you take me to Camp Brown, I'll never speak a word about you. I'll tell them about the other passengers, you can just leave the fort. Escape."

"I can't."

"But don't you see Kineson hates you? You want your gold

but what if Kineson isn't planning on sharing?" A sob of frustration caught in her throat. "I'll never give you away if you take me to Camp Brown. Save yourself. That man last night had a good heart—"

"Forget about last night," he snapped. "If you think I can change the plans, I can't. What's going to happen is going to happen. If you cooperate, then maybe we'll all get out of this alive."

Her hopes trickled away like water during a drought. She withdrew from him, staring out at the wide, grassy prairie. There was nothing more to say.

Angrily, he pulled the Ap to a halt. "What does savin' my neck got to do with you anyway? You got enough troubles just savin' your own ass."

She didn't answer; he shook her. "Why do you care so much?"

Her gaze riveted to his. She was as angry as he was. "You and I are alike, Cain, that's all. I understand you. We've both been hunted like animals. I don't deserve it. Maybe you don't either. So prove it. Take me to Camp Brown."

His grip on her tightened. "That husband of yours . . . is he the one hunting you or . . ." His words dwindled as he thought of all the possibilities.

"Go ahead, think the worst. Everyone else has." She didn't need to be reminded how bitterly true her statement was.

He searched her eyes, eyes that were crystalline blue in the brilliant sun. Slowly, he said, "No . . . you didn't kill him. You wouldn't be wearing those weeds if you'd killed him. You don't go mourning a husband you've murdered."

"No, you don't," she whispered, again feeling that troubled gratitude. She'd been running for three years. Macaulay Cain was the first person to find her innocent before proven guilty.

"What was he like?"

One simple question, impossible to answer. He asked about her husband, but she could tell he really wanted to know everything. He wanted to know why she was on that Overland Express stagecoach, where she was destined, why she had no wedding band, why she had no babies. He wanted to gauge her marital bliss, pass judgment on her past, and predict her future. If she had one.

She stared out at the breathless expanse, the sky yawning above the land in an intense blue. The prairie beckoned her. It promised space and anonymity. She couldn't give up that anonymity now, not even when something deep inside her desired to trust him, to tell him about her uncle, how he was searching for her, that she'd been accused of his crimes, of killing her parents. Perhaps she wanted to tell him about herself in the hope that he might see they were alike and that she was worthy of saving, along with the other passengers.

But she was afraid she would never convince him, and then she would have jeopardized herself for nothing.

She took a deep breath and embraced the wide open space around her. Back in New York, she'd spent three brutal years locked in an asylum, confused and tormented, afraid that all the lies her uncle told might be true. Then, as if she had awakened from a bad dream, her memory and the truth had returned. She believed one day she would find justice. Or one day her uncle would find her. Neither day had come. Until then it was best to keep her mouth shut.

"What did the son of a bitch do to you?" He put a callused finger on her cheek and turned her head so she'd be forced to look at him.

She could see he was troubled by her gaze. Most people were. Her eyes held the pain of an inexplicable and crushing blow.

"What does it matter?" she whispered. "My past is my own. I wanted you to know I see reasons for the life you lead. I have my reasons too."

"I'm an outlaw. A woman like you should have nothing in common with me."

She couldn't miss the reproof in his voice. "And what do you know of women like me?"

"I thought I knew plenty."

Her eyes locked with his. "Run, Cain. Let's save those men back in Falling Water, let's save ourselves. Then you can run and never look back. We both can."

The prairie breeze kicked at his hair, the sun glittered in his eyes, eyes like pieces of a winter sky. For one brief second, she believed they had connected, that they had formed an understanding, become like two creatures in the forest who recognize each other despite the cloak of darkness surrounding them. But the moment shattered. Cain spurred his Ap into a gallop. They rode back to Falling Water as if wildfire licked at their heels. Christal returned to the camp disheartened by the fact that Macaulay Cain was not the man she hoped he was.

Chapter Five

It was dusk when they returned to camp. Cain watered and fed his horse before he freed Christal to begin another supper of beans and biscuits. Her spirit rebelled at being a slave, but her mind wanted survival. She accepted for the moment that she had no choice but to stumble her way through the preparation of another meal for her keepers.

She stirred the beans, the heat of the campfire nauseating her. The smell made her light-headed and more than once she was forced to sit down. Besides a half-eaten biscuit that morning, she'd not eaten since she was kidnapped. She had to keep up her strength, but if tonight was like the last, the offer of food would be too little, come too late. She was supposed to serve the men their meal, prepare the pot that was to be taken to feed those up at the saloon, and put another pot on the fire to boil to wash the rancid grease from the tinware. Last night, by the time she had done everything, the meal was over with, the beans eaten; all she had left was the gang's leavings. She vowed to die of starvation rather than feast upon Kineson's rejected beans.

She served the men, then rested her head on the stones of the fireplace and closed her eyes. Cain had just helped himself to another plate, finishing off the pot. There would be no dinner for her again tonight.

She slid to the ground and tried not to think of her hunger. Every muscle in her body ached with fatigue. The ride on

Cain's Ap had made her derriere sore, the lugging of iron pots strained her back. With no food to sustain her, she could feel her energy and spirit seep from her soul.

Cain nudged her shoulder and she opened her eyes. He had finished, but instead of abandoning his plate on the needle-covered ground, he held it out to her. Half full.

He was the captor taking care of his captive. She could find the strength to eat his leftovers or starve. She looked down at the fork, the fork that he'd eaten from, that had slid between his tongue and palate, the way his tongue had slid in her mouth when he'd kissed her.

Every reason told her to save her pride and reject his offer, but the instinct to survive overruled reason. She accepted the plate and ate Cain's beans. And despite her attempts to will it away, that strange guilt-ridden gratitude came slinking back because he'd spared her from having to eat from a more vile man's plate.

He waited for her to wash the dishes before he took her into the woods. All the men watched when night fell, night that came early and cold in the mountains. Like coyotes waiting to move in on another's kill, they watched her, some licking their lips as if she were some kind of delicacy they wanted to taste again. She was almost grateful when Cain grabbed her by the hand and led her outside the ring of firelight. He didn't pull her behind the shed; instead they walked deep into the woods, and her heart pounded with renewed anxiety, the men's laughter following her like the howl of predators.

They wandered to the bottom of the falls where the water thundered down into a pool, the noise deafening because it was night and she couldn't see it. Cain led her to a boulder, moving in darkness as if he were a cat, sure and lithe. He pulled her up against him and they sat for a very long time, hearing only the Wind River tumble from above, seeing only the few stars that could wink between the silhouetted canopy of fir.

It was a strange communion. They were there because he was supposed to be raping her and by some wild mercy chose to spare her. They sat on the large cold boulder waiting for

the appropriate amount of time for the offense to be committed, Christal held prisoner by an emotion that intertwined
gratitude and hatred until she couldn't discern either, Cain
silent, his emotions, if he possessed any at all, undisclosed,
unfathomable.

He held her lightly, not touching except for his arms that
wrapped around her waist like warm chains. It was August—
the days were hot and swarming with mosquitoes—but the
nights were bitter cold. She shivered against her will and
longed for the shawl that had been packed in her trunk, last
seen lashed to the top of the Overland stage. Around her, the
woods were menacing in their frozen stillness, and she frightened herself when she thought about the creatures out there,
unseen night animals that could see them.

"Should we be here?" she asked softly. They were close
enough that despite the roar of the fall, she knew he could
hear her. "Might there be bears out here?"

"Are you bleeding?"

"Bleeding?"

"Are you wearing rags between your legs? Are you having
your monthly time?"

For one brief second she was struck by the awful terror that
he needed to know such an intimate thing because he did
intend to rape her. She stuttered, "W-why do you ask?"

He answered succinctly. "Because bears can smell blood a
mile away. It's only dangerous to sit here if one of us is bleeding. Are you?"

"No." She was grateful for the darkness because it hid her
blush. Miss Bulfinch, her beloved governess from years ago,
would roll in her grave if she knew her charge had been
forced to discuss her female nature with this outlaw.

Cain grew silent, as if he was pondering something. He'd
been brooding all evening and his mood made her uneasy.
She shifted nervously within his embrace until his arms became steel and forced her to be still.

Finally he said, "I've been wondering. . . . Why would a
woman such as yourself be traveling alone on that Overland
coach? We didn't expect to find a woman on that coach. It

wasn't planned for. Where's your people? Where's your family, Christal?"

His use of her first name made her pause. Her answers—lies—were on the tip of her tongue before his questions were out, well rehearsed after three years of use. But when she heard her name, spoken in his rough, low voice, his questions became unbearably personal. And she found she didn't want to lie to him.

"You're not answering me, girl."

"I don't want to talk about myself. I told you that."

"You have no choice. I'm making you. Tell me where you were going the other day. And tell me why you had to go there."

"No," she whispered, bracing herself for the onslaught of anger. She didn't have to wait long.

He gripped her arms. His voice had an accusatory edge. "You're running, aren't you?"

She didn't answer. He grew furious. "I want to know why and I want to know who you're running from."

She tensed, and she knew he felt it because he pulled her back against his chest, trapping her. "Tell me," he said, his breath hot against her cheek, hushed by the roar of the falls.

She again felt that strange urge to trust him. They had so many things in common. His home had been destroyed and so had hers; he was on the run and so was she; he had felt the noose around his neck, and every nightmare she had ever had about the death of her parents had ended with her at the gallows, soon to be executed for Baldwin Didier's crimes. But was that enough to trust him? She couldn't be sure.

"What does it matter why I was on that coach?" she whispered. "We'll never see each other after Tuesday. This is all for naught." *And when that ransom comes, you'll be running for your life from the marshals. In fact, I won't be surprised if they shoot you dead before you can even leave Falling Water.* The thought made her heart drop. For some reason, the thought of him dying bothered her. There was a kinship between them, an understanding that could have, in different circumstances, led to something more. She believed he was another man deep down, a good man, but hidden and scarred by a violent exterior. He'd yet to really harm her except to take away her freedom and he'd protected her, even at the risk of his own hide.

Against her back, she felt his heart beat in tandem with the rush of water, his body heat a blanket around her. She tried to erase the picture of him bleeding at her feet, mortally shot by a marshal come to save them, but she couldn't and a strange, unwanted regret filled her.

"Let's go," he said, shoving off the rock.

She followed, unable to think of anything except the dreaded moment when the hand clamped warmly on hers would turn cold.

"Gimme that mirror," Boone growled at Jake.

Cain and Christal had just returned from the falls and they stood in the shadows, watching the scene play out before them. Christal was glad there was going to be a fight. She hated both men, Boone, for his crude stares, and Jake, for his skeevy smile. Besides, the simmering hostilities between the two took the attention from her. And she didn't want the men's stares. Not after going into the woods with Cain. Her unwanted sense of shame was enough.

The tensions ran high as Boone and Jake circled each other in the glow of firelight. Boone reached for the mirror once, twice, then without warning, punched Jake right in the gut. A scuffle ensued and Jake came at Boone with flying fists. Zeke tried to split the men apart, but then Zeke caught a punch across the jaw and joined in the fray, quickly forgetting he was there to stop it. A full-scale war was about to ignite when Cain stepped into the crescent of light.

All the men paused, clearly terrified of irritating him. Cain glanced at them, his expression vaguely contemptuous, before he sat by the fire. The unspoken threat alone caused the men to drop their fists. They eyed Cain belligerently, as if they were children—albeit dangerous children—who'd just been caught by the schoolmaster. The gang members went their separate ways, Jake grumbling and tossing the mirror into a pile of clothing.

Christal stared at the pile, the clothing suddenly familiar. She ran to it, spurred on by the realization that these men had been fighting over her belongings. She frantically began to grab at the articles, hating the thought that these outlaws had touched her only possessions with their dirty hands. But before she could gather much, Kineson ambled down the path from the saloon.

"Git away from there, girlie. Them things belong to us now," he said, a nasty smile lurking behind his lips.

"But they're mine! You took them from my trunk!" she gasped, anger staining her cheeks. She clutched at her only other dress—a faded blue calico—and retorted, "You'll be getting enough money from Overland. You don't need to peddle my meager possessions!"

"If we can get a penny fer 'em, then that's a penny we'll take." Kineson stepped to her to remove the dress from her hands. She pulled to take it back and they got into a tug-of-war. He let go; she stumbled back, almost into Cain's arms.

"Have the rest of them been stripped?" Cain asked, ignoring her.

Kineson smiled. He looked behind him at the two gunmen coming down the path from the saloon. They were both holding piles of clothes. At the top of one pile was Mr. Glassie's verdigris suit.

"Left 'em with just their union suits." Kineson laughed. "And there was a mess of gold in that old fellow's vest. Yes, sirree, he was spitting mad when I found it and took it away from him."

Christal was heartsick. Pete's father's money had been taken away. All their futures were drying up faster than commerce in Falling Water.

"Take off your petticoats, girlie," Kineson said, turning to her again. "We'll take them as well. Women's things fetch a lot more than men's out here."

"I will not," she spat. She had more to lose than just her

modesty if she handed him her petticoats, and she vowed to keep them.

"I said take 'em off."

"I won't," she said, daring him to touch her.

"Take them off," Cain said behind her.

She spun and looked at him, hurt by his betrayal. For some strange reason, she expected him to stand up for her. But that was asking too much of an outlaw. Damning his soul, she faced Kineson again and said, "My possessions are mine and I'm keeping them. Stay away from me."

Kineson only laughed. His hands were on her in seconds, reaching beneath her gown to rip away her petticoats. She screeched in outrage, but before she could pummel him off her, he had her three petticoats in hand, each petticoat dropping gold pieces in the dust.

"What have we here?" Kineson said, picking up a piece.

Seven was certainly an unlucky number. For three years she'd worked to save seven ten-dollar gold pieces. She done without food in order to add to her stash because what drove her was stronger than even hunger: revenge. She was going to redeem herself and prove her uncle guilty, but she needed money to do it. Now she'd saved, only to see her seven precious gold pieces, sewn carefully into the hem of her petticoat, thrown to outlaws like worthless trinkets in a parade.

Past the point of caution, she ran to Kineson, desperate to fight and take her money back, but Cain held her back. Outraged that he would stop her, she raised her hand to strike him, but he gave her such a look, she felt as if a frigid wind had just passed by.

If she struck him, he would be forced to show his dominance in front of Kineson. He'd be forced to strike her back, and hard. Blinking back tears of frustration and anger, she lowered her hand. "That's all I have in the world. Seven gold pieces. Don't let him take it from me," she whispered, proud that she kept the tears from her voice.

"I know" was all Cain said. Kineson laughed and tossed a coin in the air, taunting her. Cain nodded for her to return to the fireplace. She stared at him for one excruciating moment, silently pleading for her gold; then she lifted her chin and walked away, refusing to let him see her devastation, or the tears that finally blurred her vision as she poked vengefully at the fire.

An hour passed as the men settled down to sleep. Kineson snored at the edge of the firelight. Christal watched him, fantasizing enormous wolves coming along and dragging him off. She should have been sleepy herself, but the tensions of the day wouldn't let her relax. She had no money now. Not a dime. She would have to begin all over again. The thought depressed her as no other. She supposed she should be grateful if she survived to have the chance to start over, but at that moment, having been stripped of every protection save the dark, brooding outlaw who sat next to her, she couldn't feel optimistic. Cain's protection was a tenuous thing at that. He could have saved her money for her. She knew he could have. The outlaws scurried away like roaches in daylight when he walked by; he had proved he could win dominance over Kineson, obviously Kineson's greatest fear. Yet Cain remained under the gang leader's orders. And why? Because he was as immersed in this gang as anyone, maybe more so.

Her gaze trailed to Cain, and she was shocked to find him staring at her. His gaze wasn't so cold in the dying firelight, his face not nearly so hard. He had a strange, taut expression as he stared, almost as if he was trying not to look at her, but was somehow helpless not to.

Her gaze met with his and held. She fascinated him, for whatever reason. Her past, which should have been unimportant to an outlaw, seemed to intrigue him. She could tell it by his questions, and now by his stare. Perhaps she was getting to him. It was playing with fire to think of becoming entangled with a man like Cain, but if she could gain his confidence, find a chink in his armor, she might convince him to see her side and assist her.

She looked down and noticed he'd been polishing his revolvers again. His energy in that matter was endless. It was as if he was always preparing for a showdown. She wondered if this unnerved the other gunmen.

She walked next to him and tried to draw him into conversation. "Those must be extraordinary guns for all the attention you give them."

"They're nothing a million men don't own." As usual, his answer was terse. He dropped his gaze to his task, appearing unapproachable and intimidating as he polished the unusually long bore.

"Those guns were Confederate issue, then?"

"Yeah." He broke one and looked down the barrel.

"You take very good care of them. I suppose you've had them since the war. You must treasure them."

He glanced at her, disgust twisting his lips. "Out here a man doesn't treasure his guns, Mrs. Smith, he's a slave to them. I'm just a more diligent slave, that's all." He snapped the revolver closed. "Besides, Yankee-issue Remingtons are better than what I have."

"Why don't you have Remingtons, then?"

His disgust appeared again. "Why bother? A dead man doesn't know the difference."

She fell silent, unable to counter this indisputable fact.

After a long pause, he said, "What were you saving that money for?" He didn't look at her. He just continued polishing and oiling his revolver as if she weren't around, but she knew if she didn't answer, those eyes would finally look her way. The threat of his stare was enough.

"I was a schoolteacher saving to buy a house."

"I see," he said, clearly not believing her.

"It came from my husband."

"No." He looked up. "You had all that gold, yet you sold your wedding band?" He suddenly smiled. It chilled her. He had caught her in a lie and there was no way to extract herself. So she said nothing. Silence was better than stumbling around for answers.

"You hated him, didn't you?" he asked in an oddly needful tone.

It was her turn not to look at him. "Don't ask me any questions about my past unless you're willing to help me."

He glanced over at the sleeping men. Snores broke in tandem with the *whooh* of an owl. He looked back at her and their gazes locked. He seemed to want to say something, but somehow he couldn't. He glanced again at the men. She wondered if he couldn't trust that the other men were truly asleep and not listening. She wanted to ask him, but he put her off. He thrust his Colt into his holster and shook out his bedroll. Then he forced her down on it on the other side of the fireplace.

Trembling, she waited for him to join her, fearing his unexpected anger. But he didn't touch her. Instead he sat with his back against the warm fireplace stones and dug out a harmonica from his saddlebag. He began the tune to "Tom Dooley" and one of the men—Kineson, she thought— shouted to him, "Cain, you are somethin', boy! Playin' that harmonica! Why, if that were my woman, I wouldn't be playin' nothing but her!"

Men's laughter echoed from around the shaft of the chimney. Christal shivered. Cain began to sing. *Hang yo' head, Tom Doolah, Hang yo' head and cry, You killed Laurie Foster and now you're gonna die.* The words rang in her head. *Now you're gonna die.*

Chapter Six

Sunday came with a vengeance. Overnight a winterlike chill permeated the air and crystalline frost covered everything including the blanket they slept beneath. Christal dreaded leaving the warmth of Cain's body, but dawn was breaking over the mountains, coloring the faces of the opposite slopes long before darkness was erased and the sun actually peeked over the eastern hills. It was one of the strange quirks of the mountains. To find dawn, she'd learned to look west.

Though he lay against her back and she couldn't see him, she knew Cain was awake; not moving as if he, too, hesitated to part from the warmth of the bedroll. There were only two days left before the ransom was paid. Two more days of hell and captivity by the Kineson gang, two more days of intense contrary emotions for the man who held her beneath the frost-covered blanket. How it would end was the only question. She pondered the different scenarios, but of one thing she was certain. Cain wasn't going to let them hurt her. He'd taken too many risks, protected her too often, to let Kineson and his gang members slay her like a lamb once they got the ransom. She only wished she could be as confident about Mr. Glassie, Pete, and the other passengers' protection. Their futures were murky, but, in truth, all their futures were. Her fate really wasn't up to Cain. He couldn't control everything. In some ways, he was a captive himself, captive of the crime he had helped to commit.

A thin light streamed over the eastern peaks, barely melting the frost. Cain moved and she waited for the gust of cold air as he threw off the covers. The cold air didn't come. Wondering what he was doing, she rolled over and met his gaze inches from her own. He still lay on his side, one hand gripping his gun belt against his chest, the other tucked beneath his dark head.

He stared at her, so close that the whisper of his breath warmed her cheek. She was captured like a bird in a snare, finally seeing where the coldness lay in his gray eyes, how the color of his irises fractured into slivers of ice blue around the pupil, an effect that seemed to drain his eyes of warmth, yet, in turn, endow them with an emotion infinitely more compelling. More dangerous.

She lowered her gaze, upset by the flare of unwanted longing. He was so near, a sigh could close the distance between them; bring them together, lips upon trembling lips in a kiss. And he wanted to kiss her, female instinct told her that. She knew that the thought of their kissing weighed as heavily on his mind as it did on hers.

She looked at his throat where the ragged scar showed above his bandanna. She wanted to feel nothing, but she was unnerved by the erotic rhythm of his pulse as it beat along one sinew of his neck. She lowered her eyes farther, this time refusing to acknowledge how the rise and fall of his chest touched another chord deep within her body.

Beneath the neck of his shirt she could see a white woolen union suit that could have done with a good washing. By all rights he should reek, but he didn't. Whether he was just cleaner than the other men or whether she'd been forced into such close company with him that she'd lost the ability to smell him, she didn't know. All she did know was that the outer layers of his smell were gone, leaving her with only the ability to recognize his essence, a scent like that of horses. Natural, animal, heated. Esthetically he'd be more pleasing with a bath, they *both* would be. She couldn't remember how long it had been since she'd seen hot water or combed her hair. But that was this outlaw's strange power. He made everything elemental. He gave her the tragic simplicity of a life with no choices. The unimportant was overshadowed by his presence. He was dangerous, protective, and ruthless all within the same breath, and he bore watching. And perhaps because circumstances were so dire, there were moments when he could pare everything in her existence down to the simple fact that they were both human, uniquely male and female. What terrified her the most was . . . it almost seemed enough.

His hand slipped beneath her chin, and she moaned. He was going to kiss her and the hell of it was, she wanted him to. He lifted her chin and her eyes met with his again. She ached to feel his hard lips on her soft ones. It was wild, insane, sinful to want something so bad for her, but she did want it and the desire for it nearly choked her.

"What do you think when you look at me . . . as you're looking at me now?" he whispered.

A sob broke into her voice. She could only tell him the truth. "I wish everything were different."

His knuckles grazed the pliant flesh beneath her jaw. She stared at him, hating her reaction to his touch, hopelessness etched onto her face like a madonna's veil.

He didn't kiss her. As if he knew just how much damage that would inflict, he simply let her go, his expression grave and preoccupied. He rose to his feet, callously pulling the blanket from her. She almost cried out when the frigid morning air rushed over her, mercifully shocking her into reality.

For the entire day Christal went through the ritual. She'd fix one vile meal after another. The men would be served. Cain would scarf down his ration, share his second portion, and settle into some task that would keep him by the chimney and thus, by her side. Twice that day he took her by the hand and forced her into the woods. Both times the men rooted for him, and she grew to despise them more each hour. To call Kineson and his gang animals would be to insult God's creatures. To call them devils was to credit them with a panache they could never possess. In truth, she'd come to discover that this gang of outlaws was a species she'd come up against only once before. In her uncle, Baldwin Didier.

But then there was Cain. Her enigma, her salvation, her damnation, a dark, brooding question mark that lurked in the shadows of her unconscious. She feared him with good cause. There was an implied brutality in his walk, a deadly potential in his eyes. He was like a gun lying useless on a table, waiting for the right person, or the wrong person, to trigger it. In Wyoming Territory she'd seen a thousand guns and a thousand violent men. Never had she seen the combination that made up the outlaw Macaulay Cain.

But as much as she feared him, she needed him. And that was part of the fear. He was Russian roulette. At any time, for any reason, he could turn on her. So she warred with conflicting emotions that threatened to tear up her insides, emotions that only got worse when he took her hand and walked her far away from the campfire. When he would hold her in silence, and she would listen to the wind chime through the aspens.

Sunday evening she was expected to serve supper not only for the outlaws but for the prisoners as well. She was exhausted. It was a lot of work hauling the pot of beans up the ravine to Falling Water. She slipped so many times, Cain finally took the heavy iron Dutch oven and carried it himself. Still, she was elated to be going to the saloon. She wanted to see the other passengers. If they fared well, then perhaps the horrors of the situation were mostly in her mind.

At the saloon, one yellow light shone through a broken glass window where the prisoners were kept. Cain held the lantern, not giving her the potential to use it as a weapon. He walked through the abandoned saloon, waiting at the staircase for her to go first.

She'd had thoughts of escaping the entire way up to Falling Water. Cain, burdened with a lantern and the Dutch oven, wasn't going to go far. She convinced herself that she might actually get a few yards, but in the end, she didn't run. The night was moonless, the forest jet black. She would stumble around and bump into boulders and trees. The man had an uncanny ability to see in the dark, and he would catch her. Worse, if he dropped the pot of beans to do so, she'd be up all night cooking for the prisoners, wasting precious time that could be used renewing her strength, thinking of ways to save herself and those seven gold pieces that now jingled in Kineson's pocket.

She walked up the stairs and knocked on the closed door. Cain nodded. She opened it and found the prisoners sitting against one wall, all in their woolen underclothes. Pete was at the end, next to an outlaw named Marmet. The outlaw leaned back in the only chair, his Winchester idle across his chest. He was drunk.

"Goddammit, I gotta take a piss. Where the hell you been?" Marmet suddenly laid eyes on Cain and straightened his chair with a screech. He stuttered, "D-didn't know it was you, Cain—"

"She's going to feed them tonight," Cain said, no reprimand but the killing look in his eyes.

"Fine." The outlaw gave him an ingratiating nod, then looked at her. "Git to it, girlie," he said, mimicking Kineson. He started to laugh, but quieted the instant he realized Cain didn't laugh with him.

Christal bent to fill Mr. Glassie's bowl and her hands began to shake. If she believed the prisoners' treatment was a reflection of the outcome, then they were doomed. Manacled, slumped on the floor, dressed in a union suit that had been worn days past its cleanliness, Mr. Glassie stared at her like an abused mongrel. He'd been unable to shave or comb his hair and he was now as grizzled as the rest of the men, outlaw or not. She was a mess, too, with her knotted hair and torn bodice, but there was no mirror for her to see herself. Instead, all she could see was the contrast of the portly, dapper salesman who had impressed them all with his fashionable verdigris suit and the man in front of her with his soul-weary expression. She could take the abuse of these men because she hardly expected better and because she'd had bad treatment before. But for some irrational reason she found it hard to bear what they had done to Mr. Glassie. Tears came to her eyes, as if he had somehow become a symbol of herself.

Trembling to fight off the emotion, she leaned near to top off his bowl. Her hands shook so badly that Mr. Glassie reached out and took the ladle from her.

With sorrow in his eyes, he said politely, "Ah, Mrs. Smith— thank God you look well, yet how it grieves me to have you see me in this state of undress."

They had taken away his fine suit; they had made him dirty and unkempt. Nonetheless, the gentleman inside endured. His spirit triumphed.

And so would hers.

Surprising even herself, she put her arms around his neck and hugged him. She buried her head in his enormous chest and fought the urge to cry. She would pay anything—all seven of her gold pieces—to see the man in the verdigris suit once more.

"There, there, my good woman . . ." he soothed, a heaviness to his voice, clearly surprised by her unexpected emotion. "We'll get out of this, never you fear. The Paterson Furniture Company won't want to lose me. They'll see to our safe return, if nothing else."

She heard his words, her eyes clamped shut as if to shut out everything she could no longer accept. He tried to hold her, but his hands were shackled, and after a tentative brush across her back, he lowered them.

She would have never moved, she would have stayed within the comfort of his chest, if she hadn't felt Cain's hand come down on her shoulder. He tightened his grip, not hurting her, but unmistakably informing her that her behavior must stop or she must pay the consequences. With a strength she could hardly summon, she drew back from Mr. Glassie and resumed filling the prisoners' bowls, her face drawn and pale, her eyes glistening with tears she wouldn't allow herself to shed. She looked at Cain only once, desperate to see even a hint of guilt cross his face for what had been done to the passengers of the Overland Express, but there was none. He only stared at her, a stare she'd seen before when they were by the campfire. A stare of possession.

She filled the driver's bowl, then the shotgun's. The preacher looked like he was almost dead from lack of drink, but she filled his bowl, too, and Pete's father's.

Pete was last. He stared at her, obviously moved by her breakdown with Mr. Glassie. She was suddenly afraid he might do something foolish again in his desire to protect her, but he didn't. Without a word, he allowed his bowl to be filled. Then he put his hand on her wrist.

It only took a second. He glanced down, motioning for her gaze to follow. In his lap, hidden between the fold of his bent legs was a six-shooter. Frightened, she glanced at the drunken outlaw sitting next to them. Marmet was saying something to Cain and once more leaning back in his chair. For the first time, she noticed Marmet's left holster was missing its revolver.

She stood, exhilarated and terrified. They were going to escape. Or be killed.

"Where's my dinner?" Marmet drunkenly asked her. She was in such shock, she didn't even realize his hands were on her until she felt his palm cup one of her buttocks through the fold of her skirt.

"Get it yourself," Cain said, an angry edge to his voice. He kicked the bean pot toward Marmet and grabbed her. Pete used the disturbance to lift the revolver. With both hands, he pointed it at the drunken lout in the chair.

"Let her go, Cain, or I'm going to put a hole through him."

In a flash, Cain had his gun from his holster, but it was too late. Pete already had a hostage. Marmet thunked forward in the chair, astonished at the gun pointed at his head. He reached for his side; his terror grew when his fingers shoved through an empty holster.

"I said give her to us, Cain. This guy's gonna die, and then you're gonna die if you don't," Pete warned, his voice cracking with the strain.

The room was dead silent. The only noise Christal could hear was the drumming of her heart against her ribs. The men didn't move. Every breath was held waiting for what Cain would do.

"Put the gun down, boy. You don't know what you're doing," Cain answered, his voice as steady as the gun in his hand.

Marmet grabbed his Winchester. He aimed it at Pete and drunkenly fumbled with the barrel. In a flash, Pete pulled the trigger of his revolver. Marmet fell dead at the prisoners' feet, a hole clean through his forehead.

Christal bit her lower lip until it bled to keep from screaming. The shot rang in her ears. Blue gunsmoke trailed from Pete's revolver and hung suspended in the air, its acrid scent burning in her nostrils. The other prisoners could have been mannequins. Not a chain rattled, not a muscle flinched.

Pete turned the revolver on Cain. His hand trembled wildly. "Let her go!" he screeched, his face filled with the horror of one killing and possibly another.

Cain hesitated a split second, perhaps on account of Pete's youth. A mistake. The rattled boy squeezed off a shot. The bullet cut across the muscle of Cain's arm and ricocheted off the wallboards.

Cain shoved her out of the way and lunged. The boy struggled valiantly to retain hold of his weapon, but he was no match for a hardened outlaw who moved with lightning speed. Marmet's revolver was in Cain's possession before Christal could gasp.

"Don't hurt my son! Don't hurt him!" Pete's father shouted as Cain held his gun to Pete. The chains rattled as the old man futilely tried to free himself. The boy cowered on the ground.

"You can't do this!" Christal cried out, pulling on Cain's arm. She then ran to the boy and took him in her arms to protect him from Cain's rage.

Cain towered over both of them, his face stone cold. He cocked the gun, and she knew the instinct to kill ran strong in him, especially now with his own blood dripping down his arm.

Christal looked at him, terror on her face. She whispered,

"Macaulay," in supplication, then turned her head away, unable to watch.

His gaze never left her. Slowly, Cain lowered the gun. The murderous rage on his face softened into acceptance. He straightened, tucked Marmet's revolver in his gun belt, and picked up the rifle where it lay by the corpse. He grabbed her to her feet rather cruelly, almost as if she were as lifeless as the Winchester. She put her arm out to stop his rough treatment and her hand met with warm, sticky blood.

She looked at him. Blood dripped from his left fingers, a carmine red so deep, it seemed black. He walked her to the door. It left a trail across the raw floorboards.

Sickened, she met his gaze. His expression brooked no disobedience. He motioned for her to leave with him. The hold on her arm was becoming painful; nonetheless, she glanced behind her at the prisoners.

All six of them were shocked at the outcome of the escape attempt. Marmet was dead, his body almost lying in their laps. Outside, through the broken panes of glass, she could hear shouts and see lanterns sway up the gulley.

"C'mon," Cain rasped. Taking her arm in a death grip, he pulled her out the door.

"Let me stay with them," she begged, stumbling down the crude wooden stairs in the dark.

"No."

"They'll kill them."

"No."

"I want to be with them." She clutched at his chest. "I knew Pete had the gun. He showed it to me when I gave him his dinner. I'm as much to blame. If they pay, I must pay also. I can't let Kineson kill those men because—"

"No," he repeated, and pushed her ahead of him.

"Oh, God. Please, Macaulay, please . . ." Her last word came out as a gasp.

Cain swayed precariously; the old banister swayed with him. He held on to it, but the rotten wood gave way. She grabbed him just before the banister clattered to the ground below. He fell against her, and she somehow kept him upright though his weight was twice hers.

He began to slur his words. "You don't understand, Christal . . . you don't understand . . . just play this out. It's got to be played out. . . ."

She didn't know what he was saying. He was an enigma. He'd always been. He'd saved her from being abused by the gang, but he was in it as thick as he could be. Was he sinner or saint?

"You—listening to me—Christal?" he whispered.

"Kineson—"

"I'll handle Kineson . . . just play this out. Goddammit— we'll all get killed—*promise* me you'll play this out."

"Oh, God, you're bleeding so much . . ." she whispered, feeling the warmth of his blood on her hand. Her insides screamed not to help him. He was the outlaw who might ultimately prove her ruin, but the woman inside her, the lady bred to a kinder, more gentle life, couldn't not help him.

Without giving him his promise, she walked him down the stairs to a ramshackle tavern chair and lit a lantern left by one of the outlaws. She reached beneath her gown and tore her petticoat to strips, unmindful that it was her last. She bound his arm, and at one point while his wounded arm rested on the table, she reached for his revolver in the slim hope that she might be able to defend the prisoners upstairs from Kineson's wrath, but Cain grabbed her, his face expressionless either from pain or from the fact that he'd expected her to try for his gun all the time. Caught, she continued to bind his arm as if the attempt had never occurred. The moment passed in silence, neither of them willing to talk about it.

"Cain, we heard shots!" Kineson barked from the saloon's broken doorway. He held up his lantern to further illuminate the dusty interior.

"Marmet's dead." Cain grit his teeth as she wound the bandages tight to stop the bleeding.

"What the hell happened?" Kineson entered, his Doberman eyes on Christal, who did her best to hide her shaking hands and keep her attention on Cain's arm.

"Marmet was guzzling the whiskey again. He was so drunk, he didn't recognize me. He shot at me—guess he thought I was one of the prisoners. I killed him."

Her hands quit shaking. She stared at Cain, who refused to meet her gaze.

"Damn fool," Kineson whispered under his breath. He sent the rest of his men upstairs to fetch the body and watch the prisoners.

Slowly, Cain's gaze rose to meet hers. She wondered if her face gave away her feelings. He was a fraud. On the outside he was the terrifying gunfighter Macaulay Cain, but on the inside he was someone else, someone possessing mercy and justice. Someone, perhaps, very much like her.

She lifted her hand to touch the hard planes of his face. Almost pleadingly, she whispered, "Macaulay . . ."

He jerked his head away from her hand and ruthlessly broke eye contact. Shutting her out, he stood and nodded for her to go to the door.

Before, she might have had to be dragged. This time, she complied. She couldn't fight a man who had saved her life and now, strangely, Pete's. Her emotions in upheaval, she walked to the door and waited while he got a lantern.

Kineson watched her, his eyes glittering with anger. She knew he'd always liked Cain's roughness with her. He'd always enjoyed the fight in her. Now something had changed between them and Christal could see Kineson knew it.

Cain took her arm and they left the saloon. Kineson's last angry words followed them as he instructed the men who'd brought down the body to dump it in the gorge "fer enough away so the fool don't stink."

Chapter Seven

*A breed which fails to honor its heroes
will soon have no heroes to honor.*
JOHN S. TILLEY ON THE CONFEDERACY
HARVARD UNIVERSITY 1959

The ransom drop was tomorrow. Tuesday would be the beginning of her life. Or the end of it.

Christal boiled coffee, serving the men who grumbled and groped at her. Supper was over and some of them were already bedding down for the night, too anxious to think any more on what the next day might bring. It had grown even colder and the weather made the men jittery. Cold fingers didn't shoot as well as warm ones. Kineson was in the foulest mood of all. He took his coffee, and when she tried to walk away, he viciously tripped her. She fell onto the hard ground and the coffeepot spilled into the fire with a hiss.

"Maybe I'll just take you with us on our ride outta here. What do you think of that, girlie? Cain can't use you forever. When am I gonna get my turn?"

Cain rose from the shadows by the chimney, but he didn't help her up.

She got to her feet, outrage burning in her eyes. She hated Kineson almost as much as she hated Didier. Unable to stop it, she let her anger have its head. "You'd better kill me now, then, because I'll never let you touch me."

Suddenly she felt Cain's hands on her, pulling her back.

Kineson stood, red fury on his face.

Cain lifted a blanket over his shoulders and without a word

dragged her into the woods. Kineson shouted behind him, "She's coming with us, Cain. I'll have a go at her sometime. You owe me that much!"

Cain said nothing.

It was too cold to go to the falls. Instead he brought her beneath the sheared-off side of the gorge, where they found protection from the wind in a grove of aspens. He flung the blanket over him and sat down, forcing her alongside. She wished she'd had the courage to pull from his embrace, but she was cold; she didn't have a shawl left to her name. Surrendering, she fell back against his chest and allowed him to pull the blanket over her.

A full moon lit the night woods. She could make out the quivering leaves overhead and, if she'd wanted to, Cain's stony expression. They'd been fortunate that it hadn't rained since she and the other Overland passengers had been taken captive. Like most outlaws, Kineson's men had no tents. Bivouacking wasn't a hardship on them.

Cain moved, throwing his arm across her chest to hold her closer. She couldn't look at his face. She knew he wouldn't have met her gaze anyway. They hadn't spoken all day, not about his stiff, hurting arm, nor about what he'd done to save them last night. He wanted it that way. But she didn't. She wanted to know everything about him. Especially what had changed him into a hardened outlaw.

"Kineson is going to take advantage of your wounded arm," she said. He didn't answer. She continued, "I'm worried that—"

"Don't be. I can take care of myself."

She turned quiet. Her voice became a monotone. She tried hard not to care. "What if he kills you?"

"He needs me."

"Not after tomorrow. I think that's why he wants me to stay with him because . . . because you won't be around."

His arm drew her even closer.

She looked down and touched it. "I don't want to see you killed. You should escape. Right now if you can. All of us owe you, Cain. No one would dispute it. Not after what you did last night—"

"Listen," he said, interrupting her, "last night had nothing to do with you or the other prisoners. I did what I did to keep my ass alive. And that's it."

"I don't believe you." Her voice was as strong as her convictions. There was something good within Macaulay Cain and she'd believe it to her dying day, despite how it angered him to bring it up.

"That's what I'm telling you and that's what you'll believe."

"How can you be loyal to Kineson? He'd just as soon see you dead." She could no longer hide the emotion in her voice.

He heard it because his answer seemed slow and difficult. "Listen, girl, don't worry about me. Kineson was in my regiment, the Georgia Sixty-seventh. We fought Federals together, side by side. We go back a long way. We understand each other. That's why he let me run with his gang."

"But that was years ago. The war is over. Kineson's still fighting, but the U.S. won."

"Yeah. You don't need to remind me of that."

His bitterness caught her by surprise. Then she recalled how he'd sung the last verse of "Good Ol' Rebel."

"Tell me about the war," she said, desperately seeking a way to get through to him. "I was too young to remember much. Tell me about it. I want to understand . . ." *the man you've become.* The words echoed through her mind. She felt as if she were talking to her lover, whispering in the dark about their ill-fated love and knowing that tomorrow they would finally be together in eternity. But they were not lovers. The analogy was absurd. He was the renegade and she, the victim. Still, the emotions fit. And they disturbed her.

"You won't die. Not if I can help it," he answered without undue sentiment. Matter-of-factly, as if it were his job to protect her.

"But *you* will die." Her words were not so calm. "If Kineson doesn't get you, the marshals will. Terence Scott isn't going to fork over that much gold and let you live to spend it." She paused. "And if you die, Cain, then I know what will happen to me." She paused again and whispered fiercely, "I won't go with Kineson."

He turned her face up toward him and the illumination of the moonlight. Their eyes met, sizzling with an understanding that was beyond even words. To seal it, she knew he wanted to kiss her. The need was there, in the way his lips hardened as if he were biting back desire.

"I want to know about you," she whispered. "Tell me about the war, tell me about Georgia."

"There's nothing to tell."

"I want to know."

He looked at her as if judging her sincerity. It took him a long time to speak. He didn't seem to want to, and there was a moment when she thought he'd pull away. But whether he decided no harm could come of talking about himself, or he just wanted to share with her at this final hour, she wasn't sure. She only knew that her heart grasped at the information as if it were bread and she, dying of famine.

"Until I was seventeen I helped my father plant goober peas at the farm." His gaze moved away, as if he were seeing another place and another time. "My family, we weren't dirt poor, but we didn't own slaves—we did the work ourselves. When the war started, I joined the Georgia Sixty-seventh and took up the Cause. They say I did it for a different reason now. Washington branded me and a lot of others as devils who fought to keep the black man in chains. But that had nothing to do with it. We were poor. I wasn't gonna die for slaves that didn't even belong to me."

"Why did you fight, then?"

He took a deep breath. "At first it was for home. You hear the Army of the Potomac's invaded Virginia and you look at your ma and you think: Soon they're gonna be in Georgia stealing your pigs and burning down your house. You've got to do something to stop it. So you join up."

His voice turned raspy, filled with anger and frustration that had long been punched down and shoved away. "Then it gets cold. You got rags on your body while you're fightin' men in blue uniforms who are warm and dry. And you get hungry, sometimes with only wormy hardtack to eat, and on the other side their blue bellies are full of white army beans that you'd give your right arm for. Then you see a boy from home get his head shot right off his shoulders"—his voice lowered— "then it gets personal. And you get hard from all that cold and starving. Fightin' becomes a way of life. I went into the war a seventeen-year-old boy and one day I woke up and I was a twenty-one-year-old man. My entire life seemed to have been spent in the Confederacy. I fought my war and I didn't pay any Irisher to fight it for me like Yankees did. But in four years, even the Cause had grown into something I didn't recognize anymore. I'd lost my father and two brothers to the war, and in the end, all I wanted was to go home and forget what had ever happened to me."

"But Sherman saw to it that you couldn't," she answered, remembering what he'd told her. Her throat constricted with emotion. The war had had no effect on her at all. All she really knew about it came from him. He'd been barely a man, asked to sacrifice everything for his homeland. He'd done it, only to be betrayed by all that he'd fought for.

He continued, as if talking was a catharsis. "When my mother lost her youngest boy, Walker, the second of her sons to die for the Stars and Bars, she couldn't endure it any longer. She was a simple woman, born in Manchester to railroad workers. She didn't understand the War Between the States and the Cause. States' rights meant nothing to her and she didn't care about issues like white man versus black. Her family was all she ever cared about and after Walker was gone, she refused to feel the loss. She took a glassful of laudanum and never woke up. She never knew she'd become a widow too." He quit talking, and she knew he was remembering the pain all over again.

In silence, he rested his jaw against her head. They sat for a long time, both immersed in their thoughts, until she felt his jaw against her crown, sliding back and forth, as if luxuriating in the feel of her hair. She had wanted to say something, to somehow let him know that his story moved her, and that she understood some things better now, but the words wouldn't come. Her mouth was useless. Until his knuckles brushed against her lips.

She turned to look up at him. The moonlight was enough to see his grave expression. Ever so slowly he bent his head down to her. "You see an outlaw here," he whispered, "talking to you, wanting to kiss you. You know you shouldn't let him, girl. You shouldn't . . ."

Then his lips came down on hers.

His kiss was just as she expected: deep and satisfying, leaving her no need for anything but him. His mouth was as hard as it looked, and deep inside she reveled in the hardness, for it hinted at strengths she didn't possess. Her mind, body, and soul told her to stop the seduction, that it could only lead to ruin. Instead, overwhelmed by the desolate yearnings of her heart, she opened her mouth, welcoming his tongue just as she welcomed the arm that swung around her backside and pulled her against him as they knelt on the blanket.

His mouth covered her, sucking on her lower lip. His teeth grazed the deep rose flesh on its underside, his tongue pushed through the barrier of her teeth. All logic told her to run. There were a million reasons to leave and no good ones to stay. She had no future with this man, and tomorrow would probably put an end to what they had. If she wasn't killed in the showdown, then surely he would be.

His tongue invaded her mouth and she moaned deep within herself. But her soul was like his. They'd both been forced to be people they were not: he, by the war, she, by Didier. And maybe they could change. Maybe if she could just trust him. . . .

"I've bedded a lot of women, Christal," he whispered against her ear, his words heated and quick after he pulled from her mouth. "But this is something more. This is wanting like I've never felt. The first time I looked at you, I wanted you."

She trembled, remembering how he'd frightened her in the stage when he'd used his gun to lift her veil. He still frightened her, but her desire for him now overrode her fear, making it trivial, to be put aside until she could think and feel something other than him.

"God, I wish I had a bed. I wish I could take you like your husband did, civilized, not here on the cold ground."

A small cry caught in her throat. Everything was moving too fast. She couldn't even tell him she'd never had a husband to bed her in a more civilized manner.

"Macaulay," she whispered, but his kiss stopped her.

He laid her back against the blanket, covering her with his long, hard body, and her thoughts grew incoherent. Her face clamped between his strong hands, he kissed her as if he would never get enough of the taste of her lips. He hardly let her catch her breath, but she didn't want to. She suddenly wanted him to take away her need for air and everything else, and leave only the need for him, which he promised to fulfill with every scorching thrust into her mouth, and every fiery trace of his fingers down her neck.

"I'll look out for you, girl. Don't you worry about tomorrow," he whispered into her ear. Then his hand slid up her chest and cupped her breast, squeezing it through the layers of bodice and corset.

It should have shocked her—she'd hated any man who'd tried to touch her there before—but it was natural the way he touched her. He treated her man to woman, his gentleness all the more compelling because she knew just how superior his strength was.

As if by instinct, she caressed his face, wanting to know all of him. She touched the straight bridge of his nose, his beard-roughened jaw. Finally she ran her finger down his neck, rimming the inside of the bandanna. Her finger slid along the ridges of his scar, a tingle running down her spine as she thought of why it was there, but the scar was warm and his pulse drummed with life against the sensitive pad of her finger. That was all she wanted to think about.

"It doesn't hurt anymore," he said quietly.

"Whatever you've done," she whispered, a sob tearing her voice, "I won't ask."

"You can ask. I didn't do it."

She didn't quite believe him, but she buried her face in his shoulder and hid from her doubts. She didn't want him to explain. She knew he kept things from her, as she did from him. There was more to Macaulay Cain than she understood, and she thought it best to keep it that way. It was less dangerous not to know. For a while anyway.

He broke away, his fingers brushing the stray blond hair that covered her eyes. Without warning, he took her right hand in his and his lips touched her palm, electrifying the scarred flesh of the rose. "Tell me about this, Christal," he whispered, every word sending chills down her spine.

She pulled her hand from his grasp. His kiss made her feel skittish and vulnerable. Branded twice.

There was a hefty bounty on her. The marshals probably didn't know about it so far away in Wyoming Territory, but the bounty would hold whether she was found here or back in New York. All she could tell Cain was that she was mistakenly wanted for her parents' death. And though she could bare her soul and plead for his understanding and sympathy, there was still a large part of her that didn't trust him. He was an outlaw; the bounty on her might be too much temptation. Perhaps he'd even believe she'd be better off back at Park View Asylum than fighting it out on her own in Wyoming. He'd turn her in, never knowing he'd given her a death sentence.

"Tell me about it, Christal."

"Please," she gasped, suddenly afraid of the intimacy they'd woven.

"You never told me about your husband. I want to know about him—" She tried to pull away but he caught her up in his arms once more. He shook her as if that would expel the truth from her. "I want to know about him, Christal. Did he hurt you? Did he give you that scar?"

"My husband had nothing to do with this—this scar." She shook her hand at him, angry that he wouldn't let her go, angrier still that her lonely, terrified heart longed to trust him.

"I want to know if you loved him."

She stared up at him, shocked by this last inquiry, her mind whirling with all the reasons why he would want to know such a thing. Then suddenly she knew why. He didn't want another man between them, dead or alive. He wanted her to be his and his alone.

"Did you love him, Christal?" he asked, his voice rough and demanding.

"No," she choked out shamelessly.

"Tell me about the scar."

"No." She pulled away and refused to look at him.

"Why won't you tell me?"

She could hear the anger beneath his words. Her past was becoming a very sore point with him. She had no other weapon but the truth. "Because you're an outlaw. A criminal. How can I tell you my secrets when I know all of that?"

He was silent, as if trying to control his temper. "Yeah," he finally said, "you see me as an outlaw, all right. That's why you can't share your past with me. But you almost spread your legs right here on the cold dirt. Don't you care you might be sleeping with a killer, girl? No, 'cause you didn't even want me to disprove it. So what kind of a lady are you?"

She gasped. Fury burned on her cheek. He had no right to say such crude things to her. He was twisting her character, he was twisting the truth. "You kiss me, then reprimand me for liking it—"

He took her jaw and forced her to meet his eyes. Nothing broke the pull of their gaze, not darkness, not the sound of the wind rustling the aspens overhead.

He growled, "I don't like that you won't talk to me."

"Get used to it," she answered icily; then she rose from the blanket, refusing to miss the warmth of his body in the frigid night air.

They walked back to camp not saying a word. The rest of the gang was already asleep by the time they crawled inside the bedroll. Exhausted and depressed, she barely felt Cain's arms around her. Everything was confused, her emotions, her desires, her future. She fell asleep, never wanting to wake to the morning, never wanting to see the moment when the outlaw next to her would be shot down like a renegade wolf.

Her escape didn't last long. She was awakened in less than an hour by a hand clamped over her mouth. She wanted to scream, but Macaulay's words soothed her. "Don't make a sound."

She complied, and he released her only to take up her hands and draw a rope around her wrists. "Why are you doing this?" she whispered, further frightened when a gang member—Kineson, she thought—rolled over in his bedroll and began to snore.

"I've got some gold hidden up in the mountains near Cirque of the Towers. I don't want you or Kineson or anyone knowing where I put my stash." Grimacing because he was forced to use his wounded arm, he fastened the rope to an iron loop that held the tongs to the fireplace.

"But why are you going now? Can't it wait until tomorrow?" She was suddenly terrified. For the very first time, he was going to leave her alone.

"I gotta go tonight."

"But—" She pulled on the rope, wanting to be free. To her dismay, the rope held fast.

He shrugged in the darkness. "Can't have you runnin' when I'm gone."

"Are you leaving, then?" *Forever* was the unspoken word.

He leaned down to her. Their eyes met. He touched her smooth cheek. "I'll be back. Don't say a word and they'll never know I was gone."

"Macaulay," she whispered, suddenly filled with grief that she would never see him again. It was obvious he was going to take his chance and run, and he was going to abandon her there with Kineson and his men. Fear shot through her heart, but she couldn't blame him. He was an outlaw. She knew his kind well. He would always save himself first.

"I promise I'll be back," he whispered, his words urgent and strange. Then, as if to comfort her, his lips swept over hers in a quick, reassuring kiss. "Not a word now, all right?"

She nodded, turning away so that he couldn't see the tears

welling in her eyes. He stood and silently walked his waiting horse into the shadows. She heard the Ap toss its head. And then he was gone.

The rider angled the rocks where the granite face of Cirque of the Towers turned midnight blue beneath the moon, his Ap managing boulder fields by tracing the narrow, almost imperceptible white buffalo paths up the mountain. He broke the treeline of the mountains, where fir gave way to tundra that finally gave way to ice, and urged the horse into a gallop. The animal took the incline at a frantic pace, its powerful hindquarters glistening with sweat, but there was no time to pause. The lamp-lit silhouette of a group of riders appeared on a perch of rock overhead, and he was hell-bent to meet them.

"What you got?" The leader, a heavyset man with an enormous gray mustache, broke ranks.

"Shit is what I got." The rider reined in his horse.

"Still mad about that hanging, aren't you, Cain?" The man chuckled.

"Oughta get me a Yankee lawyer and sue you bluebelly bastards." The lone rider grunted. "I mean, has that telegram *ever* arrived? What a goddamned thing to screw up."

"Reb, you're still sore you lost the war, admit it. And was it our fault the telegraph operator in Washington, D.C., had to go out for a pork dinner at the crucial hour?"

"That's Federals for you," Cain spat out in disgust. "Rollins, you just take me to that telegraph operator and I'll show you Confederate justice." Shaking his head, he muttered, "I gotta get outta this business . . . it's killing me."

"You do this one last job and you don't ever have to do it again if you don't want to. Overland's got a nice settlement for you and you can have any job in Washington. That comes from the President himself."

Macaulay grunted again. "Sure. Easy for them all to be so goddamned big. What are the odds of me surviving this one —one in a hundred?"

Rollins roared with laughter. He slapped his cow pony.

"C'mon son, it can't be that bad. When Kineson gets his money from Overland tomorrow, we'll be there to round 'em all up. Then you'll have done your last and most spectacular job. Terence Scott's grateful, Cain. Overland's got a million dollars riding on this one. You'll be a hero."

"A dead hero. Scott couldn't get me at Sharpsburg, so he'll get me here."

"What's got you so ornery? Were you followed?" Rollins glanced at his partners. Both men were sitting stony-faced on their horses, repeating rifles under their arms, scanning the darkness. A silent darkness.

"I know better than to be followed." Cain reined in the Ap that jogged precariously along the edge of the cliff. "There's a woman down there, came along with the other passengers. You told me there weren't going to be any women involved." His face turned hard. "I got shot yesterday by a boy who's crazy to protect that woman's honor. My arm's nearly useless. Will be till this is long over."

"Kineson planned on kidnapping some Overland Express passengers. We had all the rosters. We didn't think there'd be a woman traveling alone. . . ." Rollins turned grim.

"This one's trouble. It's all I can do to control those men when she's around." As if he was thinking of his required nightly sojourn into the woods, Cain shook his head. "I've been forced to do things you wouldn't believe."

Rollins might have smiled, made light of Cain's predicament, but they were professionals with a job to do. A woman's presence was something neither had counted on. It was an added danger.

Rollins rubbed both sides of his mustache, a nervous habit. "We'll be there tomorrow, Cain. Until then, you've got to handle it."

"Yeah, great. What a job. Shit . . ." Macaulay said under his breath.

Rollins turned his horse on its hindquarters and motioned for his partners to depart. "We'll see you at the showdown," he said almost sorrowfully.

Cain nodded, a sarcastic, irreverent smile on his face.

"Fine, but I shoulda been an outlaw. Tell them that back in Washington when I'm dead and gone. Put on my tombstone that I said there's gotta be something better than this."

Rollins let out a gust of laughter as he inched his pony down the incline. He said, "You lie, Cain. You love this job. You're the best there is and even the President knows it. Who'd ever believe that the most notorious outlaw in the West, Johnny Reb himself, is one of us."

Macaulay shook his head, thoroughly disgusted. Rollins's laughter echoed down the mountain. The three men left with the yellow light of their lantern glinting wickedly off their silver star-shaped badges. Each engraved: *U.S. Marshal.*

Chapter Eight

Christal listened to the men snore, her heart hammering in her chest while she struggled to untie her hands. Daylight would come soon, and Kineson would find Cain gone; she would be totally at his mercy if she couldn't free herself. She took a deep breath, then tried the knot again, cursing the darkness that blinded her.

She tried hard not to think of Cain. He'd taken his escape, and that was all there was to it. After all, he'd done more than could be expected to help them. He deserved to survive. But no matter how she rationalized it, she found it difficult to accept his abandonment. He'd left her alone, without any protection. And he'd left with more than fear. No matter how much it angered her, she realized she must have begun to care for him; there was no other reason for the lump of hurt in her chest. She knew if she survived the kidnapping, the fear would diminish. But she'd never forget the soul-wrenching emotion that clutched at her heart when Macaulay Cain disappeared into the night.

"Damn," she said underneath her breath, unable to see the knot. Her fingers twisted in every unnatural position, but she couldn't get it loose. Finally she used her teeth to pull on it, but the knot was as immovable as stone. She sat back, despair crashing over her like a wave.

Then a hand covered her mouth.

Terror shot down her spine. It had to be Kineson. He'd come to rape her while she was tied. He'd enjoy the abuse.

She turned her head to face him, to take her enemy head-on. And suddenly she knew it wasn't Kineson. Cain had come back. Even in the darkness, she recognized him. She knew his breathing, she knew his smell, she knew his touch.

Without a sound, he lowered his hand and untied her. She was torn between wanting to hug him and wanting to slap his terrible, handsome face. He drew her against him, she rebelliously pulled away. Without a sound, he forced her down onto the bedroll. He won the battle, as she knew he would, and soon they were lying together, both feigning sleep.

Her mind was wild with unanswered questions. She wanted to know why he had come back, where he had gone, what he was thinking, but she knew she would never get anything more than the excuse he'd already given her about hidden gold. Perhaps it was the truth. Nonetheless, she was furious that he'd left. He'd revealed emotions she didn't want and now that he was back, her terror eased, and she again felt that perverse gratitude. She vowed to do away with all her feelings for him, but that was hard while lying in the fortress of his arms. Especially because for the first time in her life, she could think of no place she'd rather be.

Until the lavender fingers of dawn crept over the mountains. Tuesday had come.

The gang rose early, keeping a fearful silence as they saddled their horses and scarfed down their breakfast. Kineson looked the most nervous. And all the while, his gaze followed Christal as if she were the ransom, not Overland's gold.

Finally, the men saddled, camp broke, Kineson sat atop his paint and mapped out the orders. "Zeke'll watch the passengers back up in the saloon while we pick up the loot." His feral gaze slid to Cain, who was astride his Ap, Christal holding on to his waist. Cain stared back, his face expressionless and hard. She knew that look well. "Cain, you and I'll get the ransom. The boys here'll cover us."

Cain nodded. Christal's heart skipped a beat. Once Kineson got that ransom, she'd bet her soul that he would return to camp alone. He was choreographing Cain's slaughter. She looked up at Macaulay, desperately hoping he saw this too, but Cain only grunted his assent.

"The woman goes with Zeke to the saloon."

"She stays with me." Cain's fingers relaxed, inches from his holster. Christal's breath suspended in her throat. Beneath them, the Ap pranced nervously, waiting for the order to move out.

Kineson's eyes lowered to Cain's fingers. "She's a liability. You can't move on that horse if she's holding on behind."

"She's insurance. They ain't gonna shoot at us when they see I've got her."

Kineson looked at Cain, then at Christal. A smile touched his lips and he said, "Sure, Cain, sure." Kineson's smile grew, and he turned his horse eastward. The men followed. Cain let the Ap have its head.

They climbed past Valentine Lake, then took a trail that wound between Cathedral and Lizard Head peaks. Mountains shot rock and snow to the heavens, a violent, awe-inspiring sight, but there was no one to notice. All were too absorbed in their own tragedies or triumphs to take note of the magnificent theater around them. Soon they reached the foothills overlooking the Popo Agie valley and in the distance they could spy smoke from the fires at Camp Brown. Only trappers and displaced Arapahoe lived there now. The government had declared the old fort abandoned, which was why Kineson had chosen the water tower near it for the drop site.

The sun rose, and it was almost warm as they descended from their mountain hideaway to the prairie below. Overhead, the sky became a huge blue dome that Christal wished was big enough to swallow her, Cain, and the rest of the Overland passengers. Like an out-of-control locomotive, the inevitable screamed toward them. Try as she might to think of a way to avoid the showdown, there seemed no escape. Her only hope had rested on Cain, that he would see the folly of going along with Kineson. But he hadn't. If anything, he'd adamantly embraced Kineson's plans. And though it broke her heart to remind herself of it, the man who had kissed her

and held her last night was still the same man who had kidnapped her. Cain was as entrenched in the Overland ransom
scheme as any other gang member who rode with Kineson.
He was an outlaw, just as Marmet had been and Boone was.
There was no denying it. There never had been.

At the edge of the plains, Christal began to remember the
path to the drop site. The day Cain had taken her there
seemed years ago. Silence had stood sentinel between them,
as it did now, but now the silence was different. When before
it had been one-dimensional, empty, mere silence, now it was
almost a living thing, a fully formed figure that sat between
them, fraught with emotion and memories of what might
have been. Draped in black.

Unable to accept what might come, Christal held on to Cain
more tightly, leaning her cheek against the soft faded fabric of
his shirt, soothing herself with the warm, hard play of muscles
on his back as he rode. The girl she should have been would
have never embraced a gunfighter this way, but the girl she'd
become was desolate. It was as if she had been given a glimpse
of something beautiful and good and right, and just as she
recognized what could be hers, the door had slammed and
she was left out in the cold with nothing, all the more discon-
solate for seeing what she now knew she could never have.

Sensing her mood, Cain said softly, "It's going to be all
right, girl."

She didn't answer, she didn't look at him. She was too
afraid of tears.

The gang arrived at the water tower long before noon. The
horses were tied in a patch of cottonwoods below a ridge out
of sight of the railroad tracks. Kineson and Cain stood in the
shade, still mounted, ready to go. Christal, also astride the Ap,
clutched at Cain's waist, feeling her terror mount as the sun
marched to its zenith. The other gang members, Winchesters
in hand, crawled through the high grass to position themselves strategically near the drop site.

They saw the locomotive five miles before it arrived. In the
distance it looked like a puny toy, no match for a gang of cold-

eyed outlaws, but as it grew closer it became more ominous. The grind of oiled steel and the flare of blowing cinders whispered fury. The release of steam was a cry to war like J.E.B. Stuart waving his plumed hat.

"We talked about how we're gonna do this. Any questions?" Kineson addressed Cain but looked at Christal. She shrank back.

"No questions," Cain answered automatically. He nodded. His eyes were frigid.

They watched the locomotive grind to a halt beneath the water tower—a strange sight with no people, no buildings, nothing but empty prairie as far as the eye could see. The train consisted of the iron engine, the wood bin, and one car, nothing more—just as Kineson had specified.

Cain and Kineson jogged their mounts to the waiting train. Cain was the one to approach the car and Christal clung to him like a frightened kitten. He inched the Ap forward and banged the butt of his rifle on the door.

The door opened six inches.

Without pause, a small canvas bag was shoved out the space, dropping with a thud to the ground. Then another, then another, until there was a large pile on the side of the tracks. Kineson released a loud, gleeful chuckle as he eyed the pleasing glitter of gold from a bag that had broken open.

The final bag shoved out, the door slammed and the train chugged to a start. Christal watched it depart, not realizing her nails dug into Cain's back. When the train was a speck miles down the tracks, Kineson dismounted. The outlaws who'd been hiding in the grass stood, whooping and shouting like Indians while Kineson filled his shirt with as many canvas bags as he could carry.

"Get them horses over here and we'll load the rest up," Kineson shouted over the din. Boone nodded, the first one to run to the cottonwoods, eagerly hitching up his jeans in his greed to have at the loot.

"Gimme the girl, Cain." In the excitement neither Cain nor Christal watched Kineson. Kineson had mounted and now stood at their side, his shirt bloated with bags of money.

Cain grabbed his revolver. It was trained on Kineson before Christal could blink. "She's not going with you, Kineson. Get that through your head."

"The only thing going through your head is a bullet. Look behind you, Cain."

Christal turned her head. One of the outlaws had a rifle pointed at them. They'd planned Cain's execution just as she'd suspected.

Her heart died in her chest. She held on to Cain and vowed never to let go. For some crazy reason her mind couldn't accept that this was how she was going to watch him die.

"What is it, Kineson? You think I betrayed you?" Cain's every word was slow and cautious.

"Hell no. You're just too uppity, Cain. Now that we've got the money, we don't need you anymore." Anger cut into Kineson's features. He nodded toward Christal. "And I don't appreciate the fact you don't share, boy. So gimme the girl, or the both of you gonna be blown to kingdom come."

Cain was silent. Then all at once, he nodded for her to go to Kineson.

"No, Macaulay," she whispered urgently. "They're going to shoot you the minute I get off this horse. Don't let them. Don't!"

"Take her, Kineson! She's all yours!" Cain said, refusing to look at her.

She clawed at his back, desperate to stay with him. "They're going to kill you!"

"Or they're gonna kill both of us." His eyes heated with anger. "Do it. Go to him."

An arm went around her waist. She held on to Cain, but Kineson was too strong. He had her in his lap in seconds.

"Let go of me!" she spat, doing her best to dismount and stop the outlaw who held the rifle on Cain.

But suddenly a man's panicked shout echoed through the prairie. She turned her eyes to the cottonwoods and gasped.

Like spectres in a graveyard, dark-coated men astride army-issue geldings had sentineled behind the trees, surrounding the outlaws' tethered horses. Christal held her breath, torn between elation and fear.

The outlaws running for their horses skidded in the tall grass. They took barely a moment to assess the situation before they scattered through the brush like ferrets.

Kineson cursed. The man who held the rifle behind Cain had run too. Cain was now the only one armed.

"Let her go," Cain said ominously.

Kineson's horse reared; he spun it on its hocks, holding her to his lap with an arm of iron. "She's my insurance now." Viciously he spurred his horse into a gallop.

Christal fought to be free, but Kineson was almost as strong as Cain. She looked behind her with frightened eyes. Cain followed, his face a mask of unadulterated rage.

They flew over the train tracks and into the wide-open prairie. "I'll take you down, Cain!" Kineson roared. He drew his six-shooter; Christal released a cry of fury. She tried to get it from his hand, but he knocked her back with his elbow. Undaunted, she fought, her fists hitting the gold stuffed in his shirt, her fingers clawing at his sweat-drenched chest. She clamped down on his wrist, but Kineson backhanded her with the arm that held the gun. She drew back, holding her cheek, moaning from pain. Kineson aimed at Cain again, but she lashed out once more and gave a violent tug on the side of the horse's mouth. The animal slowed. That was all Cain needed.

He released a savage yell and threw himself on Kineson. All three tumbled to the ground.

"You'd let yourself hang for this woman? You're a fool, Cain! Let's get on our horses and get out of here!" Kineson growled when he scrambled to his feet, gun in hand, only to come nose to nose with Cain's Colt .45.

Cain dragged her to her feet and shoved her behind him. In the distance, she could see dark-coated men loping across the railroad tracks like steers. It would only be a matter of time before the marshals caught up.

Cain said softly, "You'll never have her, Kineson. Never."

"My God," Christal sobbed from behind him. "He's right. Get on your horse and get out of here. Kineson doesn't matter anymore, Macaulay. Whatever I say in your defense, they'll hang you anyway. So go. Go!" she nearly screamed.

The two men were in a standoff, both with guns drawn beneath the bright prairie sun. But Kineson seemed to be the more desperate. He eyed the marshals again and again. Cain kept his eyes only on him.

"Forget the woman," Kineson begged. "We're men of the Sixty-seventh. We've got to stick together. We can't surrender to Yankee scum!"

"I'm sorry," Cain whispered, his face ravaged by an honor the war had torn in two directions. "It's not Georgia we're fightin' for anymore. It's just us, Kineson. Just us . . ."

Rage distorted Kineson's features.

Christal cried out and tried to pull herself from behind Cain, but he held her to his back with an arm like a manacle. She screamed that Kineson was going to shoot, but Cain just stood there. Staring at Kineson's eyes.

He'd once told her that a gunman knew when to shoot by watching a man's eyes, not his hand. But Christal was no gunman. Her gaze was riveted on Kineson's finger. Later she didn't know if the loud ringing in her ears was from the shot or her own screams.

The report echoed across the wide-open grassland. She grabbed Cain, expecting him to fall to the ground, mortally wounded, as she had pictured it a thousand times in her head. But he didn't fall. He put his unfired gun into its holster and watched Kineson.

Shock riddled the man's features. The outlaw stared down at the hole in his chest that poured gold. But it was not really gold at all. Kineson's eyes widened in horror as he looked at the ground. At his feet were chipped, gold-painted tin tokens splattered with his own blood. With a gasp of betrayal, he fell backward, dead.

"Well, I got that one just by the hair of my chinny-chin-chin," said an unfamiliar voice.

Christal whipped around to see a rotund man ease off his horse. His Winchester still smoked. He had a huge mustache and wore a red shirt common to miners, but she saw the army-issue dark blue greatcoat strapped to the back of his saddle. There was no mistaking the gleam of the silver star pinned to it. Her heart shattered.

"How are you, ma'am? Name's Mr. Rollins." He tipped his Stetson and walked to her. She drew back, helplessly watching other marshals—hundreds it seemed—trot up to them on their mounts.

"I apologize for your ordeal, ma'am. When we knew the stage was likely to be ransomed, we didn't figure there'd be a woman aboard." Rollins sensed her discomfort. He looked down at the mound in the grass that was Kineson's body. "Why didn't you pick him off, Cain? God knows you were born with the devil's hand when it comes to shooting."

Cain's words were terse and unfathomable. "You got him. Saved me from having to kill one of my own."

Rollins just nodded, as if respecting Cain's reasons.

Other marshals dismounted. Cavalry had been sent with them. They were surrounded by men in blue. Choking back a sob, Christal waited for them to take Cain away in irons. She formulated in her mind everything she could say in his defense, but when Rollins stepped toward them, her reasoning flew. She could only step in front of Cain as if to shield him and blather nonsensical words in his defense, unable to think of anything except the picture of him swinging from the gallows, his strong, scarred neck snapped in two.

"You don't have to protect me, Christal."

Cain's words broke her. She turned and threw herself in his arms. She'd always thought herself a strong woman, but suddenly the thought of them taking him away was more painful than a shot through the heart.

"What's this?" Cain asked softly, clearly taken aback by her emotion. He laid a gentle hand on her brow to brush the hair away from her glistening eyes. "You're safe now, Christal. Everything's gonna be all right."

"No," she choked, unable to take her eyes from him. "Everything's not all right. Can't you see? They're going to take you away and hang you." Desperate to find his salvation, she watched the men approach. She ached to turn back the clock, unable to accept that any second they were going to take him away and demand justice for his crimes. A bitter regret seeped into her soul. They had never had a chance. From the beginning, everything including their past and their future was against them.

The seconds ticked cruelly by.

Rollins stepped toward them; she dug her fingers into his arms to hold Cain more tightly.

"Girl, it's gonna be all right," Cain whispered against her hair.

"They can't take you. They can't . . ." she said, fiercely clinging to his shirtfront.

His arms tightened. He made a hush noise as if to reassure her. Then he said, "But I'm still armed, Christal. Think about it. Would these men let me hold you like this and leave me with my guns?"

She tilted her head to look at him. He didn't appear afraid, or even worried. Around her, marshals were tending to Kineson's body. In the distance, cavalry shackled the other gang members. She counted five. They'd captured all of them.

But Cain.

Her gaze again lifted to his. He was almost smiling.

"I—I don't understand . . ." she murmured, unsure of herself.

"He's with us, ma'am," Rollins piped up, a broad grin on his face. "Has been all along."

"But he's an outlaw . . ." She looked at Rollins, wild-eyed with confusion. "He's even been hanged once. In Landen."

"You want to explain that one or should I?" Cain said dryly to the man.

Rollins winced. "Ah, well, that was a mistake." He couldn't help himself and laughed. "But then, mistakes happen, don't they? On behalf of the U.S. Government, we're just glad that this one went off without a hitch." His gaze went to Kineson's body, then dragged to Christal, who clearly had not been in the plans. "Well, almost without a hitch . . ." he finished.

Christal stared at Cain. They weren't going to hang him.

He was safe. He would live because . . . Her knees gave way. Cain caught her; she almost fainted.

"Easy there, girl," he whispered.

"You're—you're a marshal?" she stuttered, her heart constricting with fear.

"Were you really so afraid for me?" He looked tenderly down at her.

She stared at him wild-eyed. She didn't answer.

His knuckles, rough yet tender, stroked her cheek. "We got a lot to talk about, Christal."

She still said nothing. He was a U.S. Marshal.

Unconsciously, her palm curled over her scar. If she'd wanted to escape before, now the need had multiplied tenfold. Her blood fairly gushed with the desire to run. Her gaze traveled to all the men surrounding them. She was standing in the middle of an empty prairie with more lawmen than she'd ever seen in her life. Her eyes settled on Cain. She couldn't accept it. He was a U.S. Marshal.

"We found the other prisoners and the man who held them at Falling Water," Rollins said, shattering her concentration. "The gang'll go directly to Fort Laramie for trial—we got a judge there. But we're taking the passengers to old Camp Brown to recuperate, it's closer. Then Overland's promised coaches to wherever they want to go." He tipped his hat to Christal. "That goes for you, too, ma'am. I hope you don't mind riding once more with Cain to the fort."

She didn't protest. She was numb. All she could do was woodenly comply. She had to get through the formalities and do her best to hide her identity. Then she had to *run*.

Cain put her on his saddle and they set off at a lope toward Camp Brown. Once more in his arms, stunned at the about-face of her circumstances, Christal gazed at the flat landscape, her entire being consumed with the need to flee. In truth, she didn't want to go, to leave him. Now that they'd both faced death, she knew a lot more about her feelings toward him, and the thought of leaving sent an ache through her soul.

But if he had been dangerous before, now he was suicide.

All along she'd known that a lady had no business falling in love with an outlaw.

But a woman who was wanted in New York could never even *look* at a lawman.

Chapter Nine

———⟨⟨⟨∿⟩⟩⟩———

Christal didn't know how to flee. Running from outlaws was simple. They expected runaways and they felt no moral duty to bring them safely back to camp. But the cavalry was something else. When they rescued a white woman from a band of renegades, they expected the woman to rest, to need time to recuperate from her trauma. They didn't expect her first desire to be escape. And if such a strange occurrence happened, and the girl did flee, then they would feel a deep moral obligation to go out and "rescue" the poor confused maiden, and Christal knew they would do it again and again, if need be, until she understood they meant her no harm.

Though she'd been there only a few hours, she let out a quiet moan as she despaired of leaving Camp Brown. The old abandoned fort was miles from everything. The closest settlement was the Wind River Indian Reservation and she had no business there among the Shoshone with her flaxen hair.

Raising her hands, she let the women around her dress her in a much too large ratty pink silk ballgown. Indian squaws tended to her, Mandan women, known for their free ways among white men. Christal had seen many of them in the plains towns. Their tribe had been decimated by smallpox, so they scraped together an existence by frequenting forts and mining towns, and taking the leavings of the girls in the saloons. Coarse-featured, brown, and husky, they rarely got treated well. Now Christal felt even more empathy for them.

They shared a strange sisterhood. The squaws were held captive by need as much as she was by fear.

The Mandan women left and Christal walked to the small window in her room, which she believed was the captain's former quarters. She was exhausted, but sleep was out of the question; too dangerous. Besides, there might be an Overland coach that afternoon to take passengers away. She wouldn't miss it, even if it meant giving up her seven gold pieces.

Wiping the glass of the window, she looked out into the center of the fort. The August sun hung on the horizon. Sweat beaded her brow and dust again dried her throat; she'd forgotten how hot it was on the prairie. She looked to the fort's gates and wondered if she could get past the two cavalry officers who had been posted there. They had no right to keep her, really. She could demand her gold pieces from Rollins and walk past the guards and just keep on walking. Her eyes darkened. But the marshals wouldn't like the fact she'd left without talking to them about the kidnapping. With all the cavalry at their disposal, they'd return her to "safety" in a matter of minutes. Then they'd want to know why she had run. And then she would have two choices: She could refuse to answer their questions, and thus raise their suspicions, perhaps even to the point that they would find out about her scar (the far better choice); or she could lie to them, claim abuse by the kidnappers, such terrible abuse that *any* men frightened her and all she had wanted to do was leave the fort and get away from so many of them. The marshals just might believe that story, but Cain would know she was lying. And his suspicions were far more frightening to her than those of the entire cavalry that now maneuvered on the drill field in the center of the fort.

She took a deep breath and ran shaky hands down her hair. Being surrounded by the law was her worst nightmare come true, save meeting face-to-face with Baldwin Didier. The Overland stage couldn't come quick enough, even if the prospect of leaving tore at her heart.

Macaulay Cain. Macaulay Cain. The name echoed through

her mind. She never wanted to think of him again. There was no good to come of their relationship before they'd been rescued. And now it was even worse.

A knock sounded at the door, snapping her out of her dark musings. She pulled up the shoulders of the faded pink gown, embarrassed that her bosom peeked out from beneath her chemise every time the dress slipped.

The knock sounded again, this time more urgent, and terror gripped her heart. She was consumed by the irrational thought that they'd discovered her, but sanity took over once more, and she realized it was unlikely. Twisting her hair in her hands and wishing she could pin it, she threw it over one shoulder and opened the door.

Her heart froze. Cain stood there, looking very different from the man she knew. He'd shaved and a strong jaw appeared where rough dark beard had been. With the beard gone, she realized he was far more handsome than she'd suspected. But he was still Macaulay Cain. The hard mouth and ice eyes were the same, and the combination, as always, proved mesmerizing.

She lowered her gaze to the rest of him. He'd bathed and donned civilized dress: dark trousers, white shirt, and a burgundy silk vest. His hair was slicked back and smelling of bay rum. If she'd been attracted to him as an outlaw, she had to admit she was even more drawn to him now. He was clean-shaven and restrained, and the facade suited him. Now his danger was subtle, as a whisper is more erotic than a shout.

"I hardly know you," she said in a low, cautious voice.

The corner of his mouth lifted in a smile. Looking as he did, he almost could have been one of the gamblers who'd come into the saloons she'd worked at, wanting to spend—or make—an ill-gained fortune. The gamblers she'd encountered had been powerful and violent men, men who gained on looks alone. They'd possessed enormous magnetism, and she'd always made a policy of avoiding them. But even they paled against Macaulay Cain.

She stepped away from the door, unsure of what to say. She

didn't look at him; she didn't ask him to enter. She knew he would come in whether she permitted it or not.

"That dress is too big," he said, closing the door behind him.

She hugged the faded silk to her. "I need to take it in."

"So I see." His gaze caught hers. From the gleam in his eye, it was clear he approved of the dress. He was waiting for her to fall right out of it.

She turned away, suddenly, irrationally, embarrassed. They'd kissed, they'd slept together, they'd fought. But now he was a stranger to her. A very threatening stranger. The outlaw she'd grown to care about was gone and they had nothing to talk about.

Yet so much to talk about.

Gathering her courage, she still looked steadily away and said, "You should have told me that you were a marshal. It would have made things easier."

"I wasn't sure of your acting skills. I didn't want you to get hurt. Or get myself killed," he added.

"I understand." She glanced down at the dress. One shoulder had fallen revealing an expanse of smooth skin that plumped into the beginning of a breast. She pulled the gown up, hoping he hadn't seen much. But he'd seen it all if the fire smoldering in his cold eyes was any indication.

There was a long, difficult pause while they stared at each other. She broke it by saying, "Things are very different now, aren't they? *You're* very different."

"Things are better; I'm better," he countered, running a callused thumb along her collarbone. "I can talk to you now. I can tell you anything—you can tell me anything. I'm no longer your kidnapper. I'm just a man. A man you can trust." His gaze met hers. Probing.

"I had begun to trust you anyway," she answered. Uncomfortable beneath his stare, she breezed past him to the mirror over the oak bureau and began plaiting her hair. All she thought about was running. She was afraid of his being a lawman, but mostly she was afraid of his being a man. He'd already taken her emotions and twisted them until she hardly knew what she was feeling. She couldn't let him continue. If she fell in love with him, with what she knew about him now, it would be suicide.

He came up from behind and watched her in the mirror. Not touching her, he said, "I get the feeling you trust me less now that you know I'm no outlaw."

The task of braiding her hair defeated her, and she dropped her shaking hands. A shot rang out—the cavalry going through their maneuvers on the drill field—and the noise frayed her nerves even more. Pushed to the edge, she snapped, "I just don't understand it—you call yourself a Rebel—you fought on the Confederate side—how can you work for Federals now? I just never expected—" She shook her head. Words escaped her; she worried she might have given away too much.

The ghost of a smile crossed his lips. "You almost talk like a Secesh yourself. But you're just another protected Northern lily who had to be told about the war like a bedtime story. You must have been particularly fortunate, Christal. It took ten years for that war to be done and gone before you ever bothered to ask anyone about it."

Anger flared within her. She might have been a protected Northern girl for part of her life, but after that she'd had her own war to fight; she couldn't have gotten involved in his. Tersely, she answered, "I asked you about the war because I wanted to know about you. But everything about you has been a lie. And your Rebel background must have been a lie, too, because I don't understand how you can be a Confederate one minute and a Federal the next. A Rebel just couldn't do your job. Not a real one, anyway."

"It's because I was a Rebel that I can do this job."

She expected the anger but not the bitterness. The emotion in his words made her ache.

"What do you think I got out of the war? You think I won it? You think I found honor and pride?" He took a deep breath. It seemed painful for him to speak. "I didn't find anything in that war except death and blood and loss. It's been ten years and I still can't find any meaning to it I can live with. The right and wrong is all messed up within my head. I know 'cause I look for it every day. That's why I can work for the Federals, Christal, because the damned war is long over. I'm no longer a man from Georgia, I'm a citizen of the United States, and the job I do is black and white. Right and wrong. What Kineson did was a crime. Justice has been served. I can move on to the next job without it eating my insides."

"But things aren't always that clear." She damned the panic in her voice. "Sometimes a crime isn't what it seems. You may have the facts, but the facts lie—"

"What are you talking about?"

She looked at him in the mirror. A frown marred his forehead. She couldn't tell him anything. After what he'd said, he'd have her tried and hanged before her uncle could even get to her.

"Christal, what is it?" His hands went around her waist, his warm, sure grip melting her sides. She fought the urge to draw back against his chest. But that chest beckoned her, and she longed to be enfolded in his arms, to touch him, kiss him. She wanted to make him understand things she thought the outlaw Macaulay Cain already knew: that sometimes there were reasons for crimes, sometimes crimes were misjudged.

But now there was another Macaulay Cain beside her. A man who didn't think at all the way she did, and from whom her only protection was a wall of silence.

"Don't treat me like a stranger, Christal," he said, his words a deep rumble. "I know you've been through a lot, but—"

"But we *are* strangers," she interjected. Desperately trying to distance herself from him, she said, "We went through some very difficult days, but now they're over. We can get on with our lives. I'm anxious to see that Overland coach and be off." She turned and faced him, needing to be honest one last time. "But you'll never know how relieved I am that you weren't killed. I'm—I'm glad you're a marshal. I couldn't bear to have seen you hanged."

There was an edge to his voice, as if he wanted to shake her. "You care for me, so let me care for you too. Don't pull away."

"I'm not—"

"You are." He looked at her face in the mirror. His hand came up, and he caressed one cheek. "I need to know about you, Christal—where you're from, who your husband was, where you were headed that day in the coach."

"My life is dull. My past would bore you."

"You've never told me anything—"

"There's nothing to tell."

His hand grasped her chin and forced her gaze to his. "If there's nothing to tell, then why won't you tell it? I thought you wouldn't talk about yourself because you thought I was an outlaw—a man who kidnapped you. Now I wonder if it's not something more than that."

"We're strangers who shared a bad experience," she said, closing her eyes and willing herself to be strong. She wasn't going to let him see inside her. Not while she was determined to flee at the first opportunity. "We've just got to go on with our lives. I'll be going my way and you'll be going yours—"

"No."

Her breath caught. Her eyes flew open. A small stab of fear sliced through her heart. "What did you say?"

"You heard me. I said no. We aren't going our separate ways. Not yet."

"You have no right to hold me any longer than—"

"I have every right."

She stared at him. The blood thrummed in her head. "Why?" she asked, her voice barely above a sigh.

"You know why." He turned her to face him. He ran one finger over her lips. "You know it," he whispered.

The words died on her lips.

They stood there, neither of them winning, neither willing to surrender. Finally, he nodded to the window, and the cavalry still going through maneuvers in the dust. "You're back in civilization, girl. It may not look like much, but civilization's rules apply here just as they do in Fort Laramie, or San Francisco, or Denver. You're a woman alone and tonight you'll sleep in this room, protected from any man who might want to bother you . . . like me."

A lump came to her throat. She didn't want him to continue. He was bound to make something out of their time in Falling Water, and she couldn't let him. If he gave it meaning, then it would be difficult to leave him. Even more difficult than it already was.

He lowered his voice; his eyes became shadowed. The words to stop him wouldn't come to her.

"I won't be with you tonight," he whispered. "I won't feel your softness against me, or hear you breathe deeply in slumber. I can't ruin your reputation because the rules apply now. You're what's known as a lady, Mrs. Smith; I'll treat you like one. But I want you to know I curse the rules. Whatever happened between us back in Falling Water shouldn't have happened, but sayin' that doesn't change the fact that it did. Tonight you should be in my arms. And you know that, just like you know your heart beats . . . right here." His knuckles grazed down her collarbone, then his palm opened and he laid it against the top of her left breast, where they both could feel the drum of her heart.

She looked away while tears welled in her eyes. His words scorched her with veracity. He'd said everything she prayed he wouldn't. His words made her soul weep. They made leaving him excruciating.

For the first time in years she felt one hot tear trail down her face. It had been appropriate that she'd met him dressed in mourning. For six long years she'd mourned the loss of her childhood, the loss of her former life. But mostly she mourned her loneliness, a curse that doubled as she became a woman, because now she wanted flesh not fantasy with her at night. In Falling Water she'd been taunted by the hope that she might have found someone she could be with. There'd been moments she'd looked at Cain and could almost see staying with him. He was not the man she pictured in her dreams, but dreams were for foolish young girls who could afford them. And the outlaw she'd slept with, talked to, kissed, was flesh and blood—substance not shadow—and just enough on the other side of the law to understand her.

Now he was gone. As dead as if he'd been shot by Kineson.

Macaulay had often wondered about her husband. Suddenly she discovered the one she'd mourned for. It was Cain.

"Why are you doing this?" she finally whispered, angered that he'd pushed her so far.

"Because I want you" was all he said.

She closed her eyes. Whispering, she countered, "If I whore for you tonight, is that how you think you might rid yourself of me?"

"I don't want you to whore for me. If I had, I would have had you already. I could have taken you a dozen times in the days we've been together."

"It would have been rape."

"I could have had you, nonetheless."

She began to tremble.

He encircled her in his arms. "I want you to tell me about yourself." He lifted her hand, the one with the rose-shaped scar, and traced every lush petal burned into her palm. His touch was like wildfire, consuming her. "What are you hiding, girl?"

She moaned, refusing to talk.

He gently cupped her jaw, and she was forced to meet his steely gaze. "Answer me," he said.

She looked away.

"What are you afraid of?" he whispered urgently.

"Nothing," she gasped.

He forced her gaze back to his and looked deep into her eyes, for minutes, it seemed, as if he was assessing her answer. Then, with unexpected passion, he thrust her away. "You're lying."

"No," she answered desperately.

"I can see it in your eyes. They're the color of the sky, so beautiful, so blue. . . ." His tone grew ominous. "So clouded. You lie."

Frightened, she turned and stared out the window. Her bosom heaved with a show of indignation. "You accuse me of lying, but you're the one who's lied. Who are you really? Are you one of the Georgia Sixty-seventh or are you a U.S. Marshal? Are you a Yankee or a Reb? An outlaw or a citizen?"

His expression became rock-hard. "If I ever lied to you, I did so to save your life. But when I did tell you about myself, it was the truth."

"It must be very convenient, then, to possess such divided loyalties." She knew she was stomping on hallowed ground, but in her fear and anger she didn't care.

"If you're referring to my part in the kidnapping, that was my job. But"—his words became low and angry, like the rumble of a distant drum—"if you're referring to my part in the war, ma'am, then let me tell you, I'm a Rebel, and I'll always be a Rebel. And make no mistake, if it were up to me, Georgia'd be ruling you and this whole goddamned country."

She suddenly began to cry. Why had she wanted to hurt him? All she really wanted was to get away from him, not be cruel to him. He'd been torn apart by the war. He'd said there'd been no honor in it, but there was honor. He'd stood by his country. And when that country was no more, he folded his Confederate flag and laid it respectfully to rest rather than let it become any more tattered and dirtied. He'd gotten on with his life despite the heaviness in his heart, and even then he'd done the honorable thing, by fighting his own Reb guerrillas gone bad in the lone prairies and hills of the West.

"Don't," she heard him whisper at her tears, his voice surprisingly gentle.

In unwilling surrender, she laid her head against his chest. He wiped her cheeks, her tears slick beneath his thumbs; she trembled, burying her face in his shirt. He'd bathed, his clothes were clean. He should have smelled like a different man. But beneath the starch and bay rum, his scent was achingly familiar, and she secretly reveled in it, wishing he could hold her forever.

Several practice rounds were fired by the cavalry outside the window, shattering their intimacy. Still without raising her head from his chest, she spoke the words she knew she must. "When is the Overland coach arriving?" Her voice was hoarse with emotion.

"Overland can't send one for two days," he answered woodenly.

Her shoulders slumped. She didn't know if she could last that long.

"Christal," he said, his hands tightening on her, "don't think about getting away right now. We've got two days. Let's have that at least."

"Two days is a very short time . . . or a very long time, depending on how you see it," she answered, her mind wild with the need to escape, her heart wild with the need to stay.

She wiped her tearstained cheeks with the back of her hand. His silence verified her words.

He said, "I came here to ask you to dinner. The other passengers have inquired about your welfare. I know they'd be relieved to see you at the table tonight in the mess."

She stepped from his arms to the bureau, effectively shutting him out by presenting her back, but when she looked in the mirror, his gaze captured hers and would not let go. For one short pause in eternity, her eyes spoke to his with naked emotion. Then, forced to save herself or drown, she tore away and pretended the moment had never happened. "I'd love to go to dinner. Let me pin my hair."

"You have beautiful hair. I never told you that."

She closed her eyes, fighting the ache for him to run his hand down her hair as he had in Falling Water. She again met his eyes, and in those frosty depths she could see longing, perhaps even hurt. To him, the hardship and dishonesty were over with.

To her, they were just beginning.

She whispered, "I won't be but a minute."

Chapter Ten

The old fort's mess hall was a crude log building with a dirt floor. It hadn't been abandoned long because the mud still held between the logs and the cast-iron stove was still intact.

Christal knew true terror as she looked around. The room was full of men: passengers and cavalry. And *marshals*. Their silver stars seemed to be on every chest, blinding her with their brightness whenever they caught the lantern flame.

Her body tensed for flight, her mind crying for escape, she smiled and stilled the hand that lay trembling on Cain's arm. It was imperative that she avoid suspicion until she could quietly depart with the other passengers. Still, as if by instinct, her palm curled over the rose-shaped scar, and she vowed they'd have to break her hand to reveal it in this crowd.

Without ceremony, Mr. Glassie parted from a sea of blue-coated cavalrymen. He gave her a bear hug and she found tears in her eyes once more. Henry Glassie was a kindhearted soul, and she wished they could be friends. She pulled back from him and saw he was pale, even a little thinner—though with his girth that was hard to tell—but no worse for wear. His verdigris suit had been brushed and he looked almost as dapper as the day the Overland coach had first set out for Noble.

"Thank God you're all right, Mrs. Smith. I can't begin to tell you how Mr. Adlemeyer and I worried about you," he exclaimed, holding her as if she were his long-lost daughter.

Christal smiled up at him, letting her gaze move from Mr. Glassie to the "preacher." She had never known the preacher's name. He smiled back but wearily, as if he still were desperate for a drink.

Mr. Glassie nodded toward Macaulay, who had walked over to greet some cavalrymen. "Can you believe that ruffian was actually one of the marshals?"

Christal glanced at Cain. He laughed among the men as if one of them had told an especially funny joke. His teeth were brilliantly white, his grin wolfish. There was actually some warmth in those cold eyes. He looked relaxed, even happy. Until his gaze met hers.

The smile disappeared like a miser's gold. She could see she troubled him. As he had troubled her back in Falling Water.

"He's a man full of surprises," she commented, glad that Mr. Glassie's attention was on seating her and not on their exchange. She didn't want him to see how Macaulay affected her. To divert herself, she nodded a greeting to the Overland coach driver and the shotgun, who stood in a corner. Both appeared immensely relieved to be where they were. "Where are Pete and his father?" she asked, looking around.

"Pete's watching maneuvers. Old Elias, I understand, is arguing with Rollins about when his money will be returned." Mr. Glassie chuckled. "Seems he's sore about them keeping it a moment longer than they have to."

Christal could have laughed, picturing the grizzled old man up against Rollins, but she was too absorbed in wondering when she might expect her own money to be returned. She longed to feel the weight of her precious seven gold pieces in her palm once more.

A hand on her shoulder made her look up and she found Cain standing there, drink in hand.

"Here. This will help you sleep tonight." He gave her the tin cup.

"Thank you . . ." She paused, wondering what name to call him. The name Cain didn't seem to fit him or their relationship any longer.

"Macaulay," he answered, as if reading her mind.

"Macaulay," she whispered, and accepted her drink. Then she turned away, too frightened to look at him, too frightened to let him see her eyes full of worry, her heart on her sleeve. He had gotten close to her when she thought him an outlaw. It was time, indeed it was imperative, that she back away.

Taking one small sip from the cup, she found it was hot coffee well laced with whiskey. As she refused to meet Macaulay's gaze the tension between them mounted. This time Henry Glassie didn't miss a second of the interchange.

Macaulay soon returned to the men to help them carve the venison and Mr. Glassie pulled up his chair. He took her hand and said, "I'm glad we've got a chance to speak, Mrs. Smith."

"Please call me Christal." She tried to smile, though it was difficult considering the situation.

"I'm honored to be counted as one of your friends, Christal, but . . ." Glassie's troubled gaze wandered once more to Macaulay. "I can't help but think how you looked when you came up to the saloon the other day." His kind voice lowered to a whisper. "Your clothes were torn. Cain handled you in front of us. Shoved you. Dragged you off."

"He didn't hurt me. He never hurt me," she whispered, wondering why her voice began to tremble.

"It was a terrible time. But I want you to understand whatever was done to you can be recompensed. If Mr. Cain took advantage of you during your captivity, I'll see to it that the right thing is done. I'll make him marry you—"

"No," she answered, cutting him off with more passion than she wanted to show.

"There, there, Mrs. Smith. I didn't mean to upset you."

She quavered a smile. "Please forgive me. I'm not upset. Mr. Cain did nothing he need regret. I'll be fine as soon as the coach comes. I find I must leave."

"You can't want to leave so soon!" He laughed. "Why, Terence Scott himself is coming up from the Union Pacific to give us a hefty sum to recompense us for our troubles. I understand he'll be here late tomorrow."

Christal couldn't hide the shock on her face. She never dreamed they'd get any kind of monetary apology from Overland. The money might actually be enough for her to expose Didier. It was difficult to imagine but her fortunes were actually looking up. "Do you have any idea about how much he's bringing?" she asked, knowing she was being indelicate but unable to help herself.

"No, no! But it's sure to be a fine sum. Especially for you, Christal. I understand they never thought a woman would be on that coach. They're very sorry for what they've put you through."

"I see."

He rambled, "Now, I myself must miss the presentation, but I've got Paterson Furniture to recompense me. And they'll give me a tidy sum. I'm a very valued employee, you see. They've already got me a coach so I may start out first thing in the morning and get to my accounts." He straightened the lapels of his coat. "I can't afford to dawdle here and lose my sales."

His words took a moment to sink in. Finally she sputtered, "You're leaving first thing in the morning? You're not waiting for the Overland coaches?"

"I can't miss another day at my accounts. I'm very behind."

She tapped her fingers on the splintery wooden board of the table. Her desire for the Overland money was palpable. But it would be prudent to see if she could leave in the morning. Should she do the intelligent thing and leave? Or should she throw caution to the wind, grab at the Overland money on the chance that it might be the thing to solve all her problems?

"A penny for your thoughts?"

She stared at Mr. Glassie. "I—I was just envying you your quick departure. Macaulay—er—Mr. Cain told me the Overland coaches would take two days."

"Are you in such a hurry, then?"

She bit her lower lip and thought about Cain. She could have a pleasant two days with him and he would never discover who she was. Or he could seduce her into his bed, seduce her into giving him her honor and the truth about her past, then throw her to the wolves she called U.S. Marshals. Her eyes clouded. "I—I *may* need to leave earlier."

"Well, if need be, I most certainly could take you in the morning. Paterson has telegrammed that I'll have a coach at dawn. But where do you want to go?"

She paused, unwilling to say she didn't care. That would raise too many questions. "Where is your first stop?"

"South Pass."

She smiled a beautiful, warm smile. South Pass was only a stone's throw from Noble, her original destination. "Perfect. If I decide to leave, I'll meet you at the coach at dawn."

"With no escort?"

"I'll be all right." She smiled again, dazzling him. "You won't mention this to anyone, will you?"

Mr. Glassie nodded, clearly enchanted. "Why, of course not. This is just between us."

The Mandan women began serving the meal, ending their conversation. Macaulay sat beside her, and she quickly commented on how difficult it was to find good quality furniture out west, which spun Mr. Glassie off on a twenty-minute commentary. Christal ate in silence, half listening to Mr. Glassie, acutely aware of Cain's every breath, every sip of whiskey, every shift of weight on the crude bench. She wondered if he was as aware of her, and whenever she would chance to look at him, their eyes would meet. A silent clash of lovers.

After dinner, Judd, the Overland driver, took out a fiddle and played a soothing waltz. The coffee and whiskey went down easily, even though Christal wasn't used to drinking. She wanted to relax—an impossible task while she was still in the fort, surrounded by lawmen.

Macaulay leaned back in a chair and irreverently placed his booted feet on the bench on which she sat. She looked at him, wondering how to approach the subject of the Overland money. If their compensation wasn't going to be much, her decision to leave with Mr. Glassie would be easy. If it was a king's ransom, then she'd stay, despite the risk. But now she didn't know which it would be. She had until dawn to find out.

"When do you suppose we'll be getting our possessions back?" she asked, glancing around the room as if she wasn't really that interested in his response. "You have seven gold pieces of mine, you know."

"Well, don't worry. There's nothing to spend it on here."

"Yes, but—"

"Besides, you'll have more than your seven gold pieces when Terence Scott arrives. I hear he's paying y'all pretty for your troubles."

"How pretty?" She frowned. Was there too much anxiety in her voice?

"Greedy, are we?"

She looked at him.

He gave her a rakish grin.

"No—well—all right, y-yes," she stuttered. "It's just that I haven't a lot of money. I never thought we'd be recompensed for our troubles."

"I hear he's bringing five hundred."

Her eyes opened wide. "Dollars?" she gasped.

"He ain't bringin' buffalo chips."

She took another sip of brew. Five hundred dollars split among seven passengers would be around seventy apiece—a good parcel. She again thought of her seven gold pieces and how hard they had come. She could almost taste her desire for more.

"What are you schemin' in that head of yours, darlin'?"

Her gaze returned to him. Macaulay made her nervous when he drank. Those eyes of his seemed to see right through her. It was as if he could read her mind. And his accent was much more pronounced. She really wasn't sure she liked that. His lazy words were . . . seductive.

Coolly she said, "I was only thinking about a new dress. Seventy dollars can buy a lot of new dresses."

"Seventy? I said five hundred. Apiece. And you'll probably get more, seein' as how you're a lady, and all. They feel real bad about you gettin' tangled in this mess."

The whiskey burned down her throat, nearly choking her. She was in shock. Her dreams had come true. She could get Didier with five hundred dollars. She could hire a lawyer, even a Pinkerton man to build evidence against him.

He smiled as if he knew something she didn't. "Too bad you don't have that new dress now. That pink one is fallin' right off you." His gaze lowered to a point between her chin and her waist.

She blushed and looked down. Her entire shoulder and not a little of her bosom were exposed. She discreetly pulled up the pink silk.

"Better get them Mandans to take that gown in tonight. You want to look pretty in your picture when Scott presents you with your money."

"Picture?"

"That's right." He released a cynical little laugh. "You don't think that Yankee's gonna come all the way out here to give you some reward money and not get the credit for it? That ain't the way them Yankees work, darlin'. In fact tomorrow there's gonna be so many newspaper reporters here to take your picture, you'll be famous. After Scott's through with you, Barnum himself'll probably sign you up to be an attraction at his show." He laughed, disgust all over his face. "I can just see it now: *The Wild West Widow.*" He took another sip of whiskey and said grimly, "Don't let him do it to you, Christal."

But Christal hardly heard it. Terror caused her to go deaf after he spoke the words *newspaper reporters*. She curled her branded palm around the warm tin cup, hiding it. Stuttering, she asked, "But—but how could reporters get here so quickly? We've only just been rescued."

Macaulay sat back in his chair, arms arrogantly crossed over his chest. "Darlin', this is a Yankee we're talkin' about. Terence Scott, that damned carpetbagger, had 'em sent up here days ago to get publicity from all this. Fort Washakie's just crawling with reporters. I heard tell they got 'em from as far away as Chicago. Even New York." He grunted in disgust. "The show-off."

Her hands began to tremble. She clasped them in her lap.

"What is it, girl, you don't look too well."

"I—I guess the whiskey didn't agree with me," she stuttered. Trying with all her might to stay calm in the face of catastrophe, she said, "Do you mind if I go to my room? If tomorrow's going to be as you say it is, then I'll need my rest."

She stood and didn't know if it was whiskey, fear, or just plain exhaustion, but suddenly the room began to spin. She gripped the edge of the table to steady herself and received two splinters in her palm for the effort.

Macaulay's arm came gently around her waist. His finger brushed the faint lavender smudges beneath her eyes, proof of her weariness. "I guess you oughta be in bed, girl," he conceded.

But a hostile voice halted their departure. "Haven't you bothered her enough, Cain?"

Christal looked behind Cain and found Pete in the doorway, his sullen, angry expression epitomizing his youth.

Cain didn't answer. She knew his shoulder was still sore from the wound. Fighting with Kineson had opened it again and he'd spent that afternoon with the doctor. Now here was Pete, the boy who shot him, tempting him to pull his gun.

"You shouldn't let him near you, ma'am," Pete said, snatching his hat off his head in a show of respect. "I don't care what he is now, he treated you bad at the saloon. We all saw him."

"He had no choice," she said, her head beginning to throb. She couldn't deal with Pete right now. Not when she'd just lost five hundred dollars and her chance to find justice, and reporters were descending on Camp Brown first thing tomorrow.

"Didn't he?" The boy's lip, dusted with downy adolescent facial hair, lifted in contempt.

"I'm not in the habit of shootin' boys, son," Cain interjected in a voice cold enough to freeze. "But you better know, you're temptin' me, sorely."

"Yeah, I'd love a showdown with you, Cain. You need to learn how to treat a woman."

Christal shuddered. The boy's bravado was going to be the end of him. "No, Pete. Don't even think of it. He didn't hurt me. Not really. And what he did . . . well, he had to do it. He had to convince them that he was genuine. I've forgiven him. So must you."

"He was rough with you." Pete turned to her. She could see the worship in his eyes. If she didn't know better, she'd think the boy—though barely sixteen—had somehow fallen in love with her.

She touched his arm. "What's done is done, Pete. If Macaulay was less than gentlemanly, it was because he had to be. I'm not angry about it. Neither must you be."

"He still ain't good enough for you, ma'am." He looked at her and his eyes turned hopeful. "A woman beautiful like yourself needs courtin'. I—I can do a lot of that now that me and Pa got our money back."

The boy's passion and sincerity touched her. During the entire kidnapping, during all the years she'd spent out west, he had been her only knight. Impulsively she put her hand on his smooth cheek and ached over the fact that she would never see him again. "How I've longed to hear words like that, Pete," she whispered affectionately. "You'll never know how I'll cherish them in the years to come when you've married and long forgotten me."

The boy didn't seem to have the courage to touch her back. He stood there, planted in one spot, the emotion in his eyes churning as he appeared to squelch an inappropriate confession of love. Then, unable to help himself, he blurted out, "Mrs. Smith, I must tell you—"

"Some other time, kid," Macaulay interjected, casually putting his arm around her waist. He led her away and Christal went, relieved that Macaulay had made it unnecessary for her to discourage Pete's affections; and saddened, knowing she would never see the lionhearted boy again.

"You could have been kinder to him," she admonished when they crossed the fort's drill grounds.

"The damn fool kid shot me. Why should I be kind to him?"

"He thought you were an outlaw."

"He's too uppity—playing suitor to a grown woman."

"He's not that much younger than me."

His smile was derisive. "Why are you defending him, Christal? You got a penchant for robbing the cradle?" He suddenly laughed. If she hadn't had so much on her mind, she might have laughed also.

They came to the door of her quarters. Cain halted and looked at her.

"Well, I must go now. I—I really need some sleep." She suddenly felt bereft. There was so much she wanted to say to him, but there was no opportunity, or time. She would probably never see him again. In the morning, she would be gone. And Falling Water would become just a memory.

He tapped his boot on the plank walk. She could see the frustration in his eyes. He wanted her to stay the night with him, but there was no way to do it now that they were in civilization.

"Pete's right, you know," she said, thinking about all that Cain wanted and how shockingly improper it was. "You're not much of a gentleman. I know it just by looking into your eyes."

"Damn this situation. It's foolish for me to think of bringing you posies and courting you in the parlor after what we've been through."

"Yes, it is." She was silent for a moment, thinking how painfully true those words were. With her background, she was no longer a woman to be swayed by courtship. And he was no Romeo. She had seen him kill in Falling Water. She had glimpsed a side of him that was hard and violent, too unused to mercy and gentleness. The government certainly had a good man; the war had taught him well. It had taught him how to fight; how to win and how to lose. Macaulay Cain was a man who did what he had to do no matter how difficult, and he expected the same of others. That hardness attracted her; deluded her into believing it could protect her, but it couldn't. It made him that much more dangerous. Because to him, there was right and wrong and nothing in between. Losing the war had left him nothing to cling to but that ideal, and knowing him as she knew him now, she understood why he

had become a marshal. His world had lost order; the law
restored order. If he found out she was wanted in New York,
he had a deep, personal need to see justice done. And that
was what frightened her most. Because she didn't believe in
justice anymore.

Resigned to leaving at dawn, she looked at him and wondered how she would say good-bye.

He whispered, "Will you sleep all right tonight?" *Alone*
went unspoken.

She didn't answer. If he heard regret in her voice, he'd
never let her go.

"I'll miss you tonight, darlin'," he said softly.

She closed her eyes and smelled whiskey on his breath. She
longed to taste it. Unnerved by her reaction, she looked down
and touched the splinters in her palm. Two crimson droplets
marred the rose. Teardrops. Her voice was husky. "You never
told me, Macaulay. What are your plans now? Where are you
going when you leave here?"

"I've run with my last gang. I'm gonna settle down and get
a nice, quiet job. I've heard rumors that one's waiting for me
in Washington."

"Whatever you do, you'll do it well."

"Would you come with me to Washington?"

His offer shocked her. It was so unexpected. "I—"

"We could go for a while," he said, cutting off her answer.
"We could even take a trip to New York. I'll buy you the finest
dress this side of the Atlantic."

Her heart stopped in her chest. She gave a silent prayer of
thanks they were in shadows so he couldn't see the horror on
her face. "I—I can't—go there with you. I've—I've got to be
other places."

"Where?" he asked, his tone daring her not to answer him.

"I've got to resume my life."

"But *where*," he demanded, his patience coming to an end.

She gazed up at his face, so close, so angry. Seconds ticked
by; time, all she had left, fell through her fingers like grains of
sand.

"We'll talk about it in the morning." She grasped the doorknob of the captain's room, then the finality of their parting struck deep within her heart.

She would never see him again. Never watch his lean, hard features soften in moonlight. Never hear his harsh command, or whispered need. There were no more possibilities.

Unable to hold back, she took his face in her hands and pulled him down to her, kissing him as if she could never bear to let him go. She kissed with a longing not fated to be satisfied, and that made it all the more bittersweet, all the more imperative that her lips drink fully of his, that her mind remember each tiny detail: the way his chest hardened against hers as he wrapped her in his arms, the way his breath came quick and shallow when she opened her mouth and let him in. She must seize the moment now, so that in the lonely nights ahead she would have some comfort.

He groaned, and she felt his arm go around her bottom. His excitement was all too apparent. If she'd let him, she thought, he'd take her right where they stood, skirts and rough planking be damned. But if they consummated their relationship, then she would never leave tomorrow. And if she didn't leave on that stage at dawn, she was doomed.

With near violence she ended the kiss, stepping away while her lips trembled with a muffled sob. He whispered her name like a man in agony, but she shook her head, unable to look at him and show him her tears. She left him and closed the door, wiping each moist cheek with the back of her hand. A moment of silence passed, broken only by his curse. The last thing she heard was his boot heels on the rough floorboards, walking away.

Damn him! She never cried and now it seemed she couldn't stop. She longed to wallow in her grief, but she couldn't afford the luxury. She had a million things to think about, a million things to fill her mind. But she could only think about the sound of those boot heels, echoing over and over again in her heart.

Chapter Eleven

It was almost dawn when Christal heard the door slam in the room next to her. For hours she'd been sitting on the edge of her bed waiting for the first rosy hint of sunrise. Her room was still in total darkness; she didn't dare light a lantern and arouse suspicion.

A loud curse, then the sounds of a body stumbling into a chair emanated from the plank walls. Against her better judgment, she rose from the bed and put her ear to the wall. She was sure it was Cain. There was another bump, then another curse, and she knew it was. Especially when he started drunkenly singing "The Bonnie Blue Flag."

"Hurrah! Hurrah! for Southern Rights, hurrah!" First one boot, then the other clunked to the floor. There was a pause in the singing, and she bet he was swilling from a bottle. Her lips curved in a cynical smile when he burped.

"Hurrah! for the Bonnie Blue Flag that bears a Single Star!" The sound of a bunch of coins being flung onto a bureau rattled through the wall. Then the voice became morose. Inexplicably, he changed songs. He sang in a rude drunken voice, *"In Amsterdam I met a maid, mark well what I do say!"*

A body fell onto a bed that was not six inches from her hand. *"In Amsterdam I met a maid, and she was mistress of her trade. I'll go no more a-rovin' with you, fair maid!"* He banged on the wall with his fist. If she didn't know he was drunk and irrational, she'd think he was trying to wake her up to anger her with the words of his song. *"A-rovin'! A-rovin'! Since rovin's been my ru-i-in."* The body rolled over. *"I'll go . . . no more . . . a-rovin' . . . with you . . . fair . . . maid. . . ."* She could hear deep, even breathing. He'd fallen into a drunken sleep.

Nonplussed, she sat back on her bed, but her mind kept wandering to the coins. She was as destitute as she had ever been. Sometime that day she would arrive in Noble with only the dress on her back, and one much too large for her at that. Everyone would think she was a whore. It would be hard to disprove. But if she had a few coins, she could take a room overnight in South Pass, purchase a needle and thread, and reconstruct the ballgown into something more modest. Then at least she'd have a chance at a decent job dealing faro, or pouring drinks, or selling dances.

Outside, the sky was lightening to a lead gray. There wasn't much time.

She silently opened her door. The fort's gate was closed, the sentries posted. The coach hadn't arrived yet. Sliding along the shadows, she walked to the door next to hers. She put her ear to the keyhole. The breathing was steady and loud. Cain was dead asleep.

She opened the door. It made a sorry-sounding creak and she stopped in her tracks. But Cain didn't move. Feeling braver, she walked into the tiny room. He was sprawled across a canvas army cot clad in only his black pants and suspenders. His chest, sprinkled liberally with dark hair, rose and fell with his heavy breathing. One arm was flung across his eyes, his mouth was slightly parted. He reeked of whiskey. Next to him was a small table, coins scattered across it and on the floor.

Tiptoeing to the table, she was blessed as the sun finally broke the horizon and thin gray light filtered in through the tiny window. She knew she should be about her business, but she was unable not to take just one last look at him.

Time suspended for a moment as she stood over him. Cain made a disgraceful sight. His hair was tousled, almost black against the white canvas of the cot. He'd been clean-shaven the night before, but now there was the dark shadow of a beard across his jaw. She didn't know why he'd decided to go out and get drunk. Perhaps for part of the reason she was running away. They were drawn to each other. But it never seemed right. It never would be right.

It hurt her to think about it, but she couldn't erase the picture in her mind that one day his wife would look down upon him just as she was now. She'd be up early, perhaps to make his coffee, and she'd find him sprawled as he was now. She would tenderly touch his brow and smile a secret smile as she thought of the fury of the night before. And then, when she was ready to depart for the kitchen, Cain's hand would reach out and pull her back to bed . . .

Cain suddenly let out a loud, drunken snore, startling Christal back into reality.

Quietly she began groping for each penny scattered on the floor—a pittance compared to the seven gold pieces she'd have to leave behind with him. All told, there was at best a couple of dollars. He'd probably spent most of his money on the bottle that, now empty, lay on the floor beside the cot.

She found his old bandanna on a peg with his coat and tied up the coins in it. She stuffed them down her dress between her corseted breasts. With any luck—of which she had none lately—the money would be safe there.

He groaned and her heart quickened. She took one step for the door but was so nervous, her toe hit the upended whiskey bottle. It rolled across the raw floorboards, making a clatter when it thunked against the wall.

Still as a mannequin, she watched him, stricken by the terrible thought that he'd awakened. Staring down at him, she was relieved that he didn't move, but his breathing had become quieter. Suddenly he groaned and rolled over, revealing much of his backside from the loosened lacings that fitted the waist of his pants. The snoring resumed once more.

Grimly, she wiped the sheen of unshed tears from her eyes. There was no more time. Reporters were headed toward Camp Brown even now. She looked down at him one last time. On impulse, she lowered her head and gave him a feather-light kiss on his cheek. Like his wife, she tenderly caressed his brow.

She crept from his room, heartbroken.

■ ■ ■

She placed her hand upon my toe,
Mark well what I do say!
She placed her hand upon my toe,
I said, "Young Miss, you're rather low!"
I'll go no more a-rovin' with you, fair maid.

Cain groaned and tossed on the cot. It was a dream and the reason he knew this was because his head didn't pound as it surely was going to when he woke up. He wasn't one to drink the way he had last night, but the lack of a hangover didn't make her any less real to him.

It didn't take the edge off the fear.

He sat up naked on the cot, still dreaming. She stood in the doorway in her weeds, dressed in black from hem to head, the jet-colored veil swirling around her face. An angel in thunder clouds.

He stared at her, unable to look away. The fear was like a cold ball in his gut. He wanted to protect her. She needed protection. But he didn't know how.

"Who are you?" he rasped, the need to know burning within him like the whiskey he'd drunk.

She walked toward him, her black-draped body sinfully cinched and curved, her clothes accentuating what they most sought to hide, forbidden to him, yet wanton. He held his breath.

At the cot, she paused, and he hesitantly reached out for the veil. Death. He hated it. He'd eaten it like beans and hardtack during the war. Mercilessly he ripped it from her face. Her beauty hit him like a fist in the groin. It was those eyes. As blue as the prairie sky, as haunting as a Paiute ghost chant.

"Who are you?" he whispered, unable to close his eyes to

the sorrow fleeting across her features. She was afraid, she was running from something that frightened her. She was alone.

But he was the one who was helpless. What could he do for her? Nothing—another facet to the fear. He wasn't even sure he knew her real name. He wasn't even sure she was a widow. There was a toughness about her that unsettled him. She'd seen more of the world than she wanted to.

She kissed him.

Her lips took his like a flower, petals opened wide, beckoning. Her softness had the opposite effect on him. He wanted to control it, but he couldn't. She made him do, and think, and feel, even when he didn't want to.

Another facet of the fear.

Her mouth moved lower. To his neck. Her tongue licked his scar. Her teeth pulled and sucked on his skin. She liked what she was doing to him, she liked the power. Women always did. But she was different. The sadness never left her eyes.

"Who are you?" he choked out as she kissed his flat, small nipple. Her mouth trailed down his chest to his navel. She didn't answer. He wrapped his hands in her hair. Gold silk. He wanted to see her face. Her expression. Anything but that small, pink, wet tongue that heated his skin.

"Tell me who you are. Let me help you. I'm the law . . . I'm the law . . ."

She moved lower.

"Christ, who are you?" he demanded between gnashed teeth. Groaning, he fell back against the cot.

She couldn't answer.

"Tell me . . ." he whispered, his words becoming uneven, his sight losing focus. Excitement pumped through him as acute as the fear he felt for her. She was in trouble. He knew it. But he could help her. He was no poor Southern boy looking for a handout. He was the law now. Things were finally under his control and he could help her. If she would just trust him. Trust him.

"Who are you?" he whispered, forcing an answer with every quick breath he took. "Who are you?" he demanded, caressing and stroking her hair. Until words became too difficult.

Cain's eyes shot open. He was sweating, though the room was so cold there was a transparent layer of ice in the washbowl. Disoriented, he looked around, not sure of his surroundings. Then he looked down at his pants. *Christ.*

He stumbled to his feet, his limbs leaden, his head pounding like the entire Maine 34th was thundering over it. With a shaking hand, he slicked back his hair.

He had to see her.

He grabbed for his bandanna to clean himself, but the bandanna was gone from the peg. His money was gone too. The coins he vaguely remembered throwing on the table had been picked up. The only evidence they'd been there at all was one forgotten copper penny wedged between the cracks in the floorboards.

Gritting his teeth, he broke the ice in the bowl and washed himself. He didn't know why he rushed. He knew what he'd find. That terrible feeling he'd had in the last years of the war came back to him. The Cause was hopeless. Some things just couldn't be saved, no matter how a man tried.

Dressed at last, he slammed into the room next to his. She wasn't there. He could look in the mess hall, but it was no use. In his gut, he knew she was gone. Escaped like a criminal on the run.

"Who are you?" he whispered to the empty room, wishing there was something of her left behind that he could touch, smell. He remembered something and dug inside the pocket of his vest. Seven gold pieces flashed in his palm. He couldn't understand it. In her hurry to flee, she'd taken pennies when she could have had a fortune.

His cold gray eyes sparked with anger. As if he was making a silent vow, he clutched the coins in his fist. He would understand why she fled someday.

And he would see to it that *she* personally was the one to explain.

Chapter Twelve

I gave this Miss a parting kiss,
Mark well what I do say!
I gave this Miss a parting kiss,
When I got on board, my money I missed.
I'll go no more a-rovin' with you, fair maid.

November 1875

"Obsession has many symptoms. He has all of them I fear." Rollins shifted in the oxblood leather chair, uneasy in the presence of the gentleman standing across the desk. The man looked pensively out the window. A snowstorm had hit the city. Carriages had replaced their wheels with runners, sleighs now outnumbered hacks on the avenue. Willard's City Hotel was unusually quiet in the inclement weather. The hotel's windows, which had for years stared dispassionately at the churnings of power, corruption, and—rarely—heroism, were now sheeted in falling white. In the blizzard the building looked like a squat, vacant-eyed ghost.

"I thought Cain was going to quit all that hard riding."

Rollins's answer was a chuckle.

The man caught the joke. "A woman, then, is it? God save us all. Is that what made him turn down the offer?"

"If Cain survives this one, he'll be more than ready to work for you, sir. Give him a year and he'll be scratching at the door of the Treasury to get in."

"Why is he deciding this now? I thought when he came here to Washington he was going to be ours."

Rollins shook his head. "He was going to forget about her, sir, but that's how it goes. Trying to forget an obsession only makes it grow bigger."

"We need Cain here. I've been impressed with him ever since I faced him at Shiloh. His work for the marshals has been unparalleled. He's the right man for the job."

"The Secret Service will still be here in a year. And when Cain comes back, I assure you, Mr. President, he'll be able to give it his full attention." Rollins gave a wry smile. "Unlike now."

Grant finally turned from the window. Rollins remembered him as impressive. The last time he'd seen him was in the Wilderness. Grant rode among the troops, his blue lieutenant general's uniform as soiled as the rest of them, but even with the lieutenant general's gold braid ripped and dulled by mud, there had been no one more dignified, no one possessing more valor and honor than Grant. Except maybe Lee.

Now Grant was much heavier. And he looked weary. Corruption, Rollins assumed, made a tiring bedfellow.

"So where's that Reb off to? I think I have a right to know if I've got to wait a year for him. That's a long time." Grant raised one eyebrow. "I needn't remind you—this *is* my second term."

Rollins released an exasperated sigh. Cain was behaving like a madman. Ever since that woman had disappeared from Camp Brown last August, Cain just couldn't get her off his mind. Sure, he'd vowed to. When she had trotted off, Rollins swore he'd never seen Cain so angry, so quiet. Rollins and some of the other men had offered to go after her, but Cain wouldn't budge. There was betrayal on his face when he'd said there wasn't a woman alive worth chasing all across hell and damnation.

But there was something else on his face too. And the emotion had grown every day since the girl had left him. Rollins wasn't sure he could explain to the President what Cain was about; he wasn't sure he understood it himself. All he knew was that Cain couldn't stand it anymore. The girl had a pull on him that he was finally giving in to. Cain was leaving for

Wyoming Territory in the morning. Spurred on by the fixation of his own imagination.

"So tell me about her. Tell me about this woman who has captured Macaulay Cain."

"She's in trouble. I know that for sure." Rollins cast his eyes downward. "I keep telling Cain she might be more trouble than she's worth. You should have seen her face when she found out Cain was no outlaw but a marshal. I thought she might faint right there in the middle of the prairie. The girl was more terrified of him then, than she was of the entire damned Kineson gang."

"You think she's hiding out west, running from Confederate crimes?"

"Couldn't be. Too young. Besides, she's a Northern girl. I'd stake my life on it. Something about the way she walks. Very upper class. She made me think of the women you see in Newport or Saratoga Springs. Rich. When you see her, you think rich."

"Was she rich?"

"I doubt anymore. Would she have been on that coach if she was? Besides she was wearing widow's weeds. Her husband probably left her poor."

"So maybe the family's running after her."

"We thought of that, me and Cain. But if she was some merry widow who'd up and killed her husband, why would she be mourning him in weeds? And even more important, why wouldn't she have some money?"

"The woman's an enigma, I'll hand you that. Where is she now?"

"Cain tracked her down to some dead, nowhere mining town in Wyoming. I told him to just go there and get the woman out of his system, but he's convinced that approach won't work. He's terrified of frightening her off. She could run so far he'd never find her. She's working in a saloon there in Noble—that's the name of the town—and I think she's selling more than . . . well, I hate to be indelicate . . ." ·

Grant came right out with it. "You mean he thinks she's a hooker?"

Rollins coughed. He would never get used to that word. "Yeah, I think so. And it's tearing him up. So what he did was, he wrote to the mayor of Noble and offered himself up as sheriff—hiding most of his overqualifications, of course. Well, they haven't had a sheriff in Noble for five years and they were pretty damn glad to get one. The council just voted him in. He's at the Willard packing right now."

"All this for a woman . . . it's hard to believe . . ."

"She was a fine-looking woman, sir. Beautiful, actually." Rollins stroked his mustache, a habit when he was pensive.

"Beauty is fleeting. Doesn't Cain know that?"

"Yes, he knows it. If there ever was a man who's never lacked the company of beautiful women, Cain is it. But this one's different, sir. It almost worries me. He might be headed for trouble."

"How so?"

"You know how Cain is. He took a beating in the war. It really ravaged him. All his values and morals were ripped in two when he had to put down his arms and give up the fight. He lost his family, his whole hometown." Rollins stared at Grant. "I won't kid you, sir. When he offered his services to the marshals, I didn't think he'd make it. He was a strong man, and a good fighter, I give you that, but I wasn't sure he could work with the same men he'd fought against at Shiloh and Gettysburg.

"And didn't he surprise us all. He's as loyal to the law as a man can be. I've figured it out."

The President seemed to hang on every word. "And what is it?"

Worry crept into Rollins's gaze. "It's very simple. When he lost his country, the law became his country. When he lost his family, the law became his family. He holds the law as dear as any man I've seen, and I fear he is unyielding in its interpretation. You see, he cannot bear the ambiguity the Cause thrust upon him ever again."

Grant stared at him, understanding dawning. "This girl's past seems fraught with ambiguity."

"Indeed." Rollins looked forlornly out the window at the

Pennsylvania Avenue winterscape. "Cain may find himself in the war once more. This girl's air of mystery makes her most attractive, but she's dangerous to him. Her past could be the thing to break him."

The President stood straight and commanding. "I could tell him not to go. I'm the only man he might listen to besides Lee . . . and Lee, God rest his soul, is gone from us now."

"You could ask him. But he won't stay." Rollins released a deep, resigned sigh. "Cain's going to go after her, and having seen the girl, I can almost understand his obsession. She had an aura of tragedy that surrounded her almost like the widow's veil she wore. If she were an actress, she would have made a great Ophelia."

Grant slowly turned back to the blinding white landscape, his once handsome features haggard, puffy, and sad. "I suppose Shakespeare knew human nature better than you or me: '. . . for the power of beauty will sooner transform honesty from what it is to a bawd than the force of honesty can translate beauty into his likeness. . . .'" Grant grew silent, then whispered, "'The fair Ophelia! . . . be all my sins remembered.'"

January 1876

If the town records were correct, there had been only three noble deeds ever performed in Noble. Wyoming Territory wasn't known for its altruism; still, towns like Noble sprang up, born with good intentions, then grew into something else altogether.

The first noble deed ever done in Noble was the cry of "Silver!" when old man Grizzard found a vein ten years back. Share the Wealth was his motto, and the wealth was shared until it ran out, which, unfortunately, happened just about the time it began.

The second noble deed was eight years ago when the townfolk began putting up the Lutheran church in the west side of town, where the foothills of the mountains broke through the stretch of plains to the east. It was a pretty church, with colored glass for the windows ordered all the way from St. Louis.

Back then, they even had high hopes for getting a preacher.

The third and final deed had occurred last spring.

The town had fallen on hard times with old man Grizzard dead and gone, and his silver, if you will, even more deceased. Noble was becoming more famous for its ignoble deeds than its noble ones. Folks earned their living the best way they knew how, and with a final shrug of resignation, this was written in a scratchy, illiterate hand in the town records:

April 13, 1875–Niver found no preacher. Rectory sign removed, this day, from Mrs. Delaney's cathouse.

But if some looked upon Noble, shook their heads in despair, and rode on, one didn't—a young woman who stood at the frost-covered window of F. A. Welty's Saloon, stretching her back as if she'd been sitting for a long time. This one didn't despise Noble, it was clear on her face. For now, the town was just fine with her, snow and all, and she peered down the strip of frozen mud that made a road this time of year, a strange, worried expression in her eyes, as if she were afraid some cowboy were going to lope into Noble and take the whole damn thing away.

It was kind of hard to say just what kind of lady this woman was. Her heavy black wool shawl covered a dress of blue calico, the seams worn white in the bodice from many a washing, the skirt patched with newer pieces of the same cheap cotton. That was all respectable enough, but the dress was obviously a dance hall dress, short, to reveal the petticoats, scarlet stockings, and button-top boots she wore beneath it. In Denver, maybe even in Cheyenne, her dress might have been satin. But this was Noble, and there just wasn't enough business to afford something like satin dresses.

"Christal! Has he arrived? See any life out there, girl?" The voice was booming and anxious. Faulty—F. A. Welty, the owner himself—straightened up from behind the bar lugging a jug of whiskey from the cellar.

The girl gave another long look down the street. Noble consisted of only about eight or ten wooden false-fronted buildings, not including Mrs. Delaney's, which was down the lane a piece, where they'd hoped to put the church and the town graveyard. The road through town was empty. Not a movement rippled the frozen tableau of prairie all the way to the horizon.

As if in prayer, she raised her eyes toward the sky. It was slate gray, heavy with snow, an endless howl of ice just ready to fall. A couple of flurries worked their way down and a hopeful smile tipped her lips. Maybe he wouldn't come. She hugged the black shawl closer to her, and returned to the bar to help Faulty, the bells on her ankles giving a flirty little jingle as she walked.

"Why did they go and get a sheriff anyway, Faulty?" a girl in a saffron-colored calico dress asked from the piano. She was petite with smooth, coffee-colored skin—a mulatto, some thought, but no one was quite sure; she had a mysterious ethnic beauty that could have been Cheyenne as well as Japanese.

"Ivy Rose, now don't you go complainin'," scolded another female from the corner. Dixiana always wore purple because she fancied she had violet eyes. In the gloaming her rouge would sometimes look purple, but never, unfortunately, her eyes. "Ah'm lookin' forward to this here sheriff. As long as he's under fifty and can pay his bills, Ah'll take him." Dixiana flashed dark blue eyes in disgust at the empty saloon. Last night's smoky haze still hung from the ceiling with the volatile smell of whiskey, but there were no men anywhere—except for Faulty—and wouldn't be until probably seven o'clock when the cowhands came in from the range. None if the weather grew bad. Christal braced herself for another bout of her whining. Dixiana didn't disappoint. "We had customers day and night in Laramie! Why, Ah could buy me stockin's for every day of the week! And there was a washwoman to come and do mah laundry—!"

"We've heard," Ivy Rose interrupted, drowning her out with the tune of "Lorena," which she tapped on the ivory piano keys.

Faulty looked at Christal, obviously used to turning a deaf ear to Ivy and Dixiana. The proprietor was a dapper man with a gray mustache and muttonchops, and tufted, brushed-up eyebrows that left him with a constant surprised expression. "You been quiet today, girl. You thinkin' about that sheriff too?"

A new sheriff. Christal could hardly believe her ill fortune. If the truth were known, she wanted that new sheriff gone more than the lot of them put together. "I—I guess I don't quite understand why they thought we needed one here." She polished the bar glasses to try to show she didn't care as much as she really did. The road had been long and difficult since she'd left Camp Brown and Macaulay Cain. It had taken all her resources just to get to Noble, but it had been worth it. The hiding had been good here. While it lasted.

She couldn't bury her anxiety any longer. "I just can't figure out why they thought they had to go and elect some stranger we don't even know. If they suddenly decided they wanted a sheriff, why couldn't they have picked Jan Peterson to do it? He owns the general store, and he's mayor. Why not sheriff too? That would have been so much better a choice."

"It sure is a surprise, darlin'." Faulty put his arm around her and squeezed. "But don't you worry none. That sheriff ain't gonna change this saloon. Not if I can help it. Besides, *I* can't get you girls to do what I want, so how's he gonna?"

Dixiana laughed. Christal shot her a quelling look, but before she could get out a reprimand, Faulty turned Christal away and thrust some more glasses into her hands.

She polished, every now and then giving Faulty a rebellious glance. She didn't mean to cause him trouble. He'd been the best thing ever to happen to her. His face was not pretty—red from drink and pocked from smallpox when he'd lived in New Orleans—but in many ways it was a kind face, and she'd been glad to see it when she'd arrived in town last September. Bedraggled and skinny, she was hired anyway, and so far he'd kept his part of the deal: She was only to sell dances. But all along he made it clear that he preferred she make him money upstairs and not on the dance floor.

She concentrated on a smudge and her thoughts grew dark, dwelling in places she had futilely trained them never to go. Despite Faulty's blessed appearance back in September, she knew he was not really the best thing ever to happen to her. The best thing that had ever happened to her was back in Camp Brown. He was tall, with cold gray eyes, and a smile that could blind a cougar at fifty paces. Even now she wondered if she'd fallen in love with Macaulay. The situation was hopeless. Unless she vindicated herself in New York she could never seek him out, and by the time she managed to do that, surely he would be married, perhaps with a family.

She sighed, something she was prone to do ever since she'd come to Noble. It was no use dreaming of things she could never have. But the temptation was great. Did she love Macaulay? She knew without a doubt that if she ever set eyes on him again, she would know for sure.

And then he would bedevil her the rest of her miserable days. Perhaps she was fortunate things had worked out this way.

She replaced the glass and got another, turning to Faulty. Quietly she said, "You may not be able to change me, Faulty, but I still make good money for you, just the same. You can't complain."

Faulty grumbled, appearing quite put-upon. "You're our princess. Maybe I've just got to accept that. And maybe that's good. You holdin' out keeps your price high." His words said one thing, but he never quite got that hopeful look out of his eyes. It was clear she perplexed the hell out of him. Slyly, he added, "But, darlin', don't you think there's gonna come a day when—?"

"He's here!" Ivy left the piano stool and ran to the window. Faulty, Dixiana, then Christal, last and slower, more reluctant than the rest, followed.

Through ice-covered panes they saw a man on a sleek, dark horse making his way along the frozen rutted road. The flurries were stronger now and they blurred the details. Still, Christal could see he wore a caped Federal-issue greatcoat and the buff-colored gauntlets of the cavalry. She'd seen too many men dressed like that back at Camp Brown.

"What does he look like? Oh, please say he's not too ugly— I don't even care if he don't bathe—just . . . oh, please make him a little handsome . . . just a little . . ." Dixiana pressed her cheek against the cold glass pane to get a better look. Her palms were clasped as if in prayer.

"He's a tall one, all right," Faulty said, nervously wiping his hands on his apron.

"You can't see his face for the hat," Ivy whispered in a voice tinged with fear.

Christal strained her eyes to get a better look, but the snow worked against her. The man went by, his face obscured by falling snowflakes and a large black Stetson. He stopped down the road and hitched his mount in front of Jan Peterson's general store. He disappeared into the building, but even after he was gone it took her an eternity to catch her breath. For some reason, he scared the hell out of her.

"Well . . . I guess I'd better get on over there and welcome the new sheriff to town. No sense in him gettin' the idea we're not friendly-like." Grimly, Faulty removed his apron and went to get his sheepskin overcoat.

"If he's even a little handsome, Faulty, you tell him it's on the house. Otherwise, it's half price, all right, Faulty?" Dixiana said in a little-girl's voice.

"Ohhhh, I hope he don't close us down," Faulty groaned as he slammed out the door and into the bitter cold.

The girls watched him trudge over the frozen waves of mud in the road, some as high as his knees. When he disappeared into the mercantile, the saloon was like a graveyard.

"Do you think he'll give Faulty a hard time?" Dixiana whispered.

Ivy sighed. She looked in the other direction. "I don't know but right now they're coming in early. Must be the weather."

Six men stopped their horses in front of the saloon. As if on cue, Ivy walked to the bar to get out the glasses, Dixiana primped on the piano stool, and Christal got out the dealer's box.

The whiskey was poured; Christal dealt the men their game of faro. Three of the men were up from Nevada and full of gold coins they were just aching to lose. She dealt game after game until her fingers grew stiff from throwing out cards. One of the men, a blond, handsome man with a beard, gave her a sideways look every now and then, obviously hoping to catch her gaze and be dealt something a little more than faro. But, well practiced in the art of avoidance, she just kept her eyes on the cards, with each flip counting the seconds until Faulty would be back with some news of the sheriff.

The clock ticked, the cold made her fingers stiff, the wind kicked up and blasted against the outside walls. The men quit their faro and bellied up to the bar for more whiskey. If Joe were around to play the piano, Christal was sure the blond man would have bought a dance. And something more . . . if it were for sale.

It was dark before Faulty came back to the saloon. He burst through the door, covered in snow from head to foot. His beard had icicled just during the short walk from the general store to the saloon.

Dixiana, Ivy, and Christal all stopped what they were doing to look at him. Was he angry? Afraid? As if to prepare themselves, they wanted to see it on his face before he told them.

"Christal, I got to talk to you, girl," he said, shaking his beard dry over the potbelly stove.

Christal felt her stomach drop to her knees. "Wh-what about?" She couldn't imagine what the sheriff could have said that'd make Faulty single her out. Suddenly her heart hammered in her chest. Had she been discovered? Was the sheriff somehow sent by her uncle?

"C'mon over here, girl. We got to talk." Faulty took her arm and led her up the rough wooden stairs that stood at the back of the saloon. He pulled her into her room and didn't even bother with a lamp. They stood in half-darkness, the only light coming from the hall.

"My God, what is it?" she blurted out.

He put both of his hands out in supplication. "Christal, darlin', you just gotta listen to me. I talked to that there new sheriff and by the look in his eyes, he sure ain't one I want to cross."

"But what did he say?" Her voice was calm, partly because it was choked by fear.

"I—I wanted to get some sort of understandin' from him. I told him that I had the prettiest girls in town and that dances were on the house." Faulty paused, as if he knew she wasn't going to like what he had to say next. "He told me he'd be real happy to do business with me, but he said he was partial to blondes, Christal, *only blondes*."

She felt the easing in her chest. Her heartbeat slowed. The drumming ceased in her ears. "Is that what you're talking about? You gave him a free dance with me?"

Faulty shook his head. "No, girl. That ain't it."

"Then what?"

"We weren't talking about dances. Not at all."

Suddenly she understood. It didn't surprise her that the new sheriff was already putting his hand in the till. After all, what upstanding man would want to be sheriff of Noble? Ominously she said, "You mean you tried to sell me to him?"

He grabbed her arm. "Girl, you got to see the eyes of that man! I had to promise him! He's gonna shut me down if he gets a look at you and you refuse him!"

"There are blondes over at Mrs. Delaney's. Send him there."

"Aw, Christal. You gotta help me! He'll leave us alone if we make him happy. If we don't—anything could happen. I might even lose the saloon!"

Disgusted, she turned away from him. Her room faced the street and through the window, she could see men leaving Jan Peterson's. In the darkness and snow, she didn't know which one was the sheriff. Boys had already put his horse in the livery. "You don't run a whorehouse, Faulty, you run a saloon. If Ivy and Dixiana like making some extra coins, and give you a cut for providing their room and board, well, that still doesn't make this a whorehouse. You've just got to explain to the man that not every girl here is for sale."

"Help me, Christal," he pleaded.

She took a deep breath, her mind whirling with troubles. She still dreamed of that Overland money. For months she had longed to write and have it sent to her, all five hundred dollars. But she'd been too afraid of reporters, and of Cain tracking her down, asking questions she didn't want to answer. So she was back to doing what she had done before, working like a dog because she wanted to keep her honor, and saving what little money she could so that one day, a day far off in a misty, obscure future, she could return to New York, find a way to expose her uncle's crimes, and redeem herself. Sometimes she wondered if she was mad or just dreaming.

Her chin set and she turned to Faulty. "If you made foolish promises, then there's only one thing to do. The snow isn't as heavy as before. If we don't get a blizzard, I'll leave in the morning. Then you can tell him you don't have any blondes that work for you. Not anymore."

"Christal . . . just do it once and then he'll leave us alone and you can stay."

"No." Her answer was quiet yet implacable.

". . . Oh, Christal," Faulty sighed, as if the room were caving in on him.

"I'll finish out the night. Go on downstairs."

"But what if he shows up! He'll see you and then damned Rosalie over at Mrs. Delaney's sure ain't gonna do for him. He'll never forgive me for lettin' you outta his hands."

"What kind of a sheriff is this?" she asked, suddenly angry. "He's here to protect us from gunfighting and bank robbers, not to take his fill in every saloon in town."

"I don't know what kind of sheriff he is, girl, but I'll tell you, one look into those cold eyes of his, and you can be damned sure, ain't nobody in this town gonna ask him."

He left and closed the door. She stayed behind in a dark room. A few flurries, all that was left of the storm, reflected the light from below. She looked out the window. There was a lamp burning in the building next to Peterson's—the liquor depot. Kegs were locked there, in a room that was barred and bolted from intruders. It was a good place for a makeshift jail. The light burned upstairs; probably the new sheriff's living quarters.

A figure stepped in front of the lantern and she could make out the silhouette now that the snow had fallen to a whisper. He hadn't removed his hat. It was the new sheriff. He stood looking out of the window, just as she did. Though she told herself she was standing in darkness and he couldn't see her, she'd swear he was looking right at her.

"Sheriff," she whispered like a curse, weary from running, from hiding.

The tinny sounds of the upright piano came drifting through the floorboards and she knew Joe had arrived. It was time to earn her keep. The blond man would be waiting. He had nowhere else to go in this weather.

She shook her head and wondered when it would all end. Her eyes turned back to the silhouette of the sheriff, his black felt Stetson sharp against the backlight.

Perhaps it already had.

Chapter Thirteen

Faulty's was more crowded than usual that night. The snow had been bad enough to end work early and bring in stragglers traveling on the range, but not so bad as to keep customers holed up at home. Joe, an old miner too crippled and too poor to move on, came in almost every night and played waltzes on the piano.

It was Christal's fifth dance with the blond man. He didn't say very much. He wore a fancy ruffled shirt and a dark green jacket and vest. His eyes were hazel, and not particularly kind, but that wasn't unusual. Not out west.

He flipped another nickel onto the table when the dance ended. She wanted to rest, but he pulled her to him without even asking. The bells tied to her ankles made a coy sound as they moved around the small floor. She didn't like the bells. She only wore them to please Faulty. Whores wore bells. In her mind, they got her into more trouble than they were worth. She could already see the blond man wasn't going to be too happy when she turned down his offer of a paid trip upstairs.

He spun her around, his hands cold and almost painful against her ribs. A frigid pocket of air blasted at her back as another customer entered the saloon. Joe seemed to stumble at the keys for a moment, adding to the difficulty of the waltz, but she hardly noticed; she was too involved with extracting her hair from her customer's stroking fingers. Faulty made all

his girls wear their hair down. It gave them an air of innocence, he said, and men liked that. As she looked up at the
blond man now she could see Faulty was right. The blond
man did like it. He smiled. Though he was young, most of his
bottom teeth were either crooked or gone.

The song stopped, and this time she really wanted to get
away, but the man held her tight, his arm coiled around her
waist like a snake. He bent to kiss her; she discreetly turned
her head.

"Pay first, is it?" he whispered.

"No." She tried to remove his hands from her bodice.

"C'mon. It's time. How many dances do I gotta pay for?"

"As many as you want because that's all that's for sale."

"You teasin'?" He wouldn't let her go.

Her eyes turned as frosty as her voice. "No."

His arm became a vise. For a slim man, he was strong and
wiry. "Then I want my money back."

"You'll have to take that up with the management." She
dug her fingernails into the back of his hand. His hold only
grew more painful. She almost couldn't breathe.

Faulty walked by, his gaze fixed on someone by the door,
his eyes filled with anxiety. Normally he watched his girls like
a hawk. At the first sign of trouble, he was always there. Now
he went past, not even seeing her.

She was about to call to him when he announced to everyone in the saloon, "Drinks are on the house to welcome our
new sheriff!"

At the word *sheriff,* the blond man dropped his cruel hold
around her waist. Christal backed away, thankful for the re-
prieve even if it did mean coming face-to-face with a sheriff.
She turned toward the door where all eyes were glued to the
stranger.

Her heart stopped.

If she were a blind woman, she'd have known that face just
by touch. There was Noble's new sheriff, his tall form
slouched against the wall, still wearing the blue Federal-issue
greatcoat he'd ridden into town with and the black felt Stet-

son, pulled low so that no one—just she alone—could see his cold gaze fixed on her. It was Cain.

Her prayers would have been answered if the earth had cracked open beneath her and swallowed her up whole. But the earth stayed as frozen solid as the prairie beyond town. She just stood there while Joe began playing "Dixie," unwittingly mocking her.

There were only three thoughts in her head at that moment. She would have sworn upon her life that it was the first time the Reb had ever worn blue. Her second thought answered the question that had plagued her since August. Had she fallen in love with Macaulay Cain? Now she knew.

Now she knew.

Someone poured the sheriff a whiskey, and he turned his eyes from her while cowhands slapped him on the back, welcoming him into town.

Her gaze didn't leave him. It would be like turning away from a poised tiger.

In shock, she still couldn't understand how he could be standing near the door, the new sheriff of Noble. She closed her eyes, clinging to the hope that her sight was lying to her, sure that the next time she looked the face beneath that black Stetson would belong to some other man, not *him*. But then she looked again, and her gaze met his from across the room, and there was no denying it. He'd found her. Or the most abominable coincidence ever to happen had just occurred.

Then the last thought finally hit her.

Run, it said.

"C'mon and have a drink with me."

As if waking from a nightmare, Christal blinked several times as she looked up at the blond man. She glanced over at Cain and this time found his gaze not on her but on the man standing next to her. She could see he'd seen the man dance with her. And touch her hair. And want more.

She could also see he didn't like it.

"I've got to go," she mumbled, too distracted even to look at the gent.

He grabbed her. "I still want my money's worth."

"No . . . no . . . the sheriff . . ." She nodded her head toward Macaulay.

The man looked at the sheriff and freed her. Wildly, she looked around for Faulty. He was in the middle of the fray. Men had bellied up to the bar to get their free drink. The sheriff was now talking with Dixiana. And smiling. This was her chance.

Christal slipped from the noisy, raucous crowd and tiptoed up the stairs, damning every jingle of the bells around her ankles. She got to her room and without even thinking, she pulled out a small, worn carpetbag she'd bought in South Pass. She also pulled out her "new" widow's weeds, which she'd also bought in South Pass—with Macaulay's money.

She swallowed the fear rising in her throat. Numbly she stuffed her belongings into the carpetbag, not caring whether things got wrinkled or torn. She was too frightened to be bothered with details. She had stolen his money. Did he remember?

A surge of terror passed through her. Of course he remembered. She could tell just by his gaze that he remembered.

She stuffed the remainder of her things into the carpetbag. Where she would go, what she would do hadn't yet sunk in. At the moment, she couldn't be rational. Because there was a sheriff downstairs who was bound to ask a lot of questions, questions she didn't want to answer. So it was time to leave. She didn't believe in coincidence. The only reason he'd come to Noble was to see her. If he got her alone, he was going to get his answers even if it destroyed her.

She blew out the lamp and clutched the heavy carpetbag in her hands. In back of Ivy's room was a small wash porch that had stairs leading to the rear of the saloon. She would exit there and then she would go . . . ?

Defying the impossibilities, she wrapped her heavy shawl around her and put her hand on the door. She would think about where to go when her feet hit the snow and the saloon was far behind.

Her palm slowly turned the doorknob; her mind whirled with unanswered questions. What had he been doing since

Camp Brown? Why had he come for her now? Had he found out she was wanted? Had he come to send her back to the asylum and her uncle?

She opened the door.

And froze.

He stood there, silhouetted by the lamps in the stairwell. She tried to slam the door closed, but his hand gripped its edge and held it. Her strength was no match for his. He pushed it open and walked into her room.

She backed away in the darkness like a trapped animal. The scene at the saloon in Falling Water was repeating itself, but this time the fear was different. He wasn't an outlaw come to rape her, he was a sheriff she had stupidly fallen in love with, come to drag her back to New York and betray her need for secrecy.

"You are a cool one, girl. I'll give you that," he said in that deep, scratchy voice she had thought she'd never hear again.

She stared at his familiar form, wondering desperately when Wyoming Territory had gotten too small to hide in. "Why are you here? Why did they elect you sheriff?"

He didn't answer. Instead, he struck a phosphorus match and lit the lamp she had just blown out.

In the light, she could see every angry plane of his face. There were times after she'd left Camp Brown that she wished she could see his face just one more time. The yearning had been an ache, bitter and deep, never to be erased. But she'd never imagined she'd see him again. Especially not like this.

She wanted to stammer and weep and run. Instead she stood deathly still and in a calm voice said, "You're a U.S. Marshal. You were promised a job in Washington. I don't understand why you would even consider coming here to play sheriff."

"The last time I saw you, you forgot something." He slammed it onto her bedside table.

She looked down to see what it was. To her surprise she saw one of her seven gold pieces. Another coin was slammed onto the table. Another, and then another, until all seven coins were there.

She fingered the coins, then summoned the courage to look at him. It struck her that she had never seen eyes so devoid of warmth, eyes as frigid as the hellish winter prairie.

A cold fear settled into her heart. He was angry she had stolen from him. And perhaps angrier still she had never said good-bye.

"Why did you come here?" she whispered bravely.

"I told you I wasn't going to run with any more gangs. So why not come here?" He captured her gaze. "You're here."

She swallowed. "But I don't want to be here. No one in his right mind does."

He stared at her, his eyes not missing the smallest detail of her garb. She was dressed like a prostitute, no one could deny it. Confusion ran deep in his eyes, along with a strange kind of betrayal. "Maybe I'm not in my right mind," he whispered.

She had a difficult time keeping the fear from her voice. There was no point in delaying the inevitable any longer. "Did you come here for me, then?"

His gaze locked with hers. "Come here for you? Because you stole my money and left without a fare-thee-well? No, I don't think so. If I were to come all this way for you, I think it'd have to be for something more than that, don't you?"

She could feel the blood drain from her face. He knew about New York. That was what he was implying. She'd come to the end of the line. In a whisper, she said, "What is it you know about me that you've followed me here?"

"What do I know about you?" The betrayal deepened in his eyes, along with the confusion. His lips twisted in disgust. "Not a goddamned thing. How about that? I almost died twice for you back in Falling Water and here I'm not sure I know your real name. When I last saw you, you were the virtuous widow; now I find you here, dancing willingly in a stranger's arms, acting like a common—"

"Don't." She didn't know how she summoned the strength, but somehow she straightened her back and jutted her chin. "You don't know what I am. So don't say it."

Bitter curiosity was deep in every tanned line of his face. "Why are you here, Christal? They told me you were working in a saloon and I couldn't believe it. You aren't doing it for the money—you've got five hundred dollars due you from Terence Scott. And you had an offer from me. You had me. . . ." His voice seemed to catch, but it happened so quickly, she thought it might have been her imagination.

His anger turned quiet. "I would have looked after you, girl. Hell, I asked you to go with me to Washington. Is what you have here better?" He looked around her barren little room in contempt.

She clutched her carpetbag, saying nothing. She was relieved and strangely heartbroken at the same time. He didn't know about her. She still had a chance to escape detection, but only if she could make him go back to Washington.

"Maybe you have me all wrong, Macaulay. Maybe I wanted to come here. Maybe I'm doing just what I want to do. With no man directing me all the time."

"So that's why you ran from five hundred dollars? To keep your independence?" His harsh laugh cut her. "No, girl, you came here 'cause you had to. And I've come here to find out why."

"There is no reason why. I like it here. I'm doing just what I want to do."

He grabbed her arm so tightly it hurt. The anger on his face took her breath away. "Whoring? Is that doing what you want to do? I don't believe it. The woman I knew back in Falling Water was no whore."

"Maybe you didn't know all about that woman back in Falling Water," she gasped, tugging on her arm. She hated confirming what he thought, but that was the only way she could think of to make him lose interest and go home.

"Are you a whore, Christal? Have you come to like it since I last saw you?"

His contempt hurt like a twisting pain in her chest, but she refused to let it stop her. They had no chance. They never did. So why prolong the inevitable? He needed to go back where he came from and she needed to get on with earning enough money to get her uncle. She could never tell him the truth with that tin star pressing in on her; she had no evidence to vindicate herself other than her word. A confession would shatter either his belief in the law or his belief in her. And she'd rather shame herself by confessing to being what she was not than confront the fact that his belief in her—and his feeling for her—was not that strong.

"Why don't you just go back to Washington, Macaulay?" Her voice was a low, desperate whisper. "None of this concerns you. There's nothing in Noble for you, so why don't you just head back east?"

He stared at her for an ungodly amount of time, as if trying to reconcile himself to what he feared she had become. She could see the tug-of-war inside him and she wasn't sure which side won when he reached for the carpetbag and dumped the contents out onto her thin, straw-stuffed mattress.

It was the widow's weeds that captured him. He touched the black gown, reverently running his hands along the bodice and skirt. She stepped away, frightened by his seemingly meaningless obsession, but he grabbed her by the waist and held the black gown to her as if he was trying to remember what she looked like in it.

"Please." She began to pull away, but he wouldn't let her.

"These damned weeds haunt me." He stood so close, she could feel his breath against her cheek. "You looked pretty fine in these weeds, girl. Your hair is like spun gold against the black. Your skin is . . . pink and fragile. When I saw you in these weeds I wanted to protect you. But now you tell me it was all an act. You're not a widow, are you?"

Surrendering the lies for a moment, she slowly shook her head.

He looked deep into her eyes. She could see the gleam of cynicism that was growing in his. In Falling Water, there had been a kind of respectful distance he'd kept from her because he'd thought she was a lady. Now that she'd all but confirmed his worst thoughts, the respectful distance was gone, and in its stead was a kind of familiarity that stripped her of her feelings and uniqueness. He looked at her now as if he'd seen a hundred women like her before. And though she told herself that was just what she wanted, perhaps even needed, it still sliced her to the core.

"Were you swindling someone? Is that why you were dressed like a widow? To fool them?"

She shook her head, suddenly finding it difficult to look into his eyes. "I dress that way when I travel. I'm treated better."

"I see. I guess I might've done the same. Even I have to admit, if I'd have known you were just another whore, I might not have been so chivalrous."

Her cheeks reddened with anger, but she didn't deny it. The sooner he had his fill of contempt for her, the sooner he'd be on his horse heading out of town. "I didn't ask you to cause me all this trouble. If you came here to get your questions about me answered, then they're answered. You believe I'm a whore, go ahead and believe it if that'll get you back on your horse and out of town."

"I didn't come all this distance to just up and leave." His eyebrow lifted as he stared down at her. At first it was damning, condemning her with each flicker of his eyes, but soon his gaze grew taunting. He missed nothing, not the shortness of her gown, nor the bells tied around her scarlet-stockinged ankle. Slowly he moved to her chemisette. Behind the gossamer of cotton, there was just the slightest hint of bosom, more than was proper for a lady. When he met her eyes again, she ached to slap him.

"I won't whore for *you*, Cain, if that's what you're thinking." Her fury turned her cold and aloof. If she could freeze him out of town, she would.

He only gave her a cynical twist to his lips. "I'm glad to hear that, Widow Smith. 'Cause I *don't* intend to pay."

She broke from his hold, her eyes like ice. "You're not getting anything, whether you pay or not."

"Faulty gave me a token for you. He implied the thing was just a little souvenir of the saloon, but I know what he gave it to me for. 'On the house,' he said. He all but told me I could have you."

"He had no right."

He grabbed her again, then fished through a pocket in his silk vest. When he found what he was looking for, he pressed the token into her hand. He growled, "If you really are a whore, darlin', you won't refuse this. So prove to me who you are, one way or the other. Tonight."

She opened her palm. The brass token was pierced with a heart. On one side, it was embossed: *Mrs. Buckner's Parlour House, Fort Laramie*. On the other side, which his thumb now stroked, it read in crude capitals: GOOD FOR ONE SCREW. Faulty had a coffer of them, all useless, from an out-of-business cathouse. Dixi and Ivy didn't honor them, so she sure as hell wouldn't.

"Give this to Dixiana." She threw the token at him, her face alive with indignation and anger. The brass coin clattered to the floor.

He stared at her, his expression just as angry, just as desperate. "So are you or aren't you?"

"What you're suggesting, *Sheriff*, is illegal." She spat out, "I don't think the circuit judge would be pleased to hear about it."

His arm lowered to her waist and he roughly pulled her against him. "And you'd just love to go against the circuit judge, wouldn't you, darlin'? With your penchant for running from the law . . ."

His words struck her like a knuckle across the face. By his expression, she knew he hadn't seen the wanted poster. Most likely he believed her a whore who'd committed some petty thievery, then run from the law only to end up in Noble. But she couldn't allow his speculation to continue. If he hung around, digging into her past, it wouldn't be long before he discovered who she really was.

"So what's it to be, Christal, truth or dare? Are you going to tell me why you left Camp Brown the way you did, or are you going to lie back on that bed and honor this here token?"

She didn't even breathe.

His hand rode up her waist until it rested beneath the swell of one corseted breast.

"If you're a whore, you'll honor that token just to be rid of me," he whispered against her hair.

His hand rode higher.

Her heart beat harder. Inside she felt a war was being waged. He might go away if she relented. But if she relented—

"Stop." She pushed his hand away before he cupped her breast. Stumbling from his arms, she went to the bed, where her possessions lay scattered across the mattress. Without forethought, she began stuffing them inside her carpetbag.

"You aren't a whore, are you?" he asked softly, watching her.

She didn't deny or confirm his words. She just kept packing.

"You're still the woman I knew back in Falling Water," he whispered reverently. "You're still fighting to keep your honor. So why are you here, Christal? Faulty's not beating you into working for him—he's too good-natured. There's no apparent reason on earth for you to be here, doing what you're doing. So why are you here, Christal? Why?"

Tears threatened. She didn't dare answer; she just kept cramming all her worldly belongings into the small, worn carpetbag.

He put a hand on hers and stopped her. Slowly he lifted her hand and turned over the palm. The scar gleamed in the yellow lamplight. He met her gaze. Her eyes glittered with unshed tears. The questions went unspoken.

Laughter from the barroom filtered through the floorboards, shattering the moment. Hastily she pulled her hand away and, like a madwoman, continued packing.

He laughed. "What do you think you're doing? You think you're just going to ride out of town like you did last August?" He nodded to the window, which had three inches of snow clinging to the sills. "You're not going to get out of here till the spring thaw." He stepped over and took her bag. He set it on the bureau, far from her reach. "That's right, it's just going to be you and me. . . . For months, darlin' . . . That oughta be time enough to get you out of anybody's system."

"I can leave whenever I want to."

"You'll leave when I let you leave." His smile never reached those ungodly cold eyes. "I'm the sheriff, remember? Nobody here wants me angry and snooping into their business. If it means they've got to tell me when you left and where you were headed, then so be it."

She stared at him, defiance hot in her eyes, but she could find no way out of his trap. She wasn't going to get far in winter, not in Wyoming. Until the thaw and until his back was turned, there seemed no other choice but to play the game his way.

"You've nothing to gain by staying in Noble. I won't honor that token." She tightened her lips.

"When it's time, I won't need a token."

Angered anew, she held her breath and walked past him to leave the room.

His arm shot out to stop her.

"I've got customers," she said through clenched teeth.

"I told Faulty when he suggested—ever so legally, mind you—that I might enjoy the company of one of his girls, that if I liked one in particular, my girl wasn't to be with any other man but me. That was our little understanding."

Her words crackled with fury. "I sell dances. Nothing else."

"Fine. You won't be sleeping with anyone else anyway. Faulty will keep his eye on you. By now he knows I like you."

"How could he possibly know that?"

He released a dark laugh. "What do you think he thinks we're doin' up here? Talkin'?" He tipped his head back and laughed some more.

She wanted to strike him. In a low, harsh whisper she said, "I don't know why you came here, but I promise you, you will rue the day. If I don't get out of here for months, I swear my only purpose will be to make your life miserable."

He grasped her chin and forced her to look at him. "Go ahead. Make my life miserable. But don't think I can't return the misery. I'm not a stupid man. I noticed it wasn't until I put on a marshal's badge that you decided you couldn't stand me. When I was a damned criminal, you didn't seem to care near as much. There are a lot of ways to be a whore, girl."

Before she could stop herself, she cracked her hand across his cheek. The violence horrified her. It should have brought relief, but it didn't. It was no panacea at all, not for the anger or the agony. Unbidden, tears sprang again to her eyes, perhaps because he'd found her, or perhaps because she still felt the same despair she'd felt when she'd gotten into Mr. Glassie's coach at dawn and left him behind.

He rubbed his cheek, anger glittering in his eyes. "Christal, just you tell me why you left me last August and I'll leave this shithole town right now."

"I'm not going to tell you anything," she whispered, staring at the six-pointed tin star on his chest, desperation nearly choking her.

He nodded, still rubbing his cheek. "Then I'll be here until you do."

"You'll be here till hell freezes over, then."

He looked to the window. It was snowing again; a pattern of fractured ice clung to the panes. A strange desire flickered in the depths of his chilly gaze when he looked at her. "Well, darlin', if this ain't hell freezin' over, then I don't know what it is."

Cain departed her room without another word. Christal could barely pull herself together to return to the customers in the saloon. Though she didn't want to admit that he'd gotten to her, it took almost fifteen minutes for her to stop trembling.

Morosely, she picked up her seven gold coins and the black gown that had fallen to the floor. Her heart sank every time she pictured Macaulay. She wanted to trust him. It meant something that he had come for her. Perhaps it was only to ease the unresolved questions in his mind. Still, it meant something.

But she couldn't trust him.

She stepped to the window, clutching the black gown to her bosom, her thoughts dwelling darkly on the past. She could tell Macaulay the truth, place her very soul into his hands and beg for mercy. But she knew she'd never do that. And she knew the reasons why.

Against her will her mind played out an imaginary conversation.

"Christal, trust me, girl, and I'll help you." Cain stared at her, silently demanding she answer.

"My uncle killed them. He gave me the blame, but he killed them," she sobbed.

"I believe you. I'll find a way to absolve you. You know I will, girl. If you're tellin' me the truth, I'll move heaven and earth to see you're free."

"Macaulay . . ."

"Yes, darlin'? Is there something more?"

"I didn't go to jail for his crimes."

"What did they do with you, then?"

"I've been in an asylum. An asylum for the insane."

Christal shut out the picture of Cain's reaction. She closed her eyes and hugged the weeds, but that didn't ward it off. The picture of his face haunted her. She could bear almost any reaction but not the sudden doubt she would find in his eyes. And the revulsion that would follow. The revulsion that he'd almost trusted someone whom society had labeled utterly untrustworthy. Someone locked away from society not just because of her wrongdoing, but because of her inability to understand her wrongdoing. Someone who had never learned the boundaries between right and wrong. Between truth and lies.

Her mouth formed a grim line. She could plead she had had no memory of the crime and therefore no memory to defend herself. But memory was ephemeral. With a will of its own. Unimportant details can be recalled with diamond sharpness, but the name and face of a man who destroyed lives could remain in a fog for years. Memory had damned her at one point in her life, freed her in another. Macaulay would always wonder: Did she escape the asylum because her memory came back . . . or had her memory never left her? Was it memory that was elusive, or just her ability to understand what she had truly done?

She laid the dress on the bed and smoothed the wrinkles in the jet-colored silk. She would never tell him. Whether or not he was the law, whether or not she loved him, she couldn't tell him. He could chase her all over the world, but he was never going to get his answers.

Because she was never going to watch him turn away.

She spent the rest of the evening gaily dancing with whomever had the nickel to pay for it, her only distraction the stormy brooding expression on the new sheriff's face as he stood by the bar and watched her.

By the time Faulty closed down the saloon, her feet hurt, her ribs were sore from too much manhandling, and she was exhausted. Cain went to his rooms, silent and oddly sober for all his shots of whiskey. She watched him go, as silent and sober as he. Then she went straight up to bed without even helping Ivy with the dirty glasses.

But rest eluded her. Three times during the night Christal rose from her bed and walked to the window, clutching her shawl to keep away the bitterly cold drafts. Three times she saw Cain's silhouette in his room above the new jail, sitting by the lantern, drinking. Taking long, pensive pulls on his whiskey glass. Like something was driving him slowly mad.

Finally, when the night melted into dawn, she was able to relinquish some of the shock and horror at his finding her and accept her situation. Leaving Noble in the dead of winter was useless. The weather made it impossible, dangerous, even with the best of conveyance. And she had none. For now, she would have to stay. But she didn't have to talk. Until he knew the truth, he would never hear it from her.

The sun rose and sleep embraced her in long, dark shadows. But she dreamed of being the new sheriff's bride, dressed in white satin and tulle. Behind them Baldwin Didier hung from a scaffold, his stately form limp in the breeze. She married the man she loved. And never again did she wear black.

* * *

"Can't you come down on the price just a bit?" Christal asked Jan while admiring a bolt of sky-blue wool. It was the next day, and she had defied her fear of the new sheriff and gone to the mercantile. Now she pulled her shawl closer and licked her chapped, cold lips, all the while coveting the beautiful fabric. A gown fashioned out of the wool would be becoming. Better than that, though, it would be *warm*.

Jan wrinkled his forehead and looked down at the ledger in front of him to see what he'd paid for the cloth. During the pause, Christal glanced around the store, nervous at the thought of running into the sheriff. Peterson's was crowded with cowhands out of work because of the snow and lonely old miners with no where else to go but the stools near the black potbelly stove. Nowhere did she see Macaulay. She gave a small prayer of thanks.

"I just don't know, Christal," Jan said, shaking his blond-gray head. His lined Scandinavian features clouded with doubt. "It cost me almost ten dollars for the whole bolt. If you want half of it for five dollars, I just can't see how—"

"If you must have six, then what if I pay you three dollars now and three in a few weeks?" She looked at him hopefully.

"Don't you mean a few months? The last time I gave one of you girls credit, I never did get all the money."

She ran her hand along the soft wool, a melancholy wistfulness on her face. She couldn't spend her gold pieces on luxuries. That was her savings. She would need those seven gold coins in the future to find Didier. To run from Macaulay. But the bolt of wool would cost too many dances.

Too many. Always too many.

There was always an easier way. Dixiana and Ivy Rose had many nice dresses.

Slowly, she drew back her hand. "All right. I'll bring you the money as soon as I have it." Her words possessed a hope that she knew was a lie. There would be no warm new gown for her this winter.

"I'm sorry, Christal. I'll try to save it for you."

"Thank you." She sighed, put on her gloves, and turned

around. Her gaze collided with that of the new sheriff of Noble.

"Good day to you, ma'am," he said quietly, tipping his black felt Stetson. The ice in his eyes left her breathless.

"Good day, Sheriff." She made haste to walk away but he followed. Bitterly, she wondered why she even tried. His threats last night had made it clear she was never going to depart Noble without him knowing all about her. Until she could shake his interest, he was going to be like a ghost at her side. There, even when he wasn't.

"I need you to come to the jail with me, ma'am. There's something I want you to see."

A poster with Christabel Van Alen's face on it. The thought ran over her like a full-steam locomotive. Forgetting herself for a moment, she stared up at him as if he'd just pulled his six-shooter.

"Darlin', you don't look too well."

She calmed herself and tried to think rationally. He wasn't going to show her the wanted poster. He didn't know anything about it. Because if he did, he'd have ridden into town and arrested her last night. Besides, even he admitted that the only reason he'd even taken the sheriffing job was to find out about her. He knew nothing; she meant to keep it that way.

"I really can't go with you. Faulty needs me to—"

"It's just next door." He took her by the elbow.

She looked around the general store, but there was no one who could intervene. Macaulay was the sheriff. They'd bow to his desires every time. She wasn't the only one in Noble with something to hide.

"What is this about?" she asked woodenly as he led her to the door.

"You'll see" was all he offered.

They walked next door in silence. The bitter cold weather didn't help her uneasiness. The wind whipped down the center of town, skimming across the frozen ruts in the road, whistling through loosened clapboards, rattling unpainted false fronts. From the east to the west, there was no one in sight on the road. The frozen silence in the middle of town was eerie.

"In here," he said, and waved his hand through the door. She stepped into the jail. She already knew it well. Many a time Faulty had had her pick up the saloon's liquor there. It was now converted to a jail, and she was surprised how little had changed. The walls were still crumbling whitewashed brick, steel bars still divided the room where the kegs used to be stored. She stared nervously into the new jail cell. A canvas army cot and a bale of hay were the only things it contained. A rush of anxiety passed through her. She wouldn't let him— or anyone—put her in there. After the asylum, she wouldn't be locked up again.

"Sit down."

A table and chairs had been brought from the store. Reluctantly, she allowed him to seat her. On the opposite wall, a store-bought calender caught her attention. The picture of a rosy-cheeked blonde dressed in ermine and blue satin stared at her from the top of the calender. The date "1876" was printed in gold embossed letters across the girl's plumed chapeau.

1876. It was going on four years since she'd run away. The thought depressed her. She had so much to accomplish, and yet all she did day after day was struggle for survival. Dismally she wondered if she wasn't being a fool in thinking that she'd get revenge on Didier. Without money she was powerless, and her time and energy were overwhelmed in fighting for subsistence. Suddenly she was as close to giving up as she'd ever come. That blue wool at the mercantile beckoned her. It was so warm . . . so soft . . .

But then her eyes met Macaulay's and she knew the fight was still in her. She wouldn't let him see her shame herself. He already had a low opinion about her character. He thought her a whore. She wasn't about to prove it to him.

To prove her nonchalance, she loosened her shawl, letting it drop around her arms. The room was well heated, a delightful change from the drafty saloon. During the winter, the liquor depot was always the warmest place in town. Jan kept the stove burning night and day to keep the whiskey bottles from shattering.

Macaulay walked to a small desk where some papers were stacked. He retrieved something. Without a word, he slid it in front of her. As if he simply wanted to see her reaction.

It was a daguerreotype of her and her sister. Alana had been perhaps fifteen; Christal, twelve. Christal had taken the picture with her when she'd fled New York. It was the only memento she had of her family. The daguerreotype was in the trunk that Kineson and his gang had pilfered after they'd removed it from the roof of the Overland stagecoach.

"You've returned my money. And now this. So where are the rest of my things?" she asked in a controlled voice that hid how unsettled she was.

"I can wire Rollins and have them sent here. There's not much."

"What Kineson stole from the coach was everything I have in the world."

"You could have had all your belongings and five hundred dollars if you'd only waited an extra day at Camp Brown. Now you'll have your things in due time." His hand rested on her shoulder. For strength, or intimidation, she didn't know. "Tell me about the picture."

She stared down at the daguerreotype. "Why did you bring it with you and not the rest of my belongings?"

"I'm not a courier. The picture's what interested me."

His hand lowered to her own. He slowly removed her right glove. One instinct told her to pull her hand away, the other told her to stay and not look guilty. Without even glancing at the scar on her palm, he grasped her hand in his. The warm shock of his skin against hers sent a tingle down her spine.

"Tell me about this," he said, his voice a coaxing deep rumble in her ear. "The girl next to you must be your sister. She looks like you. What's her name?"

"A—" She closed her mouth, unable to speak. She couldn't tell him. Revealing even a little detail like Alana's name would be stupid.

"Who is Sarony?"

She stared down at the picture. The name *Sarony* flowed across the lower right-hand corner. Napoleon Sarony was the premiere New York daguerreotyper. Just going to have the picture taken had been a momentous occasion; there weren't many of her social class who had stood for a daguerreotype. Knickerbockers had had their portraits done by great painters like Stuart and Copley. Photography was something most members of their class dismissed as fleeting and inconsequential. Nonetheless their mother insisted the two Van Alen girls be photographed.

Sarony's studio was at the top of a four-story building with bays of La Farge stained glass and skylights flooding it with sunshine. It was an entrancing place, but what had captured her thirteen-year-old heart was Sarony's collection of exotica. Leopard skins dotted the floors, potted palms swayed over doorways, and in one corner, Persian couches upholstered in red and purple flanked a strange fox-red monkey called an orangutan that was trained to cool seated guests with an ostrich fan.

She smiled to herself at the memory. Their mother had thought Sarony was crazy, but she was still insistent upon the daguerreotype.

Feeling a tightness in her throat, Christal forced herself to look at the picture. Both girls were dressed in serious umber-colored satin gowns, an indicator of their exalted family lines. Her sister, Alana, though barely sixteen, appeared calm and serene, even regal. But not Christal. In her eyes there was such a twinkle of happy mischief that she couldn't help but wonder if it was still there, ready to come alive again should her fortunes change.

She tried to hide how much the daguerreotype meant to her, but that was difficult, especially when she could relive that day completely in her mind. When Mr. Sarony had all his apparatus in front of them, she could remember, a twinge of anxiety had passed through her. It was as if she were worried that the magic of taking their images might also take something they could never get back. But just as she was ready to ruin the picture, Alana had reached over and taken her hand in her lap, somehow possessing a big sister's instinct that she needed reassurance.

Even now Christal could see the "ghost" image of Alana's arm as she pulled her sister's hand into hers. And now Christal was grateful to Sarony, so grateful that if she ever met the man again she would throw her arms around him and kiss him on both cheeks. He hadn't taken anything from them at all; he'd given them a moment that would remain forever, undimmed by cruel mortal memory.

Her gaze rose from the daguerreotype to Macaulay's hand wrapped around her own. Sisters held hands. Friends and families. She missed it. It was comforting and genuine: one hand perfectly meshed into another, as hers was in Macaulay's.

She stared at the physical bond of their hands. It looked so right. Her hand, fragile and pale, covered with another, one strong, corded, the back sprinkled with dark hair. These were the clasped hands of lovers.

Lovers.

"Thank you for bringing this to me. I must be going now." She stood and shakily pulled on her glove.

"I know she's your sister. Why won't you even tell me her name?" His face was taut with repressed anger and frustration.

"Her name is unimportant."

He slammed the door closed just as she opened it. She shivered in the gust of frigid air.

"If it's unimportant, you would tell me. So I can only conclude it's of supreme importance." He looked down at her and she could see every silver fleck in his eyes. "What—is—her—name?" He paused. "Is she dead?"

She was silent.

He looked as if he could beat her. "What must I do to get you to talk? Jail you on some offense and starve you with bread and water?"

"I'm never going to tell you anything. Don't put us through this torture."

"You were rich, weren't you?" He ripped the daguerreotype from her hand and pointed to the gowns. "These dresses are satin. Only rich girls wear satin."

She was silent. He looked down at her, his handsome features ravaged by frustration. She almost toyed with the idea of telling him all kinds of lies so that his curiosity might be satisfied and he might go away. *Might.*

Contempt curled his lip. "I can't help but get the feeling if I was some lonely renegade you'd be purring every night to tell me all about yourself." He shoved her aside. "You're just like every other fallen woman I've known. You don't like a man unless he's criminal and treats you bad."

Her eyes sparked with fury. There was nothing more to say. "I've got to go. I've got people waiting for me."

"I'll bet," he spat out in disgust.

"I meant Faulty!"

"Fine! You go back to that saloon. It's where you belong anyway."

"I'm not a whore. You know it," she said, blinking back angry tears.

"Then prove it." His voice was low and desperate. "Tell me something about yourself and *prove* it. 'Cause if you don't, I'm going to put Faulty's, and every other establishment like it, out of business for prostitution."

She ached to slap him. "Don't bother with Faulty. I won't be working for Faulty anymore. He's shown me too much kindness for me to let you ruin his livelihood. I'm leaving tomorrow when the wagons arrive from Fort Washakie. Go ahead and follow. We'll just go from town to town destroying each other."

They stood, braced for combat, glaring at each other.

Finally he shook his head in resignation. "If you run, I can outlast you. But I believe you'd rather die than tell me anything, and I don't hanker to bury you out there on the prairie."

"Then why don't you go back to Washington? Nobody here wants a sheriff anyway, except Jan."

"I looked forward to this job. It's peaceful and there's no

runnin'. I'm here to stay for a while. I'm not ready for Washington."

"You're a one-man club, then. Nobody wants to be here but you." She glared at him. "May I leave, Sheriff?"

"Yeah, sure. Go on. But don't think this is over. You'll talk someday."

"I won't. I've already proved it."

"No, girl, not at all. You were close to talkin' when we were in Falling Water. You trusted me then; you'll trust me again."

She glanced at the tin star pinned to his chest. "I doubt it."

He shrugged and took out a coin from his pocket. He began flipping it. She could see it was the whore's token Faulty had given him. Newly enraged, she opened the door.

"Christal."

She paused.

"Save a dance for me, okay?" he said, a nasty gleam in his eye.

She slammed the door in her wake.

"Now he don't want you to be too friendly with the customers, Christal. He told me that last night. I guess he wants you all to hisself." Faulty wiped his hands on his white apron and poured another gent a whiskey. The evening's business was light. The new sheriff had been in town less than a week and already things were slowing down.

"You're making him think I'm a—" Christal eyed Dixiana and Ivy. She didn't like saying the word around them. *Whore* had no meaning other than the physical one. It had no heart to break, or dreams to tarnish. She finished, saying with ire, "You just shouldn't have implied that I did that kind of thing, Faulty. You've given him expectations. He's going to be mad when I don't honor the token."

Faulty clasped his hands in surprise. "Didn't he already use the token?"

"No," she answered, disapproval on her face.

"Oh, my saloon!" he gasped, looking heavenward. He grabbed her. "Is that why he comes here every night? He's waiting to use the damned token? Christal, you gotta get him to use it! He's ruining business. Folks just don't want to come here with him sitting there every night, glaring at every man who touches you. You got to be nice, girl. You gotta save my saloon!"

"I'm not going to be that nice, Faulty." She glared at him. "Besides, I'll be gone as soon as I can get a wagon to take me out of here."

"And where would you go? Come on, Christal, the other girls do it."

"But I don't! You should never have given him that token!"

"How was I to explain you're different? He wouldn't have believed me."

She hid her wounded feelings. Perhaps she no longer had a right to her pride. But she was a Van Alen, a Knickerbocker from one of the most illustrious families of New York. Pride was something she would never relinquish.

Handing him her tray, she ordered three whiskeys. Faulty poured them, his forehead lined with worry. Suddenly she couldn't be angry with him over the token. He'd been a godsend when she'd had nobody to help her. Saloon owners weren't known for their charity. Once in Laramie, one had tried to beat her into going upstairs with a customer. She had left that night and never looked back. But running was a difficult life. Coach fares were costly; it cost her a ten-dollar gold piece every time she went on one. In many ways, Noble offered respite. Faulty wasn't too ambitious. He couldn't afford to be with his cheap customers.

She took the three whiskeys and gave two of them to a pair of cowboys who were playing a hand of poker. She walked with the last one over to a table in the corner and set it down, pointedly not looking at the customer. Joe played gaily in the background and a drunken cowhand pressed a coin into her hand and dragged her to the dance floor.

In the corner, Macaulay took the whiskey, kicked a chair in front of him and put up his feet. He eyed the men in the bar, but none of them held his attention like the one who had Christal in his arms.

But he made no protest; started no fight. Instead, he did exactly what he'd done the night before. And the night before that.

He drank and he stared.

Chapter Fourteen

SOMEBODY'S DARLING

Into a ward of the whitewashed halls,
*   Where the dead and dying lay,*
Wounded by bayonets, shells and balls,
*   Somebody's darling was borne one day.*
Somebody's darling, so young and so brave,
*   Wearing yet on his pale, sweet face,*
Soon to be hid by the dust of the grave,
*   The lingering light of his boyhood's grace.*

Matted and damp are the curls of gold
*   Kissing the snow of his fair young brow;*
Pale are the lips of delicate mold,
*   Somebody's darling is dying now.*
Back from his beautiful blue-veined brow,
*   Brush all the wandering waves of gold,*
Cross his hands on his bosom now—
*   Somebody's darling is stiff and cold.*

Kiss him once for somebody's sake,
*   Murmur a prayer soft and low;*
One bright curl from his fair mates take—
*   They were somebody's pride, you know.*
Somebody's hand has rested there:
*   Was it mother's, soft and white?*
Or had the lips of a sister fair
*   Been baptized in their waves of light?*

God knows best! He has somebody's love,
  Somebody's heart enshrined him there,
Somebody wafted his name above,
  Night and morn, on the winds of prayer.
Somebody wept when he marched away,
  Looking so handsome, brave and grand!
Somebody's kiss on his forehead lay,
  Somebody clung to his parting hand.

Somebody's watching and waiting for him,
  Yearning to hold him again to her heart;
And there he lies with his blue eyes dim,
  And his smiling, childlike lips apart.
Tenderly bury the fair young dead,
  Pausing to drop on his grave a tear;
Carve on the wooden slab at his head,
  "Somebody's darling slumbers here."

PENNED BY MARIE REVENEL LA COSTE,
WHO TENDED CONFEDERATE SOLDIERS IN THE WARDS OF
SAVANNAH AND WHO LOST HER BETROTHED TO THE CAUSE

Macaulay closed his eyes, grasping for sleep that seemed always beyond his reach. The whiskey was keeping him awake, he rationalized, but he knew what it really was. It was the girl. She was in his blood, a heat pounding through his veins. She ran through him, capturing him. He couldn't let her go.

He placed his hands at the back of his head and stared at the dark ceiling. The night was silent. Across the street the lights at the saloon had long since gone out.

Was it lust that had driven him here? She was beautiful. God, she was beautiful. Classic blond perfection. But he'd had women that were just as beautiful, and far less trouble.

As if seeking the answers, he let his mind wander. He found himself in the past. Growing up at the farm in Georgia, they'd had a dog, an ugly, scarred mongrel that looked as if God had put it together from leftover parts of other more sleek and beautiful breeds. The thing had appeared in their lives one day dragging itself onto the property, starved and chewed up from a fight. His mother had taken pity on the creature and nursed it back to health. For twelve long years the cur was his mother's shadow, trotting happily at her side as she swung her willow marketing basket on her arm, or sleeping by the stove as his mother cooked when its joints became stiff with age. He himself must have been nine years of age when he looked up from his morning porridge and watched his mother feed the hideous thing potatoes and bacon grease. "Why do you care for that creature, Mama? He's hard on the eye," he'd said smartly, always all too sure of himself. But then his mother had stepped up to him and caressed his smooth, boyish face, resting her hand beneath his jaw. "'Caulay," she'd said, tenderness for him in her eyes, "remember this well: There's no face more beautiful than one well loved."

The memory burned into him. So did he love Christal? Was love what had brought him here? He didn't think so. He cared for the girl, and he sure as hell lusted after her. But love—not yet. He didn't know enough about her yet. All he knew was . . .

Memory came back again, this time of war. Unwanted pictures assaulted him. Armies of skeleton boys on crutches—all of them with faces like his brother—defeated yet not dead, with war in their eyes. Because as obscene as they looked, what they had witnessed was even more obscene.

Their ghostly memory trudged by, hundreds of them moving in an imaginary line through his room, all young boys betrayed by the notion that manhood and war walked hand in hand. He whispered in the dark some lines penned by a Confederate patriot,

> *And in our dream we wove the thread*
> *Of principles for which had bled,*
> *And suffered long our own immortal dead,*
> *In the land where we were dreaming.*

He said the last line twice, feeling his gut twist in longing and remembrance. And then he knew the lure that had brought him here. The girl had something he'd rarely seen in a woman. And because he'd looked once, now he found he couldn't look away.

She had war in her eyes too.

Chapter Fifteen

"Ivy, you're just talkin' that way because Jericho's in town tonight. My, my, don't you get uppity when he comes sniffin' around Tuesday evenings? Well, Ah don't care. Give me some fine-looking young cowboys and you can have all your Jerichos and then some." Dixiana fell onto the bed, clad only in her knickers, chemise, and corset. She studied her fingernails, each filed to a sharp point.

"You just leave me and Jericho alone." Ivy sat on a wooden bench staring at her face in a tarnished vermeil hand mirror. Christal stood behind her, weaving her thick, dark hair into a chignon.

Though at times Christal was very conscious of all their differences in background and upbringing, for the most part it didn't seem to matter. Each of them had taken a very different road to Noble, but they were all lone women in a cruel, violent land. By all rights, it should have been difficult for her to understand them. Yet somehow it was not.

"Why are you two always fighting?" she asked, pulling Ivy's hair tight at her temples. "Dixiana, sometimes I think you're jealous of Jericho and Ivy."

"*Jealous?*" Dixiana raised herself from the bed, revealing a breathless amount of bosom. "How could Ah be jealous? Why Jericho's a—" She abruptly stopped, then started laughing. "Oh, go on! What are you tryin' to do? Fool me?"

Christal pinned some more of Ivy's curls. "You might not

want Jericho. But you sure are jealous of his attention. Come on, Dixi, admit it. You want a man to court you, just as much as that old Miss Blum wants Jan Peterson to come calling on her with a posy of violets."

Christal watched Dixiana roll onto her back and stare at the unvarnished boards of the ceiling. Their bedrooms weren't as luxurious as the saloon downstairs, which had canvas tacked to the walls in an attempt to look like plaster. Upstairs was plain and raw. Strangely appropriate.

"Ah'm not like that old maid Sarah Blum." Dixi sighed. Her pretty, heart-shaped face held a faraway, melancholy expression. "Besides, Ah had a man court me once. Ah met him in Laramie." Her voice lowered as if she were saying a prayer. "Oh, he was somethin' fine. With thighs as hard as iron and a face like an angel." She stretched her hand out to the ceiling, as if reaching for him.

"What happened, Dixi?"

Dixiana shrugged. If she were any other kind of woman, she might have had tears in her eyes. "He said he was going to marry me. Ah followed him up to Noble 'cause he thought there was still minin' goin' on here, and he wanted to strike it rich. But the minin' didn't work out and the day before we got to the preacher, he just up and left. Oh—Ah don't mind that he didn't want to marry me." Dixiana's face turned rock hard. "Ah know Ah'm not the type to have a passel of brats hangin' on to mah apron. But why didn't he take me with him back to Laramie? Why did he just leave me here, with no-where to go and no money? Ah even understand his leaving. There are so many girls in Laramie . . . and—their faces are so smooth." Dixiana touched her face as if she could feel every damning line on it. She'd told them once that she was twenty-eight, but everyone figured she was hiding ten years.

"Dixi," Ivy whispered, turning around on the bench. "I'm sorry I told you you couldn't borrow my snood. Jericho's seen enough of it. You go on and wear it. It'll look prettier with your lavender gown than with my yellow one."

"Maybe he'll come back, Dixi. Maybe it was all a mistake,"

Christal added, wanting to help, maybe just because Dixi hid the pain so well.

"He's not coming back. He's a good-for-nothin' cowboy. They never return." Dixiana gave a little hollow laugh. "The only thing good about 'em besides their looks is that there're so blessed many of 'em! And them baby cowboys, they can be so sweet—when they're fawnin' on you, they're so in love, why—you're just their mama, their sister, and their sweetheart all rolled into one!"

Ivy smiled and threw her the snood. Even Christal smiled. There were more and more young men coming west every day. Dixi liked to set up court with the pretty ones in her special corner they'd all dubbed "the bullpen." Even a hardworking saloon girl couldn't run through them all. Maybe for Dixiana, that would be enough.

"Come on. Ah got to git dressed." Dixi rose from the bed.

"But wait! We haven't heard about the sheriff." Ivy looked at Christal. Christal dropped to the edge of the bed in an attempt to pretend she didn't know what Ivy was talking about.

"That's ra-aht!" Dixi stared at Christal too.

Christal fiddled with her fingers.

"Come on, you Yank! Tell us! If you don't snare that man, Ah'm gonna snare him for ya!" Dixiana pinched her.

Christal shot up from the bed and retrieved Ivy's wire bustle from a chair. She handed it to Ivy, saying, "There's nothing to talk about. You can have him, Dixi. He's nothing but trouble. Faulty's getting mad, and I've got to find a way to get rid of him."

"But why don't you want him? He's a handsome one. Right takes mah breath away to look at him. Though he's a little cold around the eyes—kinda makes you pause—never did like the mean ones. . . ." Dixi looked at Ivy, who was tying her bustle. Though still useful, Ivy's arm was slightly crooked and had been ever since she'd arrived in Noble a year ago. All she ever said was a man broke it who accused her of stealing from him. She told them all she never thieved in her life. Faulty had been nervous hiring her, but time had proven Ivy out. They never had any trouble. No customers ever complained of lost money at Faulty's saloon. Still, Ivy's arm was a sorry reminder of how badly men treated women of their profession.

Christal studied both Ivy and Dixiana. They were just like all the other prostitutes she'd known: children. They wanted to be nice and they desperately wanted to be treated nicely in return. But most were lambs to the slaughter, victims of their customers and their own passive natures. Christal looked around Ivy's room at the magazine cutouts of cupids and pink floral hearts tacked to the rough wood-plank wall. It was typical. These women had ideas of love that were amazing in their innocence and sweetness. Love was a fairy tale to them, something they dreamed of and wished for, a knight in shining armor to come and erase all the bad things men did to them day after day. But it was a fairy tale nonetheless. Christal knew that better than anyone. Her knight in shining armor had arrived and instead of saving her, he'd switched hats and turned into the villain. A villain with a tin star.

Christal returned her gaze to Ivy. The girl was absentmindedly rubbing her arm as if somehow it ached. They were all a little afraid of the new sheriff. Sheriffs got anything they wanted—a power easily abused. But as much as she herself had to fear of Macaulay, she knew enough of his character to know he'd never physically hurt them, and she felt compelled to ease the other girls' fears. "Ivy Rose, Dixi—you don't have to be afraid of him," she blurted out. "I can tell you, I know he'd never hurt you."

Ivy frowned. She stared at her. "How do you know that?"

Christal didn't want to answer, but she didn't want them to be unnecessarily fearful either. They had enough fear in their lives.

With more emotion than she wanted to reveal, she said, "Because I knew him before." The look on her face must have told them she didn't want any questions. They both stared at her in shock, then suddenly became absorbed in donning their clothes.

After a moment, as if to ease the tension, Dixi taunted, "So you think Sheriff Cain's the type to be standin' at the door with a bunch of posies after all, do ya?"

Christal could have laughed. Macaulay Cain was definitely *not* the kind of man to go sheepishly calling on a woman with a bunch of limp violets grasped in his sweaty palm.

Dixi continued. "Like Ah said before, he's a fine-lookin' man, even if he ain't pretty like my babies that come ridin' in here off the range. If you don't want him, Christal, you say the word. Ah think Ah could do pretty well in the saddle with a big buck like him. . . ."

It was on the tip of Christal's tongue to deny she had any hold over Cain, but a strange feeling came over her. It was a hot, sick feeling almost like jealousy, and it kept her silent. Fool that she was. All logic told her that if Dixiana could get his attention off her, she would be stupid not to let the woman try. But somehow she couldn't cough up the permission. Not when she pictured Macaulay kissing Dixi on the mouth, just as he had kissed her.

But then she turned inexplicably angry. She needed him off her back and she couldn't afford to be weak and jealous. Like ripping a bandage from a festering wound, she said quickly, "Just take him, Dixi. I don't want anything to do with him. I wish he'd go back where he came from. He's hurting business with his sitting there in that corner night after night, just staring with those cold gray eyes at—at—everybody—"

"At you, Christal," Ivy interjected. "He stares just at you."

"Ah think you must like him a bit," Dixi said, her face almost gleeful. "You cain't have that much passionate hatred for a man and not care at all. So what went on between you two before Noble? Ah'm dyin' to know."

Christal stared at both of them, shocked. She was about to deny everything when the piano started up downstairs. Joe was already playing for customers and neither Ivy nor Dixiana was dressed.

The women scrambled for their gowns and petticoats. Much to Christal's relief, there was no more talk of the sheriff.

With Faulty, however, she was not so fortunate. The evening was young and she was in the back making dinner for those who had the pennies to pay for it. Faulty slammed into the back of the saloon, a paleness to his ruddy features.

"You got to get rid of him tonight. He's killing business," he whispered to her. Slowly his eyes turned to the door. Through it she could see Cain step into the saloon. He took off his hat and settled into the corner where he sat every night.

She swallowed, finding the words difficult to say. "Dixi says she likes him. Why not let her get him off your back? He won't go arresting anybody if he's partaking of the fun."

Faulty turned his gaze to the piano where Dixi sat with Joc. Even Christal could see the way Dixiana was eyeing the sheriff. Confused, Faulty asked, "You think he'll take her? Seems he's got his eye on you."

"He's not ever going to have me."

Faulty opened his mouth as if to plead with her once more, but sensing it was useless, he sighed and went to go get Dixi.

Christal turned from the door, pointedly refusing to watch. She didn't know how she would handle it if during the evening she saw Macaulay take Dixi by the hand and walk upstairs.

A soft knock interrupted her misery. She went to the back door and found Jericho there, hat in hand, fresh from his weekly supply trip to Jan Peterson's. He was a tall man, young and strong. No woman would consider him handsome, but he had a warm, quick gaze and a polite manner. Christal could understand why Ivy was in love with him.

She put her finger to her lips. She tiptoed to the kitchen door, being careful not to look at either Cain or Dixi. She closed the door, then let Jericho into the kitchen.

"Would you like some beans? Have you had supper?" she whispered.

Jericho shook his head. "No, ma'am."

"You want me to fetch Ivy and then maybe you two could have supper together? I'll make sure Faulty doesn't come back here. I think I can give you an hour."

"That's mighty nice of you, Miss Christal."

Christal smiled. She nodded to a chair, then left to fetch Ivy Rose.

Ivy's whole face lit up when she told her Jericho had arrived. She eyed Faulty, making sure his attention was elsewhere, then she left with Christal for the kitchen.

Christal served them dinner and watched for Faulty, the whole time thinking what a strange world they lived in. Unlike Faulty, or Dixi and Ivy, or most of the saloon's customers, she had grown up wealthy, well aware of the classes considered "beneath" her. But her experience out west taught her that even a low man could find another below him to crush. The country had fought an entire war so black men could be free. But they still couldn't walk into a saloon in a crummy little town like Noble and order a drink and talk with a pretty girl. Instead, they had to knock on the back door and hide in the kitchen. When the weather was warm, Jericho had to settle for just sitting on the back porch for twenty minutes while Ivy took a break from customers, and when it was cold he didn't even have that. The only way Jericho could see Ivy these days was behind Faulty's back.

"You want a whiskey?" Christal asked the muscular black man.

Jericho nodded. He laid the necessary coins down on the table.

"I'll get it." Ivy stood from the table and squeezed his hand. Hers looked almost white in his; he was very dark.

"No." Christal stopped her. "I'll get it. If Faulty sees you walking back here with a whiskey, he'll know what's going on."

"Thanks." Ivy smiled, then looked at her man. Jericho was a homesteader, freed from Missouri. He lived in a shack east of town and had come to Wyoming with only a mule to plant wheatgrass. He'd been fairly successful. The soil hadn't lasted enough seasons to make him rich, but when the ground petered out, he'd saved enough money to buy some cattle. Many said that was going to be the future of the territory, but the future hadn't arrived yet. Jericho was still living in his log shack, unable to purchase the lumber for a real home, and though all the girls knew he hated what Ivy did to earn her room and board, he couldn't bring himself to take her from the warmth and comfort of the saloon until he had the proper place for her.

But even now, Christal could see Ivy didn't care about waiting. The girl would go tonight if Jericho would only let her. No man had ever been so nice to her as Jericho was. He talked to her and asked about her feelings. He made her laugh. He told funny stories about roughing it out on the homestead, sometimes not seeing the sky for days when the shack was buried beneath ten-foot drifts of snow, and watching the contents of his chamberpot freeze before he was even finished with it. Christal couldn't understand the logic behind barring Jericho from the saloon. Being a black man, he would never be allowed upstairs, yet as mean as some of the cowpokes could get, especially when they were drunk, the cowpokes were white and therefore the only men "good" enough to use Dixi's or Ivy's bedroom.

But they talked that this might be the spring when they would finally be free. Jericho hoped to make good money on his cattle, that was, if the cold and the wolves didn't take too many down in the meantime. If he could make a good sale, he'd have enough money to marry Ivy proper. Christal kept her fingers crossed for both of them. If Ivy could marry, then someone would escape. And every time Christal thought of the man drinking whiskey in the corner of the saloon, in his black Stetson, she was no longer sure it would be her.

"I'll be right back with that whiskey," she said, untying her apron. She wished she could get it without entering the bar. For some reason she had a terrible thought that she was going to walk into the saloon and Dixi was going to be swinging her leg, sitting in the sheriff's lap.

She closed the door behind her, doing her best not to look in the corner. Business was picking up and Faulty was busy pouring at the bar. She ordered a whiskey, still not looking for Dixiana, still not looking in the corner.

"Another one for that damned sheriff?" he cursed, sliding a glass to a cowhand.

She didn't answer, glad he'd been so busy he hadn't seen where she'd come from.

He poured two fingers in a glass and slid it to her. She took it, dismayed that he was watching her, waiting for her to give it to Cain.

She turned. With a strange, unspeakable relief, she saw Dixiana dancing with a cowhand—very far away from the brooding man in the corner.

"Well, go on. Give it to him. All I need is for him to decide we ain't serving fast enough." Faulty angrily clanked the bottles on the bar.

Christal walked to Macaulay. She could see him staring at her, his eyes glittering beneath the black brim of his hat.

"Business is good tonight," he said before she put the whiskey down.

"It should be," she commented coolly. "I heard you shut down Mrs. Delaney's."

"It isn't legal to run a cathouse. It's only a matter of time before this one goes too. The minute I see one of you girls accepting money—"

"The girls have got to make a living. What else are they going to do?"

"They can run a saloon or a penny opera. I told them when they're ready I'll even go in with them and they can give me part ownership."

"So you're cleaning up the town. Just what everyone wants." She didn't bother to hide the disdain on her face. She felt bad for Mrs. Delaney's girls. Some of them were real nice. She hoped the opera house worked.

"This place is next." He fingered a coin lying in front of him on the table; his eyes glittered with shadowed emotion.

She looked down. It wasn't a coin he was fingering, it was the whore's token Faulty had given him. Faulty had told him it was just a souvenir, and most men looked at them that way. Whore's tokens were a joke. They were notoriously never honored. Faulty had only given the thing to Cain in a clumsy attempt to try to read the new sheriff's attitude. Her lips twisted in a derisive smile. Faulty probably thought he was being cagey by giving Cain the token, but Cain wasn't stupid. He knew what was going on at the saloon. And soon he would get whatever cold, hard proof he wanted and shut them down.

She watched his thumb stroke back and forth along the surface of the token. Her gaze met his and she could barely repress the fury that suddenly seized her. When he had acted the outlaw, he'd treated her with some deference. Now that he was sheriff, he seemed to be just waiting for a turn, as if she were a piece of venison on a spit.

"Why do you keep that thing when you know I'll never honor it?" she whispered to him, her eyes glittering with anger.

He covered the token with his palm and slid it into his pocket. "I haven't decided what I'm going to do with you yet."

She stared at him, her face as emotionless as alabaster. He'd made her care for him in Falling Water. Back then, she knew they had had something good between them. But now he'd returned and all she wanted to do was hate him. And the curse was that she couldn't.

Faulty was behind a crowd of men at the bar, his attention consumed by demands for whiskey. Without saying another word to Macaulay, she turned and took her chance to sneak back to the kitchen.

But his hand shot out and stopped her. "Where you going with my whiskey, girl?"

"Who said this was your whiskey? Get it from the bar like everyone else." She tossed her head in the direction of the dance floor. "Or have Dixiana get it for you. She'll honor that token and with my blessing."

"If I thought that'd get a rise out of you, I'd take her tonight." He pulled her near to him, even though he was still seated. He whispered, "But I'll tell you true, Christal, I'd rather take you."

She met his gaze. If she were the girl she had once been, she would have dropped the tray and whiskey, and slapped his face, then walked away with all the dignity of a dowager duchess.

But she wasn't that girl any longer. She'd slept with this man, clung to him for protection, and now feared him as she feared few others. If things were different, and he asked her to be his wife and have his children, she believed she might be the happiest woman alive. But things were all messed up, and her feelings for him were all stirred into the mess. And now all she wanted was him to be gone. She had too much to lose to allow herself to be intimate with him.

"Excuse me," she said coolly, refusing to look at him. With slow, wooden steps, she returned to the kitchen.

She silently gave Jericho his drink. Ivy and he were whispering and laughing so much, they hardly noticed her pensive mood. She was about to return to the saloon, when Faulty burst through the kitchen door.

"Where the hell are you girls? Dixiana's out there trying to please the whole of 'em while you two are back here just sittin' —and—" Faulty's gaze found Jericho. Jericho stood, his mouth tense, his eyes defiant. Ivy nearly fainted. Christal just looked on in horror.

"What the hell are you doin'?" Faulty gasped. In a knee-jerk reaction, he skittered to the kitchen door to close it to the view of his customers. Then he nearly knocked Ivy over in his fury. "Are you stupid, girl? I can't have no darkies in here! That'll bust up business surer than a tornado!"

"They were only spending a moment together," Christal interrupted. "Jericho comes to town on Tuesdays to get his supplies. He just stopped by to say hello. I invited him in. It was my doing, not Ivy's."

"No—Christal—don't—" Ivy stood, her entire body trembling in fear. "You know he was here for me."

"Yes, but I invited him in."

Faulty turned to her. "Christal, if you do this again, I'll beat you, girl. You understand that? I'll beat you senseless."

Christal didn't answer. She couldn't. She didn't understand any of this.

"Answer me, girl. You know what I'm talkin' about or do I

have to take a hand to you now to show you the error of your ways?"

She still didn't speak. She wasn't going to say she understood why Jericho couldn't come in the bar and visit with Ivy when she didn't and never would.

Faulty raised his hand to her, but a voice at the kitchen door nearly made him leap to the ceiling.

"I wouldn't do that."

Macaulay stood at the kitchen door. In the fray, he had entered without anyone even seeing him. Now he lounged against the closed door, arms crossed casually over his chest, as if he were surveying a bunch of bickering children.

Faulty pointed to Jericho. "Sheriff, arrest this man for trespassing. There ain't no darkies allowed in this saloon."

"No!" Ivy cried out, running to Jericho's side.

"That's ridiculous!" Christal gasped. She turned to Macaulay. "I invited the man in. He isn't trespassing. You can't arrest him."

Faulty chimed in, "This here is my saloon and I'm not gonna let people think I'm servin' Negroes. Arrest him, Sheriff."

Macaulay looked around the room, his gaze coolly surveying the situation.

By now several customers were peeking through the kitchen door. Faulty had no choice but to make a show of protesting Jericho's presence and demand that the sheriff take the trespasser away. He began to rant, "Ain't no darkies allowed in this saloon. Take him away! Ain't no darkies allowed in this here saloon, no sir!"

Finally Cain turned to Faulty. "This man isn't in your saloon. He's in your kitchen. There's no law that says this man can't be in your kitchen if invited."

"Well, he weren't invited! No sirree!"

Christal stepped forward and glared at the men crowding the saloon door. "But he *was* invited. *I* invited him in."

Faulty let out a wince and began shaking his head, as if he were watching his saloon fall right down to the ground.

Cain looked at the customers crowding the doorway. "Go

on, go back to your drinkin'. Nothing's gonna happen in here tonight."

The men slowly left the doorway.

Faulty slammed it closed again. "What do you mean, Sheriff, by not arresting this man? There ain't nobody gonna come to this saloon if they think I'm serving darkies."

"This man was in your kitchen, not out in the bar, and I'm not going to arrest a man for something he didn't do."

"But he's a Negro and Negroes ain't allowed in here!"

Macaulay nodded to Jericho. "I'm not going to take this man out of here like he just robbed a bank. He didn't. All he did was come here, thinkin' he had some friends."

"Well, don't that beat all." Faulty dropped his jaw. "Never thought I'd see one of you Rebs stickin' up for a darkie."

Cain's mouth hardened. Christal's gaze riveted to his face. If there was ever a sore subject with Cain, Faulty had just gone and picked it. She knew how passionately Cain viewed his role in the war, how guiltless he'd felt about it during the fighting, and how guilty the North had branded him afterward.

"It's the law. I go by the letter of the law. This man broke no law. I'm not going to arrest him."

"Then take him out of here!" Faulty snorted. "I just uninvited him!"

Jericho looked as if he could have slammed his fist into Faulty's face. Instead, he looked at Cain.

Cain nodded. "C'mon. Let's go. If it's whiskey you want, I got a bottle warming at the jail. No reason to stay here any longer."

Christal almost admired Cain at that moment. He'd saved the day. Even Ivy was looking at him with something akin to hero worship. A weaker man wouldn't have stood his ground for a black man.

Jericho whispered a reassurance to Ivy. He then followed Cain out the front door—ironically, the first time he'd ever been allowed to walk through the saloon.

Joe began playing a lively tune and men began drinking

and talking again. Dixi was heard laughing somewhere in the crowd, but in the kitchen, no one was laughing.

Faulty muttered something about tending his customers. He warned both girls to get to work, but Ivy started crying and Christal could find no way to leave her. Faulty left them alone, bursting into the saloon with the chant, "Ain't no darkies allowed in here, no sirree!"

"Someday things will be different," Christal whispered to Ivy, who was weeping into her hands.

"He's so angry, I just know he's going to get himself arrested one day. He'll come back here and they'll throw him in jail until the judge comes to town in the spring. Then all his cattle will die and then he'll never have enough . . . enough . . ." She broke down weeping anew.

"Macaulay won't let that happen," Christal soothed.

Ivy looked at her, tears marring her smooth coffee-colored cheeks. "How do you know? Do you know him that well? Because I heard tell he was a Confederate. My mama was colored and she said the Confederates hated her."

"No . . . he's not like that . . ." Christal whispered. Deep in her heart she knew he wasn't. Perhaps it was his acutely honed sense of justice, but she could not see him stripping Jericho of all he held dear just because of a stupid incident and the man's skin color.

"Are you sure, Christal? I love Jericho. I couldn't stand to watch the law go and ruin him."

She patted Ivy's hand, forcing herself to believe the words, if just for the moment. "You won't. The law . . . the law . . . well, it just isn't there to ruin lives."

Chapter Sixteen

I'll choose me then a lover brave
From all that gallant band;
The soldier lad I loved the best
Shall have my heart and hand.

"The Homespun Dress"
Carrie Belle Sinclair,
Confederate niece of Robert
Fulton, inventor of the
steamboat, 1872

At half past three in the morning, Faulty kicked out the last drunken cowboy and latched the front door to the saloon. Two more customers lingered, but they were upstairs. The girls would let them out when they were through.

Exhausted, Christal walked to the kitchen with pieces of a broken glass, telling herself she'd sweep up the rest in the morning. There was nothing she longed for more than sleep, but when she walked through the darkened saloon to the stairs, she noticed the lights still burning at the jail.

She stifled the impulse to see him. Cain had handled the situation tonight with Jericho well; he'd been scrupulously fair. It tempted her. She wondered if he could also be fair with her.

Her eyes rested on Ivy's black cape, draped forgotten across a chair. Without quite pondering what she was going to do, she grabbed it.

The cold sucked away her breath even going the hundred feet to the jail. Flurries fell from a starless sky, coyly drifting down as if playing with the idea of a snowstorm. Even Ivy's heavy cloak was poor shelter from the frigid night. By the time Christal reached the jailhouse, she longed to be invited inside, if just to stand by the stove and thaw.

With anxiety pumping through her, she gave a knock. The door flew open. Macaulay stood there, a vague annoyance on his face. He looked at her small form huddled in the cloak. His annoyance quickly melted into a wicked pleasure.

"Why, if it isn't Widow Smith . . ." His gaze flickered down her black-clad body as if somehow he was remembering how she looked in her weeds. The only thing visible was her face, a pale oval against the heavy folds of the dark hood.

He stared at her long enough to let the snow dust her shoulders and lashes, long enough to allow the icy air to further sting her cheeks and redden her lips.

She grew uncomfortable. By his expression, he looked more than capable of warming her up.

"I—I just wanted to thank you. You handled the situation back at the saloon very well," she said softly, wishing he wouldn't look at her with that gaze which seemed to pierce through to her very soul. "I saw your lights burning. I couldn't come until I was finished for the night. I know it's late so—"

"Come in." He stepped aside and let her enter. To her surprise, the room wasn't empty. Jericho was sitting at a table strewn with playing cards and whiskey glasses. Cigar smoke hung on the ceiling as if the men had been playing an intense game of poker.

"I guess I'll be headin' out now, Cain." Jericho glanced at Christal. "Tell Ivy Rose I'll be back next Tuesday."

She frowned. "You know Faulty will be on the lookout for you. You'll just be caught."

Jericho gave a defiant shrug. He donned his enormous bearskin coat and hat. With a nod to Macaulay, he stepped out of the small jail and disappeared into the cold night.

"He shouldn't have to sneak around to see Ivy. She loves him, he loves her. It isn't right they can't be together." She watched Macaulay.

"It's the law. He can't go into a saloon that won't accept coloreds."

"It's an unfair law. I'm glad you don't really believe in it."

"Whether I believe in it or not makes no difference. Until the law's changed, I'll enforce it."

"You're not that cruel."

He stared at her, placing his hand against her cold cheek. "But I am cruel, darlin'."

Fear began to twitter in her stomach like a trapped butterfly. His threat didn't bother her so much as the tone he used. She looked deep into his eyes and an ominous feeling of foreboding took hold. "But if you're so cruel, you would have arrested Jericho tonight and you didn't."

"He wasn't in the saloon. You invited him into the kitchen —and, I might add—proved stupidly brave in confessing that you had. Faulty could have caused a lot of trouble on that point, you know. I might have had to lock you and Jericho up."

A chill ran down her spine. She never thought he might have arrested her for defending Jericho. "Must you be so literal? You know as well as I do what happened tonight was ridiculous—"

He touched her lips to quiet her. "I'm the sheriff and I uphold the law. That's all I did."

"But you saw that the end was just."

"The end is usually just when you follow the law."

She stared at him, unable to agree.

He slowly smiled. "Why'd you come here tonight, Christal?"

"Just to thank you. I was glad you didn't hurt Ivy and Jericho."

"And you were wantin' to talk, weren't you?"

Her stomach dropped. He seemed to be waiting for a confession. Suddenly she no longer felt like talking. "I must be going. It's very late."

He slid his hand beneath the cloak and put an arm around her waist. He pushed her against him and said gently, "Answer one question. If you do that, I'll let you leave."

Her eyes glittered with anxiety. "What's the question?"

"You must promise to answer it without knowing what it is. Otherwise I think I might keep you here indefinitely." His arm tightened. He almost smiled.

She stared at him. He was bound to ask her where she came from, or her sister's name, or such. But she could get around the question somehow. Surely she could. "Go on, ask your infernal question."

"You'll tell me the truth?"

She watched him, her gaze direct and cool. "If I lie, it's only by omission."

His smile was strangely not reassuring. He pulled her down to a chair at the table. With both hands capturing her face, he said, "Tell me, who is the one person you love most?"

She couldn't hide her surprise. It was an unexpected question. The answer was Alana, of course. All she had to do was utter the words *my sister* and she could leave the jail.

But when she met his gaze, a sudden and terrible emotion hit her. She loved her sister deeply, yet perhaps because she hadn't seen Alana in four years and the despair of ever seeing her again ran deep, she wondered if the answer was as simple as she thought. Her sister might have forgotten her by now. Alana Sheridan had a life in New York complete with husband and by now, no doubt, babies. Sometimes Christal even wondered whether Alana would want her back. Christabel Van Alen was different now. Didier and Wyoming had made her hard. She didn't fit into the Knickerbocker life anymore. Maybe, despite everything, she never would again.

And maybe that was why she couldn't say her sister was the true and only answer to Macaulay's question. But she knew it wasn't. Her love for her sister was still as strong as ever, yet looking into Macaulay's eyes, she knew there was another answer to his question. It echoed through her heart, whispering, *You.*

He lifted her chin, her silence clearly bothering him. Gently he said, "What's wrong, Christal?"

She didn't look at him. "I can't answer your question after all."

"Does the memory"—his voice grew husky—"hurt?"

She shut her eyes in despair. *I was in an asylum for the criminally insane. Do you believe me? Do you believe me?* She shoved aside her tortured thoughts. "I won't talk about it. Really, I must go—"

"Was it a man who led you astray?" His voice turned quiet. Jealous. "If a woman's come out here, the cause is always a man. They either die on you or abandon you. Which was it happened to you?"

"I can't talk about this—"

"Is he comin' back for you? Is that why you left Camp Brown the way you did? Are you covering for him? Or are you covering for yourself?"

She stood, the chair screeching violently across the raw floorboards. "I won't talk about it. I've told you that a million times."

"Goddammit, I'm sick of begging! Is he coming back? What kind of trouble are you in, girl?" The desperation in his voice made her look at him. He held on to her arm until she nearly moaned with pain.

"Please . . ." she whispered, knowing any second she was going to confess what was in her soul and doom herself. *I was in an asylum for the insane, the demented, the mad. I didn't do it, I tell you. . . . You do believe me. . . . Why, you must believe me. . . .*

"Tell me, just tell me . . ."

She put her hands to her ears to shut him out. On the brink of tears, she said, "There is no man. No one's coming for me. No one I care about."

He studied her for a moment, as if trying to decide for himself whether she was lying. Then, as if he couldn't decide, or no longer cared, he pulled her down to him, branding her mouth with his own. A kiss that said he would never relinquish her. She could taste the whiskey he'd been drinking, and though it should have repulsed her, it didn't. Deep down she wanted him to kiss her. She wanted to taste him, touch him, hold him. She was in love with him. She wanted intimacy.

"Let's go upstairs." He roughly took her hand.

She studied his face in the flickering lantern light. He'd never know how much she wanted to say yes. If there was a man for her, the one she wanted was the one standing before her. Her need for him was like an ache only he could ease. She was so desperately weary of standing and fighting all alone. And he was so strong.

"Make me trust you, Macaulay," she whispered.

His breath was heated and quick against her temple. "If it's fear stoppin' you, girl, then know this: I fear you equally. I want to be free, but you're my obsession. And if I want you above all else, so must I fear you above all else."

"Is obsession love?" she whispered almost to herself. She stared deep into those fathomless cold eyes, and couldn't find the answer. She wasn't sure he knew himself.

Silently he took her hand and pulled her toward the stairs. She hesitated, wanting to follow, at the same time wanting to flee. Perhaps it was the drink, but he handled her more roughly than necessary. As if he were the outlaw and she, again, his captive, he pulled her ahead of him and gestured for her to lead the way upstairs.

"No, not tonight," she whispered, sentencing herself to another night of unfulfilled desire and dreams.

"Yes. Tonight."

"No," she answered, pulling away.

"I want you. You want me. If there isn't another man, what's stopping you?"

Her gaze slid to the star still pinned to his shirt. Six little points of tin. It stopped her more resolutely than a gun.

Slowly he followed her gaze. He reached for the star and unpinned it from his chest. It dropped to the ground almost noiselessly.

"Removing the star doesn't remove the sheriff."

"Tonight it does."

"It's only pretend."

"It's always pretend." He stroked her hair, her cheek, as if unable to get his fill of her.

"No, you said yourself you abide by the law. You don't know who I am, Cain. You don't know what I've done."

He grabbed her by the arms and shook her. There was gentleness in his touch but the restrained violence in his actions made her think of the outlaw Cain. "Maybe I don't want to know. Maybe I've sat here for nights on end wondering whether I should telegraph Rollins and put out a description of you. I've wondered about it until even the whiskey couldn't make the questions go away. But I haven't done it. Why, Christal, why?"

"The wires are down all over the territory because of the snow. If you haven't wired maybe it's because you can't," she whispered.

"You know it's a lie." The edge in his voice frightened her, so did the sheen of desire and desperation in his eyes. Doubt tortured him. Strangely, she could understand. It was just like when she was at Falling Water needing to trust a wild renegade. But now the roles had reversed. Now he was the law-abiding, and she the renegade.

"Maybe everything's a lie," he answered, his words low and harsh, "but this isn't a lie. Even you know this isn't a lie." His lips came down on hers, moving roughly in a gesture of possession. She wanted to resist, but he spoke the truth. What they had between them had been wrought out of danger, fear, and need. He was like no other man she had ever met, would ever meet. Their future, even if they had one, was bleak. But as he thrust into her mouth, and the heat of his onslaught built a fire in her loins, she didn't know how she could fight him when she wanted this moment with every breath she took, every mile she'd run.

He broke away and dragged her up the stairs two at a time. His bedroom wasn't much fancier than hers: bare plank floors and walls, a brand-new varnished bureau the likes of which Henry Glassie sold. An iron bed.

She closed her eyes and tried to think. If she surrendered her virginity to him, she would lose everything she'd spent years protecting. She would give him her body and her heart and when he walked, she'd have nothing left at all.

She took an unconscious step back from the bed. But before she could even take a deep breath, he had bolted the door and was crushing his lips over hers.

The kiss was deep, and if she'd been ready for it, wanted it, it might have even been sweet. But all she could think about was him leaving, taking everything she'd ever had to give a man and packing it up with him when he rode out of town. She struggled to release herself from his embrace, and when finally free, she gasped, "No," but the man she was with was no longer the chivalrous lawman. He had become the outlaw Cain again, taking her captive within arms of iron.

Her hand rose to shove him away, but he was like a lead weight against her. She glared at him and said, "This isn't right. I'm not ready for this. Let me go—"

"Let you go?" he rumbled against her fragile neck. "I've followed you here, I've tortured myself with your identity. Is obsession love, Christal? I'm damned sure going to find out." His tall, lean body tensed for fighting, his mouth took hers with a desperate heated rhythm. She tried to strike him, but she couldn't get her hand at the right angle with his body shoved against her. In frustration, she clawed at his face until he broke away.

In the flickering lantern light, he stared down at her. They were in a standoff, gazes locked, chests heaving for air. His eyes asked only one question: Why must it always be like this? but his mouth was set, as if he was determined to have her and nothing, not even his own heartache, was going to stop him.

Slowly she turned her gaze to her raised hand. They'd danced this dance before, but this time she knew their coupling was inevitable. It was the tension in the atmosphere when their eyes met, it was the gentleness of his hand as he touched her, it was the beat of her heart that quickened when she thought of him naked above her, pounding all of his anger and love between her thighs. Making love to him was destined to hurt her, but if she was truthful, she wanted it more than even he did. Deep in her heart she dreamed of holding him close. If she could only admit it, she knew she longed for him to make love to her so that she could forget New York and Park View Asylum, even the abominable weather outside her window, and just for one sweet moment believe there was nothing in the world to think and feel and taste but him.

Slowly she lowered her hand to her side. Her heart shattered. The price of surrender was too high, especially for the high-born girl who expected marriage before bed, who had fought long and hard to keep her honor above all else. But that had been before love. She'd always assumed cruelty and violence would be the things to break her. But love was more cruel and more violent.

And now love had won.

Cain found her lips again, releasing a deep, throaty growl of satisfaction at her submission. She gave no fight; instead, she opened her mouth, moaning with pitiable, traitorous need as he filled her with his thrusting tongue.

They kissed and he shrugged out of his greatcoat and red flannel shirt, not once releasing her mouth. She raised her hands to touch his hair and inadvertently knocked the Stetson to the ground. His arms went around her waist and his kiss became so intense, demanding and needful, he nearly lifted her off the ground.

Anxious to go further, he unbuckled his gun belt and slung it over the iron post of the bedstead. He next shrugged off his suspenders, then broke the seal on her mouth to unbutton her chemisette. His fingers were quick and nimble despite their size, and unforgivably too familiar with a woman's dress and undress. In seconds, her chemisette fluttered to the ground, a frothy white lace flag of truce, in marked contrast to the black felt of the Stetson that lay beneath it.

"Come here." He took her hand and led her to the bed. He kissed her, then stooped to take off his boots. She watched, her lips red and tender from his rough kiss, her emotions glittering in her eyes, unable to hide them any longer.

His boots hit the floor with two solid thunks, and he turned back to her, gathering her in his arms for another kiss. She gave it to him this time, moving her lips upon his own as if she, too, were seizing destiny.

Their mouths played upon one another while he painstakingly undid the buttons that ran down the front of her calico gown. His hands, greedy for her corset, began to unhook it even before he removed her dress, then, swallowing a groan, he dragged his mouth down her throat, leaving a burning trail to the two mounds of flesh overflowing her chemise.

She released a soft whimper, wanting the intimacy yet terrified of it at the same time. Unconsciously, she grabbed his bent head as if needing something to steady her; he continued, never seeing her tears. Not until his hand reached once more for the corset and one single tear fell and caught on the hair sprinkled across the back of his hand.

As if it were an intruder, he just stared at the tear suspended like a diamond on his hand. Then he looked straight into her eyes, his own in the lamplight a cool, unfathomable Confederate gray.

She almost didn't know she was crying. Her tears came not with sobs and wails, but with an emotion that went beyond her ability to express. She touched her cheeks, wiping away the moisture as if it had caught her by surprise too. She waited for him to kiss her again. He didn't.

"Tell me what this is about," he whispered, as if in agony.

She didn't answer. Instead, she just continued to wipe the tears that trickled down her cheeks.

He pulled her hands down and locked them at her side. Urgently he whispered, "I've never hurt you, girl. I don't want to rape you. As mean as I can get, you know I'll stop. . . . You're gonna make me crazy . . . still I'll stop . . ." His words seemed to choke him. "But Christ, I wished you'd either give to me or take the feelings away."

He had handed her the choice, as she knew he would. And that was why she had fought. Given the choice, her heart was going to take the wrong one. She was going to sleep with him, and when he left her behind, the toll would be exacted. Having been his lover would make her sorrow tenfold what it was now.

She touched his lips. They were every bit as hard as they looked. He kissed her fingers, licking the saltiness of her tears from the tips. Then she took her hand away.

And replaced it with her mouth.

They kissed and this time he was no longer forcing her. Instead, she was the one to kiss him, just as she had kissed him at Camp Brown during her farewell. Yet now she was not going to stop. For once she would have a memory worth saving.

He pulled her down on the bed, then broke from her to search her gaze. As if he could finally decipher the enigma in her eyes, he unbuttoned the front of his woolen union suit and shrugged out of it.

She didn't remember having seen his bare chest and she shivered at the sight. It was muscular, broad, and well sprinkled with dark hair, and so incredibly warm, she melted when she placed her palms against him and ran them along the muscle wrapped to his ribs.

He knelt on the bed to unbutton his jeans. Unbidden, the picture came to mind of him above her, arching back in ecstasy to reveal the mortal expanse of his neck. In her fantasy, she placed her hands along the rope scar and pulled him down for an aching kiss. It was a gesture of total possession.

Unashamed of his nakedness, as if he'd been in a hundred brothels and with as many women, he pulled her to him and began on her clothes. The first thing he removed was the string of bells around her ankle. He untied them and gave her a look that said *Never wear these again,* then he tossed them into the corner and began on her corset.

His skilled hands told her of the women he had undressed before. She desperately tried not to think of them, but a sick, burning jealousy crept up on her anyway. Thankfully, he was merciful. He covered her mouth in another kiss and in no time, emptied her of the pain and all her bad memories, and filled her instead with desire.

Like a magician, his hands worked her corset, her stockings, her garters, until they lay on the foot of the bed, discarded. Her dress was wrapped around her waist, the worn fragile cotton no match for his demanding fingers. He pulled it from her hips and she heard more than one rip. But she didn't care. Especially as he knelt above her, his naked body a magnificent specimen of the male animal: tall, lithe, muscular. And obviously ready for mating.

She shivered as he reached beneath her chemise for her white cotton knickers. He untied them and pulled them down, his knuckles erotically bumping along her soft buttocks. All she had on now was her cotton chemise, worn almost translucent from numerous washings. The thin fabric lay taut against her chest and clearly outlined her nipples. She wanted to put her hands across her chest to hide herself from his intense stare, but the gesture seemed falsely coy. She was a virgin in body but not in mind. She'd seen too much, been subjected to too much, to be unfamiliar with what went on in the bedroom. So she kept her hands at her sides and let him trace silver-dollar-sized circles around her nipples until they were as hard as buds and she, breathing fast from unfulfilled want.

He kissed her once lightly on the lips, then grasped the hem of her chemise and lifted. With a thumb, he brushed the triangle of her sex, making her gasp from shock and the rush of desire. The lines on his face deepened as he concentrated on removing the last vestige of modesty. He dragged the hem of the chemise up over her hips and waist and finally over her breasts. Bunching it at her neck, he lowered his mouth and captured one nipple, his tongue licking until she released a short, breathless moan.

He next pulled the chemise over her arms, letting the fabric twist at her wrists. She lay beneath him with her arms in bondage over her head while he gazed at her. His free hand skimmed her waist, as if pleased by its narrowness, then it moved upward, as if her generous pale breasts were too much a temptation. He cupped one, branding her with the heat of his palm and the heat of his gaze.

Turning away, she closed her eyes, feeling shameless and wanton, then arched against him, unable to lie about her need for his touch. When his hot mouth found another nipple, she struggled against the hold on her wrists, then moaned with the need to be free. But he didn't want her free. As he ran his hands along the curve of her belly, then entwined his fingers in the hair of her femininity, it was clear he only wanted her to be his.

She thought she might go mad as he stroked her. Turning away again, she bit her lip until she tasted the rustiness of her own blood, unwilling to surrender to the pleasure he created. When he bade entrance to her with his finger, her thighs instinctively slammed tight, but not before he'd wet his finger. In a strange trance of horror and awe, she watched as he touched her nipples with her essence, then covered each with his mouth as if he, too, was immersed in the need to devour.

He continued their lovemaking in much the same way, shocking her, pleasuring her with every caress. His scent covered her skin everywhere they touched and she reveled in it, loving the male smell of saddles and dust, and another scent totally different from her own, a scent that made her impulsively open her legs to this dangerous, unpredictable man.

Preparing for the finale, he jerked the chemise from her wrists. "Touch me . . . everywhere . . ." he whispered as he settled his hard length between her pale thighs. She complied, loving the feel of his beard-roughened jaw, his muscle-girded belly, his bulging, rock-hard forearms; giddy with appreciation of her sense of touch only because he'd withheld it from her.

He breathed hard now, his face taut with the need to complete the act. His fingers found the recess between her thighs and without pause, as if his desire for her had pushed him beyond the limits of his better nature, he violently thrust himself inside her.

Only to find an unexpected barrier.

As if struck by lightning, he abruptly stopped, his entire body rigid and panting. Though he was inside her, her virginity was still retrievable and there was now an unwanted decision.

She longed to hide from the displeasure on his face. All the old lies had eloquently been revealed. She was no widow, she was no whore. Her past was once more an undecipherable puzzle.

"Damn it, Christal," he whispered, burying his head between the tangle of her hair and the soft skin of her throat. "Damn everything," he whispered again like a curse, then, as unexpected as her intact hymen was to him, he thrust up inside until she could feel her maidenhead tear like a bedsheet.

She might have dwelled on the pain, but he gave her no time. He moved like a bronc trying to rid itself of a saddle. He pushed and withdrew, taking her with a frenzy that diminished her pain and forced it to blossom into pleasure. The unfamiliar tension in her loins mounted with his every thrust, until she could hardly stop herself from reacting. Almost against her will, as if she was afraid she might like it too much, she tried to hold back, but it was no use. He held a secret that she knew would drive her mad if she didn't discover what it was.

Slowly she released herself to him and let him take her where she longed to go, amazed that his pleasure could increase just by heightening hers. He worked hard, his body glistening with a sheen of sweat though the stove in the room needed stoking. She wondered at the compatibility of their bodies—as he pumped, she instinctively gripped; as he thrust, she surrendered until both of them seemed ready to explode.

She had no warning of the blackmail in his heart, but with a sudden grunt of agony, he stopped his movements, proving once and for all that he had molten steel running through his veins and not blood. She cried out, hurting every bit as much as he did, and then she knew he had her. At that moment, she would promise him anything, give him anything, to make him continue and give her the ecstasy he promised.

"Never run from me again," he rasped, finding words difficult. He shuddered within her, and she thought he had to be made of ice given his ability to stop despite how his body was racked with the pain of denial. "Promise me, girl—say it— you'll never run from me again—"

She moaned and looked at the iron bedpost, at the gun

belt, heavy with his steel six-shooters. She was giving herself a death sentence. "I promise—I'll never leave you—I'll never leave," she repeated, trying to make him start again.

He complied. He thrust several times more, then ground his teeth and pushed deep inside her womb. She felt his seed shoot up inside her and that was what finally drove her over the edge. She dug her nails into his back, threw back her head and embraced her pact with the devil.

Chapter Seventeen

Christal found it painful to open her eyes. The morning sun shone brightly through the window, its glare intensified by the snow. She covered her eyes and rolled over. Though she knew she was not in her own bed, she might have been on the moon for all that she found familiar. There was an ache between her thighs, a well-satisfied ache perhaps, but foreign nonetheless, and every muscle in her body seemed spent of energy, as if she had just walked across the divide. But these were only symptoms. Her eyes finally adjusted to the brightness of the sunshine streaming across her bed and she found the cause.

Macaulay lay asleep next to her, his limbs entwined inextricably with her own. The sheets and blankets were scattered over them as if a storm had just come through and blown them off the bed. Then, when she thought of the exact nature of the storm, she could feel hot color on her cheeks.

She turned her gaze to Macaulay. It was strange to have a naked man next to her. The warmth of his skin was delicious, particularly since the stove had burned out long before dawn, but it was frightening too. He was too close. It was like lying next to a sleeping wolf. Any minute he might awake.

Afraid of disturbing him, she lay quietly and studied him, an odd, unwelcome tenderness seeping into her heart. She was unused to seeing him with his defenses down, and she delighted in the luxury of it. No longer was he the cold-eyed outlaw of the notorious Kineson gang or the strong-willed sheriff ready to scour the town of vice. Instead, he was just a man—albeit a very handsome one—sprawled possessively across her bed in slumber, breathing deeply and well after a night's vigorous activity.

His mouth was slightly parted and his brow was clear of the stresses that ate at him. She longed to reach out and trace the lines that ran down his cheeks, to touch a lock of his dark umber–colored hair, hair that she noticed for the first time was streaked tawny, a testament to his years spent in the saddle beneath a hot prairie sun. His chest, partly covered by the blanket, rose and fell with his deep breathing, creating a temptation for her hand once again to feel his muscles harden at her touch, to feel the erotic crispness of the dark hair that ran in a stream down his belly, to parts she now gratefully found hidden.

He groaned and rolled away, onto his back, giving her the opportunity to rise. She wanted to be dressed and gone before he awoke. It had unsettled her last night having his man's gaze on her nude body. Now, beneath the sun's bright glare, she seemed even more naked.

She slowly rose up on one elbow. The exertion of the night made her movements slow and cautious. She tried to sit up, but the length of her hair was hopelessly caught beneath his meaty shoulder.

She stared, puzzling how to extricate it without waking him up. If she had had scissors available, she would have cut it all off rather than face him nude across the bed, her emotions running the gamut of embarrassment, anxiety, longing, and fear. He had forced a promise of no more running, but in the harsh light of morning she didn't know how well that promise could be kept. *It was an asylum . . . an insane asylum . . .* She didn't want him to look into her eyes and see the lie she still needed to tell. Not yet.

Finding no other way, she reached across the mattress and pulled on her hair. It gave an inch or two and still he slept, heartening her. She tugged again and again, getting a bit more hair out from beneath him with each pull. Then, with a final lusty heave, she freed her hair, but not before his hand reached out and pulled her naked onto his chest.

"Mornin'," he rumbled, repressed laughter warming his normally cold gaze.

"Good morning," she said, the formality of her words making her feel stupid, especially while she was buck naked atop him, her breasts crushed against his hairy chest, her buttocks an appallingly convenient place for him to rest his hands—unbelievably warm hands.

"What time is it?" His voice was a deep vibration through his chest, titillating her own.

"Late," she whispered, not brave enough to scramble away and reveal more of her nudity.

"Then let's not get up at all." He bent his head and kissed the top of her breast.

She wanted to pull away but if she did, she knew he'd have her nipple in his mouth before she could gasp a protest. Then she'd be lost. "I—I really have things to do—please—"

"Faulty's not going to come over here and drag you away from me. You know it, darlin'." He squeezed her bottom. She couldn't believe the strength in his hands.

"But—"

He took her face and brushed the hair from her eyes. "But you're not used to making love in the daytime. Or ever, are you?"

She was silent, remembering how he'd risen from the bed after he'd taken her the first time last night. Using a chipped pitcher and bowl, he'd washed the blood from himself, then handed her a damp cloth so that she could do the same. The entire episode was performed without a word, without questions. He was solemn, almost grave, as if taking her virginity had been an undesirable, unavoidable task. But then, accepting it as done, he'd returned to bed and taken her twice more, almost as if he were trying to convince himself she'd never been a virgin at all.

"What were you saving it for, Christal?" he asked quietly, bringing her out of her thoughts.

You, she wanted to say, but didn't.

"Let me see you." He sat up in the bed and pulled her from him. She clutched the sheet, but he took it away. Kneeling before him like a slave, she felt his gaze wander freely over her breasts and thighs. She was so mortified, she couldn't even look at him.

He tilted her face up. She finally met his stare, wishing hers could be as cool and detached as his; knowing it could not.

His hand brushed the knots at the back of her head, further evidence of the fury of the night before. He looked straight into her eyes. "You're beautiful, Christal. Hide yourself from every other man, but don't hide from me."

Unable to stand his scrutiny any longer, she grabbed the twisted sheet and held it to her chest. "Please . . . you leave me no modesty."

"It's too late for modesty now." His gaze flickered over her maidenly pose as she clutched the sheet to her breasts. He suddenly smiled. "What are you afraid of? You think I'm looking for flaws?"

"Maybe. I just don't see what you find so fascinating. And it's so damned light in here." She looked around, cursing the sunlight that poured through the two long windows of his bedroom. Now she knew why Dixi and Ivy shunned the east bedroom. The morning was just too hard to face in the glare.

"I'm not looking to see flaws." He still wore that irreverent smile. "But I will say this: You're too thin. And I don't need the light to know it."

Her eyes flashed at him, her nerves taut with nervous anger. "It hasn't been easy for me since Camp Brown. What do you think, that I dine at Delmonico's every night?" She snapped her gaze away. "You just want me fat so my bust will be as big as Dixiana's."

"It's not your bust I'm complaining about." He ran his fingertips lightly along the portion of her rib cage that wasn't covered by the sheet. There was just enough rib showing to prove his point.

Disconcerted, she covered her side with the sheet, but then it fell from one breast.

He took possession of it before she pulled away.

Bending over her, his thumb doing wild things to her nipple, he whispered, "Ah, girl, don't you worry . . . your bosom is big enough . . ." His eyes flickered down to the flesh overflowing his cupped hand. "Dixi's got nothing on you . . ."

"And how would you know?" she asked, breathless at his touch, anguished at the thought he might get personal experience.

"I don't know a whore from a virgin, or a widow from a runaway, but if there's one thing I can judge, darlin', it's the size of a woman's breasts." A dark, wry smile tipped the corner of his mouth. He forced her down to the mattress with a kiss, then took his sweet time adding to the knots already in the back of her hair.

Chapter Eighteen

The half-breed took his time dismounting in front of the hotel. Traffic congested at the entrance while velvet-bustled ladies were helped from carriages, their delicate white hands stuffed into mink muffs, and thus rendered useless. The Fairleigh Hotel was the finest in St. Louis. It sat back from the railroad so that the ashes and cinders wouldn't dull the gilding. It could boast of such famous visitors as Henry Tompkins Paige Comstock, Mark Twain, and General and Mrs. George A. Custer. The Fairleigh advertised that it was just like a hotel in Boston or New York, with every modern convenience and tasteful Louis XV decor, and to the people who could afford a night on the Fairleigh's feather mattresses it was indeed a heavenly respite from the endless jarring of the Pullman car headed west.

But though the hotel rose above the muddy roads and the riffraff drinking heavily in the saloons between wagon trains, it didn't intimidate the half-breed. Not much did. Perhaps it was because of his height—White Wolf was well over six feet tall—but most likely it was because of his cold-blooded stare, given to him by his Pawnee father who had raped his mother while attacking and setting her wagon train to flames.

No indeed, White Wolf was not a man most wanted to go up against. To the misfortune of many, his mother survived her burns to give him birth. But then, because of what his father had done, she'd felt no compunction in beating her

half-breed bastard until he ran away or stopped her. At fifteen, the boy chose to stop her. He clubbed her to death, then
roamed the prairie forts and reservations, and grew into a
man, a man who had now been ushered to the Fairleigh Hotel. A man proficient in the skills of no mercy.

"May I help you?" An effeminate hotelier shuffled up to the
half-breed and discreetly placed a hankie over his nose, soft-
ening the stench of rancid bear grease.

The half-breed ignored him. He looked around the gilt-
and-crystal lobby as if searching for someone he knew. In the
far corner a man stood up from a ruby damask banquette. He
was a handsome man in his fifties, with startlingly blue eyes
and a gray Vandyke beard. Reaching into his sapphire silk
vest, the man took out a gold watch, noted the time, then
nodded.

The hotelier shook his head while the half-breed walked
past, a Winchester slung over his shoulders as if he were in
the wilds of the Dakotas and not in the middle of the great
city of St. Louis.

Civilization has to come soon, the dapper little man tsked to
himself. There was more and more building every day following the railroad, so much so that the pounding of hammers
could be voted the state anthem. But in the meantime—the
hotelier's shoulders slumped as he perched himself once
again behind the richly inlaid walnut counter—in the meantime, it was no use trying to convince men they were in a
place as cultured as an East Coast city. This was Missouri.
Men could enter a hotel with their rifles. It was still the West.

The half-breed refused to sit at the banquette, probably
because he was more comfortable on an ant-riddled tree
stump than fine French damask. The other gentleman resumed his seat, dismissing the half-breed with a glance that
said he considered him little better than the help.

"How much do you want to find her?" The gentleman
lifted a gray eyebrow, his detached gaze trained on a garish
gilt-framed oil painting of Prometheus.

White Wolf looked around the lobby as if judging the worth

of a person who could afford to stay there. "One thousand dollars."

The man with the Vandyke beard laughed. He met the half-breed's eyes. "I'll give you two hundred and not a penny more. I've barely enough to afford this rattrap." He swept his hand in the air, gesturing to the lobby. "For the same price I could be staying in New York at the Fifth Avenue Hotel, ensconced in the finest of suites."

The half-breed took another look around the lobby. He'd never known a finer hotel than the Fairleigh. The man's disparagement confused him.

"Do we have a deal? I was told you're the one who can find her, but I know there are others who would like the chance. Look at all these Mormons who can't get to Utah. I hear they'll do almost anything—"

"Two hundred, I bring back her hair. Three hundred, I bring back this." White Wolf wiped his hands on his rabbit fur vest, then extracted a greasy piece of paper from within it. Carefully he unfolded it and placed it on a rosewood table next to the banquette. It was a drawing of a scar shaped in a rose with the word WANTED blazed across the top.

Suddenly the gentleman began to laugh. He picked up the piece of paper. "You mean, for three hundred dollars you'll bring me back her *hand*?"

White Wolf nodded. "For three hundred you'll know she's dead."

The gentleman possessed a handsome smile and he turned it on the hotelier. "Over there—bring us champagne, will you? We have something to celebrate."

The hotelier nodded. With pursed, disapproving lips, he went to fetch the champagne.

The gentleman turned back to the half-breed. "I'll get you a room here in the hotel tonight. I've only heard a rumor this girl's out in Wyoming, but if the rumor's true the money's as good as yours. You'll go first thing in the morning."

"I'll go tonight." White Wolf didn't care about luxury. He couldn't have an opinion on something he didn't know.

"Delightful. Delightful." Beneath his Vandyke, the man

smiled like a jackal. "I'm anxious to return to New York and seek my fortune on the Exchange once more, but until I find this girl, I'm an outcast. I left town with all the gold I could carry, but I'm used to better. The sooner you find the girl, the sooner I can return. No one can blame me for anything if she meets her end in the wild western territories and I can return to New York without worry that her memory might convict me. And then I can claim her share of the Van Alen estate, whatever that cursed mick didn't already take. After all, I cared for the girl for years. I paid every dime for that expensive asylum. Am I due nothing?" His jackal's smile widened.

White Wolf watched the man pour the champagne that appeared on the rosewood table. He didn't care about this man's problems. All he was thinking of was the bounty. "Do I bring the proof to this hotel?"

The gentleman nodded. "The name is Didier. Baldwin Didier. Don't forget it."

White Wolf finally smiled. "I won't."

In the fading light of evening, Christal watched Macaulay buckle on his gun belt. He was dressed in everything but his red flannel shirt—that, she wore. She sat against the iron headboard of the bed, her knees tucked against her, her eyes saddened that it was finally time to face reality.

He went to the bureau and found a wool shirt. Shrugging it on, he said, "Let me check on things downstairs, and then we'll have some supper at the saloon after I talk to Faulty."

"T-talk to Faulty?" She tried to brush the hair out of her eyes, but the long shirtsleeves kept falling over her fingers.

He sat on the edge of the bed and pulled on his boots. "You think I could let you stay there and sell dances? After what we've done?"

"It's nothing that Dixi and Ivy don't do every night."

He turned to her, his eyes stern. "Exactly."

She looked out the window. The setting sun painted the clapboards of Faulty's saloon a brilliant fuchsia. "This won't last forever. It can't. You know that."

She looked back at him. He'd donned his dark blue greatcoat. The cape made his shoulders look even wider; its length made him look taller. He was a large, muscular man; compared to her, he was a giant. But his heaviness between her thighs had been delicious. He'd ruined her for anyone smaller.

"Let's not think of forever. Let's just think of right now."

She nodded and looked away. "All right. We won't think about tomorrow. That is, until tomorrow comes. And it will come. Soon."

He picked up his Stetson where it lay by the door. Quietly he removed the lacy chemisette from its top and laid it on his bureau. "I'll make you a deal. You don't talk about tomorrow and I don't talk about New York."

Her blood froze in her veins. He'd never given her any indication he knew something. But he knew about New York. "How—how did you find that out?"

"You mentioned Delmonico's. I know where that is. It's a restaurant on Union Square in the city of Manhattan."

She stared at him, naked fear on her face.

He was silent for a moment, then he said, "I've never been there myself. Couldn't afford it. I was told nobody but Vanderbilt can."

She wrapped her arms around herself to keep from trembling. Mentioning Delmonico's had been a foolish detail to reveal. Now he knew more about her from that one slip than he would have in a month's interrogation.

"Well . . . I'll be back in an hour." He suddenly seemed weary. She wondered if he was losing the fight against telegraphing for information about her. After all, he'd gotten what he wanted. One mystery about her was solved. That left only one more.

"Are you going to check up on me?"

He paused but didn't face her. "I know you're running from something. Known it all along. If I check on you, what will I find?"

She stared at his back, helpless. There seemed no way to explain it all. Her story was fantastic, and he would be obliged by his duty as sheriff to bring her back to the asylum.

"I thought so," he mumbled when she didn't answer.

"Wait," she whispered, her voice trembling as violently as her hands. "My uncle—my uncle—" She choked, unable to finish, unable to surrender her fear.

"Tell me about your uncle."

She opened her mouth, but the words wouldn't come. She was damned by the picture of his eyes; of the betrayal she would find in them when they took her away, back to the asylum, back to her uncle looming in the shadows of death.

"Christal, tell me about him." His voice brooked no disobedience.

She clasped her hands to keep them from shaking. Still the words wouldn't come.

He finally faced her. His features seemed carved in stone. "Christal . . . if you'd just taken Terence Scott's money and left town with the rest of the passengers, I might have let you alone. I would have figured you just couldn't fall in love with a man who'd played outlaw with you, kidnapped you, and held you against your will. But you didn't let things work out the way they were supposed to. You took my money and left behind even more of your own, and you ran away, as if something had terrified you out of your mind. . . . So I couldn't let it be. I had to find you." He was quiet for a very long time, studying her, his eyes glittering with need.

"I want to tell you," she whispered, her voice full of unshed tears, her heart so tired of fighting alone. "But—but you're a sheriff. Your duty—the war—you need to do the right thing —I want to tell you . . . but I can't. I just can't." She dropped her face in her hands. The game was up. He knew just enough about her to telegraph New York. The scar would give her away. He could find out anything he wanted to in a matter of hours. In the end, it would be better just to confess. What he would find out from the authorities in Manhattan would be much worse than her explanation. And maybe, just maybe, he cared enough about her to believe her.

She looked down at the rumpled sheets all around her. Her heart felt heavy in her chest. One thing was certainly true: If he didn't care for her now, he never would.

"Tell me," he demanded again, chiseling away at her resistance.

She choked on a sob, unable to face him. "You want to know this terrible thing about me, and I'll tell it to you. But first answer me this: Would you still want to know if it meant I would be taken from here, taken away never to be heard from again? Would you still want to know if it"—she swallowed a sob—"if it caused my death?"

He became gravely quiet. He didn't move. He didn't touch her. He offered no comfort, only cold, calculating silence.

She broke down in choking sobs, but to her shock, she felt his hand run down the tangled length of her hair.

"Then it's my choice, isn't it?" he said in a voice husky with emotion. "It's my honor as a lawman, or it's you."

He was silent for a long time. She couldn't bear to look at his face. Finally, in a whisper, he said, "So I choose you, Christal. God save me, but I choose you."

She began to weep quietly into her hands, relief washing over her like waves from the ocean. It was not a moment for celebrating; there was no need for him to hold her or for her to rush into his arms. It was a melancholy time when a man gave up all he believed in for a woman who might turn out not to be worthy of the honor.

He watched her forlorn figure and ran his hands once again down the long golden strands of her hair. "Get dressed," he said solemnly. "There's a lot to do. I got to talk to Faulty."

He walked to the door. But before he left, he spoke what seemed to be pressing on his mind. He paused and choked out the words. "I just want you to know, girl, that one day you're gonna tell me. I'm gonna believe you and then we're never going to speak of it again. I just want you to know that." He left the room as if anything else that needed to be said could wait until they were again holding each other.

Minutes later, Christal rose from the bed, her thoughts fearful and unclear. She wasn't sure what to do next. It tore through her insides to see Cain turn his back on all he believed in. Her instinct was to flee, to run as far away from him as she could and lose herself in another territory where they could forget they had ever known each other. But that would never happen. She would never run far enough away to forget him. When Macaulay had first arrived in Noble, she was scared and shocked and crazy with the need just to get away. But now she had ties to him that would not break. She loved him, and with nowhere to go and no way to get there, she resigned herself to dress and wait for his return.

He came within the hour and took her to Faulty's. The saloon was empty of drinkers save an old miner named Brigtsen and Jan Peterson. Dixiana was up in her room; they found Ivy in the kitchen and she served them dinner. Conversation was sparse. Christal could see Ivy was terrified of the sheriff and whatever Macaulay had said to Faulty had scared the hell out of him. The old saloonkeeper nearly bowed as she entered the kitchen. There'd never be any more talk of her taking customers to her room; in fact, by the look on his face, she thought Faulty would kill her if she even suggested the idea.

Ivy quickly departed and Faulty went into the saloon to tend to his customers. Christal and Macaulay ate their supper without exchanging a word. It was not Delmonico's; there were no virgin-white linen tablecloths or silver candelabrum, just a rough wooden table, a sputtering lantern, and a warm seat by the stove, but strangely, Christal didn't mind. The future frightened her, it was an unformed spectre off in the horizon. One day she would know what it was, but for now she looked into Cain's eyes and saw no coldness there. And for the moment that was all she needed.

When dinner was over with, Macaulay took her to her bedroom. They could hear Dixi with a customer talking and giggling through the rough board walls. Quietly Cain undressed her and made love to her in silence, as if he was so unwilling to share their coupling, he wouldn't even allow another to hear their sighs. But his silent caresses brought her fulfillment quickly, and by the second time, her heart burst with greed for him and with the bittersweet joy of experiencing something wonderful that she knew couldn't last.

The passion died slowly. Eventually he gathered her in his arms and fell asleep. His breathing was deep and comforting, and she nestled against his sure, strong heartbeat, content with the lie that tomorrow would be just as fine. And that an honorable man could abandon his honor forever.

Chapter Nineteen

Macaulay was gone when Christal awoke. She opened her eyes to another morning of sun. The light reflected off the snow and blazed into her room, forming windowpane shadows across the blankets. Outside she could hear the familiar *drip, drip, drip* of water as it melted off the icicles on the eaves. Today would be warmer, but there would be no promise of spring yet.

She reached across the mattress and touched the pillow still bearing the concave depression where Macaulay's head had lain. The indentation was cold. He'd been up for a while.

She rose and dressed quickly, anxious to see him again, but hesitant. At some point she would speak about what she knew must finally be confessed. Pondering this, she sat for a long while by the window and stared at the daguerreotype of herself and her sister. It was difficult even thinking about telling him of her past, but only because of the bad things. The good things, the joy, she was anxious to share with him.

She touched the picture as if stroking her sister Alana's cheek. In truth, there had been much joy. Maybe too much. Maybe God was so cruel, he had wanted her to pay for all that happiness.

She shook off the notion and returned her gaze to the daguerreotype. A small bittersweet smile tipped her lips as she remembered one of the better times when she and her sister were still little girls. Their mother would come home with the

latest edition of *Godey's Lady's Book*. Mrs. Van Alen made her
girls promise every time to be neat with their cutting, then
she would pass them her sewing scissors and allow them to
cut out the paper dolls in the back. Even now Christal could
remember the elaborate fashions created for their dolls: blue
velvet riding habits with pert top hats frothed with netting,
pink taffeta ballgowns flounced with alençon lace, and best of
all, wedding gowns made with yards and yards of white satin.
With the old-fashioned caged crinolines, her bridal paper
dolls had looked like the tiny bellflowers of lily-of-the-valley.
She'd loved them. But especially she loved her mother for
bringing them home to her girls every month and never forgetting.

Christal's eyes glittered with memory. The day the magazine arrived was made even more special. If she and Alana
were very careful with their cutting and didn't slice through a
concoction for a cure for gout or the latest chignon style from
Paris, their mother rewarded them by sending tea up to their
rooms. They would have a tea party with all their dolls, including Mary Todd, the doll her father had bought for her
after he returned from Paris. He brought back a very expensive gown of blue satin for Alana, which their mother had
made Alana promise not to wear until next season—the
Knickerbocker tradition of aging their possessions so that no
one could mistake them for the nouveaux riches—but he'd
forgotten to bring something back for Christal. Crushed,
Christal had silently longed for the day when she, too, would
be old enough to wear gowns from Paris. Though she never
let anyone see her disappointment, her father must have
sensed it. The next day he surprised her by bringing home
Mary, a fashionable doll with a china head, kid body, and a
gown of blue satin, one very much like Alana's. Christal remembered loving the doll until its clothes were threadbare
and there were tiny cracks in its porcelain face. She also remembered naming it after the president's wife, and when her
father found out, he'd come into the parlor, kissed her on the
forehead and hugged her in a tight grip, his voice shaking as
he told her that he was proud of her patriotism.

She never knew until later about the terrible loss of Union boys at Antietam reported in the *Chronicle* that day. And she never knew what he meant about being quiet around Mrs. Maloney, their laundress. She only remembered the poor lady weeping all day into her apron. She found out later both of her grandsons had died in the battle.

But Cain had not. Christal took a deep breath and tried to hold back the hope blooming deep inside her. Cain had been at Antietam and lived to tell. A Confederate, he called the place Sharpsburg, but it was all the same battle. The bloodshed had scarred him but he had survived . . . and found her. They'd both been through so much. It couldn't all end with betrayal and Baldwin Didier. It couldn't.

She reverently placed the picture back on the bureau. She closed her eyes and made a wish, then went to seek out her lover.

White Wolf stalked his prey like his namesake, but whereas the wolf used scent and hunger to drive him toward his victim, White Wolf used cunning and anticipation of the kill. He was most times successful. Perhaps it was his Indian blood; he had an instinct for the hunt. But it was his particular mix of blood that drove the instinct awry and made him a ruthless assassin.

The sun broke the horizon of the prairie and yellowed the grasses with the first watery light of dawn, and he could feel the draw of his prey. It was like a knot in his gut that tightened and released depending on how close he was. He cast his gaze down on the wanted poster, touching every curve of the rose as if he were touching the girl's hand. She would not be hard to find. He was already on her trail. There weren't many women in Wyoming Territory. As he'd thought, one as beautiful as she was had been noticed by everyone.

He stuffed the paper beneath his rabbit fur vest. The knot was easing; a good sign. Laramie was far behind him and he continued moving west, toward the mountains, toward his game.

* * *

"Stop!" Christal giggled and ran farther into the snow-covered prairie. A snowball pelted her back, then another and another. If she hadn't borrowed Ivy's cloak, she'd be soaked.

"We don't get much snow in Georgia, but we Rebs know how to make the most of it!" Macaulay scooped up another handful of the freezing white stuff and ran toward her.

She screamed and ran into the endless plains. Behind her, Noble was just a tiny weatherboard outpost in a calm, flat sea of white. "This is war!" she squealed, and tried to get her own ammunition before Macaulay could catch her, but she didn't have a chance. She barely had a handful of snow before he tackled her to the ground, laughing.

"Villain!" she cried out.

"Yankee!" he retorted, as if that were the worst insult of all. But then he smiled and kissed her. And she was so distracted, she didn't see the fistful of snow until he had smashed it in her hair.

"Oooooh!" She shoved him off and sat up. Her hair was a thick, wet tangle, its pins scattered in the snow like pine needles.

"I win," he whispered, and kissed her again.

They'd had a wonderful morning. No one in the saloon had risen yet, so they had the luxury of breakfasting alone. Christal had fried eggs with salt pork and made a pot of thick black coffee. Macaulay had been the one to offer a walk. The sun was bright and warm, and the snow wasn't too deep; she couldn't refuse. She'd borrowed Ivy's cloak from the peg in the kitchen and off they'd walked, hand in hand. Until Macaulay had pelted her with a snowball.

"You beast, it'll take an hour for me to dry my hair," she said to him when they broke apart. In playful revenge, she gathered a fistful of snow and poised to hit his head with it. But his hand shot out and froze hers in midair; his Stetson didn't even slip from his head.

"Unchivalrous Rebel!" she whispered as he forced her hand to her side.

"That's a contradiction in terms, ma'am." He smiled and tipped his hat to her.

A fatal error. She flipped the black Stetson off his head and, with her free hand, broke the snowball in his hair, rubbing it in for good measure.

He tumbled her back onto the ground. The snow made a cold, downy mattress. She was laughing as she struggled within his arms.

But then something in her face—an expression maybe— seemed to move him. He took her face in his hands and his gaze became solemn and piercing, as if searching to see the expression again.

Her smile began to fade.

"There's that girl," he whispered, his own expression troubled, yet exhilarated.

"What girl?" she asked, unsure what he was talking about.

"The little girl in the picture . . . when you laugh, I can see her."

Their eyes locked. Her heart filled with an old familiar pain. She wished what he said were true, but somehow it seemed impossible. The girl was gone forever. Slowly she turned away so he wouldn't see her eyes fill with homesickness and hurt.

As if a wall had been built up between them, he silently rose from her. He stood like a thrown bronco rider, stiff, broken, and defeated, his wet chaps skintight from the melting snow. He brought her to her feet and, arm in arm, they trudged back to Noble, the unasked questions a dark, thundering cloud on the horizon.

"It's a lie! A lie, Ah tell you!"

Christal and Macaulay entered the saloon to find Dixiana near tears.

Again she sobbed, "It's awl a lie!"

John Jameson, a wealthy rancher from outside the town, stood between Dixi and Faulty. He was a rusty-haired man in a black suit and scarlet cravat. He shot Macaulay a glance, then muttered, "You the sheriff?"

Cain nodded.

Jameson pointed to Dixi. "Arrest her, Sheriff. She stole all my money. I kept it in a green silk purse. I had it last night and now it's gone."

Faulty interjected, "Now there ain't no reason to go and accuse Dixi of nothing. She don't steal, sir, I know it."

"Arrest her, Sheriff. I had three hundred dollars in that purse!"

Macaulay slowly removed his coat. "When did you last see it?"

"I had it in the whore's bedroom. I remember quite clearly I removed the purse from my vest pocket and put it next to the bed."

"No, no, you never did! Ah never saw any purse!" Dixi began sobbing. Her rouge trickled down onto her chin.

"There, there," Christal whispered, and clasped her hand in her own. She looked to Macaulay for help.

Macaulay said nothing.

"The slut ought to be hanged for stealing a man's money. No-good whore," Jameson spat out.

"Don't talk to her like that! She didn't steal your damned money!" Christal could have bitten her tongue, but Jameson's words were too cruel. Saying those things about Dixi was like kicking a child.

"You don't have any proof she stole your money. I can't arrest the girl with no evidence of a crime," Cain said, taking a seat at one of the tables.

"Oh, yes, I have evidence." Jameson pointed to Faulty. "This man right here saw me with the purse not a minute before I went up to the whore's room. I paid my tab and he commented on the amount of money in my purse."

"Is this true?" Macaulay asked.

Faulty looked rather sick. "Yes."

"And the whore saw me put on my clothes this morning. There's no green silk purse anywhere. So where did it go? She stole it, I tell you!" He pointed to Christal. "These girls are probably all in cahoots!"

Hesitantly, Christal looked at Macaulay. His face was a cipher; she didn't know what he was thinking, and it bothered her. She, Dixi, and Ivy weren't in cahoots, but she couldn't shake the feeling a seed of doubt had suddenly been planted. She had, after all, stolen money from him once.

"I still don't think that's proof this woman stole anything," Macaulay said finally.

Jameson turned beet red, his face clashing with the red in his hair. "That's for the judge to decide, not you. Your job is to put this girl in jail until the man arrives. If I may remind you, Sheriff, I am on the town council. I was one of the men who brought you here to Noble."

Cain was silent. Finally he said, "I'll need to check out her room." He turned and went up the stairs. Christal followed at his heels.

"She didn't steal that man's purse. You know she didn't," she whispered as Cain entered Dixi's room. He went over to the rickety bureau and forced open a drawer. There was nothing in there but stockings, garters, and a patched cotton corset. He opened another and another. There was nothing but clothing.

He walked to the neatly made bed. He ripped off the covers and upended the thin mattress. No green silk purse anywhere. Quietly he looked around in every barren corner. There seemed no other place to hide anything.

"She wouldn't steal from that man. I know Dixi—"

"Christal, it doesn't matter," he said ominously, "Jameson's a pillar of this community—such as this hellhole is—and there isn't a judge in the world who's going to believe Dixi over him." He looked at her. "If you know anything about this purse, or you can persuade Dixi to tell us something about it, that's the best you can do for her. Jameson's going to put her in jail, if not."

"No, not Jameson. *You*. You're going to put her in jail," she spat out, tears glistening in her eyes. "And you know she didn't steal the purse!"

Cain took her by the arms. "Listen carefully to what I have to say. It may not be pretty, but it's the truth. The judge is going to come in here and see Dixi as a known whore, a woman with a shadowy past. Nobody will believe her; everybody will believe Jameson. My protests in this matter will be a howl in the wilderness unless somebody can find that purse."

"What if he's lying?" she asked numbly. "What if John Jameson has some grudge against Dixi and he's just lying about the purse being missing because he wants to hurt her?"

Cain stared at her. "Why would he do such a thing?"

"I don't know. You'd have to ask him, and he'd never tell the truth. So Dixi's as good as convicted. Whether she took his money or not, she's going to go to jail."

"Not if you can convince her to find the purse."

"You talk as if you don't believe she didn't steal it." Christal stared at him, trying hard to hide the pain in her eyes. *An asylum for the criminally insane. You do believe me?—oh, you must believe me!*

Suddenly she turned away from him, unable to meet his gaze. The end had finally come. If he couldn't believe Dixi, then he'd never believe her, no matter how emphatically he said he would. *An asylum for the criminally insane.* Would she see revulsion in his eyes? Her heart cracked and shattered.

"C'mon," he said grimly, taking her arm. She followed.

Downstairs Cain confronted Jameson. "I didn't find the purse upstairs. When the judge gets here you can press charges. Until then Dixiana will remain here under my supervision."

"Is that all you'll do?" Jameson turned red again.

Macaulay nodded.

Jameson glanced at Christal, then gave Cain a nasty smile. "Fine. Do nothing, Sheriff. But when I go before the judge I'll see all these girls prosecuted. This was too crafty a theft for Dixiana to do it all by herself. They were all involved, I know it, including the whore on your arm."

Cain grabbed the man around the throat, screeching a chair across the floor with a violent shriek. Christal gasped and ran to him to keep him from killing the man. She didn't know what triggered Cain's anger—whether it was his fear that the man wanted to prosecute her or whether it was because he had called her a whore—regardless, he quickly had Jameson in a death grip.

"What are you going to do, Sheriff?" the rancher choked. "Kill me? My money was stolen and here I'm treated like the criminal!"

Sanity seemed to take hold once more. Macaulay released his hand. He looked at Christal and seemed to weigh the circumstances.

She could feel the blood drain from her face. If she were prosecuted with Dixi, the judge would probably ask the sheriff to wire their last place of residence to see if they'd committed any other crimes. He'd be obligated to wire New York, then everything would be over.

His face was taut with frustration. In a hard voice, he said to Dixiana, "C'mon. I've got to lock you up."

"Oh, God . . ." Dixiana sobbed into her hands.

Christal was numb. She couldn't stand seeing Dixi locked up. She was sure she was innocent. But if Cain didn't lock up Dixi, Jameson would see the rest of them prosecuted, their pleas be damned.

"No, wait!" she choked out to Cain, wondering if she was committing suicide. "Cain, you know this man doesn't have enough evidence to prove Dixi stole anything. Don't do this for me. . . ." In desperation, she lifted the hem of her gown and began ripping the seven gold pieces from her petticoat. "Here," she said, turning to the red-haired man, her voice trembling with desperation, "take this for your lost money and go away!" She thrust the coins into the man's hand.

"This isn't enough," Jameson complained.

"But that's all I have!"

Cain took the gold pieces from the man and placed them into Christal's palm. She was about to protest when he pulled her aside and warned, "Stay out of this. It's more trouble than it's worth."

Her gaze was riveted to his. He was trying to protect her. Even at Dixi's expense. But if Cain could brand Dixi a thief on circumstantial evidence, then what would he do if he should ever come across the wanted poster with her face on it? A searing panic shot through her. Cain would go crazy, was what.

"You can't do this to Dixi, Cain. You just can't," she whispered helplessly, her eyes begging him for mercy. "She didn't do anything. You know she wouldn't steal."

"I don't know that. All I know is that Dixiana's a saloon girl and saloon girls are known for stealing their customers' money." He looked at her. "And you had nothing to do with this and I'm not going to let Jameson drag you into it."

Devastated, she watched him step to Dixiana and take her by the arm. Dixi was still crying; Christal felt tears well in her eyes also. It had all been a dream. Her hopes of confiding in Macaulay and believing he might help her were gone. The dream had ended. She was fooling herself to think his love for her would override Cain's duty as a sheriff, and his weakness as a mortal man. He would react to her supposed crimes as any man would react. And as a sheriff, he'd proved more than once he'd do his duty first and foremost. And he would find his duty easy to do when he saw that wanted poster.

Christal watched in silence as they left the saloon. Deep inside she could feel her fragile, vulnerable heart grow cold. She had opened herself to him and let him briefly glimpse inside, but now she could never be so foolish again. The lesson was learned. She had to keep away from him. He'd made her promise to never run from him, but she would break that promise and run as fast and far away as she could. No matter how hard and lonely running made her, she had no choice but to protect herself.

"What will happen to her?" Ivy whispered behind her.

Christal turned around, her face pale and desolate. "I don't know."

"Lord have mercy . . . this is going to destroy Dixi . . ."

Christal didn't deny it. It had already destroyed her.

Chapter Twenty

⁓⁓⁕⁓⁓

"Lord, you are the coldest man!" Dixi came down from her tiptoes. Cain walked away from the other side of the bars.

He folded his arms across his chest. "What can I tell you, Dixi darlin', you can't get out of jail this way. We're just going to have to see the judge on this one."

Dixi started bawling. Her tears came in great dramatic breaths.

Cain was unmoved. Perfunctorily, he said, "C'mon now. It won't be that bad."

"Yes! Ah'm a prisoner! Ah have to stay in this filthy jail cell!"

"Filthy? Dixi, it's never been used!" Cain chuckled.

"Oh, you cruel man. Isn't there anything Ah can do to get out of this?" She turned tear-reddened eyes to him. "Anything?"

He shook his head.

Hurt creeped into her eyes. She turned away and bravely wiped at the tears on her cheeks. "Is it because Ah'm a mite older than the other girls? Is that why you don't want me? You think Ah'm—too old?" The last two words came out hushed, as if she were speaking of the dead.

"You're a fine-looking woman," he said gently. When she didn't respond, he put a hand through the bars and touched her shoulder. "You know, there were times, Dixi, I was running with the gangs up in the Wind River and I'd have paid a fortune for a night with a woman like you."

Dixi took a peek at him and sniffed. He handed her his bandanna.

"I'm just not looking right now, is all. It's Christal. She makes it hard for me to think of other women."

"You in love with her?"

He was silent, as if he'd been asking himself that question for a long time. Quietly he answered, "Whatever it is, I know I got it bad." His expression lightened. "C'mon, Dixi. Spend one night here and I'll wire to Fort Laramie to find out when we can expect the judge. I think I can convince Jameson to let you stay in the saloon until then. I'll ride out to see him tomorrow."

She gave him a tremulous smile of thanks. "You goin' to the saloon in the morning? Could you ask Christal to bring me my perfume and a change of undergarments?"

"It'd be my pleasure, ma'am," he answered in his most seductive drawl.

Dixi smiled behind the bars. "Thank God for Georgia gentlemen like you, Macauley Cain. I do believe the South is not dead after all."

He shot her a blinding smile and tipped his hat. "No, ma'am, she's not dead at all."

The bar was like a morgue that night. Everyone in town knew about Dixiana. Macaulay didn't return from the jail and Christal told herself she was glad. Much to Faulty's distress, she'd gone back to selling dances. It was mostly to fill the void Dixi's absence created, but also an act of defiance. Cain wouldn't like what she was doing, but that was probably for the best. She wanted anger between them because with anger there was distance, and she was desperate for distance.

She swallowed the lump in her throat. Macaulay had seduced her into trusting him, and through want and need she had desired the seduction. Every minute with him had made her want to tell him the truth. Thank God she hadn't. In perspective, she could now see that she had toed right up to a precipice and stared down at her doom. But she hadn't walked off the edge, nor would she. She had pulled back. Though to walk away meant to walk away from love, she steeled her heart and knew she would do it. Her instinct to survive was too strong, too well honed from years on the run.

There was no need to search for dance partners that night. Dixi was at the jail and Ivy had walked a customer upstairs. The girl was taking much longer than normal and Christal had asked Faulty at one point if she shouldn't go knock on her door, but Faulty had said the gentleman had paid a goodly sum up front and there was no point in upsetting him. Ivy could take care of herself.

"Gimme another drink, will you?"

As if snapping out of a trance, Christal looked down at the half-drunk man seated beside her. He repulsed her. More than anything in the world she wanted to get away from men like him, and never again feel them paw her during a waltz. But for now, that was the price of freedom. And she would pay it.

"Another whiskey, Faulty," she said at the bar.

"Christal, Cain's gonna kill me when he walks through that door. He told me no more dances."

"I don't care what he told you. It's my business and I know it's perfectly legal to sell a dance. He has no say in the matter."

"God save me! Why'd I hire all you girls? All of you, you're nothing but trouble with a capital T!" Faulty slid another whiskey to her.

She handed the drunkard his drink and surveyed the room. The men were all regulars tonight, except one. The newcomer sat at Cain's table, off in the corner, by himself. He was unusually tall, with dark hair plaited like an Indian's. If he was a half-breed, he was a handsome one, but despite his physical appearance, she hadn't enjoyed her dances with him. There was an animal odor about him that nearly made her gag when she waltzed too close, and his clothing was dirty, especially his vest, a patchwork of thin, greasy rabbit skins. But the worst thing about him was his stare. His brown, rather inhuman eyes hadn't looked away from her all night, and it was becoming unnerving.

"You're just working this one night while Dixi's gone. Now, you promise, won't you?" Faulty nervously handed her another whiskey.

"Don't worry, Faulty. I won't be working long." She walked away with the drink, not having the heart to tell him about her plans to escape with the next cowpoke who could give her a ride to South Pass.

Christal delivered the drink, but not without catching the eye of the half-breed. He motioned for a refill. She went to the bar for the bottle.

"No. Another dance."

She inwardly cringed. Returning the bottle, she walked back to the table, mentally forming her excuse.

"I'm—I'm rather tired—"

Without warning, the half-breed grabbed her hand, running his grimy forefinger along the ridges of the scar on her palm. She pulled it away as if burned.

"Can—I get you—something else?" The words were hard to choke out. He frightened her, but it was difficult to pinpoint why.

He nodded to the stairs.

She shook her head. "No, I—"

"Another dance, then." He stood and handed her a nickel. There was no way to refuse without him starting a fight with Faulty. Reluctantly she let him put his hand on her waist while Joe played "Devilish Mary."

"What's your name?" he grunted.

"Christal," she whispered, growing more afraid of that stare with every passing second.

The expression on his face was one of deep satisfaction.

"Where are you from?" For some reason, she had a burning need to know about him. Her instincts told her it was important.

"I just came from Laramie. Before that, St. Louis. You been to St. Louis? Women there aren't near as beautiful as you."

His thumb ran along her scarred palm, and for some reason Christal felt her knees give way. Terror ran liquid through her veins. Suddenly she couldn't wait for Macaulay to darken the door.

"Please—let me give you your nickel back—suddenly I don't feel well—"

"I want to keep dancing. I don't get chances to be with women like you . . . and time's almost up."

She stumbled. He kept his hand locked on her waist. He turned the corner with her, his inexperienced feet treading on her own as if he didn't care at all about the pain he caused her.

"No—please—we must stop—"

"I like it." The half-breed answered as if he wasn't really talking to her, but to himself.

"No, no . . ." She tried to stop, to gracefully pull out of his arms, but he was a big man and she, only a petite woman. The only way she was going to get away from him was to cause a scene.

"We must stop right now. I don't feel well." She looked at him, but he didn't even see her. He was running his thumb again and again along the ridges of the scar on her palm.

She froze, inexplicably terrified, every muscle in her body tensed as if for a fight. He started to waltz again, but she tossed his nickel at him, the coin bouncing off his shoulder and clattering to the floor, a noisy, humiliating rejection. He wasn't even angry. He just kept on dancing, dragging her with him like a predator with prey.

Until a voice cracked like thunder behind her.

"What the hell are you doin', girl?"

One by one, heads turned until even old deaf Joe quit playing the upright and wheeled around on his stool to stare. From the corner of her eye, Christal saw that Faulty looked about ready to roll back on his heels and faint dead away. She watched him take a fortifying gulp of firewater and amble from behind the bar.

The half-breed released her, picked up his coin, and retreated to his table like a kicked dog. Christal was flooded with relief. But then she faced Cain.

He stood by the door, his arms crossed ominously across his chest. Even though she expected it, the fury on his face daunted her.

"I told you no more dances," he said, a deadly calm in his voice.

"I was helping Faulty," she answered as defiantly as she could beneath that cold stare.

"Faulty can go to hell."

"A lovers' quarrel, now don't that beat all!" Faulty came running up, releasing a nervous, high-pitched laugh. "Christal, you gotta be nice to Sheriff Cain here. If he don't want you dancin', then—"

Macaulay turned his eyes to Faulty only once, but the one cold glance was enough to cut off Faulty's words as if Cain had reached into his throat and pulled out his vocal cords.

He turned back to Christal. "I suggest we take this discussion elsewhere. Upstairs would be my preference."

From the corner of her eye she could see the half-breed staring at them. Macaulay particularly seemed to interest him.

Faulty scurried back to the cover of the bar. It was as if everyone in the saloon were preparing for a gunfight. There would be a showdown all right, but it would take place here in the saloon, not upstairs on her mattress. She would make sure of it.

"No, Cain. You can't tell me what to do. I want to help Faulty tonight and that's just what I'm going to do." She hid her gaze from the angry question in his eyes. She understood his bewilderment. He'd arrested Dixi in part to shield her. Now he'd come back from the jail only to find her coldly accepting his company and defying his every wish.

"If you think I'm just going to stand around while any man who wants to puts his hands on you, you've gone loco, girl." He lowered his hat over his predatory eyes. "Go get your things, you're coming with me to the jail."

"Are you arresting me?"

"Do you want me to?" There was more than an imagined threat in his words.

"No," she whispered, backing away.

"Then go get your things, Christal."

"No. I have rights. You may be sheriff of this town, but you're not a slavekeeper."

He took a step toward her, his expression angry bewilderment.

She backed away.

He took another step.

She turned to the staircase to bolt, but she stopped in her tracks. Ivy stood there, as pale as death.

"Oh, my God, what happened to you?" Christal whispered.

Ivy lifted her face. There were bruises on both cheeks and one eye was puffy, swollen, and purple. She appeared faint and had to steady herself on the wooden banister.

"Who did this?" Christal exclaimed, growing irrationally angry. If it wasn't for the memories of her father, she'd hate every man who walked the earth at that moment.

"That cowboy from the Henderson ranch." Ivy's words were a bit garbled. Christal could see her jaw was nearly swollen shut.

Macaulay gave Christal an angry stare, as if to say, *we're not through,* then gently led Ivy down the stairs to a nearby chair. "I'll go after him."

Ivy caught his hand. "No."

"What do you mean, 'no'?" Cain snapped. "A man can't go beating on a woman as if she were some kind of green horse that refused to be broke."

"He's gone. There won't be any justice for me anyway. You know it as well as I do, Sheriff." Ivy wiped the tears that began falling. "He told me never to tell anyone and he'd not come back."

"He ought to be horsewhipped. I'll see to it he is."

Faulty appeared with a rag stuffed with snow and Christal began ministrations on Ivy's face. The men in the saloon spoke in low whispers. Except for the half-breed. A chill ran down Christal's spine when she saw his gaze still trained on Cain.

Ivy clutched Christal's hand. "Don't tell Jericho. He's supposed to show up tonight. Just tell him I'm ill. He'll go crazy if he sees me like this."

"How can I hide this from him? I've got to tell him," Christal pleaded.

"No need now." Macaulay nodded toward the back of the bar. Jericho stood there in his bearskin coat, his features hardened with rage as he stared at Ivy.

"You go home now, Jericho! You ain't got no cause to be here! You know the policy!" Faulty shouted at him.

Macaulay shut him up with one glance. Then he turned to the customers and said, "Go on home. The saloon's closed for the night. Y'all can come back again tomorrow night."

"Yeah, that's right," Faulty chimed in. "Ain't no darkies allowed in here. Tomorrow night you'll see it's so!"

Slowly the men dribbled out the door. The half-breed was last, shuffling his large feet, strangely reluctant to go. He paused only once. He stared at Macaulay and this time Macaulay stared back. The instant dislike between the men was almost palpable.

"Go on with you," Cain growled.

The half-breed shuffled out into the freezing night, his destination unknown.

"Take me with you, Sheriff. I know better than you where the Henderson ranch is," Jericho said, ignoring Faulty's glare.

Cain nodded. "We'll go right now, before the bastard's got time to run." He looked at Faulty. "Lock this place up tight." He pointed to Christal without even looking at her. "She's your responsibility while I'm gone. I want you watching her every minute. And don't take any lip. If you have to, lock her in her room."

"What?" Christal gasped. She could hardly believe her ears.

"That's right." Cain turned to her, his face still harboring a previous anger. "I don't know what you were up to tonight, but from this moment onward, you're in my custody. Consider Faulty your guardian till I return."

She stared at him, mute with fury.

He and Jericho left without another word.

Chapter Twenty-one

Cain and Jericho were back by morning, conspicuously absent a prisoner. They had taken so long that Christal had begun to worry. Even the fright of the half-breed dimmed in the wee hours of the morning as her anxiety grew. There were a hundred innocuous reasons for Cain and Jericho's delay, but instead of thinking of lame horses and bad weather, she thought of grizzlies and gun-toting renegades unwilling to be captured.

Christal had stayed with Ivy all night. She'd tended to her with compresses and hot broth, but the girl cried until she fell into an exhausted sleep. Deep inside, Christal cried too. They'd all had enough of the misery of their lives. At least Ivy's misery would end when Jericho took her away.

From the window, Christal watched Cain dismount. His spurs cut into the ice of the road as he handed the horses to a boy from the stable. He hadn't shaved that morning and his jaw was covered by a dark beard that only accentuated the icy gray of his eyes. He wore a battered fringed jacket she remembered from Falling Water, and chaps, those same chaps worn smooth along the inside of the thighs, and that now made her want to slip her hand between his legs to remember just how slick and hard and warm those chaps were.

He turned around toward the saloon, and as if by instinct he looked up at her window. Their gazes locked. A grave error. Christal saw too much, she revealed too much. Her love for him left her breathless, but it sliced through her heart to think of the future. In the small dark hours of night, she'd longed for him to slip into bed beside her and erase all her tortured imaginings. But now in the cold light of morning, she was glad he had not come. Her practical side had taken hold once more and she was convinced it was best. He could only betray her. Keep him at bay, she told herself. His anger was a good thing.

After Cain had entered the saloon, there were muffled voices down the hall near Ivy's room. She expected it; still, the knock at her door made her jump.

"Who is it?" she called out, already knowing who it was.

"Macaulay." His voice was unusually somber.

She slowly opened the door. By sheer dint of will, she refrained from flinging herself into his protective arms.

"Did you catch him?" she asked.

He entered her room and closed the door behind him. "He's dead."

"But—?" She turned silent. "Did you shoot him?"

Cain rubbed his unshaven jaw. It was ten o'clock in the morning, but he looked as if he could use a drink. "Jericho killed him. Shot him clean through the head. Maybe I shouldn't have let him come with me."

"Did he murder him?"

"I'll tell the judge in my report that it was in self-defense. If you look at it in a certain light, well, it was self-defense."

She stared at him, wondering about his words. "It's impossible to make a just and perfect world, even for a sheriff." She looked away. "What's to happen to Ivy?"

"Jericho's taking her out to his cabin. In a few years, things'll be better for them. His cattle should do well. They'll get married, have a few kids. It won't be so bad."

"It sounds wonderful."

Their gazes met. A muscle in Macaulay's jaw tensed. The moment was painful and uncertain.

"Girl, I didn't like what you did last night." His words were like an icy wind rushing through her. The old anger and fear came back to her. "I told you never to do that again." Each syllable was enunciated with scathing anger.

"How am I to earn my room and board here if I don't work for Faulty?"

"I don't want you here anymore. I want you to come to the jail."

"I'm not living with you at the jail."

"What's gotten into you?"

A terrible lamenting pain settled in her chest. "I don't want to be with you anymore, Macaulay. I want you to go back to Washington. There's no future for us. I see that clearly. You must too."

"When did you come to this conclusion?" His question was quiet, foreboding.

"I've known it all along."

"Why?"

One small question that needed a lifetime to answer. She took a deep breath. There was really no way to explain except to tell him everything, and that was something she could never do. Not when she'd seen how he'd treated Dixiana— guilty before proven innocent.

"*Why* doesn't change the inevitable, Cain," she whispered.

"No." He grabbed her, unnerving her by the desperation in his eyes. "The only thing that was inevitable was our coming together, not our parting. You gave your word you would stay, remember?"

She closed her eyes. It hurt to remember it. "You blackmailed me. You elicited that response from me. I won't keep it."

"You *will* keep it."

She opened her eyes and stared at him. There was a wildness in his expression, that same wildness that once made her believe he was an outlaw.

"I'm not going to go chasing you from place to place. I've already done that. You're going to stay with me until we've finished our business and if that means locking you up so you can't go anywhere, I will."

"You can't keep me against my will twice. And need I remind you, you're a sheriff now, not an outlaw. If you make me a prisoner you have to come up with a charge." Her gaze snapped with ire. She hated it when he played sheriff. That damned badge was already a fortress between them, he needn't abuse his powers more than he already had.

"If I wire New York, instinct tells me they might come up with a charge." His words were like acid burning into her heart.

She turned from him, unable to let him see how upset she was. She had never felt more desolate. "If you wire New York, they'll take me from you. The result will be the same."

He touched her, drew her back against the warm, hard planking of his chest. She found it very difficult to be strong. "Get your things together, girl. We're leaving."

"Where?"

"Someplace where we can be alone. Where the rest of the world won't ever bother us. We'll be there by dawn. Get your things."

Her silence was damning; her reluctance palpable.

He cupped her chin. "You'll be going of your own free will, Christal. Because even now that free will of yours is tellin' you to go with me. I am your only salvation. Without me I give you two months before you start whoring for your coins. Without me, they'll take you back to New York because there'll be no one to hide you like I'm willing to do."

She stared at him, shocked by his offer and the risk he was willing to take. An uneasy gratitude seeped into her, just as it had back at Falling Water. She didn't want the answer to her next question, but she had to have it now. It was fight or die.

"Do you love me, Macaulay?" The words were barely a whisper. She refused to meet his gaze and let him see her heart in her eyes. If his answer was yes, she would go with him. If it was no, she didn't care what happened to her. She might even surrender herself to the authorities.

She forced herself to glance at him. There were so many lies between them, she didn't know how one single answer to one single question could change everything. But it could, she knew it could. She waited in terror.

"Yes, I love you."

The answer and, more so, his delivery caught her by surprise. He used the same tone as when he cursed.

She looked up. Her gaze locked with his. His eyes were angry and crystalline cold.

"Don't ever ask me that question again."

"I've the right to know. If I'm to go away with you—"

"You've no right to know. None at all. I've risked everything for you. Even death. And the result is that I love you, but my love is not tender and sweet. It's angry and dark. You'd do well not to explore it."

Raw, fearful emotion choked her. "You sound as if you hate me more than love me."

"I hate your shadowed past and your subterfuge. In every breath that I love you, I can't escape the hatred for your lies that lives there as well, and so my love for you has become my own personal hell. You once asked me if love was obsession. I can finally answer you with a resounding yes. The cruel part is, that's only half the answer."

She stood like a statue in front of him, her heart turned to marble, her tongue unable to refute anything he said. His words were an unbearable, inescapable truth. He said he was her only salvation, but he was her ruin too. She could never really have him with her past standing between them, yet if she revealed all, tore the wall down, she knew he'd no longer be there for her, standing on the other side.

"I would rather a man love me or hate me than feel the way you do. Discover the truth about me, then," she said quietly. "Wire New York."

He backed her against the wall, then took her face in his hands. "You're coming with me, Christal. Because as long as I don't know about your bad past, I can still love you. And as long as you have something to hide, I can still make you do the things I want. Like this . . ." His lips came down on hers, a hot, seductive kiss, utterly manipulative. Utterly powerful.

"No . . ." She moaned when his hands braced her rib cage, then slid to her breasts.

He whispered against her hair. "Will you fight me, then?

Do you want me to wire New York? Do you want me to hate you?"

"No . . ." She sobbed, wanting him to love her. Desperately wanting him to love her.

"Kiss me, then. Take me to your bed and love me with all the fury I've seen before. Take me between your thighs and in your mouth, then let me take you, where I will keep you safe."

Her chest heaved with deep, ragged breaths, her heart torn with her need for survival and her need for him.

But surrender closed in quickly. As did his mouth. And his hands. His kiss was deep, hard, rhythmical, his lips daring her to remain cold and unfeeling, every movement of his hands a burning sweet torture, until inch by painful inch he began to win, spiriting away her independence like an Indian on the raid, and leaving nothing behind but a shuddering, melted woman who kissed him back with all the passion in her soul.

"You're a wise woman, Christal, a very wise woman." He groaned as her lips dragged across his neck, feather soft against the hardened flesh of his scar.

"No, I'm a fool." She touched his face with her hand, wanting to know every hungry line on his cheeks, every dark slash of his eyebrows, every straight ridge of his nose. Then, with a deep, wrenching sadness in her soul, she took his hand, led him to her bed, and did all that he asked.

Chapter Twenty-two

"But Sheriff, what am I gonna do without Christal here? You've gone and taken all my girls away!" Faulty was not pleased at the news Christal was leaving. He normally slept until well past noon and they had to wake him up. Now he stood behind the bar in a nightshirt, a weary blanket full of holes wrapped around his shoulders.

"She wasn't going to sell any more dances, so you don't need her anymore." Cain's expression brooked no argument.

"I'm sorry, Faulty." Christal could hardly meet his gaze. She felt everything showed, her fear, her love, her kiss-bruised lips, the raw skin in the hollow of her throat where Cain had marked her in a moment of passion.

She gave him a guilty glance. "I know it's an awkward time to ask you, Faulty, but I don't know when I'll be back, if ever, and before I go, there is a matter of thirty-five cents that you held for me that night I discovered a hole in my pocket . . . ?"

Faulty nodded wearily. "All right, all right. You went and broke me. All you girls. Take the whole damned kitty, Christal. It ain't gonna help now."

She cringed at his dramatics; it only increased her guilt, but she told herself again and again, she was doing the right thing. With her gone, Cain wouldn't have any need to bother him. Faulty didn't know it yet, but her leaving was his good fortune.

The money was in a tin box hidden behind the jugs of sarsaparilla. She retrieved it, then counted out her due—exactly seven nickels—with Faulty's gaze monitoring her every move. She then put the canister back, but one coin slipped from her hand and rolled beneath the bar. Shuddering to explore the dusty, unclean darkness beneath the bar, she reached for it nonetheless, unwilling to let even one precious nickel out of her possession.

In the void, her hand came in contact with a silken object. Dismayed, she drew it out. It was, indeed, a dirty green silk purse.

"Whoooeee, is Dixiana gonna be mad at you, Sheriff," Faulty murmured as Christal handed him the purse. "Looks like the thing's been here all along. It must've fallen off the bar when Jameson went to pay his bill, then it got kicked underneath." He opened it and counted out three hundred and two dollars and change.

Cain took the purse. "I'll take it back to him."

"Sure." Faulty scratched his head. "But do you think, Sheriff, you could send Dixi back here right away, if it ain't too much bother? I could sure use a girl around here tonight. I had three of 'em just yesterday, you know," he added accusingly.

Cain nodded, not acknowledging he was the one responsible. He took Christal's hand in his and they went to the jail.

Mechanically, as if moving in a trance, Christal helped Dixi dress while Macaulay went to Jameson's to return the purse. Dixiana complained the entire time, though Christal's thoughts were elsewhere, somberly dwelling on Cain and their future.

"Men!" Dixi groused, straightening her black knitted stockings and rebuckling her garters. "Ah told that sheriff Ah had nothing to do with that man's money being gone. And does he believe me? No!"

"He needed proof. You know that." Absentmindedly Christal hooked the back of Dixi's corset.

"Why do they always have to have proof? Why can't they just take your word for it?" Dixi faced her. "That damned

Macaulay Cain! He could have asked Faulty, he could have asked you or Ivy. Ah don't steal. Ah don't have to. Mah gentlemen are good enough to me without me stealing from them. Why do they never believe us, Christal?"

Christal didn't answer. She just stared down at the scar on her palm, her face drawn and somber.

"Darlin', you never did tell me where you got that scar."

Christal closed her palm. With a bitter curve to her lips, she drew Dixi's dress over her. "I don't know, Dixi. All I know is that some people will never be convinced of the truth."

"Don't Ah know it." Dixi adjusted her corset, a maneuver that required a fair amount of shimmying and jiggling. All the while she ranted and raved like a politician. "But someday that's all gonna change! Mark mah words, Christal, Ah'm gonna go out and vote in that there next election, yes sirree! We're lucky we live in the territory. We've had that vote since '69 and Ah'm takin' it seriously now. Things is gonna change 'round here. Ah might even run for justice of the peace just to show 'em all. They had a woman do that down in South Pass, why not here?"

Dixi stared at her, indignant, as if somehow Christal could answer that question.

"I'd vote for you, Dixi," Christal offered.

"Well, Ah'm thinkin' about it, don't you think Ah'm not." She hooked her front, shoved her skirts down over her garters, and walked out of the jail, a free woman.

"Faulty's waiting for you at the saloon, Dixi." Macaulay entered the jail, a hard, unyielding expression on his face whenever he looked at Christal.

"No apology, Sheriff?" Dixiana sniffed.

"I did my job, that's all." He turned to Christal. "Are you ready?"

"Where y'all goin?" Dixi gazed at Cain, then Christal.

Cain crossed his arms over his chest, as if defying Christal to refute his answer.

She didn't.

"I'm taking Christal away for a while. I've got a cabin up in the mountains. She's going to stay with me there."

"So you're leavin' us too, Sheriff? Why, you just got here." Dixi looked at Cain and raised an eyebrow. Christal wasn't sure if Dixi was sorry Cain was leaving or not. He was an unpredictable, intimidating man; Dixi preferred inexperienced, adulating boys. Still, Dixi was attracted to Cain. Even now Christal could see it. Dixi had always done a poor job of hiding it.

Cain cleared his throat. "I'll be comin' down now and again to take care of what needs to be done. This town doesn't need a sheriff on hand every minute. I'll be around if you need me."

"Oh, Ah hope so," Dixi answered, a sarcastic smile playing on her pretty lips. "Ah mean, Ah wouldn't want someone else around here missin' something and me gettin' away with another crime."

His mouth twisted ruefully. "There wasn't any help for it. If it'd been up to me, I never would have made you come here, you know it."

"Yeah, yeah, tell that to the justice of the peace. Ah'm runnin' for office, haven't you heard?"

As if he couldn't help himself, he chuckled. Dixi gave him a swat, and Christal felt a strange jealousy burn her insides.

"You take care now, Christal. All right?" Dixi said in farewell.

"You too, Dixiana." Almost forlornly, Christal watched her go, the jealousy having burned itself away. She didn't think she'd ever forget her. Dixi was a memorable sort. But Dixi would be all right. She might even win that office.

Christal's eyes slid to Cain. There was nothing more to take care of, except to leave.

He nodded to the table. "Take that package and bring it with us."

"What is it?"

"Look."

She opened one corner of the large package. A sky-blue wool fabric peeked out of the tear.

"Do you like it? Jan told me you were admiring it. It'll make a pretty dress. Better than the one you have on." He moved closer and caressed her upper arms, his hands like warm wrought iron.

"It's beautiful. Thank you." Slowly she rewrapped the fabric and wondered if this trip they were about to take was only a delay, an artificial manufacturing of time. She never told Cain about it, but the half-breed still haunted her, touching an innate fear even when all logic told her he had moved on. Still, when she closed her eyes he was there, staring at her with the same soulless expression as her uncle's, reminding her that at any time, all she had to live for might be taken away.

"We got a long ride to the cabin." He took the package from her.

"Whose cabin is it?"

"It's just a place I used to go when I rode with Kineson. We'd hide out there after a robbery. It's a trapper's cabin in the middle of goddamned nowhere. If you want to lose yourself, girl, it's the place to be."

He led her outside. His old Ap was waiting, loaded with saddlebags full of provisions. Above, the night sky was scattered with stars so white and radiant, they seemed as unreal as fairy dust.

Macaulay helped her mount, then swung up behind her. "Say good-bye to Noble, Christal," he said as the Ap began to jog eastward. "If it's up to me, you'll never see it again. We'll go to Washington in the spring."

She gazed at the snow-patched prairie tinged indigo in the moonlight and thought of her uncle. Where was he now? Hot on her trail or halfway around the world? She didn't know. That was the nightmare.

"You're so sure about everything, Macaulay, but you don't know what waits ahead."

"The only thing waiting is this."

He turned her head and surprised her with a kiss, one that was long and lingering and made her forget everything but her need for him, a need she resented as much as she embraced because it was not under her control. Proof of this fact came when she found her hand clutching the scratchy wool of his greatcoat as if begging for more, and ultimately, it was he who ended the kiss, to calmly rein the Ap eastward, where the mountains rose above the night clouds like a great blue heaven.

By morning they had reached the cabin, following the North Popo Agie River to its source, a lake breathlessly suspended between glacier and mountain. The log cabin stood in a valley that in springtime would be covered by tender green grass. Now it was only a snowy crevice, wedged between cathedrals of rock.

At first, Christal wondered how they would fare in the one-room cabin with no windows or comforts, but after Macaulay built a fire in the hearth, she found the stone fireplace large enough to keep the room quite warm. And at least there was furniture, if one counted chairs made of twigs with the bark still on the wood, a rickety table as scarred as the Southern army, and a bedstead, again made of rough timber, the corners held together with rawhide. Outside, there was timber to burn, and the lake held plenty of fish. They would do all right. For a while.

She placed the bolt of sky-blue wool on the dusty table. Sunlight streamed into the cabin through the open door. Outside, she could see Cain hobbling the Ap. The sun was just appearing over War Bonnet Peak and on the other side of the valley, the top of Pingora was tinged a rosy pink, the colors in the sky a sight no painter could ever capture. Beneath the blue granite, an azure lake was alive with light bouncing off the snow. Cain had called it Lonesome Lake, and Christal could understand why. The little valley was surrounded on three side by walls of stone that shot into the sky. It was the perfect hiding place, even more isolated than Falling Water. She doubted even Indians had showed up here but once a millennium.

Cain stepped into the cabin, temporarily blocking the light. The fire crackled and spewed in the hearth, casting his face in shadows.

"Can we stay here forever?" she asked quietly.

He heaved the heavy saddlebags onto the table, his eyes warming as he looked at her. "That's fine with me."

"Are you hungry?"

"The better question is: can you cook? I still remember those beans back at Falling Water."

She bit back a smile and stepped to the saddlebags.

He closed the door, plunging the windowless cabin into night, the only illumination the fire dancing at the hearth.

They were alone. Utterly, completely alone. Adam and Eve in a snowy paradise. For once she didn't have to worry about the outside world intruding; there was no outside world here, just the fire, the darkness, him.

He touched her hair first. His hand ran down its length, as if paying homage to a deity. He hadn't let her pin it up before they left. He'd said he liked it down and wild. She didn't bother to fight him about it.

He bent to kiss her. He tasted good. She blushed, recalling how shameless she'd been the last time they'd made love. His power over her disturbed her.

He pressed his lips against her hair. His arm crossed her chest, holding her back against him. "You love me, Christal," he whispered. A statement, not a question.

She met his gaze, never knowing all the hurt she showed in her eyes. "I could tell you I don't."

"But you do."

She looked away, unable to take his honesty. It left her unprotected.

"C'mon. Let's go to bed."

She shivered and hugged her arms. Though she had done everything imaginable with this man in bed, it still filled her with reluctance. There was something not right about it. No matter how wild Wyoming had made her, the need for marriage was still ingrained in her.

Sensing her hesitation, Cain whispered in her ear, "I know we're different, Christal. I see that every time you speak, every time you lift that chin in defiance. I know you come from a good background—rich, even—I can see the wealth in the picture of you and your sister, and in your manners. But for some reason, a reason I may never know, all that wealth's gone. Holding on to your rich girl's morality won't bring it back."

"And you grew up with no morals? No wonder Georgia lost the war." She turned away from him, unwilling to show him the contrition in her eyes. When would she quit flailing him with the war everytime they argued? She hated herself when she did that, but he bull's-eyed her emotional target every time; he left her so defenseless, she resorted to cowards' tactics.

"You may think I'm poor white trash, but I'm not the one running." He didn't bother to hide the bitterness in his voice.

She felt the stab, as if he'd just sunk a knife into her heart. They were even.

He caressed her cheek. Slowly he took her into his arms, slowly she acquiesced.

"We're here not to think about this," he said quietly.

"It's there. How can we not think about it? Fight about it?"

He laughed. "My parents fought like the devil. In fact, I don't remember a day when they didn't have a knock-down-drag-out fight. My ma one time beaned my pa on the head with a frypan, and he didn't wake up for two whole days."

She looked at him in horror. Not in her wildest imaginings could she picture her parents doing such a thing.

His mouth twisted in a wry grin. "I know that's a bit out of the realm of your experience, but I'll tell you this: when they made up, they sent me and my brothers packing. Sometimes all day. I can only guess what they did in all those hours in the bedroom. I can still hear them laughing and carryin' on." He took her face in his large hands. "You know, my ma must have known Pa was gone. She just gave up."

The sorrow in his voice moved her. It made her think of her own parents. They had died together and she took comfort in knowing they would have wanted it that way.

He took her hand to lead her to the bed, but still she paused.

"What's stopping you? Don't you like it? I want you to like it."

She turned away. "You know I like it. I like it too much. I can hardly keep up with you."

"You can. And you did. And you will."

Her gaze locked with his. In some ways he might claim to be a simple Georgia boy, but the man who looked at her now was hardened and schooled by bloody battle. He knew what he wanted; he saw no point in wasting time. The thought left her breathless, frightened, and unaccountably intrigued.

She felt the comforting circle of his arms, and she was afraid of getting used to their protection, when his love for her hung by a silken thread, one that could snap the second he saw the wanted poster.

"The mattress is dirty," she whispered, feeling the hot trail of his lips down her vulnerable neck.

It was. The soiled ticking was stuffed with dried grasses that poked through the worn material. There were no blankets and no sheets.

Undaunted, he tossed his blue greatcoat over the mattress, covering it. Slowly he lowered her down, wrapping her in the intimacy of his warmth that lingered in the coat. They made love slowly, believing that the world would never intrude upon the one that they were forging. Afterward, lying safe in his arms, she closed her eyes and began to dream.

Her lover was Cain. But he was no longer a renegade or sheriff. In her dream he was a gentleman caller, arriving at the doorstep of the Van Alen brownstone on Washington Square. He wore a black coat, an equally restrained cravat, and no hat. Her mother didn't quite approve.

"He's not quite tame," her mother told her, eyeing Cain at the open door as if he couldn't see or hear her. Christal could only agree. Nonetheless she invited him inside, thinking that black suited him, it suited his moods, and his eyes, pale like ice.

He had a drink with her father in the library while she and her mother took their cordials in the parlor. Not once, during her dream, did she think this odd. In life she had never had a beau come to call, she had been too young. Even so, it was not difficult to imagine how it would be choreographed.

Father, naturally, liked her beau. His laughter boomed through the oak pocket doors, encouraging her. Cain was a man other men either liked and respected, or feared. There was no in-between.

"Will I have his sons, Mother, and will they be strong and wild and handsome as he?" she asked, the nonsensical nature of dreams giving her freedom to ask questions she never would have dared ask in real life.

"We always wanted sons in addition to you and your sister. Yes, my dear little Christal, you must have Macaulay's sons." Her mother patted her hand. Her angelic smile beamed upon her. Then she returned to her needlework.

"But will he ever love me, Mother, as Father loves you?" Even she could hear the sorrow in her voice.

"Of course, of course, or we won't let him marry you. How foolish you are, child." Her mother patted her hand again. Christal turned back to her own needlework, something she was never very good at. Alana was the artist with her needle, not she.

"See here!" Suddenly her father's voice boomed out, angry and tingeed with fear. "I said see here, my good man! You can't do that to this fine fellow! He's going to marry my daughter!"

Her mother leapt from her cushion by the fireplace and slid open the pocket doors. A scream curdled in her mother's throat, sending icy shivers down Christal's spine.

Slowly, as if fear made her aged and gouty, Christal shoved aside the needlepoint frame and rose to her feet. Somehow, knowing what she was going to encounter, she reluctantly walked to the library entrance.

Didier had arrived.

The library was cast in darkness, the only light from the fireplace illuminating her uncle. He wore a blue coat and a paisley silk vest that elegantly covered his expanding paunch. Seeing him now, she could understand how her aunt could have been attracted to him. Baldwin Didier was a handsome man, regal in his Vandyke beard, arresting, with a cold, piercing gaze much like Cain's. But in Didier's eyes there was no soul that cried out for salvation, no boy who needed warmth and love, as she had seen, rarely, in Cain's. When she looked deep into Didier's eyes there was only an icy void from which there was no return.

She spun around, clawing at the shadows to see her father, to find help, but her father was gone, disappeared into blackness, with her mother.

Then the shadows parted. And she saw what had made her mother scream.

Macaulay was gagged and blindfolded, a noose around his neck with Didier poised to kick the stool from beneath his feet.

"You've been a bad girl, Christal. . . . How will you take your punishment?" Didier asked, his blue eyes shooting chills down her spine.

"How—how have I been bad?" she choked out, her own gaze glued to Cain, who stood motionless on the stool.

"Perhaps if you'd been a better child I wouldn't have killed your mother and father. Perhaps if you had come into their bedroom sooner, you might have interrupted me, kept me from doing away with them. What have you to say for yourself, young lady?"

"How was I to know you were going to kill them? I awakened. I heard a noise and I came. I wish I could have saved them. I loved them." Her voice was harsh with longing and despair. "I beg of you, don't take Macaulay too. I beg of you. He's all I have now."

"What do I care?" Didier placed his spit-polished shoe on the top rung of the stool, pretending to push it away. "You've been a bad girl, Christabel Van Alen. You could have saved your parents, but you didn't. You didn't come in time. You don't deserve this man. I'm taking him away."

"Don't! I beg of you! I *beg of you!*"

She screamed. The blackness around her rushed in.

Didier pushed away the stool.

"Christal . . . Christal . . ." The voice cut through her crying, a rough, deep murmur that made her weep.

"Don't take him away. I beg of you!"

"It's only a nightmare. Don't be frightened."

She fought with the greatcoat that was wrapped tight around her. Struggling, she opened her eyes and sat up in the cabin's crude bed, clutching at Macaulay as if he were still the outlaw ready to be taken away in chains.

"Don't let him take you away! I'm sorry! Oh, God, I wish I'd gotten there sooner!" She gasped for breath. Tears poured down her cheeks.

"You've had a nightmare. That's all it is, girl. Nothing's going to hurt you. I swear it." Macaulay brushed away the hair that clung to her sweaty brow. "You see? You're here with me. You're safe. No one's going to take me away."

"Make love to me," she whispered against his chest.

"You've had a fright."

"Make love to me," she repeated, holding on to him as if she couldn't quite believe he was there, warm, vibrant, and alive.

"Tell me about the dream—"

He couldn't finish. She rose on her knees and kissed him, demanding he do as she asked. If before she had been a reluctant maiden, now she was a fiery siren. She wanted to forget. She would do anything to forget.

He groaned and stiffened beneath her hands, as if he was afraid of taking advantage of her. But the gentleman in him had his limits. With every soft, needful kiss upon his mouth, his resolve seemed to weaken. Until finally the gentleman disappeared, and in his place was the outlaw Rebel she knew so well, the one with proven carnal appetites, the one who took before asking.

With a moan of satisfaction, she felt him return the kiss, his arms iron-hard with the fury of his desire, his lips rough and devouring, his tongue grinding against her teeth until she shook with the pleasure of his first thrust into her mouth.

"More," she demanded, breathless after they separated.

"Tell me what frightened you."

Her hands trembled as she reached for him. She needed to feel him on top of her, his hard body pounding life into her. "Afterward."

He took her hands captive in his and stopped her roaming, even though his eyes flickered down at her breasts. "Tell me now, Christal. I need to know what frightened you."

"Afterward." She twisted her wrist, frustrated that he was stopping her. Eventually she quieted, and looked into his eyes. He wanted an answer. Slowly she broke down. "Promise me there'll be no other time, no other place but now and here."

His face was grave, etched with concern. "If that's what it takes. Just tell me. For once, trust me, Christal."

"I will," she sobbed. "I will trust you. But now take me and make me forget. Just for a little while."

He nodded, then kissed her, long and deep, moving his lips to her face, her neck, her breasts, as if his passion might take away some of her fear.

"Take me," she whispered, wanting nothing more than to feel his heart beat against hers, feel the cold air racing her blood, his naked body, racing it even faster.

He uttered the words like a vow. "From now on, there is no man but me, no place but this, no past but the one we are going to make right now."

He brought himself up on his arms. She parted her thighs, desperate for him to fill her, to take away the emptiness she felt whenever she thought of life without him.

"I love you, Macaulay. No matter what happens, I love you. I love you," she whispered as he thrust into her, as his lips burned in the hollow of her throat, as his hungry soul assuaged her own.

The half-breed followed the Appaloosa's tracks in the snow, his own paint not nearly so nimble, or so quick. Still, he made progress. He was halfway down the valley, past Dog Tooth Peak and the Meadows. Cirque of the Towers lay ahead, the setting sun blinding him as he headed west.

He'd found her. The girl he'd danced with last night was the girl the man in St. Louis wanted dead.

Dead. He thought upon it, his eyes squinting as he did. He'd never killed such a pretty girl before. There was that woman in Laramie. She'd been pretty too. But not quite as pretty. The blond hair made all the difference. Perhaps because he was dark, he wanted to see what that girl's blond hair looked like twisted in his hand. If he could have, he would have touched her hair last night, but he knew she wouldn't have let him.

He smiled. There was something about killing a woman that made the power of it rush through his veins like the wind rushed through the grass on the prairie. Even as a child he'd thought about killing women.

Stopping the paint, he let it drink in the shallow waters of the Popo Agie. He was going to have to kill the man too. It'd been a stroke of luck finding him. He'd asked about the girl in Camp Brown. Nobody really knew her. But they remembered a man brooding after a girl with her description a few months back. The man's name was Macaulay Cain and they told him he was now some kind of sheriff up by South Pass. It had taken less than a day to find him in Noble. And less than an hour for him to find the girl herself, guilelessly selling dances in a two-bit saloon.

He reached the cabin near dark. There was a horse hobbled in front of it, an Ap. The half-breed felt the blood surge in his head. He became almost light-headed. The thrill was intense and sweet.

He dismounted and huddled beneath a granite overhang. The cabin door was outlined in firelight. He wished he could invade the cabin now, but he knew the cabin door would be bolted from inside. It was a white man's cabin and white men didn't sleep with the doors unbolted. Not if they liked their scalps.

The bolted door was no bother. He could wait. The door would open eventually, and in the meantime it wouldn't be a bitter-cold night. Already the snow was getting too soft to dig into and form a shelter.

He untied a bearskin rolled up behind him and wrapped it around his torso, his eyes seeking the outline of that door. A firelit rectangle. The passage to hell.

He waited.

"Are you warm?"

"Mmm." Christal snuggled deeper into Macaulay's shoulder. The fire crackled and hissed, releasing azure flames that licked at the hearth.

"Tell me about the dream."

She tensed. It was a luxury to lie by the fire in the arms of the man she loved, her body sated by lovemaking, her thoughts quiet and introspective. She was reluctant to see the moment end.

"It was a dream about my parents. A suitor came to call at my parents' house."

"Who was the suitor?"

"You," she answered, locking gazes with him.

His mouth twisted in a bitter smile. "And because I came to call on your parents you woke screaming? I could see some fathers doing that, but not a daughter."

She almost laughed. "No, it wasn't because of that. They approved of you, in fact." She rolled over onto his chest. "I was glad."

He touched her hair, twisting it in his hand. A sensuous gold rope. "So what frightened you?"

Her eyes darkened. Her gaze lowered to the scar circling his neck. She touched it with her finger, surprised that he flinched. "You said they hanged you by mistake. You could have been killed. It was a miracle you survived."

"I had an angel on my shoulder that day, I guess."

She laid her head on his bare chest, reassured by the steady beat of his heart. "If they had killed you, I'd have never found you." She paused, swallowing the emotion that threatened to make her cry. "I dreamed I saw you hanged."

"Were you hoping to save me? Is that why you cried out? Were you too late?"

"Yes," she whispered desolately. "Too late for everything."

He held her, his strong hand running the length of her hair until he squeezed her bare buttock. "Christal, why can't you take me to your parents?"

She shut her eyes, unwilling to remember the details. Not now, while they were so far from everything that might intrude. "They're dead. They died in a fire. I might have saved them, but I didn't get to them in time."

He was silent for a long moment, his hand still stroking her hair. Finally, as if to ease the tension, he whispered, "I love your hair, Christal. It always smells of roses."

"There was an old woman who sold roses on Washington Square. My father bought my mother one every day. Until he died." She released a long, heavy breath. It was difficult even to think of the happy times without the nightmares.

"It's guilt that hurts you, girl, isn't it?"

A tear ran down her cheek, then another and another.

"Tell me the rest."

"It's—terrible." She wept.

"I want to hear it."

"I'm afraid."

"Don't be. You and me in this cabin will change your mind."

"Change my mind, Macaulay." She lifted her tear-streaked face and he kissed her. For the moment, he asked no more questions and she offered no more confessions. They just lay by the fire, his hand petting her hair until, at last, she fell into a deep, dreamless sleep, in his arms, safe even from nightmares.

Chapter Twenty-three

"Where are you going?" Christal whispered as Cain rose naked from the bed and pulled on his jeans. It had to be the middle of the night, the day had come and gone, unnoticed in the darkness of the cabin.

"Something's botherin' the Ap." He spoke as if his thoughts were elsewhere, and his accent slipped into his words.

"Could it be wolves?"

"No . . ." Outside, the Ap gave a nervous nicker. Cain stared at the bolted door, worry creasing his brow. "Maybe a bear. Maybe it's hungry after the long sleep."

"Don't go." She held out her hand. "I saw a grizzly once take down a deer. The thing had it ripped apart before you could blink."

Cain strapped on his guns, his movements clean yet uneasy. "Bolt the door when I'm gone. If it's a bear, it'll smell the food and be in here before I can stop it." He glanced over at the table where the saddlebags lay, still packed.

Christal slipped on her chemise. "Are you going to kill it?" she whispered as he shrugged into a flannel shirt and his fringed jacket.

"Maybe. Let me see what it is."

"Be careful. Please." The last word was like a prayer.

He took up his old Sharps repeater and unbolted the door. With the greatcoat wrapped around her, she ran to the threshold, surprised to see it was dawn again. The entire valley was awash in gray light.

The Ap had wandered near the lake. Even in the dimness she could see its ears pricked forward, its tail up in fear and excitement. It smelled something in the air. Something dangerous.

Cain turned to her, his eyes dark with warning. She closed the door as much as she could without totally blocking her view. If it was a bear, she'd see it charge the door long before it could get to it. In the meantime, Cain would have to endure her surveillance. She wasn't going to let him disappear without knowing what happened to him.

She watched while he stealthily made his way down the lake's embankment. The Ap seemed relieved by his appearance; the animal gave him no trouble at all when he grabbed its mane and led it toward the cabin.

But suddenly there was a disturbance. Branches waved and snapped above an embankment of half-melted snow. Christal held her breath, the scream swallowed by sheer will. Cain didn't move. The Ap danced around, terrified by whatever lay in the brush to their left.

Against her better judgment Christal ran out of the cabin, nearer to Cain. She was thirty yards away when she skidded to a halt, her fear freezing her as much as the snow froze her bare feet.

It was a grizzly. The animal appeared at the top of the embankment, grinding through the brush with all the finesse and serenity of an earthquake. It was thin, its heavy gold-tipped coat hung loose on its frame, its claws were unbelievably long, proof it hadn't killed in weeks, not since snow had blinded the valley and frozen it into a wasteland.

The Ap released a high-pitched whinny, and Cain threw his arms around the horse's face and forced its head down into his chest. If it couldn't see, it wouldn't be as frightened.

"Cain. Cain." She whispered the words. She was surprised he heard her.

"I told you to stay in the goddamned cabin." His words were even and showed no fear.

The grizzly stopped on the embankment and looked straight at Cain.

"Shall I make a diversion, Cain?" she asked in a low, trembling voice.

"No, goddammit." The Ap threw its head. It took all of Cain's strength to hold it down.

"Should I—" Her words choked in her throat.

The bear rose up on its hind legs to a height of more than eight feet. Up on two feet, it looked unnervingly human. Below, Cain struggled with the Ap, clearly taking great pains not to lock stares with the bear.

"Go back to the cabin, Christal." His words were calm and gentle. "Don't look into his eyes, don't make any loud noises. It'll irritate him."

Christal thought he'd gone mad. "Shoot him!" she rasped in a harsh whisper.

"Back yourself up, girl, and get into that cabin. *Do it!*" He held down the Ap's head and looked at her.

She glanced at the towering bear and swallowed another scream. "He's going to attack. I can't leave you. . . ."

"He smelling me, that's all. If he were going to attack, you'd know it. He'd be snarling and angry like a dog. Now he just wants to know what we are, so go back to the goddamned cabin. I need you to do that."

She backed up slowly, her bare feet slipping in the snow and ice. Suddenly she could see the bear was indeed trying to discern Cain's scent. Its nose was up, its huge front paws limp and useless in the air. The Ap gave a weary nicker. Cain tried to muffle it in his chest.

She was in the doorway when the bear finally dropped to all fours. Its eyes were too small for her to read any of its thoughts, but its face was screwed up into an expression of extreme repugnance, as if it had detected a dark, alien stench. But then, the bear turned away. It slid down the other side of the embankment. She, Cain, and the Ap stayed perfectly quiet while they watched it lope up the incline to Warrior Peak.

Christal grabbed the doorway, weak from relief. Cain still stood frozen by the lake until the bear was far enough away that the Ap wouldn't irritate it. She almost laughed with relief when she heard another of the horse's weak nickers.

Then the sky fell on her. At least she thought it was the sky. Something heavy dropped from the roof of the cabin, covering her body with a heavy, muscular weight. Her breath knocked clean from her chest, she lay on the floor of the cabin, gasping for another lungful. And staring at the large shadow of the half-breed.

He drew a gun, kicked her into the cabin, and bolted the door. She scrambled to a corner, leaving Cain's greatcoat in the middle of the floor.

"Why—why are you here?" she panted, every breath giving her pain and renewed terror. "What do you want?"

"Another dance."

He laughed, and the sound sent stabs of fear through her heart.

His shadow fell on her. She huddled into a ball. Doomed, she knew what he was going to say before he said it.

"A man in St. Louis told me to find you. He paid me gold." He knelt and touched her hair as if he'd waited for a long time to do it.

"My uncle." Her words were hardly a whimper. Terror choked her.

"I don't know who he is to you, but he paid me to kill you. So I'll kill you."

"It's you who'll be killed," she said, somehow summoning the courage. She couldn't let this man kill her and destroy whatever happiness she would have with Cain. "The man outside will kill you if you hurt me. I've seen him kill before. He won't let you live."

"He did not kill the bear."

The half-breed's expression, or lack of expression, froze her. The bear had more humanity than he did. She could see the man had no thoughts other than his goal, however perverse that goal might be.

"The—the bear went away," she stammered. "If you leave here and leave me unharmed, Cain will let you go too." She stared at him, desperate to find some compassion in his eyes.

"I waited all night for the cabin door to open. When I saw the bear, I was glad. I'm not afraid of the bear. I'm not afraid of *him*." He nodded toward the door.

Huddled in the corner, she looked up at him. She'd forgotten how tall he was. How muscular. He was like the grizzly in every respect, but there was malice in his eyes, whereas the grizzly knew none.

"The bear went away. You must go too. Save yourself," she whispered, her heart hammering against her chest.

"Christal! Open the door! Why have you locked it?" Cain called angrily from outside.

"Help—" Her answer was muffled by the half-breed's filthy palm. He stared down at her a long time, his eyes captured for some reason by her hair.

"Goddammit, open the door, Christal!"

She could hear Cain's fury now. And the edge in his voice that said he was worried.

"Do not speak." The half-breed put a finger to his lips.

She watched the half-breed while he stared entranced by her hair. It was the end of the line. Her uncle had caught her and won. The half-breed would kill her, and as soon as Cain came through the door, the half-breed would kill him too.

"Don't do this," she whispered, her eyes imploring him for mercy.

The half-breed smiled. He had crooked yellow bottom teeth. "What choice do I have? You think he'll let me take you away?"

Helplessly, she thought of all the times Cain had protected her. Even when she thought he was an outlaw, he'd always protected her. He didn't deserve to die for her now. For all that he'd done, she owed him a life. If her end had come, then so be it, she would instead fight for his.

She grabbed for the pistol, suddenly leaping to her feet, fighting like a wildcat. Shock crossed the half-breed's face. He lost his grip on the gun. She pointed it at him, but he hit her and she fell against the wall, stunned. He grabbed the gun. Dominant once more, he stared down at her while she lay panting in the corner, defeated.

Then she realized Cain had stopped shouting. It was artificially quiet. Ominous.

The half-breed took her wrist and dragged her to her feet. He ran his dirty fingers through her hair. His rancid smell burned through her nostrils. Her gaze searched every corner of the cabin for a weapon, but there was nothing.

"I'm going to take your hair with me."

The idea shot icy fear through her. "A hank of hair is not much company." She forced the panic from her voice. "Wouldn't—wouldn't you like the whole—the entire woman to come with you? Why, I—I can cook for you—" She groped for something more to entice him. "I—I can even keep you warm at night. You see—I've run with outlaws before. Why—I could run with you."

He looked down at her. She wasn't sure but she thought she finally saw the mortal flash of emotion in his terrible dark eyes.

"You lie to me. You know you won't stay with me and give me comfort. You'll run the first chance. Then I'll have nothing."

Bewilderment set in. She hadn't expected his reaction. "No, no . . . I would stay. I would owe you for my lover's life."

"When we leave this cabin your lover will try to kill me. Then I will kill him. I won't spare his life."

She closed her eyes, weak with terror. "Unbolt the door. Let me talk to him. I'll tell him I want to go with you. That I met you at Faulty's."

He stared at her for a long moment, then he placed the pistol to her head. "Open the door."

She slid back the bolt, her heart near to bursting.

The half-breed walked her out, the barrel of the pistol resting at her temple, a hair's breadth from firing.

"I'm taking her with me!" the half-breed called out to the wilderness.

They turned full circle. Cain was nowhere to be found. The silence was chilling.

He poked her in the head with the pistol. "Call him."

"Cain!" she yelled. The half-breed poked her again. Her eyes teared from the pain in her temple.

"Let her go!"

The voice came from a ledge in the rock high above them. She looked up and saw Cain, his rifle trained on the half-breed.

"Tell him," the half-breed prompted.

"I'm going with him, Cain." Tears streamed down her cheeks and this time she wasn't sure it had anything to do with the bruising pain of the pistol barrel. "I have to. He's come to get me."

"Let her go or I'll shoot you dead," Cain growled to the half-breed.

The half-breed laughed. He pulled her to him, jamming his forearm underneath her chin and putting her in a headlock. "You shoot me, you shoot her too."

"My aim's not that bad. Let her go."

He poked her temple again with the iron shaft of the pistol. She visibly winced.

Then a shot rang out.

The half-breed's arms fell away from her like a puppet's. She spun around and watched him fall back in the snow. There was no blood. Just a small black hole in his forehead where the bullet had entered.

Cain loped down from the granite face of the mountain.

Sick and frightened, still unable to accept what the half-breed's presence meant, she silently watched as Cain leaned down toward the body.

"He's an Indian, isn't he?" she asked.

Cain turned grim. "The moccasins are Cherokee, but he's not Cherokee."

"How do you know?"

"Because I know this man. He's a bounty hunter. Every lawman in the territory knows him."

She froze. The truth would have to be out now. And in the worst set of circumstances.

Aching to stop him, she watched Cain begin to remove a piece of paper that stuck out from the half-breed's vest. It had one small drop of blood on it, old and dark. Someone else's.

"Don't look at the paper." She couldn't hide the fear in her voice. Desperately she tried to think of the way to explain.

"You know what the paper says?"

She nodded, unable to look at him.

He gazed at the body. "So he was coming here for you." It was not a question.

"My—my uncle sent him. He told me." In despair, she turned away from him. The end of the line had come.

Cain slowly withdrew the paper from the half-breed's dirty vest. As he read it, his face turned hard and pale, as if he was battling some internal war.

There was not much more she could tell him. He knew everything now, except the part about Didier, and that she would have to convince him of, but with no other evidence than her character and her pleas, she didn't know if she could.

"Is this true?" His words were harsh, choked. He smoothed the wanted poster with his hand.

She looked at it, damned by the sketch of her face and the outline of the rose-shaped scar, damned by the vicious crimes of which it accused her.

"Is this true? That you were in an asylum for three years?"

She couldn't meet his eyes. Her answer was barely a croak. "Yes."

"An asylum for the criminally insane?"

"Yes."

The silence was morbid. A nightmare. More deafening than a roar.

"Were you . . . treated well there?"

"My family connections are very good. I was treated as well

as one could expect." She finally broke down. "I didn't do it, Cain. I didn't. My uncle—my uncle blamed me for his crimes, and they convicted me falsely—"

She found the courage to look at him. He studied the paper in silence, as if somehow it might explain what had happened to her parents better than she could.

"Please believe me. You've got to believe me."

He stared at the wanted poster as if he couldn't take his eyes from it. "This explains so much—your odd behavior at Falling Water—your fear of the law—your dream—your guilt . . ."

"I didn't do it. Oh, God, you've got to see I loved my parents. It's my uncle who did it. Please, please believe me. I'm not insane." A sob caught in her throat.

He took a long time to speak. "It's all right, Christal. If you tell me you didn't do this, I'll believe you." His voice lowered to a hard whisper. "I love you. I've got to believe you. I *will* believe you."

"But you won't even look at me."

"Just give me the proof of your innocence. That's all I need."

"I'm innocent. Or else why would my uncle send this man here to kill me?"

"He's a bounty hunter. For all I know he could have come here just to collect the reward on this wanted poster." He seemed to force his gaze to meet hers; his eyes remained shuttered. "Tell me more about the asylum—about why they put you there."

"It was a compromise to jail. My uncle made everyone believe he was helping me." She looked down at her hand and the cursed rose branded into her palm. "This scar proved that I was in the room when my parents died. Because of the trauma of seeing the crime, I didn't remember anything of that night until four years ago. Then I remembered that Didier was the one who killed them . . . and locked me in the flaming room to die also. . . ."

"There must be evidence—"

"If there were evidence, I would have found justice and I

wouldn't be running. There is no evidence but my word." She kept her eyes lowered, hiding the pain. "I know what you're thinking. You're thinking I could indeed be insane. My memory of the truth could be nothing more than a dream I had one night, absolving me of my guilt and pinning it on my uncle." Silent tears ran down her cheeks. "I don't know what else to tell you. I believe I'm innocent, so much so that I've been saving for years to hire a detective to find my uncle and prove I am. But maybe I am insane. Maybe my memory is all wrong and I just can't accept . . . what I've done."

"No!" He raked his hand through his hair. "You didn't commit this crime." He balled up the paper and threw it on the ground. "I'll believe you and there will be no more talk like this."

"If you believe me, let me see it in your eyes." Her voice was filled with anguish.

He didn't look at her.

Slowly he answered, his voice low and gutteral, like a wounded animal's. "I went through hell during the war believing in right and wrong. In the end, everything got twisted. I can't let everything get twisted again. We've got to prove your innocence."

"And if you cannot?"

He looked at her, the emotion in his eyes unfathomable. "The decision to go to war is simple. The result is not. But if we're to have a future, you must return to New York and face the charges. We'll find a way to prove your innocence. We'll find your uncle." He finally touched her, taking her in his arms. "Will you return to New York with me?"

"Yes," she whispered, her heart filling with despair. He was doing everything she knew he would. There was no way to prove her innocence without Didier's confession and getting that was unlikely, if not impossible. She would rot in Park View for the rest of her days or, if the judge decided to punish her for her escape, be hanged. Either way, the damage was done. She'd lost him. He'd never prove her innocence and until that innocence could be proven, she never have him again.

"I wish you were an outlaw, Cain, do you know that?" she said bleakly. "I wish you really had been a member of Kineson's gang, and I wished we'd escaped that night I begged you to."

"If you didn't do this terrible thing, Christal, we'll find a way to prove it."

"Then let's return to Noble. You can wire New York and send for a marshal to take me there."

"I'll take you there."

"No." She stood her ground. "You won't come with me. There's nothing you can do. I couldn't bear to have you see me—locked up—" She lost her voice for a moment. "If I'm freed, I'll come back to you. If not. . . ." She didn't finish. There was no point. She would not come back. Her sister, Alana, had fought for her freedom for years. It was a futile effort to renew the battle, but she would for his sake. Even though this time she might be truly driven insane.

"I'll have someone in Noble in a couple of weeks to take us to New York. Argue if you must, but I'm going with you to face the charges. Get your things. We'll need to return to town." He glanced at the dead half-breed. "There's no point staying here any longer."

She nodded. Reality had come and found them anyway. She shivered, finally realizing how cold she was in just her shift.

Cain saddled the Ap while she dressed. She walked out of the cabin with the bolt of sky-blue wool clutched to her chest.

He looked at her, puzzlement in his eyes, as if he wondered why she still cared about the fabric.

"I'll make a dress while we wait for the marshals." It was the only answer she offered.

He helped her mount. They rode out of the valley, the mountains' blue icy peaks beckoning behind her, hinting of unreachable, mythical places.

Her thoughts were not so lofty and faraway. She held on to Macaulay's back and thought of the gown she would fashion from the sky-blue wool. If she could prove her innocence, she wanted it to be her wedding gown. If she could not, whether she died by the hangman or aged infirmity, at least the gown would be done.

She drew closer to Macaulay and placed her scarred palm on her throat. Her skin was smooth, warm, undamaged. It heartened her. Perhaps there was still hope.

Chapter Twenty-four

The gentleman who arrived in Noble on the Overland Express coach was the subject of everyone's gossip. It was no secret he was searching for Christal. He went into Faulty's, his dignified manner at odds with the rough-and-tumble atmosphere of a saloon, and he asked about a blond girl with a rose-shaped scar burned into her palm.

Christal and Cain had been back from the mountains for two weeks. A winter storm delayed the telegraph, which, in the end, had to be sent from Fort Washakie. Jericho had ridden out with the message. He was due to arrive any day, U.S. Marshals in tow.

The stranger's appearance temporarily diverted the townfolk from the fact that Christal was being held at the town jail waiting for marshals to come and take her away. Some speculated she was wanted elsewhere and that the sheriff had discovered her crimes, while others thought the trouble began when Sheriff Cain took her to the undisclosed cabin in the mountains. Everyone knew he was in love with her. Something tormented him. He had grief in his eyes. The lights in the jail burned late into the night.

Now they had a mysterious stranger to contend with. Faulty knew right away the man wasn't one of the awaited U.S. Marshals. For one thing, the stranger's clothes were much too fine for a marshal. For another, U.S. Marshals did not arrive by

Overland Express stagecoaches, especially when Overland Express had no station in Noble.

"She's over at the jail, sir. The sheriff's watchin' her," Faulty had been quick to volunteer.

The man nodded. He offered no thanks, as if *thank you* were two words rather foreign to him.

"There's a stranger in town asking for Christal, Sheriff. Just saw him go into the saloon." Jan Peterson stood in front of the smithy's, shivering in his shirt sleeves.

Cain straightened and dropped the Ap's hoof, the one he'd wanted the smithy to look at. "Who is he? What does he look like?"

"He looks powerful and rich. I wouldn't want to cross him."

Cain eyed the quiet street up and down as if looking for others. There wasn't a soul in sight. The spring mud was more than even a cowpony could handle. The coach must have let off passengers down the road at Delaney's.

Without a parting word, Cain left the smithy's and walked to the jail. Jan watched him go, sensing the unease in the man's every step.

"Christal, girl, there's someone in town to see you." Cain stepped into the jailhouse. Christal sat at the table, blanketed in sky-blue wool. The dress was almost complete.

"What's your uncle look like, girl?" He flashed a tense expression.

"He's—"

"He's shorter, fatter, and older than I am."

Cain whirled around.

Christal gasped at the stranger standing at the threshold of the door. He filled the frame with his tall, lithe form. She had never seen him before, but she would never forget him. He was ungodly handsome, with dark flashing eyes and nearly black hair that was slicked back with macassar oil. He entered the jail stiffly, using a black ebony walking stick with every step.

"What's your business here?" Cain crossed his arms over

his chest and moved in front of Christal. Distrust darkened his features.

"It's Christabel Van Alen I've come for." The man paused by the table, as if respecting Cain's need for distance. There was a slight accent to his words. His roots were Irish.

"Do you know this man, Christal?" Cain glanced behind him, clearly uneasy.

She shook her head, but she didn't take her eyes from the stranger. He'd captured her, somehow.

"She doesn't recognize me, because we've never met," the stranger said, "but I recognize her. She looks like her sister, Alana . . . my wife."

"Oh my God." Christal sat down in her chair, shock running through her body. She couldn't take her eyes from the stranger. He was her brother-in-law. Her sister's husband. Their marriage had been hasty and secretive, Christal had certainly not had the freedom to attend the wedding. She'd never met the man her sister had fallen in love with. She only knew he was an Irisher of the name Trevor Sheridan and that Alana loved him as no other. Every time Alana had spoken of her new husband, though their exchanges had been pitifully brief in the asylum, Christal had seen the passion in her eyes for him, the man who stood before her now.

"How is my sister, Mr. Sheridan?" She couldn't hide the excitement in her voice. "Is she fine? What has she done all these years?"

"The only thing she has done, Christal, is pine for you." The man took a step toward her, but Cain blocked his path.

The two men eyed each other for a long time. Anger flared in Sheridan's eyes, but then he seemed to see something in Cain that gave him pause. He noted Cain's unyielding, protective stance, then glanced at her, studying every detail of her appearance from her unbound hair and cheap, threadbare gown, to her slim nose and full mouth, each an exact replica of her sister's.

Enlightened somehow about their relationship, Sheridan stepped back and took a seat at the table, his gold-tipped walking stick laid across his thighs. "Where do we go from here, Sheriff? I must take this girl back to New York."

"Return to New York alone. I'll be the one to bring her there."

"Let him take me back, Cain." Christal turned to Sheridan. "Please tell me about Alana. How is she? Has she had—?"

"She couldn't accompany me, Christal, although it almost killed her for me to be leaving her behind." The man's accent slipped in again. Christal could understand how her sister had fallen in love with him. He was dark, even a little terrifying, but there was something fine and honest about him, something in his slight Irish accent, in the way he gave Cain the respect he was due. "She's with child. Our third."

Her mouth opened in awe. "Nieces or nephews?"

"Two nephews. This last one we hope to be a girl. I won't know until I return. Alana was due two weeks ago. I've been gone a very long time on this trip."

"How did you find me?" She couldn't begin to utter all the questions that filled her mind.

"Alana and I have been looking for you for all the years you've been gone. Then last fall, I had a long talk with an old friend of mine named Terence Scott. His mother was from Galway, as I was. He's become rich transporting payrolls and passengers in the territories. The detectives I hired led me to believe you might be out west. I told Terence years ago to let me know if ever he might help me. Last fall he told me of a girl involved in the Overland kidnapping. She disappeared before he could compensate her. It was very strange. Her description fit you. I had no choice but to find this girl. If I hadn't gone, I know my wife would have, despite the child growing within her. Alana has never given up hope of finding you, Christal."

"And you did find me," she whispered in amazement. She reached to him, wanting to touch the hand of the man who was her only contact with her sister. She scowled at Cain, who was in the way. "Let me talk with my brother-in-law, he's come so far!"

"No." Cain's face brooked no rebellion. "You've never seen

this man before, Christal. If Didier sent him, he could have come with the same purpose as the half-breed had."

"He's married to my sister!" she exclaimed, surprised at his distrust.

"You didn't attend the wedding. This man could be lying. He could be telling you these things, meanwhile waiting to get you alone. Waiting to kill you." His voice lowered. "You want me to believe in your innocence, then this is the only course."

She looked at Sheridan and could not bring herself to believe he was anyone but who he said he was.

But there was no convincing Cain, though she made one last effort.

"Surely, Mr. Sheridan, you can convince us of who you are. You must know details of Alana's and my childhood." She looked at the Irisher expectantly.

Sheridan smiled a dark, enticing smile that she knew had entranced her sister. "I could tell many things about your childhood, but nothing that Baldwin Didier couldn't have found out in the years he spent with you and your sister. I'm afraid the only proof I can offer is that Alana is indeed my wife, but to speak publicly of our intimacies, even with you, Christal, her sister, would be too indelicate."

"Return to New York, Sheridan, if that's who you really are. Christal and I will be arriving right after you. We're going to get her a new trial. She'll be acquitted."

Sheridan stared at Cain once more. His smile became more open. "I do believe, sir, that between us, we just might be able to acquit this girl."

Cain's face hardened. He didn't seem as optimistic. "I mean to see it done. So if you're who you say you are, you'll leave Noble right now and not show your face to us again until this girl embraces her sister. Because only when Christal's sister acknowledges you as her husband, will I ever trust you."

Sheridan nodded. "I understand. I know you've been through a lot with her. Terence Scott told me a man named Cain ran with the Kineson gang and saved everyone on the stage. I'm indebted to you, sir, and I have faith you'll deliver

Christal to her sister safely, but still I ask you to let me take her now. I promised her sister that I'd find her. Now that I have, don't deny me the satisfaction of bringing her home."

"I'll be the one to take her to Alana Van Alen. And no one else."

The two men stared at each other, locked in a battle of iron wills. At last, Sheridan began to relent. There was something in Cain he seemed to respect. Perhaps it was only Cain's implacable need to be the one to protect Christal. Nonetheless, it seemed to impress Sheridan.

"I have only one thing to say before I leave to meet you in New York," the Irisher said.

"And what is that?" Cain didn't soften one bit.

"Christal's sister's name is no longer Alana Van Alen. She is Alana Sheridan now. Mrs. Trevor Sheridan in her circles."

Cain paused, as if Sheridan's comment almost made him believe him. "I'll remember that when we meet again."

Sheridan gazed at Christal. He bowed and flashed his dark eyes.

With a cry dying in her throat, she watched him leave the jail.

"Oh, I know he was my brother-in-law! I think we should have trusted him! Cain, why didn't you let him talk more—I wanted to hear more about Alana and the babies. My nephews," she whispered reverently, still unable to believe she was somebody's aunt.

"I wasn't going to take the chance. If he's who he says he is, you'll see him at your sister's side when the train pulls into Manhattan."

She looked at him. There were lines worked deep into his cheeks. She couldn't remember him looking so tired, so worried. "Don't be afraid for me, my love. I'm no longer afraid. What's going to happen will happen." She locked gazes with him. She had never told him how useless the appeal was. He would find out the hopelessness of her case soon enough. In the meantime, she had found some happiness in his arms, late at night when he was angry at the world, but gentle with her.

He tore his gaze away, then walked to the door to lock it.

She watched, knowing he was hurting with every protective gesture he made. He couldn't protect her forever and that was what was eating at him.

"It's out of our hands."

"No." He walked to her and paused, inches away. His voice was raspy and full of emotion. "I'll fight to the death to see you free, you know it, girl."

"But it's like the war, Cain. You just may not win."

His hand cupped the back of her head. He kissed her, his mouth hard and angry as if somehow he could purge his frustration with the violent possession of her mouth.

"This is just like the war," he groaned, burying his face in her hair. "If I can't see you freed then there's no right—no wrong—no end."

She brought his head down to hers and placed her lips softly on his mouth. "I thought once I would have you run from this, as I've done all these years, but time for running is past, and you, my love, are not a man to run away. If you found nothing in that war, you found your honor and that is why I love you."

"Christal," he groaned, his hand rough, possessively cupped over her breast as if she were his and he was suddenly desperately afraid he would lose her.

She whispered, "There is an end, my love. New York will be the end. But I wish you wouldn't come with me. Remember me now, like this. Oh, God, I can't bear to have you see me otherwise . . ."

She could no longer speak. His lovemaking became too fierce. It was as if he was seeking catharsis for an old and deep pain. He whispered her name only one other time. Just before he found his peace. Just before she felt her cheek damp with her own tears.

Chapter Twenty-five

We have shared the incommunicable experience of war.
We felt—we still feel—the passion of life to its top . . .
OLIVER WENDELL HOLMES

The marshals were late. Jericho had left weeks ago and still there was no word on his whereabouts.

Meanwhile, springtime dripped all over town and ran in little rivulets out to the prairie, feeding the tender shoots of green that thrust up bravely through the snow. From the back window of Macaulay's bedroom Christal watched the patches of snow diminish, every day taking on a new and lesser shape, like clouds after a thunderstorm. But the promise of spring didn't cheer her. It didn't stop destiny. If anything, the better weather should have spurred it on. But still the marshals did not arrive.

"Should you ride out and wire them?" she asked Macaulay, turning away from the window.

He stared at her from a chair, his arms crossed, his legs stretched out, feigning an indolence she knew he did not feel.

"They'll come eventually," he said, a grim cast to his mouth.

"Something might have happened to Jericho. I worry about Ivy all alone at the homestead."

"I'll go out there this afternoon."

"Take me with you." She looked at him, hope in her eyes. What wouldn't she give for a ride out on the prairie. One last moment of strong winds, wide sky, and freedom.

"I won't leave you here. We'll go in an hour." He stood and

stared at the bed. The blue dress was carefully laid out on it. "You finished the dress. Why aren't you wearing it?"

"I'm saving it for a happy occasion."

He glanced at her, his cold eyes filled with anger and pain, like those of a wolf caught in a trap. "You'll wear it soon. I promise, girl."

She only smiled, hoping the sadness wouldn't show.

Ivy nearly wept when they showed up at the homestead. She was worried sick about Jericho, and though the shack was well supplied, it was not nearly as comfortable as the room in the saloon. Without Jericho, Ivy was having a difficult time managing.

Ivy and Christal drove the mule cart while Cain, on the Ap, scouted the driest path ahead. By evening they rolled into Noble, the mule covered with as much mud as seemed to lie at their feet.

The smithy was ready to take the wagon and the animals, then he gave Cain a short message that caused Cain to turn his head toward the jailhouse.

There were five horses tethered at the rail. The marshals had arrived.

"C'mon, darlin'. It's time." Cain wrapped his arm around Christal's waist while Ivy stared at the marshals' horses, unable to hide the worry in her eyes.

Christal walked with him along the boardwalk as if they were just a couple taking a stroll. Cain felt strong and sure beside her. She made a point not to look at his eyes.

"Are you sleeping?"

Christal shook her head and continued to look out the train window. They'd ridden south and caught the Union Pacific at Addentown, and now they bulleted east across the plains. Flat, snow-patched monotony.

"You don't ever seem to sleep anymore, girl. You've got to be tired." Cain shifted in his seat. The car was crowded with people. Two women nursed their babies by the stove while strings of woolen laundry dried above their heads. In the coldest corner Rollins and some other marshals she'd never seen before played cards on the wooden benches with the other men. The car generally stank of cigar smoke and wet sheep ready for the shears.

Macaulay and Christal sat apart from the rest of the people in the car. They had quiet conversations broken only when Christal would lapse into slumber and loll her head on Cain's chest. Everyone seemed to leave them alone, as if knowing that to intrude upon them was to intrude upon lovers.

"Where do you think he is right now?" Christal whispered, gazing sightlessly out the window to the sun-flooded grassland.

"Your uncle?"

"Yes."

"I don't know."

"He could be anywhere. Anywhere at all."

"I'll find him. I've got every man who owes me a favor asking around for him. With me and your brother-in-law looking, it won't take long."

She didn't answer. She just snuggled closer and closed her eyes, letting the clackety-clack sound of the train soothe her tired body and weary heart.

The Fairleigh Hotel was packed that Wednesday night with a whole trainload of wealthy passengers from Pittsburgh. There wasn't a room to spare but when one certain gentleman entered the establishment, his suite seemed to appear on the register as if from nowhere, causing no small amount of dismay and dissatisfaction among the persons milling in the lobby on the slim chance a registered guest might not appear.

The gentleman had an edge the others did not. He was regular as clockwork, appearing at the Fairleigh on the third of every month, a paying guest come good times and bad, snow and sunshine. So he was treated like a king.

Thus, the gentleman's luggage, which consisted of strange and numerous pieces, was hefted into the arms of no fewer than three bellboys and taken to his room, and the gentleman, with nothing but leisure time on his hands, took to the bar, as if longing for the comfort of the bartender's famous rum punch.

The gentleman commented to the man next to him as he eased his large girth behind the table, "It's certainly been too long since I've been in such elegance."

"Where have you been traveling?" the other man asked.

"Oh, here and there and everywhere. Wyoming Territory mostly."

If the man were a dog, his ears would have pricked up. "Wyoming, you say? I suppose you've seen just about all of it the way you travel. Name's Didier, Baldwin Didier, of New York."

The gentleman smiled, always ready to make an acquaintance, and thus a potential customer. "Very good to meet you, sir. And I am Henry Glassie of the Paterson Furniture Company, Paterson, New Jersey. That makes us practically brothers way out here."

"So it does, so it does." Didier stood and neatly smoothed down his well-cut Vandyke. "May I?" He gestured to the chair at the salesman's table.

"Certainly. I need a good conversation. On this trip, I've seen one too many corrupt Indian agents and one too many sad redmen to shun jovial company. What do you do, Didier?"

"Right now, I'm looking for someone. In Wyoming actually. Perhaps you may help me. It's my niece. I fear she's come to a bad end. It's been almost four years since she's been gone and I find myself desperate in my search for her."

Mr. Glassie put down his drink. "What a tragedy. How did she end up way out there?"

"Ran away."

"Eloped?"

Didier smiled. He didn't quite give an answer.

Henry Glassie shook his head as if not quite able to understand the impetuosities of youth, at least, impetuosities that didn't concern buying furniture.

"If you wouldn't mind my scouring your mind. Any news at all would be most appreciated."

"I'd be happy to oblige. What does your niece look like?"

Didier rubbed his palm. "She's very pretty, fair, about twenty years old. Blue eyes. The color of the sky."

Glassie grew solemn. "There was a girl who fit that description I met once. But if her eyes were blue, I didn't notice. They were too filled with sadness and grief."

"My niece is quite distinctive. Beyond her beauty, she possesses a unique mark." He began to draw concentric circles into the palm of his right hand, as if demonstrating. "Christal has a scar, a most unusual scar on the palm of her right hand, in the shape of a rose."

Mr. Glassie sat straight up. "Christal did you say her name was?"

"Yes, Christabel Van Alen. Have you seen her?"

"I am most sorry to tell you, sir, she has lost her husband. She was wearing weeds when we met."

Didier's chilling eyes grew wide in wonder. "Are you certain it was her?"

"Indeed. The woman I know was named Christal and she had the scar. I only saw it once, that night we had dinner in Camp Brown, but it was there, right on her palm as you describe."

"I must go to her." Didier stood, concern too dramatic and deep in his expression to be totally genuine. It was the first pang of uneasiness Mr. Glassie felt. "You say you saw her at a place called Camp Brown? Where is this Camp Brown? How may I get to it? It's of the most dire urgency. I cannot wait another minute."

"My good man, there's no hurry. Unfortunately, your dear niece's fate has already been decided."

"What are you talking about?" Didier snapped.

"The papers. The *St. Louis Chronicle*. Haven't you read today's headlines?"

"Where can I get a paper?" Didier snapped.

"Why, I have one right here." Glassie handed him the one folded inside his suit breast pocket.

Mr. Henry Glassie had seen a lot of things in his travels, he'd even been kidnapped by an outlaw gang; but he had never seen a man's face drain completely of all blood, not even a man ready for the hangman. "Are you all right, man?" he asked suspiciously.

Didier threw the paper onto the table. The headlines blared:

> *Missing Heiress Found!* Christabel Van Alen to face charges in New York—Trevor Sheridan vows millions for her defense!

Mr. Glassie cleared his throat. "Of course, this is all quite a shock. Anyone who's met the poor child knows she must be falsely accused. When I knew her, she was a most respectable woman. The charges drawn against her cannot be true. I'll never believe them. But not to worry, my good man. If the Sheridan fortune can't resolve this matter in the girl's favor, then nothing can help her."

"I've got to go." Didier suddenly looked around the bar as if any moment he might meet someone he knew and dreaded. Glassie wondered who it might be.

"But you're not going to meet your niece? You search for her for four years then flee the moment she's due to arrive?"

"What are you talking about?" The concern was leaking out of his voice, quickly being replaced with a strange anger.

"The paper. You didn't finish reading the article. The Union Pacific pulls in tomorrow. Your niece will be on it, headed to New York."

Glassie wasn't sure, but he read joy all over Didier's face. It could be joy over seeing a long-lost niece, but suddenly he doubted it.

"Of course, I must see her." A smile cracked Didier's face. Glassie thought the sight decidedly unpleasant.

The men stood, a sudden chill between them. Glassie

dropped a twenty-five-cent piece down on the table, not offer-
ing to buy the other man's drink as he might have done if the
uneasiness were gone from his gut. "Good night to you, sir. I
wish you luck in your rendezvous with your niece."

"Thank you." Didier's eyes were like the ice off a pond.

Henry Glassie left the bar. Suddenly all he wanted to do
was warm himself by the stove.

Chapter Twenty-six

The train stop in St. Louis was to take over two hours. Passengers were invited to step outside and partake of the fresh, cold spring air, or perhaps a rum punch at the famous Fairleigh Hotel.

Christal was offered no such luxury. She remained in the custody of the marshals in the stuffy car, content simply to doze against Cain's chest while he read the St. Louis newspaper.

They were on their way in no time, the train lurching and chugging to a start while steam billowed across the muddy, torn-apart station. It had just been built and it was already under construction to be expanded. The great wild West was soon to be tamed.

Hours passed as they railed along more open prairie, the ground broken more and more often with farmland and trees. Christal was fast asleep when the familiar voice rang in her ears.

"My good man! And Mrs. Smith—or should I say Miss Van Alen! How wonderful it is to make your acquaintance again! I have thought of you both often! Often!"

Christal opened her eyes. It wasn't a dream, it was true. Mr. Henry Glassie was standing before them, looking as dapper as when he'd first boarded the Overland Express.

"Glassie," Cain greeted, standing. "What brings you here? You board at St. Louis?"

"I did indeed. I'm headed back to Paterson to have a meeting with the company president. Sales have been good, you know—quite delightful, actually. Yet I was saddened to read about Miss Christal's circumstances. How have you been, Miss Van Alen?"

"I'm holding up and getting good at it, as you might guess, especially given the circumstances of our last meeting." Christal wavered a smile.

Henry Glassie nodded in sympathy. "Never fear, Miss Van Alen. I see you've the famous lawman Macaulay Cain behind you. I've heard much about him since our days in Falling Water and all of it is impressive. I've no doubt you will be fully vindicated, my girl."

Christal gave him a tremulous smile. She figured Glassie knew the whole story by now. There was talk that she was in the papers, but she hadn't had the heart to read the ones brought aboard.

"I was just taking a walk. My berth is in the front of the train and I said to myself, 'Glassie, old boy, it's time for you to seek out your old friends.' I must say, Miss Van Alen, you have me surprised. I thought I'd find you with your uncle."

Christal's blood froze. She felt Cain stiffen. "What did you say, Mr. Glassie? Have you seen my uncle?"

"Baldwin Didier was his name. A nice enough fellow. Don't care for his eyes though. I met him at the bar in the Fairleigh. He was beside himself to find you. I thought he'd be aboard."

Christal's hand went to her throat as if for protection. Her words were choked and forced. "You met my uncle in the Fairleigh—back in St. Louis—where we just stopped?"

"He's not your uncle, is he, child?" Glassie's plump, fatherly face shadowed with doubt. "I thought there was something untrustworthy about the gent. I'm glad I came aboard so I could tell you about him."

"He is my uncle, Mr. Glassie, but he is not to be trusted. He is the one who committed the crimes of which I am accused. I fear he wants me dead."

Mr. Glassie looked deeply troubled. "It was I who pointed out to him that you were to be on the train. I hope I haven't endangered you, but when he asked if I'd ever seen a woman such as yourself in the territory, I fear I wasn't thinking. I figured his concern was real. At least I thought so for a while."

"Have you see him on the train?" Cain broke in. Christal looked at him, surprised by the blood lust in his eyes.

"I have not. Perhaps he didn't board after all."

"Or perhaps he's in disguise." Cain turned to her. "Christal, you're the only one who knows what he looks like. We'll have to go through the train person by person. We've got to make sure he's not aboard."

"Let me help. I feel responsible to a degree. If I had only kept my mouth closed, the train might have come and gone without this man seeing Christal's schedule in the papers."

"Fine." Cain nodded behind him. "You check out the baggage car. The men, Christal, and I will walk forward and check out all the passengers. If it's all clear, we can rest easy until we stop again. If not, we have enough men to take care of it."

Mr. Glassie rolled back the door to the baggage car. He stood between the cars, the ground rushing below him, the wind whistling in his ears. All that stood between him and disaster was a tiny platform with a thin railing that couldn't have held back a child let alone his generous girth should he slip. He found it a relief to enter the baggage compartment.

There was not much room to walk. Canvas sacks stamped *U.S. Mail* were piled high in one corner. Along the sides, row after row of wooden boxes marked in Chinese filled the compartment. Excelsior peeked out of many of them, a clue that they contained porcelain imports taking the short route across the prairie from San Francisco. The passengers' baggage filled in wherever there was free space—except in one corner where a leak in the roof constantly dripped melting snow. The only other baggage of note was a fine leather trunk or two, but the rest of the compartment was filled with common wicker baskets and large raggedy portmanteaus that had clearly belonged to ancestors.

Glassie sighed. There was no one here. He turned to go back to the forward cabin.

He never saw the billy club come down on his head.

"There doesn't seem to be anyone on this train who could be this girl's uncle," Rollins whispered to Cain. He peeked at Christal, who was nervously surveying the farthest-forward cabin. "We've checked the entire train out. I think it's safe to return to our car. When we stop at Abbeville, I'll make sure every new passenger passes inspection."

Cain glanced at Christal. He nodded.

Rollins stared at Christal too. "You know, Cain, they say—"

"I don't care what they say. She didn't do it." Cain's whisper was like a hiss of steam.

"But what if she did? What if this story about her uncle is just fiction—a diversion so she can find an escape?"

Rollins stepped back from the arctic blast of Cain's gaze. "I'm going to tell you only once: *She didn't do it.*" Cain resumed his detached manner. "Besides, Henry Glassie spoke to her uncle. If the man doesn't exist, how could Glassie have seen him?"

"Perhaps the uncle was trying to find her. If she escaped from an asylum—" Cain gave him another icy stare, but Rollins continued bravely, "She *did* escape from an asylum, you can't dispute that, and her uncle could have been genuinely worried about her welfare and gone to look for her. Now that she's found, he's headed back to New York to be with the rest of the family." Rollins softened. He nodded to Cain with commiseration. "She's a beautiful girl, Cain. A real heartbreaker. Anyone could understand your falling in love with her. But, you know, she could be a little tetched. She's been through a lot—seen her parents die in a fire, been put into an asylum— God only knows what she went through in there—maybe these stories about her uncle are just delusions."

"When we get to New York, I will discuss things with her sister and brother-in-law. They will confirm her story."

"No one else in the family has ever spoken up about Baldwin Didier. I wired New York to get the story before we came to Noble. It's true, Cain. I just can't stand to see you—"

"There was a half-breed sent by her uncle to kill her. He had the poster. That proves her story."

"There was an enormous bounty on her head if her whereabouts could be found. He wanted the bounty. He probably never even met Didier."

"Why are you saying all of this?" Cain shot a glance at Christal, who was again walking down the carpeted aisle of the first-class car to check each passenger's face. His eyes flooded with worry and another unnamed emotion that burned with passion.

"I'm saying this because I think you ought to remove yourself from her. You can't do anything that her family can't do ten times over with their money. Sheridan's one of the richest men in New York."

"I know that—"

"What can you do for her that they cannot? Why are you letting yourself be torn apart by this girl's problems? It's not worth it, the conclusion will be a bad one. The girl's going to go to prison, I don't see any way around it. There's no evidence she's innocent."

"She *is* innocent." Cain closed his eyes, as if he could no longer bear the sight of Christal's face as she desperately searched the car.

"I was at Fredericksburg, Cain. I was in Hooker's regiment when we went to take the sunken lane. We lost half our troops to you Confederates that day. You men were just as snug as a snail in a shell behind that wall and we were like lines of prisoners before a firing squad every time we tried to advance."

"What does this have to do with—?"

"I saw you, as did everyone else in my regiment who survived the advance. We heard the cries of Jimmy O'Toole with his legs half gone, whimpering for one blessed drink of water before he died. We still talk about the Georgia Gentleman as if he were some myth spun by our forefathers. You know the man, Cain. The Reb who came over that ridge and crawled on his belly beneath the wall of fire to quiet the enemy with a sip from his canteen . . ."

"As I said, what does this—?"

"A man who has honor like that, even if he is a damned Secesh, shouldn't have to lose twice. You lost the war, Macaulay, don't lose this one too. Extract yourself now. Christabel Van Alen is a heartbreaker, but she's a lost cause. She's going to go to jail. Maybe forever."

Cain was silent. He watched Christal, carefully shuttering away the emotion in his eyes. "I stood by my country when it was a lost cause. I abandoned it only when I was forced to. I won't do less now."

Rollins stared at him like a Yank staring at a crazy Reb, until finally he sighed and nodded to gather up his men. "We'll do whatever you think is necessary, then. You just give us the word, Cain, and you know we'll do it." After this cryptic statement, he added, ". . . until we reach New York and it's out of our hands."

Macaulay understood.

Inside the baggage car a man was just finished dressing, while another, Henry Glassie, was once more stripped down to his union suit, and bound and gagged, hidden among the bags of mail. That was where the man had come from, Glassie surmised, finally coming out of the darkness caused by the blow to his head.

He peered at Baldwin Didier through the dirty canvas sacks of mail. Didier was not so portly as Henry Glassie, but he did fit his suit rather well, once the suspenders were in place holding up the too large trousers. The coat was too large also, but if it was left unbuttoned there was enough doubt about its cut that one could surmise, briefly, that it had been made for Didier.

Didier removed the coat and stepped to the bags of mail, throwing aside one that hid Glassie's face. Henry Glassie's eyes shut in the split second when light hit his face.

Didier studied him a long time, then he covered him with another bag of mail. Through a part in the bags, Glassie shifted his head ever so slightly and resumed his spying. Didier had rummaged through one of the fine leather trunks and removed a silver cup. He dumped a white powder into it and filled it with water from the leak on the roof of the car. Glassie hadn't a clue as to what Didier was doing, until he removed a small brush and mirror, and proceeded to shave.

Chapter Twenty-seven

When Christal, Cain, and the marshals returned to their train car, Mr. Glassie was seated at the back near the baggage door, fast asleep, his face partially covered by his fine beaver hat. Cain motioned to wake him. Christal knew he wanted to ask about the baggage car, but she stopped him. "If there was anyone in there, would he be asleep like this? We were gone so long, he probably fell asleep waiting for us."

Cain removed his hand from Glassie's shoulder. "All right. Leave him be. We need to talk anyway. No sense having to get rid of this busybody to do it. Come over here." He took her hand and led her to the opposite bench, as far from the marshals circling the stove as he could get.

Across the way, on the opposite bench, Glassie let out a loud, snoring gasp and shifted positions. Cain ignored him.

"What's wrong? I saw you speaking with Rollins." She quietly waited for the bad news. Because it was always bad news.

Cain picked up her hand, the one with the scar, and traced every petal with his finger. His expression was pensive, determined, fear-inspiring. He was an awesome sight in this mood, she thought. But then he'd always taken her breath away.

"The train will be stopping in about an hour in Abbeville."

"Are you afraid Didier might get aboard?"

"No, Rollins and the other marshals will make sure he won't."

Christal locked gazes with Cain. She was able to read the

frosty depths of his eyes more easily now. Something was definitely wrong. He had more to say to her, but he didn't seem ready.

"At Abbeville I want you to escape."

The muscles in her body grew rigid with shock. She stared at him, disbelief on her face. "But—but—why now?" she stammered.

He squeezed her scarred hand as if he needed desperately to hold on to it. "I know better than anyone that some battles you just can't win. Rollins pointed that out to me just now. I don't know if we can win, Christal. And if I lose this one, I don't think I could take it. The law be damned, I *know* you didn't do this and I'll believe it until the day I die. So at Abbeville, get off the train when I nod and lose yourself in the town. I'll be back for you in an hour. When we cross Big Crimloe Creek, the train has to slow and mount the rise to the bridge. I'll jump off the train there. It'll be a day before Rollins can catch up. The next stop after Abbeville isn't for hours."

"Rollins knows about this, doesn't he? He's going to help because he's your friend. You're all breaking the law for me—"

"No, not for you, Christal. For us. Do you understand? For us. The war took away my whole family, it took away my home and my country. I don't have anything left but you. If I lose you, I have nothing."

"We'll be running forever."

"I know the life well."

She looked at him. He smiled bitterly. A renegade smile.

"With my brother-in-law's help, I might be able to get a new trial. Shouldn't we give it a try?"

"When we get to New York, they aren't going to let us breathe, girl. There'll be no more opportunities after this."

"Do you really want to do this? It's against everything I know about you." She looked into his eyes, her own eyes pleading.

"I have to do this." He looked at her as if he were searching her soul through her eyes. Softly, he touched his lips to hers.

"It's not the life I choose, Christal, but I'd choose no life to a life without you."

The train slowed. The whistle blew, signaling Abbeville.

"Oh, God, are you sure?" she whispered, frightened. The plan seemed crazy, doomed to fail. Though it hurt, she even wondered if he'd decided she was guilty.

His face had turned into a stony mask. "I'm going to walk to the front of the car and begin a hand of poker with Rollins. The marshals will follow. When the train stops, exit out the rear. I'll join you in Abbeville in an hour. We'll have a horse and be gone before nightfall."

He stood and she clutched his hand. Then she let him go, watching in mute desperation as he moved to join the other men at the front of the car.

Mr. Glassie let out another rumble beneath the hat. He was still fast asleep. There would be no time to say farewell.

Slowly she stood and watched Macaulay. He adamantly refused to look at her, as if that might betray her escape. She slid back the rear door between the passenger car and the baggage car. It gave a miserable creak. Almost artificially, none of the marshals turned their heads to look.

For a brief moment she stood on the small platform between the cars, breathing the fresh air of freedom. Her heart pumped in her chest, a sign of her fear and exhilaration.

The door to the passenger car slid open.

She spun around, sure that Rollins or another marshal had seen her leave, but the face that met her was unfamiliar. Yet familiar. She thought for a moment the man was Mr. Glassie come to join her for some air. It was not. She looked at the man's eyes.

She knew.

"Oh, Christabel, at long last, our time has come."

The door closed behind him. She stepped back and briefly lost her balance on the precarious edge of the platform. He caught her arm and shoved her into the baggage car.

"Where is Henry Glassie?" she choked, suddenly realizing how they'd been duped. She stared at Didier. She hardly knew him without his trademark Vandyke.

"Our friend is napping among the mail. Shall I wake him and do away with you both?" He smiled.

Before she could answer, a commotion ensued outside on the platform. A woman was arguing with her husband.

"But I did bring it! We gave it to the conductor and he put it inside this car, right here."

"You didn't bring it, Martha, I would have remembered," he husband explained, exasperated.

"Conductor! Open this car! We have baggage inside!"

Didier clamped his hand over Christal's mouth and drew her into the shadows behind the Chinese crates. The car door slid open.

"There it is!" the woman exclaimed, her arm extending into the car, pointing to an orange carpetbag. "I told you I brought it, Howard, you old fool."

"Yes, dear." They heard the sounds of Howard as he climbed into the car and dumped the bag onto Abbeville's crude wooden platform.

"Anybody else want their bag?" the conductor cried out, looking for other passengers.

Christal struggled against Didier to call out, but he held her firm, crushed against his chest, his hand silencing her. In despair, she smelled the English lime water he bought from Lord and Taylor. Only the best for Baldwin Didier. She and Alana had bought a bottle for Didier as a wedding present when he was to marry their spinster aunt. She could still remember their aunt's face, so beautiful and serene, her dream of marriage come true at last. She wondered if her aunt ever knew she had married a monster.

The conductor slammed the door shut. They were in darkness except for the light shining through the roof where it leaked melting snow.

"You thought you had eluded me, didn't you, my darling niece?" Didier let her go. She fell against the side of the car when the train lurched to a start.

"My sister knows the story," she panted, trying to keep her balance in the moving train. Her mouth was dry from fear. "Before I ran from New York I wrote her a letter telling her everything about the night you killed our parents. If you kill me, it doesn't matter. The end will be the same. She'll see you hanged for your crimes even without me."

"If your sister had anything but your word against mine, her rich and powerful mick of a husband would have seen to that long ago."

"No doubt they couldn't find you to hang you with the evidence. I heard you disappeared shortly after Alana's wedding." It took all her courage to answer him. Trapped in a boxcar with her uncle was like being in the belly of the beast.

"I went looking for you, my girl. I went all over the damned world . . . looking for you. I spent all the money I had left to bring me here. Oh, well, there are other lonely, wealthy women like your aunt. I have a prospect in Paris, and there was a widow in Spain, a Basque with quite a gourmet appetite for the bedroom. I shall enjoy them all, as soon as I have rid myself of you."

"How do you think you mean to get away with this?" she asked, terror streaming through her blood like a narcotic. "There are five U.S. Marshals in the next car and one in particular—"

"Ah, yes, *him.* I've heard a lot about your paramour. He's almost legend out here, isn't he? Yet imagine his surprise when he jumps the train and enters Abbeville only to find you not there—yes, I did hear your plans as I took my little 'nap.'" He chuckled.

"Macaulay will know you got to me. He knows I would meet him unless I was unable to." She was glad it was dark and he couldn't see the doubt and fear in her eyes.

"On the contrary, my dear. He will think he gave you a chance to flee, one which you embraced wholeheartedly. There will be quite a bad taste in his mouth, I imagine, when you don't meet him in Abbeville. Surely then he will know the heinous crimes they convicted you of in New York were true. He will go mad thinking how you duped him."

"No . . ." she whispered, her terror springing to life anew. She shook her head, as if denying his words might make them untrue, but there was no fault to his logic. She was going to die by Didier's hand and the worst was that, in the end, Macaulay, her love, would believe she was a murderess.

"Don't think about it, lovely girl. You and your sister were always such lovely girls. I really didn't want it to end this way. I thought you would all die quietly in the fire. It's distasteful to me to have to take such an active role in your death. I hope you can forgive me." He touched her cheek, leaving the scent of limes, the same smell he left in the wake of a visit to Washington Square. It lingered in the parlor and trailed into the foyer, a presence unto itself. The fresh, tropical scent of death.

"My aunt was in love with you. You fulfilled her every dream when you asked her to marry you. Did you ever make her happy? Did you ever like my parents? Have you no remorse at all for what you've done?" Her words were accusing, yet little girl–like. In her naiveté, she wanted answers. She wanted to take solace in the knowledge that all the pain in her life had been governed by more than one man's whim. If she were to die without even that, it would be a cruel death indeed.

"On the night your aunt died, Christal, she forgave me. If I never loved her, she at least loved me. And isn't that what brings us true happiness? To have what we love?"

"Did you kill her? Did you kill my aunt too?" The question had burned through her mind all the years since her memory returned.

"No," he whispered gravely. "In some ways, our marriage provided my happiness too. Your aunt was not an impoverished woman, you know, Christal. Her fortune gave me moments of pleasure—on Wall Street—and at the hotel where I kept my mistress."

He stepped toward her, his heavy build swaying with the motion of the speeding train. "But upon your aunt's death, I discovered my terrible appetite. I was a creature who fed on money. Your aunt's fortune was spent and there was no more to come. I was in dire straits. Unless"—he cocked one gray eyebrow, his words ending in a hiss—"unless I found a way to get the entire Van Alen fortune. With you and your family dead, I would be the one to inherit. Ah, what choice did I have but to kill your parents and torch their bedroom?"

"You're a monster," she said, her hatred finally overcoming her fear.

He smiled bitterly, still quite handsome for his age. "Yes, a monster. You've pegged me well, Christal. You're an intelligent girl, I've always known it. I want you to know I did not enjoy putting you in Park View. I did not enjoy breaking your spirit. It was a messy, unplanned end, even for a man such as me—a monster. You see, I wanted you and your sister dead. I wanted the Van Alen money without the Van Alens, but after the fire when I discovered both you and Alana had lived, I became too cowardly. Then, when you were convicted of the murders I, myself, had committed, I feared my fortune was too good to test by trying to murder the survivors. I left you and your sister alone, and now I pay the price for that, because look what it's brought me."

He stared at her. She found a strange intimacy for her in his eyes, like the intimacy of lovers. But this intimacy was tinged with blood. It was a killer's intimacy with his victim.

"It is not easy being a monster, Christal," he whispered.

She said nothing. She simply stared at him with grave blue eyes and searched futilely for compassion.

"I'm a monster cursed with intelligence. I understand all too well what I do and why I do it. And lo, it gives me night terrors I would not wish on any of my victims." He met her gaze. "I killed your father first. He was asleep. I hit him on the head with that heavy brass candlestick and he never opened his eyes. It's your mother who haunts me. She was so beautiful. So kind and gracious. When I killed her I knew I was a monster. She awakened and we struggled. She begged me not to—"

"Don't—oh, God, don't—" she uttered, unable to hear it. Hurt and anger swelled in her throat like bile.

"Don't be like her, Christal," he whispered, drawing her against him. The scent of limes was overpowering. "Don't beg me for mercy. Let this be quick. I want you brave and pure and defiant, as you are now—"

She broke loose and ran for the door. She threw it open and screamed, but he yanked her back. He slammed the door behind them and silence reigned once more on the prairie, the only unnatural noise the *chug chug chug* of the train rolling over steel-girded tracks.

Chapter Twenty-eight

"What was that noise?" Cain looked up from his hand of cards and stared sharply at the back of the car.

"Nothing—just the squeak of wheels," Rollins answered hastily. "Go ahead and bid, Cain, you're winning. I can't afford to lose this hand."

"Look—she's gone." The three words hung in the air spoken with all the drama of a Shakespearean actor, not a U.S. Marshal forced to state the obvious.

Reluctantly, all five men raised their heads and stared at the back of the car, now devoid of their prisoner.

"Well, I'll be. She *is* gone." Rollins looked at his men.

"She just up and left the minute our backs were turned. How about that?" another marshal piped up.

Cain stood and ran his hand through his hair as if exasperated by their bad acting skills. "I'm going to check that noise."

"Ah . . . wait, Cain." Rollins scuttled up to him and whispered, "Let my men go back there. Then nobody can say you had anything to do with her disappearance."

Cain stared at the door that led out to the baggage car. "Where's Glassie? Did he get off at Abbeville? He told me he was headed for New Jersey."

"Maybe he went back to his own car—"

"No." Cain walked to the rear door, his holstered guns swaying with every pump of the engine's driving rods. "He

didn't leave by the front of the car. If he left, he left here."
Cain touched the oak panel of the rear door.

Rollins watched him, concern furrowing his forehead.
"What's wrong? Tell me what you're thinking."

"I don't know what it is . . . but something's wrong. Tell
the conductor to stop the train. I'm going to check out the
baggage car."

Rollins nodded.

Cain opened the door between the cars.

"How would you like your death?"

"You can't get away with this—they'll find me—they'll see I
was murdered—" Numb with terror, Christal backed away
from the fine Spanish dirk that Didier held elegantly in his
hand.

"If I simply push you from this train, I could break your
neck. The end would come quickly, mercifully." He turned
sober. "But then you might only break a leg or an arm. You'd
lie in the melting snow, every wind, every chill, sapping the
warmth from your body while you lay helpless from your in-
jury. It could take days to die. Slow, terrible days. And I'd
never be sure you were dead. After all, someone could find
you."

Her hands were trembling as she held them out in supplication. "And *he* will find me. You think Macaulay will believe
the worst—but if he's confronted with a terrible truth, I know
him, he'll go to his grave searching to disprove it. He'll ride
every inch of these tracks. When he finds my body, he'll know
you killed me."

"Then he must not find your body."

"How—?"

"When Cain jumps at Big Crimloe Creek, you will be dead,
my dear. The creek runs into the Mississippi and it's fast
enough to move a body well out of reach of this train. By the
time they find you, no one will know who you are." He
touched the pointed dagger to his thumb. To prove its razor
edge, he pricked himself. A crimson droplet fell to the
wooden floor. "Come here."

"No!" she gasped, backing away. She glanced at the baggage door. Didier blocked passage to the other cars, but if she could swing open the side door, perhaps a jump wouldn't be fatal. One thing she knew, Didier wouldn't jump after her; he was too much of a coward.

He walked toward her, the knife gleaming in the shafts of sunlight streaming through the holes in the roof. She ran to the side door and unlatched it. It swung open by the sheer forward force of the speeding train. The noise was deafening. Thousands of tons of black steel and wood propelled forward in tandem by the use of steam. The prairie whipped by, a white-and-gold blur.

"It's no use, Christal. Jump if you must. You know if you survive, I'll get you one day. You'll always have to watch your back. One day I'll be standing there. Your death is inevitable. Give it to me now!" He lunged forward. She screamed. The knife seemed to shoot for her heart.

Then suddenly, it fell. And Didier was thrust backward in the strong arms of her lover.

"Oh my God!" she cried out, tears streaming down her face as Cain took Didier into a headlock. The dirk was at her feet. She picked it up, just to make sure.

"Baldwin Didier?" Cain demanded through clenched teeth.

"Let me go, sir! This woman was trying to rob me. She was trying to escape the train when we prematurely pulled out of Abbeville."

"No," Christal whispered, shaking her head. She looked at Cain and knew he believed her.

"We have a passenger who can identify you as this girl's uncle. Christal claims you're responsible for the murder of the Van Alens, her parents."

"No! It's not true!" Didier choked through the iron headlock. "You have no proof! And where is this passenger you speak of? I know of no one on the train who can identify me!"

"You've done something with Henry Glassie. These are his clothes you're wearing. We'll get to the bottom of this. I'll have every lawman within fifty miles of here to search for evidence. So confess. We've come to the end of the line."

"Never!" Didier reached inside his vest. Cain grappled with him for the weapon. It was a tiny Derringer, much like the muff pistol she had once held on Cain. The men struggled for possession of it, their shouts and grunts muffled by the violent noise of wind passing outside the open car door. Christal held her breath. Didier was able to point the small pistol at Cain, but Cain swiftly grabbed Didier's wrist. She heard a cry, then the pistol, too, fell to the ground.

"You'll never catch me, I tell you!" Didier backed away from Cain's menacing form. He turned and fled through the connecting door. Cain opened the door to follow, then paused as if he could not believe his eyes.

Christal ran to him. Beyond, her uncle was down between the cars, grappling with the coupler. He was not an agile man, nor was he slim. Baldwin Didier was used to servants and waiters, but when it came to his freedom, even he could lower himself to manual labor. He labored now to separate the car. Already he had worked the pin more than halfway.

"Don't do this!" Cain cried out, his face taut with shock. The train was moving full speed. Uncoupling the cars might cause a derailment.

"Good-bye, Christal. Until we meet again!" Didier unpinned the coupler. He grasped it in his black, greasy palm and laughed. Then he lost his balance. He clung to the railing on the other side of the train, but it was just wire beneath his weight. It bent and bent, until he lost his grip. Though the baggage car was separated from the engine, it still moved at a quick clip on its own momentum. As if in slow motion, Christal saw Didier fall to the tracks. He screamed and she buried her head in Cain's chest. There was a loud, grisly bump, then silence as the car rolled to a halt, and the body of the train sped on, the conductor not yet notified by Rollins to halt.

"Shit."

The silence of the prairie was awesome after the thunderous noise of the train. The boxcar sat like a house on the tracks, immovable. Cain pulled her from his chest and repeated his curse. "Shit."

"What is it?" she asked, wiping the tears from her cheeks. She couldn't believe Didier was dead. But he was. Behind the car, he lay like a gray pinstriped boulder wedged to the side of the tracks.

"We got no confession, no proof. I knew something like this would happen. I should have tried to save him."

"You would have been killed yourself."

"C'mon. We gotta go. When Rollins stops that train and comes looking for us, I want to be gone from here. Without a confession they'll take you to New York and take you away from me—"

"What's that noise?" Christal turned worried eyes to the corner of the car. The mound of mail bags was moving up and down, like a cat under a comforter.

Cain began throwing off bags. Underneath lay Mr. Henry Glassie, of the Paterson Furniture Company, tied and gagged, and looking embarrassed, because for second time in his entire life he was once more caught by the same lady, clad only in his union suit.

"Thank God you weren't killed," Christal whispered as she went to him. She helped Cain untie the bonds. When the gag was off, he let loose several expletives.

"So sorry, Miss Van Alen. Your uncle is a devil. Worse than that Kineson fellow."

"Henry, they'll be back for you. But we gotta go." Cain helped him stand, then he took Christal's hand. Peering out of the car, he saw, miles in the distance, the train stop just before the rise across Big Crimloe Creek.

"So you're taking up the life of an outlaw after all, eh, Cain? And all for Miss Van Alen?"

"Where's the choice?" Cain snapped, eyeing the prairie as if scouting the escape route.

"Oh, there's a great number of choices." Mr. Glassie chuckled. "And I would suggest starting them all with some marriage vows. You've treated this girl much too casually, for all her position in society."

"She won't have much position in society when they lock her back up in that asylum. Sorry, Glassie, but we gotta run."

Christal felt Cain's pull. She looked back at Mr. Glassie, her eyes giving a silent farewell.

Henry Glassie only laughed. "I don't think this woman's brother-in-law is going to appreciate your galloping off to live like a renegade. I want to tell you, Cain, you've no reason to do it. I was awake most of the time I was underneath those bags. You say you haven't a confession from Didier—but that's false, because you do have a confession. *I* heard him confess his crimes, every word, and I will testify as such. From this moment onward, consider Christabel Van Alen a free woman."

Cain stood rigidly still, as if he needed time to absorb what Glassie was saying. Then suddenly he let out a loud Rebel yell and picked her up like a rag doll.

Her mind and body were numb with shock. She was free. *She was free.*

Chapter Twenty-nine

Manhattan. It had changed in four years. Christal had left the city when the tallest structures were church steeples. Now there were office buildings and stores, some higher than six stories. And there was an elevated train being built to circumvent the knots of carriages and public omnibuses on the street. The farmland north of Central Park had been graded for town houses. There was even talk of building—of all things—an apartment house for the wealthy, and the plans were to put it on the west side of the park, in an area still so desolate, people jokingly referred to it as Dakota Territory.

The city had changed. *She* had changed. Christabel Van Alen had returned, yet not entirely. She was not the girl she once had been. But then . . . her gaze trailed to Macaulay, who sat silently beside her in the rented hack. She didn't really want to be that girl again. The pain she never wanted repeated, but now she knew if she had not run from her uncle, she never would have met Macaulay Cain. Her love. Her salvation.

"You're very quiet, my love," she whispered to him as she squeezed his hand.

"Are you excited? It's been a long time since you've been home." He smiled down at her, but his eyes were shuttered. He was holding back something, she knew it. Ever since they'd arrived at the Grand Central Depot, he seemed as quiet as if he were attending a funeral. She wished he would tell her what was bothering him.

"Everything is very different. The city has grown so rapidly, I can't quite get my bearings." She looked out the window. Telegraph wires etched the sky like tangles of clotheslines, the sidewalks were dotted with the iron covers of coal chutes, even the alleys were now paved. It was a modern city in every sense of the word.

"Christal."

She turned to face him, her eyes glistening with happiness and anticipation. He seemed somber in comparison. "Why are you so pensive?" She laughed. "You look as if we're headed for the gallows."

His mouth tipped in a wry grin while his gaze took in the sight of fashionable shoppers on Broadway. "This is all so new, that's all." He didn't look at her. "I never expected all . . . this." He waved his hand toward the window.

"You told me you'd been to New York. You knew about Delmonico's."

"I came here a long time ago—right after the war. And God knows I might have known about Delmonico's—everybody who's come here has heard about it—but I sure as hell never ate there."

"We could go there if you like."

"You know I can't afford a place like that. You'll just have to go with Sheridan and your sister."

She placed her hand intimately on his thigh. "My sister is wealthy. Not me. Remember that."

He glanced at her. "You have your inheritance and I'm not talking about wealth—I'm talking about upbringing, background, family ties and traditions. No matter what you say, Christal, this place is a part of you. I can see it in your eyes."

"So it's a part of me. What does that change? Nothing."

"It's a part I hardly know."

She touched his cheek. He turned to her. They locked gazes. "Then let's get reacquainted. . . ."

She kissed him tenderly on the lips—a sweet, loving kiss that was meant to be as chaste as it was quick. But she soon found out he had different ideas. He wrapped his arms around her and pulled her to his lap, shamelessly deepening the kiss as if she were still some kind of saloon girl and not the famed missing heiress of Washington Square. Despite the privacy of the cab, she heard some men jeering on the granite sidewalks.

"Stop . . ." she gasped when she finally broke free. Her cheeks were red, and she glanced embarrassedly out of the window to see if anyone else were watching.

"You see you have changed."

"No. I've never wanted to be treated like a whore."

His mouth turned into a rock-hard line. "Girl, that's not how I treat a whore. That's how I treat the woman I love."

She sighed. She knew he was a man not destined to be tamed. Now, in the midst of the city, he seemed wilder than ever.

"Fifth Avenue!" the driver called out, knocking on the door of the carriage.

"Alana." Christal whispered her sister's name.

"C'mon." Cain helped her out of the carriage. If he was shocked by the enormous marble mansion in front of them, she didn't see it. She was too busy running to the door and pounding on it.

"Yes?" An old, austere butler answered the door. Beyond, a marble foyer loomed like a mausoleum.

"I'm—I'm here to see Alana." Christal held her breath, disoriented. She didn't expect to recognize things. She'd never seen the Sheridan mansion, but everything seemed so foreign. Perhaps her sister wasn't home? Perhaps she had the wrong house?

"Miss Christabel?"

Christal widened her eyes. The butler was almost smiling, and his eyes held a warmth for her he couldn't have for a stranger. He knew Alana, and Christal looked enough like her sister that he could recognize her. She had the right house after all.

"Is she home? Oh, don't tell me I've missed her!"

"No, miss. I'll tell her you've arrived. Please do come in and

allow me to settle you in the library. My name is Whittaker."
The butler stepped aside and let her pass. When Macaulay
followed, the men exchanged suspicious looks.

"And who, sir, may I say is calling with Miss Christabel?"
The butler waited for Cain to introduce himself, as if he were
a general waiting for a lowly lieutenant. He missed nothing of
Cain's appearance, not the barely civilizing veneer of gray
wool suit that the man wore with an invisible savagery that
strained at every seam, and not the clean, starched collar that
just barely covered a terrible scar around the man's throat.
The old butler took particular note of the strange black felt
hat the man had yet to remove.

"I said, who may I say is calling?" Whittaker repeated dis-
dainfully.

Cain tapped himself on the forehead. "Well, I'll be
damned! I forgot my calling cards!"

Christal shot him a quelling look. "Just tell them U.S. Marshal Macaulay Cain is accompanying me."

"Very good." Whittaker bowed to Cain, keeping his facial
expression calculatedly neutral. "May I take your hat, sir?"

Cain took off the Stetson and ran his fingers through his
hair. He handed it to the butler, but just as Whittaker was
about to retreat, he said in a mocking twang, "Hold on there,
partner."

Whittaker imperiously raised his eyebrows at the word
"partner." Cain smiled and unbuckled something beneath his
suit jacket. He reached down and untied the thongs that
wrapped around his wool-covered thighs. Casually, Cain
dumped the heavy holster into the butler's hands.

Whittaker looked down. The six-shooters looked well oiled
and well used. The holster was replete with cartridges,
enough for one rip-roaring shootout. He gulped. "Will that
be all, sir?" He looked at Cain, his eyes wide.

Cain crossed his arms over his chest. "Yep." His answer was
as slow as molasses.

The old butler nodded. He held the holster out from his
body. "The library is the door to your right, miss." Without

another glance at Cain, Whittaker stiffly walked away, holding the holster as if it were a bomb.

"Do you think she'll recognize me?" Christal turned worried eyes to Cain.

But Cain wasn't looking. Instead, his gaze was focused on the Corinthian pillars that lined the foyer. He touched one as if to see whether it was real marble. By his expression, she knew he had his answer.

"These people live in a bank."

Christal finally looked around the foyer. It was indeed the most lavish entrance she had ever seen, but somehow she couldn't care about it one way or another. She was too excited about seeing Alana.

"Come into the library. Surely we'll be more comfortable there." She took his hand and led him through the doors that Whittaker had pointed out to them.

The library was far from cozy. The walls were adorned with sixteenth-century Flemish tapestries depicting the Union of Utrecht, the floor was covered with English Axminster carpet, the furniture was overly carved and well-gilded. When Christal chanced to look at Cain, she thought he looked about as comfortable in the Louis XIV chair as he would on a bed of nails.

"Christal?"

Christal turned her head toward the whisper. A cry welled up in her throat. Alana stood at the door. Her blond, buttery hair was in a discreet chignon. She wore a gown of leaf-green taffeta, the exact color of her eyes. Christal couldn't believe how she mirrored their mother.

"Oh, Christal," Alana suddenly cried, dispensing with formality. She ran up to her and Christal began to sob. The two women wrapped their arms around each other and held on as if they would never let go.

"I was so worried. In all these years, I don't think I ever slept well, but I shall sleep well tonight." Alana held her for almost a minute, then she pulled away and looked at her.

Christal didn't find her sister had aged at all. The only thing different about Alana was the deep contentment to be found in her eyes, whereas before, when Christal saw her in the asylum, she could only remember the pain.

Christal could hardly get her words through her tears. "Has Alana had her baby? A girl, as she had hoped?"

"Yes. Shall we go to the nursery? I'll introduce you to her and the boys."

Christal laughed and wiped at her tears. She held her sister's hand. "I can't think of anything I'd rather do at this moment! Mother and father would be so proud. Grandchildren! How I wish they had seen them."

"Then let's go."

"Wait." Christal turned to Cain who stood silently by the mantel. She could see the uncertainty on his face. It puzzled her. She didn't like it.

"Alana. This is Macaulay Cain. He—he . . ." She could hardly begin to describe all the things he meant to her. Thankfully, her sister took her cue.

"Mr. Cain." Alana held out her hand. When Cain took it, she brazenly kissed him on the cheek. "My husband told me you protected my sister. I can never thank you. As long as I live, you will always be our dear friend."

"Thank you, ma'am," he answered solemnly. His gaze trailed to Christal. "Go on and see the children, Christal. Don't pay any mind to me. I'll just make myself comfortable here and give you some time to be with your sister."

"Thank you." Christal squeezed his hand. "I won't be gone long."

"Don't worry." He repeated, "I'll just make myself comfortable."

Christal only looked back once before departing with her sister. Cain was once more sitting in the Louis XIV chair. She almost laughed. He was never going to make himself comfortable there.

"He's very handsome," Alana said as they walked the stairs to the third-floor nursery.

"Macaulay?" Christal's lips tipped in a secret smile. "Yes, he is handsome."

"Do you love him? Oh, of course you do. I see it on your face." The expression in Alana's green eyes turned bittersweet. "He'll take you away from us."

"If we marry, we could stay in New York. Why, of course we could!" Christal didn't like the way the conversation was going. She had so many years to catch up on. How could there be talk of leaving already?

Alana tried to hide her smile. "Macaulay Cain looks about as comfortable in this house as Trevor Sheridan would look trying to rope a steer. Mr. Cain's not going to want to stay here for long."

"But surely he can wait for the wedding."

"Will he?" Alana arched one perfect dark-gold eyebrow.

Christal stared after her as she entered the nursery.

In the library, Cain rose from the gilt chair and wandered around looking for a drink. The library was, after all, a man's room, replete with desk, leather sofas, and, hopefully, liquor.

He spotted the crystal decanters in an anteroom draped with curtains of gold-fringed green velvet. He sloshed the contents of one into a heavy, cut-glass tumbler, then took a stiff gulp, not caring what kind of liquor it was.

"Christ." He closed his eyes to keep them from watering. His throat was on fire. Sniffing the contents of his glass, he suddenly chuckled. What the hell was rotgut doing in Sheridan's decanters?

He took another sip, this time easing his haste. It went down about as smooth as a serrated knife, but the effect was decidedly good. Already he felt better.

"Where are the women?"

Cain looked up. The stranger who'd arrived in Noble claiming to be Christal's brother-in-law stood in the library's door. Stiffly the man entered the room, leaning a bit too much on the ebony walking stick he sported.

"You weren't lying, I see," Cain said, returning his attention to his drink.

"I was who I said I was." Sheridan's eyes lowered to Cain's glass. "I have better, if you'd prefer it."

"No, this is fine—whatever it is."

"It's from the old days. Château Margaux has yet to impress me."

Cain wasn't sure what Château Margaux was, but he sure as hell wasn't going to let Sheridan know. "Christal and your wife went to the nursery."

Sheridan lowered himself onto a settee. Cain thought he didn't look all that comfortable there himself. He looked like a man who commanded his surroundings but hadn't quite assimilated into them. But Sheridan's wife, Alana, she was another story. Cain remembered how she looked standing in the doorway to the library calling to her sister. Alana Sheridan seemed born to gilt furniture and marble pilasters and European tapestries. And so did Christal. Christal looked quite at home here.

Cain took a long, dismal swallow of his drink.

"There's a lot I have to ask you."

Cain turned his eyes to Sheridan. "Such as?"

"Such as your sleeping habits. Particularly those concerning my sister-in-law . . ." Sheridan's eyes glittered. They were a strange color of hazel, not quite brown, gold, or green, but an arresting blend of all three.

"I'm not going to tell you anything about my sleeping habits, Sheridan. You may as well know that right now."

"I'm her only male relative. It's my responsibility to be protecting her." There was a hint of Irish accent still in Sheridan's speech.

"You protect her all you want. But whether I've slept with Christal or not is not something I'm going to discuss with you. Not now. Not ever."

Sheridan laughed. It was a rather unwholesome sound. "Good answer. I like it."

Cain blessed Sheridan with a look, as if to say he didn't give a damn one way or another.

The Irishman nodded, giving Cain a wide berth for his mood. Pensively, he studied the gold lion head gracing the knob of his cane. "What would you do if you were me, Cain?"

Cain shrugged.

"You've slept with her, I know it. But you saved her life too —more than once, I'm told. I should make you marry her, but I'm grateful to you for bringing Christabel back to her family. So how can I strong-arm a man I'm indebted to?"

"You think I don't care about her?"

Sheridan became silent. Gravely he said, "No, I know you care about her. I saw how you feel in Noble. It's just—"

"It's just she's a whole new girl. A girl I don't know." Cain looked around the opulent library. "Maybe a girl I could never know. . . ."

"Inside she hasn't changed. That's all there is, anyway."

"You say that, Sheridan, but when you offered for Christal's sister you weren't depriving your wife of all this." Cain waved his hand around the room.

Sheridan gave his unwholesome laugh. "I was depriving my new bride of much more—a place in society and her reputation. Here in New York they don't look too fondly upon Irishers marrying one of their own."

"Alana doesn't look like she's suffering."

"She set society on its ear when she married me. It was the scandal of the century." Sheridan stood and refilled Cain's glass. "But society came around after a while, and only Alana could have done it."

"She's a remarkable woman."

"Both the Van Alen women are."

"Yes." Cain set down his glass. In the mood he was in, he wanted to smash it against those damned hoity-toity tapestries. "Christal has been through hell. No one knows that better than me. She deserves all the comforts and luxuries she's been denied all these years. She deserves the life that was snatched away when Didier killed her parents."

"Christabel doesn't need all of this." Sheridan motioned to the room. "Believe me. It won't make her happy."

"How do you know that?"

"I know it better than anyone, Cain." The ghost of a smile touched Sheridan's lips. "My wife taught me."

* * *

Dinner was served in the dining room. There were fifty people present—a tiny, intimate gathering by New York standards—a huge, unmanageable crowd by Cain's. The children were now tucked in the nursery, but before dinner they were brought down to meet the guests. Cain was amused to note that the eldest two boys were the spitting image of Sheridan, with dark hair and those arresting hazel eyes. The newborn child, however, favored the Van Alens. To Cain's shock, Christal had walked up with the babe in her arms and handed the newborn to him. Helpless to do anything else, he awkwardly held the child until it began to howl and the women laughed. Christal laughed too and quickly took back the babe. With the child quiet in her arms, Cain studied the newborn. She was but a few weeks old, blond and pretty like her mother and aunt. Christal had whispered the girl's name in awed delight: *Christabel.* Cain heard the name with a strange longing in his gut. The babe was only further proof that Christal's life was inextricably entwined with the Sheridans'.

After dinner, Christal made a point to seek Cain out in the crowd. It was a cold night, but she had wrapped herself in one of her sister's satin capes. She took Cain's hand and stepped out onto the stone loggia overlooking Fifth Avenue.

"Are you beginning to remember everyone's name? It seems there are too many people in there." She picked at a piece of lint on his lapel, the intimate gesture of a wife.

"Everyone is very nice."

"I especially like Eagan—Trevor's brother." She laughed. "What a flirt. If he wasn't so in love with Caitlín, I'd call him hopeless."

"Yes."

"And can you believe Sheridan's sister is a duchess? Of all things! I can't wait until she and the duke return to New York. I've never met a duchess—"

"Yes."

Christal quieted. She gazed at Cain's profile in the dim lamplight off the avenue. It was taut, handsome, and not a little disapproving. She took a deep breath. "Why are you so unhappy? Ever since we came today you've looked like a bull caught in the corral."

Cain ran his hand through his hair. He had it tied back, but several strands had escaped, making him look downright savage. "I'm leaving here, Christal. It's time I returned to Wyoming."

She was shocked, but by some strange instinct she almost expected his words. He'd been so moody and out of place in New York. Quietly she asked, "When do we leave?"

He looked at her. The darkness hid his stare. "We?"

"I'm going with you."

He took her by both arms. "Are you a fool? You just got here. You haven't seen your sister in years. Why would you leave with me now?"

"Because I love you. I want to be with you."

He dropped his hold as if it burned him to touch her. "You have a life to return to." He looked down at her. She was a girl right off that calender that hung in the jail. Her evening gown was borrowed from her sister, a deep azure-blue satin with cascades of French lace at the bustle. Reluctantly, he touched the heavy sapphire-and-diamond necklace at her throat—a gift from her sister. "Look at you, Christal. Where is the girl I saw in Noble who wore that worn calico gown and those bells on her ankle? She's gone, as well she should be. Because you were born to look like this, to wear these priceless jewels, to clothe yourself in satin. Don't you see? My love won't give you any of this. The best I could ever do is in Washington. And even a job with the Secret Service won't get you any mansions."

"I don't need mansions." His talk confused her. He made it seem that her home was the end-all of her existence, and in truth, it had been for many long, lonely years; but then she'd fallen in love with him and now he was the end-all of her existence. It seemed impossible that he couldn't understand it.

"You don't know what you need. Or what you want." He heaved a sigh. "Look at you, girl. Just a minute ago you walked in here dazzled by the thought that Sheridan's sister is a duchess. You should have the chance to explore the life you were denied. I'm not going to keep you from it."

Panic suddenly coursed through her. He couldn't be talking of leaving her. "Of course you're not going to keep me from it. It's my choice to make. And I choose to go with you."

"I'm leaving tonight."

"All I ask is for you to stay a little while longer—"

"No." He looked out toward Fifth Avenue. A light rain had begun to fall, giving the cobbles an oily sheen like a raven's wing. Neither of them moved to go inside. He talked in a low, rough whisper. "It doesn't feel right being here, seeing you the way you used to be, not the way I know you. I've got to return to Noble and finish out my job there. Then I'll go to Washington. Anytime, you know you can return to me, girl, but stay here for now and test your desires for this life." His voice grew strangely heavy. "You just may like it, Christabel."

She stared at him, her real name on his lips sounding foreign and unfriendly. Holding back tears, she whispered, "Tell me when you're leaving tonight. I'll be with you on that train."

He glanced behind them through the French doors and into the drawing room. Alana was searching the room. "I think your sister wants you."

Christal turned her head. Alana waved.

"Just tell me when it's time to go. I'll be with you, Cain. I swear I will," she said.

"Sure," he whispered as he watched Alana take Christal's arm and introduce her to a group of women who wore enough emeralds and diamonds slung around their necks to have financed the entire Confederate army.

"Sure," he repeated to no one as he turned back to Fifth Avenue.

Chapter Thirty

You choose the rose, love, and I'll make the vow
And I'll be your true love forever.
                                    TOMMY MAKEM

"Have you seen Macaulay?" Christal had a tight, almost desperate expression on her face as she sought out her sister in the crowd. It was past midnight. She'd been up in the nursery with Alana while her sister fed the baby. She'd asked to rock the child back to sleep, and when she'd returned back to the drawing room, she couldn't find Macaulay anywhere.

"Darling, he's got to be around here . . ." Alana turned around. Her eyes sought her husband in the crowd. With the instinct of lovers, Trevor immediately looked up and found his wife across the room. "Trevor will know where he's off to. Oh, Christal, you look terrible. Why are you so worried—perhaps he went to bed."

"No." Christal wrung her hands and searched the crowd once more. Macaulay's tall form was not among the glittering jewels, gleaming satins, and black swallowtail coats. "Oh, don't tell me he's gone. Don't tell me!"

"Where would he be off to at this time of night?" Alana turned to her husband, who was suddenly at her side. "Trevor, where is Macaulay?"

"Cain? I saw him at midnight. He was talking to Whittaker."

Christal paled. "May I speak to the butler?"

"Come." Trevor took her arm. Alana watched, concern marring her smooth forehead.

The butler was in the dining room instructing the footmen on clearing the table.

"Whittaker—we're looking for Mr. Cain. He spoke to you?" Sheridan's booming voice easily traveled across all the marble in the dining room.

Whittaker bowed to Christal. "I just saw him, sir. He requested his firearms."

"He wanted his guns?" Christal gasped.

"Is he planning on shooting someone?" Sheridan asked dryly.

"No . . ." Christal hung her head. She fought the urge to cry.

"Is something amiss?" Whittaker interjected, the worry in his eyes betraying his professional demeanor. "Should I have kept Mr. Cain's weapons? I thought he requested them because he was retiring—I hear cowboys sleep with their boots on, and such. I assumed that was why he wanted his guns."

"He's—left—me." Christal barely choked back her sobs. She looked once at Sheridan's shocked face, then ran to the foyer and lifted her heavy satin skirts to mount the marble stairs, two at a time, to flee to her bedroom.

"Oh, he can't have left! You only arrived today!" Alana exclaimed as Christal stuffed her few belongings into a valise.

"He probably looked for me"—Christal swallowed her tears and shoved another petticoat into the bag—"while I was in the nursery—he thought I was—I was—having too much fun!"

"Whatever are you talking about, Christal?"

"Oh, how can I explain it?" Christal looked around the room to see if she had forgotten anything. She had. The sky-blue dress was draped across a tufted mauve satin ottoman. It looked ridiculously cheap and homemade against the artistry of the furniture, but it was the most beautiful dress in the world to her. She lifted it to her chest and hugged it.

"Does he not like us?" Alana looked quite vexed. "Oh, but how can that be? He doesn't know us!"

"I think he's trying to help me. He told me he was leaving, that I was better off here in New York, resuming my place in society—but I told him I loved him—how could he leave without letting me know?"

Alana helped her fold the sky-blue dress, not making any comment as to why Christal was forgoing all the costly Worth satin gowns she had donated to her in favor of a crudely fashioned wool gown.

"I wanted to dance at your wedding, Christal. If you leave and marry him in Wyoming, I won't be there." Christal was packed and Alana was in tears. "I wanted to give you such a beautiful big wedding."

"I think I'm going to have a baby."

Alana stared at her, stunned.

"I've missed my monthly time and with everything that has been happening these past weeks, I just couldn't think about it." Christal dropped her head to her hands. "What should I do, Alana? If you were me, what would you do? Call him back here and make him miserable? Or go to him and love him?" She shook her head. "Don't you see, he knows he doesn't fit here—and now I see I don't either . . . anymore."

No words came from Alana's lips. She only stood there and let the tears fall silently down her cheeks.

"I haven't told him about the baby. I wanted to be sure." Christal felt the tears renew in her eyes. "I don't want to leave you. I love you, Alana. I love the children and Trevor. But what can I do? I love him so much."

"Go to him." Alana took the valise and put her arm around Christal's waist. "I'll forgo dancing at your wedding to be at the birth of *my* first niece or nephew. When will that be?"

"In about eight months—seven? Oh, I don't know!" Christal suddenly laughed through her tears. "There just never seemed to be a moment to sit down and calculate the time."

"If we get to Wyoming and that man hasn't put a ring on your finger, Trevor will kill him—"

"Don't worry. Just let me find Macaulay. I have a feeling the rest will take care of itself."

"Telegraph us the moment you have a chance or we'll set out looking for you all over again." Alana hugged her, misery and love glittering in her eyes. "And know that I love you, Sister. I wouldn't let you go if I didn't."

Christal began weeping in earnest. Anguished, she forced herself to break away, then ran down the marble stairs to the waiting carriage.

The train to St. Louis was pulling out just as she ran to the platform. She walked in a fast clip alongside, peering into every window she could find to see if Macaulay was on it. She got to the halfway mark and still she couldn't find him. Tears of frustration sprang to her eyes. She'd been through too much in the past days to have it end like this. She could join him later, but she wanted him, needed him, loved him. *Now.*

"Where are you, you damned Reb!" she screamed at the slowly passing train, shocking the bystanders on the platform. In a fit of anger, she ran past two more cars. He wasn't in either of them.

And then she saw him. He was leaning against the railing between cars, a morose expression on his handsome face while he lazily watched Grand Central Depot ease by.

"I hate you!" she cried out, running to keep up with the slow-moving train.

Macaulay's eyes widened. He nearly slipped from his perch. "What in God's name are you doing?" he cried out, rushing to the other side of the railing nearer to her.

"I'm going with you, you bastard! How could you leave me behind?"

"You're not giving it a chance!" His expression turned dark. She could see the lines deepen in his face. "You don't yet know what you'll miss. I don't want you unhappy. I got better things to do with my life than saddle myself with an unhappy woman—"

"You don't want me unhappy?" She was losing patience more quickly than she was losing platform to run on. Angrily, she threw her valise at him. It landed with a thud against his chest. Next, she reached behind her and unclasped the sapphire-and-diamond necklace. "Then take me with you to Wy-oming! Let me leave all this behind. I don't want it!" To prove her point, she handed the priceless necklace to the first person she saw, a frumpy older woman with a black shawl covering her head. The woman nearly fainted when she saw what had dropped into her hands.

"Jesus Christ!" He almost fell off the train. Shock and disbelief were painted all over his face.

"Take me with you! I lied—I don't hate you—I love you. Don't let these things come between us!" She continued to run alongside the train, but it was gaining speed. She dropped her sister's satin cape on the platform and began ripping from her ears the diamond earrings, which she handed to another shocked bystander.

"Damn, girl, what are you doing?" he said, amazed by her crazy behavior. She'd given away a small fortune.

"I'm proving I love you!" The train gained even more momentum. Her chest ached with her need for air. She was quickly running out of platform. If he didn't put out his hand and help her up, she would miss the train.

And her life would be over.

Because there was no way she could live without him. She loved him, and all the Sheridan wealth was paltry consolation if he didn't love her back.

"If you come with me, you might be making a big mistake." His gaze darted between the end of the platform and her running figure.

She didn't answer; she only looked at him, her love in her eyes. The train of her dress was soiled by the dirty platform and her hair, previously dressed, smooth and chic, now flew behind her like a banner of golden tangles. The proud, wealthy heiress was gone. In her place was a woman whose heart was near to breaking because Macaulay Cain thought it best she remain in New York with her empty wealth and useless society prominence.

"No, I *do* hate you!" she cried in despair as she hit the end of the platform.

Then a hand reached out and took her by the back of her dress as if she were a dirty stray kitten. It plucked her from the platform and threw her against Cain's hard, warm chest.

"You crazy Yankee," he whispered, looking deep into her eyes.

"I lied—I don't hate you."

"I don't want to hear any complaining. If you marry me, you won't be living your sister's life, that's for sure."

"Take me to Wyoming. I want to see the mountains. I want to see the water lilies bloom on Lonesome Lake. I want to be your wife. I want you to love me."

His cold, wolf-gray eyes filled with emotion. He clasped her scarred hand and drew it to his chest. "Girl, if you want me to love you, you got it. I don't have anything without you. And I know it."

She smiled and dug into her valise, glad that she'd been able to hold on to it.

"What are you doing?"

She drew out the sky-blue dress. "Do you think this is a good enough wedding gown? We might find some Indian paintbrush to make a bouquet. Who knows, when we get to Noble, Dixiana might be justice of the peace. Then *she* can marry us."

"That'll be the day." He rolled his eyes.

"But we can't take too long."

"And why not?"

She laughed and threw the dress at him. "It ain't gonna fit forever, cowboy, that's why."

He pulled the dress away. "What . . . ?"

She smiled a beguiling secret smile.

"Oh, Jesus . . ." It slowly dawned on him.

"I have it on good authority the Sheridan men will come for a lynching if there isn't a ring on my finger in due haste."

He suddenly laughed and let out a Rebel yell. It echoed beneath the iron and glass canopy of the train shed. Then he kissed her, deep and sweet, as the train broke from the depot. The moon shone overhead, competing against the sparkling gaslights of the city, and the train headed west, to the mountains, where heaven kissed the earth.

> *God bless Wyoming and keep it wild.*
> FINAL ENTRY IN THE DIARY OF
> HELEN METTLER, AGE 15,
> WHO DIED IN THE TETONS

If you enjoyed
FAIR IS THE ROSE
and would like to read Trevor and Alana's story,
be sure to ask your bookseller for
LIONS AND LACE,
now available from Island Books.